The
Firebrand

Also by Susan Wiggs
in Large Print:

Halfway to Heaven
The Lightkeeper
Passing Through Paradise
The You I Never Knew
The Drifter
Enchanted Afternoon
Home Before Dark
The Hostage
The Ocean Between Us
A Summer Affair
Summer by the Sea

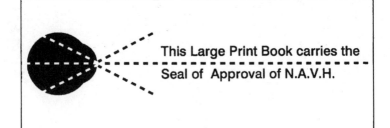

This Large Print Book carries the
Seal of Approval of N.A.V.H.

The Firebrand

Susan Wiggs

WHEELER
PUBLISHING

L.T.

(1)

NORTH

Published in 2005 by arrangement with Harlequin Books S.A.

Wheeler Large Print Romance.

The text of this Large Print edition is unabridged.
Other aspects of the book may vary from the original edition.

Set in 16 pt. Plantin by Al Chase.

Printed in the United States on permanent paper.

Library of Congress Cataloging-in-Publication Data

Wiggs, Susan.
    The firebrand / by Susan Wiggs.
        p. cm. — (Wheeler Publishing large print romance)
    ISBN 1-58724-945-6 (lg. print : hc : alk. paper)
    1. Great Fire, Chicago, Ill., 1871 — Fiction.   2. Custody of children — Fiction.   3. Loss (Psychology) — Fiction.
    4. Adopted children — Fiction.   5. Chicago (Ill.) — Fiction.
    6. Rescues — Fiction.   7. Bankers — Fiction.   8. Fires — Fiction.   9. Large type books.   I. Title.   II. Wheeler large print romance series.
    PS3573.I38616F57 2005
    813'.54—dc22   2005000384

I have a great desire to see a variety of employments thrown open to women, and if they may sell anything, why not books? The business seems to partake of the dignity of literature.
— Miss Elizabeth Peabody,
Boston bookseller, 1848

This is for booksellers everywhere, including Tamra, Beth Anne, Donita, Dean, Jennie, Terry, Gerald, Michael, Mary Gay, donNA, Donna, Sally, Lucinda, Marge, Rose Marie, Lois, DeeDee, Stefanie, Ruth Ann, Tanzey, Judy, Judy, Kyle, Charlie, Elaine, Char, Mary, Sharon, Virginia, Anne Marie, Leah, Yvonne, Tommy, Bobbie, Tina, Mark, Maureen, Cathy, Kathy, Rose, Dawn, Bronwyn. And of course, Fran at the Safeway. You enrich the lives of readers beyond measure.

National Association for Visually Handicapped
--------------------------- *serving the partially seeing*

As the Founder/CEO of NAVH, the only national health agency solely devoted to those who, although not totally blind, have an eye disease which could lead to serious visual impairment, I am pleased to recognize Thorndike Press★ as one of the leading publishers in the large print field.

Founded in 1954 in San Francisco to prepare large print textbooks for partially seeing children, NAVH became the pioneer and standard setting agency in the preparation of large type.

Today, those publishers who meet our standards carry the prestigious "Seal of Approval" indicating high quality large print. We are delighted that Thorndike Press is one of the publishers whose titles meet these standards. We are also pleased to recognize the significant contribution Thorndike Press is making in this important and growing field.

Lorraine H. Marchi, L.H.D.
Founder/CEO
NAVH

★ Thorndike Press encompasses the following imprints: Thorndike, Wheeler, Walker and Large Print Press.

Thanks to Barb, Joyce and Betty for knowing what's right and finding what's wrong, to Martha Keenan for her expert editing and to the Chicago Historical Society for keeping bygone days alive.

Part One

I suppose I need hardly say that I like Chicago — like it in spite of lake-wind sharpness and prairie flatness, damp tunnels, swinging bridges, hard water, and easy divorces.

— Sara Jane Clarke Lippincott
(aka Grace Greenwood), 1871

Prologue

The city was like a matchstick, waiting to be struck. The shipyards were stacked with lumber from the north woods, soon to be transformed into warehouses, tenements, breweries and shanties. In just a few short years, the prairie town had sprawled into an ungainly maze of wooden structures.

Many of the buildings looked grand. Some even appeared rock-solid. But in fact, most structures were clad in the false and fancy dress of ornate facades. Their insincere faces were painted to resemble stone or marble, copper or tin. But scratch beneath the surface, and the flimsy substance would be revealed — wood, as dry as tinder, capped by a deceptive veil of shingles glued on by flammable tar.

The roadways radiated like arteries from the giant, churning heart of the lake. Six hundred miles of wooden sidewalks and sixty miles of pine-block roadways spread through the business district and working-

11

class neighborhoods where immigrant mothers tried to hush their fretful children, suffering in the unseasonably dry heat. Rickety boardwalks and causeways spread across manufacturing centers and even dared to encroach upon the fashionable wealthy areas north of the river.

The barons of industry and commerce had put up varnish factories, alcohol distilleries, coalyards, lumber mills and gasworks with more regard for fast profit than for fire prevention. They lived for show, in houses built to resemble the centuries-old manors of aristocrats. Blooded coach horses occupied stables crammed with dry straw and timothy hay. Avenues of trees, stripped dry by the summer-long drought, connected neighbor to neighbor, each trying to outdo the other in ostentation. Those who had established themselves in the city a mere fifteen years ago liked to call themselves Old Settlers, and the new arrivals had no grounds to challenge the designation. Instead they set to work earning their own fortunes so that one day they might buy their way into the ranks of the merchant princes.

Many of these newcomers stayed at the Sterling House Hotel, which was considered the very height of fashion. Literally. Crowned by a dome of colored glass, the five-story structure boasted a steam elevator and commanded an impressive view of the river.

Feverish and impatient with ambition, no one cared that Sunday was supposed to be a day of rest and reflection. No one heeded the fire alarms that had been shrieking through drought-choked neighborhoods all week. The wheels of commerce ground on with dogged relentlessness, and only those too timid to dream greatly would pause to worry that Chicago was a city built of tinder; or that sparks from a hundred thousand chimneys infested the gusting night air; or that the fire-fighting companies had already worked themselves into exhaustion.

To be sure, no one could have predicted the vicious speed with which the fire took hold. No one could have imagined that, with such a modern system of alarms and waterworks, the Great Fire would burn without interruption Sunday night, and on through Monday, and deep into the middle of Tuesday. No one looking at the falsely solid brickfronts could have believed the city would be so vulnerable.

But like anything built on an unstable foundation, the city had only the thinnest of defenses. Chicago was not long for this world.

Part Two

We hold these truths to be self-evident;
that all men are created equal; that they
are endowed by their Creator with certain
inalienable rights; that among these are
life, liberty, and the pursuit of happiness.
— Thomas Jefferson,
"Declaration of Independence," 1776

We hold these truths to be self-evident;
that all men and women are created equal;
that they are endowed by their Creator
with certain inalienable rights; that
among these are life, liberty, and the pursuit of happiness.
— Elizabeth Cady Stanton,
"Declaration of Sentiments," 1848

One

Lucy Hathaway perched on the edge of her seat, pretending to hang on every word spoken by the evangelist. Anyone in the crowded salon who saw her attentive posture would admire her piety. Observers would find the sight of the dark-haired young woman, with her hands clasped in religious fervor, uplifting. Inspirational, even. Commendable, most assuredly.

"Your eyes are glazing over," said a deep, amused voice beside her.

She didn't recognize the voice, which was unusual, for Lucy Hathaway made it her business to know everyone. The man must have slid into the seat beside her after the start of the lecture. But she didn't turn to look at him. She pretended not to notice that he'd spoken at all.

". . . St. Paul is clear on this point," Reverend Moody intoned from the podium. "A wife must submit to her husband's leadership in the same way she submits to the Lord. . . ." The message rang through the room full of people who had braved a dry windstorm to attend the event at the fashionable Hotel Royale.

Lucy blinked slowly, trying to unglaze her eyes. She kept them trained straight ahead with unwavering attention. She tried to govern her mind as well, batting away the preacher's words like bees at a picnic, when she really wanted to leap to her feet and object to this claptrap about the superiority of man over woman.

And now, despite her best intentions, she found herself wondering about the insolent man sitting next to her.

The man whose whisper had come so close that she could feel the warmth of his words in her ear.

"You know," he said, leaning even closer. "You might try —"

"Go away," she said between clenched teeth, not even moving her lips as she spoke. He smelled of bay rum and leather.

"— leaning on me," he continued insolently. "That way, when you fall asleep from boredom, you won't attract attention by collapsing on the floor."

"I will *not* fall asleep," she hissed.

"Good," the man whispered back. "You're much more interesting wide-awake."

Ye gods. She mustn't listen to another word of this.

The Reverend Dr. Moody came to a lull in his address, pausing to fortify himself with a glass of lemonade from a pitcher.

She sensed the man next to her shifting in his seat and then leaning back to prop his ankle on his knee in an easy, relaxed pose. By peeking through lowered eyelashes, she caught a glimpse of his pantleg. Charcoal superfine, perfectly creased, fashionably loose-fitting.

Lucy herself was being slowly strangled by a corset designed, she was certain, for use in the Spanish Inquisition, and she resented him more than ever.

"We should leave," he suggested, "while we have the chance."

She glared stoically ahead. This was the first lull in forty minutes of the stultifying lecture, and the temptation to flee burned like a mortal sin inside her. "It's interesting," she said, trying hard to convince herself.

"Which part?"

"What?"

"Which part did you find so interesting?"

Lucy was chagrined to realize that she could not recall one single word of the past forty minutes. "All of it," she said hastily.

"Right." He leaned in closer. "So now I

know what bores you. Suppose you tell me what excites you."

She narrowed her eyes in suspicion, for no man had ever voluntarily made small talk with her. He was probably setting her up for some sort of humiliating moment. Some social faux pas so he and his cronies could have a chuckle at her expense. So what? she thought. It wouldn't be the first time someone made her the butt of a joke. She'd survived moments like that before. Many moments.

"Ha," she muttered. "As if I would tell you."

"I'm leaving," he said. "Come with me."

Lucy ignored him. If she got up now, people would notice. They might think she was following him. They might even believe she had "designs" on him.

As if Lucy Hathaway would ever have such a thing as designs on a man.

"Quickly," he urged, his whisper barely audible. "Before he gets his second wind."

The audience, restless and trying not to show it, buzzed with low, polite conversation while the evangelist refreshed himself. At last Lucy could resist no longer. She had to see who this rude, mellow-voiced stranger was. With the bold curiosity that caused her such trouble in social situations, she turned to stare at him.

Heavens to Betsy. He was as handsome as a sun god.

Her eyes, no longer glazing over, studied him with unabashed fascination. Long-legged. Broad-shouldered. Deep brown hair, neatly combed. An impeccably tailored suit of clothes. A face of flawless, square-jawed strength and symmetry such as one saw on civic monuments and statues of war heroes. Yet this particular face was stamped with just a hint of wicked humor. Who the devil was he?

She didn't know him at all, had never seen him before.

If she had, she would have remembered. Because the unfamiliar warmth that curled through her when she looked at him was not a sensation one would easily forget. Lucy Hathaway was suddenly contemplating "designs."

He smiled, not unkindly. She caught herself staring at his mouth, its shape marvelously set off by the most intriguing cleft in his chin. "Randolph Birch Higgins," he said with a very slight inclination of his head.

Guiltily she glanced around, but to her relief noticed that they sat alone in the rear of the salon. She cleared her throat. "I beg your pardon?"

"Please don't. I was simply introducing myself. My name is Randolph Higgins."

"Oh." She felt as gauche as a schoolgirl unprepared for lessons.

"I believe the usual response is 'How do you do?' followed by a reciprocal introduction," he suggested.

What a condescending, pompous ass, she thought. She resented the marvelous color of his eyes. Such an arrogant man did not deserve to have perfect leaf-green eyes. Even more, she resented him for making her wish she was not so skinny and black-haired, pinch-mouthed and awkward. She was not an attractive woman and she knew it. Ordinarily that would not bother her. Yet tonight, she wished with humiliating fervor that she could be pretty.

"Miss Lucy Hathaway," she said stiffly.

"Pleasure to meet you, Miss Hathaway." He turned slightly toward her, waiting.

She had the oddest sensation of being alone with this man. On some level she perceived people milling around the large outer salon behind them. Through the arched passageway, she vaguely noticed ladies laughing and flirting, men stepping through the French doors to light up their cigars in the blustery night. In the lecture room, people spoke in low tones as they awaited the next portion of the address. Yet a strange electricity stung the air around Lucy and the man called Randolph Higgins, seeming to wall them off into a place of their own.

"Now you're supposed to say 'It's a pleasure to make your ac—' "

"I don't need lessons in idle conversation," she said. Lord knew, her mother had taught her that well enough. Ensconced in a North Division mansion, Viola Hathaway had elevated frivolity to an art form.

"Then we should move on to meaningful conversation," he said.

"What makes you think you and I could have a meaningful conversation?" she asked. Her parents had spent a fortune to drill her in manners, but all the deportment lessons in the world had failed to keep Lucy from speaking her mind.

She wished Mr. Higgins would go away. Far away. A man who produced this sort of discomfiting reaction in her had no possible use except . . .

Lucy was nothing if not honest with herself. Perhaps she should quit trying to feel peevish and admit that she was most inappropriately intrigued. A sudden, sinful inspiration took hold. Perhaps he *could* be useful. As a New Woman who adhered fervently — if only in theory, alas — to the radical notion of free love, Lucy felt obliged to practice what she preached. Thus far, however, men found her unattractive and annoyingly intellectual. Mr. Higgins, at least, seemed to find her interesting. This was a first for Lucy, and she didn't want to let the opportunity slip away.

"You're looking at me like a cat in the creamery," he whispered. "Why is that?"

She snapped her head around and faced front, appalled by her own intoxicating fantasy. "You're imagining things, sir. You do not know me at all."

The lecture started up again, a boring recitation about the ancient founders — male, of course — of the Christian faith. She tilted her chin up and fixed an expression of tolerant interest on her face. She'd promised Miss Boylan not to argue with the preacher; her radical views often got her in trouble, tainting the reputation of Miss Boylan's school. Instead she kept thinking about the stranger beside her. What wonderful hands he had — large and strong, beautifully made for hard work or the most delicate of tasks.

Lucy tried to push her attraction away to the hidden place in her heart where she kept all her shameful secrets.

Men were trouble. No one knew this

better than Lucy Hathaway. She was that most awkward of creatures, the social misfit. Maligned, mocked, misunderstood. At dancing lessons when she was younger, the boys used to draw straws in order to determine who would have the ill luck to partner the tall, dark, intense girl whose only asset was her father's fortune. At the debutante balls and soirees she attended in later years, young men would place wagers on how many feet she would trample while waltzing, how many people she would embarrass with her blunt questions and how many times her poor mother would disappear behind her fan to hide the blush of shame her daughter induced.

In a last-ditch effort to find their daughter a proper place in the world, Colonel and Mrs. Hathaway had sent her away to be "finished." Like a wedding cake in need of icing, she was dispatched to the limestone bastion called the Emma Wade Boylan School for Young Ladies, and expected to come out adorned in feminine virtues.

Women whose well-heeled papas could afford the exorbitant tuition attended the lakeside institution. There they hoped to attain the bright polish of refinement that would attract a husband. Even those who were pocked by imperfection might eventually acquire the necessary veneer. Lucy found it bizarre that a young woman's adolescence could end with instructions on how best to arrange one's bustle for sitting, or all the possible shades of meaning created by a crease in a calling card, yet she'd sat through lengthy lectures on precisely those topics. To her parents' dismay, she was like the wedding cake that had crumbled while being carried from oven to table. No amount of sugar coating could cover up her flaws.

Whenever possible, Lucy buried her social shortcomings between the delicious, diverting pages of a book. She adored books. Ever since she was small, books had been her greatest treasures and constant companions, offering comfort for her loneliness and escape from a world she didn't fit into. She lived deeply in the stories she read; caught up in the pages of a book, she became an adventuress, an explorer, a warrior, an object of adoration.

And ironically, her many failures at Miss Boylan's had endeared her to some of the other young women. There, she'd made friends she would cherish all her life. The masters at the school had long given up on Lucy, which gave her vast stretches of free time. While others were learning the proper use of salt cellars and fish forks, Lucy had discovered the cause that would direct and give meaning to her life — the cause of equal rights for women.

She certainly didn't need a man for that.

"We stray too far from the virtues our church founders commanded us to preserve and uphold," boomed the Reverend Moody, intruding into Lucy's thoughts. She stifled a surge of annoyance at the preacher's words and pressed her teeth down on her tongue. She mustn't speak out; she'd promised. "The task is ours to embrace tradition . . ."

Lucy had a secret. Deep in the darkest, loneliest corner of her heart, she yearned to know what it was like to have a man look at her the way men looked at her friend Deborah Sinclair, who was as golden and radiant as an angel. She wanted to know what it was like to laugh and flirt with careless abandon, as Deborah's maid, Kathleen O'Leary, was wont to do belowstairs with tradesmen and footmen. She wanted to know what it was like to be certain, with every fiber of her being, that her sole purpose in life was to make a spectacular marriage, the way Phoebe Palmer knew it.

She wanted to know what it would be like to lean her head on a man's solid shoulder, to feel those large, capable hands on her —

Exasperated with herself, she tried to focus on the mind-numbing lecture.

"Consider the teachings of St. Sylvius," the preacher said, "who taught that 'Woman is the gate of the devil, the path of wickedness, the sting of the serpent, in a word a perilous object.' And yet, my friends, it has been proposed that in some congregations women be allowed to hold office. Imagine, a *perilous object* holding office in church —"

"Oh, for Pete's sake." Lucy shot up as if her chair had suddenly caught fire.

Moody stopped. "Is there some discussion, Miss Hathaway?"

Unable to suppress her opinions any longer, she girded herself for battle. She'd promised Miss Boylan she wouldn't make waves, but he'd pushed her too far. She gripped the back of the empty chair in front of her. "As a matter of fact, we might discuss why our beliefs are dictated by men like St. Sylvius, who kept paramours under the age of fourteen and sired children concurrently with three different women."

Scandalized gasps and a few titters swept through the audience. Lucy was accustomed to being ridiculed and often told herself that all visionaries were misunderstood.

Still, that didn't take the sting out of it.

"How do you know that?" a man in the front row demanded.

Well-practiced in the art of airing unpopular views, she stated, "I read it in a book."

"I'd wager you just made it up," Higgins accused, muttering under his breath.

She swung to face him, her bustle knocking against the row of chairs in front of her. Someone snickered, but she ignored the derisive sound. "Are you opposed to women having ideas of their own, Mr. Higgins?"

Half his mouth curved upward in a smile of wicked insolence. He was enjoying this, damn his emerald-green eyes. "So long as those ideas revolve around hearth and home and family, I applaud them. A woman should take pride in her femininity rather than pretend to be the crude equal of a man."

"Hear, hear," several voices called approvingly.

"That's a tired argument," she snapped. "A husband and children do not necessarily constitute the sum total of a woman's life, no matter how convenient the arrangement is for a man."

"I reckon I can guess your opinion of men," he said, aiming a bold wink at her.

"But don't you like children, Miss Hathaway?"

She didn't, truth be told. She didn't even know any children. She had always considered babies to be demanding and incomprehensible, and older children to be silly and nonsensical.

"Do you?" she challenged, and didn't bother waiting for a reply. "Would you ever judge a man by that standard? Of course you wouldn't. Then why judge a woman by it?"

He made the picture of masculine ease and confidence as he stood and bowed to Reverend Moody. "Shall we remove this discussion to a more appropriate locale?" he inquired. "A sparring ring, perhaps?"

Laughing, Moody stepped back from the podium. "On the contrary, we are fascinated. I yield the floor to open discussion."

Fine, thought Lucy. They all expected her to disgrace herself. She could manage that with very little effort. She swept the room with her gaze, noting the presence of several prominent guests — Mr. Cyrus McCormick and Mr. George Pullman, whose enterprises had made them nearly as wealthy as Lucy's own father, Colonel Hathaway, hero of the War Between the States. She spied Mr. Robert Todd Lincoln, son of the late great Emancipator and one of the leading social lights of the city. Jasper Lamott, head of the Brethren of Orderly Righteousness, sat in smug superiority. Watching them, she felt an ugly little stab of envy. How simple it was for men to stand around discussing great matters, secure in the knowledge that the world was theirs for the taking.

"I believe," she said, "that women have as much right as men to hold office in the church or the government. In fact, I intend to support Mrs. Victoria Woodhull's campaign for president of the United States," she concluded grandly.

Higgins's brow descended with disapproval. "That woman is a menace to decent people everywhere."

Lucy felt a surge of outrage, but the heated emotion mingled strangely with something unexpected — the tingling excitement touched off by his nearness. "Most unenlightened men think so."

"Her ideas about free love are disgusting," Jasper Lamott called across the room, instigating rumbles of assent from the listeners.

"You only think that because you don't understand her," Lucy stated.

"I understand that free love means immorality and promiscuity," Higgins said.

"It most certainly does not." She spoke with conviction, trying to do honor to the great woman's ideas, even though she knew her mother would be calling for smelling salts if she heard Lucy debating promiscuity with a strange man in front of a crowd of avid listeners.

"Isn't that exactly what she means?" Randolph Higgins asked. "That a woman should be allowed to follow her basest instincts, even abandoning her husband and family if she wishes it?"

"Not in the least." In the audience, heads swung back and forth as if they were watching a tennis match. "The true meaning of free love is the pursuit of happiness. For men and women both."

"A woman's happiness is found in marriage and family," he stated. "Every tradition we have bears this out."

"Where in heaven's name do we get this tradition of pretending a marriage is happy when one of the parties is miserable? Marriage is a matter of the heart, Mr. Higgins, not the law. When a marriage is over spiritually, then it should be over in fact."

"You're almost as much of a menace as she is," he said with a harsh laugh. "Next you'll be telling me you approve of divorce."

"And you'll be telling me you believe a

fourteen-year-old girl forced to wed an alcoholic should stay with him all her life." That was precisely what had befallen Victoria Woodhull. But rather than being beaten down by circumstances, she'd begun a crusade to free women from the tyranny and degradation of men.

"People must learn to live with the choices they've made," he said. "Or is it your conviction that a woman need not take responsibility for her own decisions?"

"Like many women, Mrs. Woodhull wasn't allowed to decide. And sir, you know nothing about me nor my convictions."

"You're a spoiled, overprivileged debutante who deals with boredom by stirring up trouble," he stated. "If you really cared about the plight of women, you'd be over in the West Division, feeding the hungry."

A smattering of applause came from some of the men.

"Women would be better served if men would simply concede their right to vote."

"You should relocate to the Wyoming Territory. They allow women to vote there."

"Then they don't need me there," Lucy insisted. "They have already won."

"Such passion," he said.

"Whether you'll admit it or not, the entire

universe revolves around feelings of passion."

"My dear Miss Hathaway," Mr. Higgins said reasonably, "that is exactly why we have the institution you revile — marriage."

A curious feeling came over Lucy as she sparred with him. She expected to feel offended by his challenges, but instead, she was intrigued. When she looked into his eyes, a shivery warmth came over her. She kept catching herself staring at his mouth, too, and thinking about the way it had felt when he had whispered in her ear. The feeling was quite . . . sexual in nature.

"The institution of marriage has been the cornerstone of mankind since time was counted," he said. "It will take more than an unhappy crackpot female to convince the world otherwise."

"The only crackpot here is —"

"I beg your pardon." Like a storm of rose petals, Phoebe Palmer entered the salon, her face a mask of polite deference. The finishing school's self-appointed doyenne of decency always managed to reel Lucy in when she teetered on the verge of disgrace. "Miss Lucy is needed and it's ever so urgent. Come along, dear, there we are." For a woman of the daintiest appearance, Phoebe had a grip of steel as she took Lucy by the arm. Without making a scene, Lucy had no choice but to follow.

"There is a name for the institution you advocate, Mr. Higgins," she said, firing a parting shot over her shoulder. "Fortunately, slavery was rendered illegal eight years ago by the Emancipation Proclamation."

Phoebe gave a final tug on her arm and pulled her through the doorway. "I declare," she said, scolding even before they left the room, "I can't leave you alone for a moment. I thought a Christian lecture would be safe enough, but I see that I was wrong."

"You should have heard what they were saying," Lucy said. "They said we were the gate of the devil."

"Who?"

"Women, that's who. You would have spoken up, too."

Phoebe's mouth twitched, resisting a smile. "Ah, Lucy. You're always shooting your mouth off and getting in trouble. And I am constantly trying to stop you from committing social suicide."

"I think I did that already, last August when I burned my corset at that suffrage rally." Lucy extracted her arm from Phoebe's grip. "Speaking of trouble, how is

Kathleen getting along?"

"That's why I came to get you." Phoebe gestured toward the French doors, draped by fringed velvet curtains. "She is flirting outrageously with Dylan Kennedy."

Lucy followed her gesture and spied Kathleen O'Leary in an emerald gown, her head of blazing red hair bright against the backdrop of Mr. Dylan Kennedy's dark suit. Watching them, she felt a keen sense of satisfaction. Kathleen was much more than a lady's maid. She was their friend. And tonight, she was their pet project.

Their prank was a social experiment, actually. Lucy claimed it was possible to take an Irish maid, dress her up in finery, and no one would ever guess at her humble background. Phoebe, an unrepentant snob, swore that people of quality would see right through the disguise.

Framed by the French doors, Kathleen tilted her head and smiled at Mr. Kennedy, one of the most eligible bachelors in Chicago. The night sky in the background seemed to glow and pulse with the city lights. As she watched, Lucy felt a tug of wistfulness. They were both so attractive and romantic, so luminous with the sparkling energy that surrounded them. She could not imagine what it would be like to have a man admire her that way.

"Well," she said briskly to Phoebe. "One thing is clear. I have won the wager. You must donate a hundred dollars to the Women's Suffrage Movement."

"There's still time for Kathleen to stick her foot in her mouth." Phoebe sent Lucy a wry smile. "However, tonight that seems to be your specialty."

Lucy laughed. "Only tonight?"

"I was trying to be polite." She linked arms with Lucy again. "I wish Deborah had come with us this evening."

A frisson of anxiety chased away Lucy's good humor. "She seemed quite ill when we left Miss Boylan's."

"I'm sure she will be fi— Good heavens, it's Lord de Vere." Without a backward glance, Phoebe sailed off to greet the weak-chinned English nobleman, whom she hoped and prayed she might marry one day.

Lucy caught herself thinking about Mr. Higgins, and the way their public disagreement had led to private thoughts. It was a rare thing, to meet a man who made her think. She should not have antagonized him so, but she couldn't help herself. He was provocative, and she was easily provoked.

As more people filed out of the lecture salon, she spotted him moving toward the adjoining room, and felt herself edging toward an admission. An admission, followed by a plan of action, for that was Lucy's way. She saw no point in believing in something without acting on that belief.

What she admitted to herself, what she had come to believe, was that she was wildly attracted to Mr. Randolph Higgins. Until tonight, she'd never met a man who made her feel the lightning sting of attraction. It had to mean something. It had to mean that he was the one.

That was where her plan of action came in. She wanted him for her lover.

When he went over to a long table, laden with punch and hors d'oeuvres, she marched straight across the room to him. He gave no sign that he'd seen her, but when he turned away from the table, he held two cups of lemonade.

"You," he said, handing her a cup, "are the most annoying creature I have ever met."

"Really?" She took a sip of the sweet-tart lemonade. "I take that as a compliment."

"So you are both annoying *and* slow-witted," he said.

"You don't really think that." Watching him over the rim of her cup, she added, "I am complimented because I have made you think."

Lord, but he was a fine specimen of a man. She felt such a surge of triumph that she could not govern the wide grin on her face. She'd found him at last. After a lifetime of believing she would never meet someone who could arouse her passion, share her dreams, bring her joy, she'd finally found him. A man she could admire, perhaps even love.

"Do I amuse you?" he asked, frowning goodnaturedly.

"Why would you think that?"

"Because you keep smiling at me even though I have just called you annoying and —"

"Slow-witted," she reminded him.

"Yes," he said. "Rude of me."

"It was. But I forgive you." She glanced furtively from side to side. "Mr. Higgins, do you suppose we could go somewhere . . . a little less public?" Before he could answer, she took his hand and pulled him toward the now-empty lecture room. The dry windstorm that had been swirling through the city all evening battered at the windows. Gaslight sconces glowed on the walls, and orange light flickered mysteriously in the windowpanes. Rows of gilded chairs flanked a central aisle, and just for a moment, as she led him along the crimson carpet runner toward the front of the room, she had the fanciful notion that this was a wedding.

"Miss Hathaway, what is this about?" he asked, taking his hand from hers.

"I wanted to speak to you in private." Her heart raced. This was a simple matter, she told herself. Men and women arranged trysts all the time. She should not get over-wrought about it.

"Very well." He propped his hip on the back of a chair, the pose so negligently masculine and evocative that she nearly forgot her purpose. "I'm listening."

"Did you enjoy the lecture tonight, Mr. Higgins?"

"Honestly?"

"Honestly."

"It was a crashing bore."

Clearly he didn't share her passion for debate. She pulled in a deep breath. "I see. Well, then —"

"— until a certain young lady began to speak her mind," he added. "Then I found it truly interesting."

"Interesting?"

"Yes."

"And . . . provocative?"

"Most definitely."

"Did you think it was . . . stimulating?"

40

He laughed aloud. "Now that you mention it."

Her spirits soared. "Oh, I am glad, Mr. Higgins. So glad indeed. May I call you Randolph?"

"Actually my friends call me Rand."

She most definitely wanted to be his friend. "Very well, Rand. And you must call me Lucy."

"This is a very odd conversation, Lucy."

"I agree. And I haven't even made my point yet."

"Perhaps you should do so, then."

"Make my point."

"Yes."

Ye gods, she was afraid. But she wanted him so much. "Well, it's like this, Mr. — Rand. Earlier when I spoke of passionate feelings, I was referring to you."

His face went dead white. His mouth moved, but no sound came out.

"You see," she rushed on, "I've always wanted to have a lover. I never did encounter a man I wanted to spend my life with, and if I took a lover I would simply have no need of a husband."

"Lucky you." Some of the color, and arrogance, returned to his handsome face.

She could sense suppressed laughter beneath his wry comment. "But I wouldn't want a love affair just for the sake of having one. I've been waiting to meet a man I felt attracted to." She looked him square in the eye. "And I've found you at last."

The humor left his expression. "Lucy." The low timbre of his voice passed over her like a caress.

"Yes?"

"Lucy, my dear, you are a most attractive girl."

She clasped her hands, thoroughly enchanted. "Do you think so?"

"Indeed I do."

"That is wonderful. No one has ever thought me attractive before." She was babbling, but couldn't help herself. "My mother says I am too intense, and far too outspoken, and that I —"

"Lucy." He grasped her upper arms.

She nearly melted, but held herself upright, awaiting his kiss. She'd never been kissed by a man before. When she was younger, Cornelius Cotton had kissed her, but she later found out his older brother had paid him to do it, so that didn't count. This was going to be different. Her first honest-to-goodness kiss from the handsomest man ever created.

Late at night, she and the other young ladies of Miss Boylan's would stay up after lights-out, whispering of what it was like to kiss a man, and of the ways a man might touch a woman. One thing she remembered was to close her eyes. It seemed a shame to close them when he was so wonderful to look at, but she wanted to do this right. She shut her eyes.

"Lucy," he said again, an edge of desperation in his voice. "Lucy, look at me."

She readily opened her eyes. What a glorious face he had, so alive with character and robust health and touching sincerity. So filled with sensual promise, the way his lips curved into a smile, the way his eyes were brimming with . . . pity? Could that be pity she saw in his eyes? Surely not.

"Rand —"

"Hush." Ever so gently, he touched a finger to her lips to silence her.

She burned from his caress, but he quickly took his finger away.

"Lucy," he said, "before you say anymore, there's something I must tell you —"

"Randolph!" a voice called from the doorway. "There you are, Randolph. I've been looking all over for you."

Lucy turned to the back of the salon. There, in the doorway, stood the most stunning woman she'd ever seen. Petite, blond and willowy, she held her lithe body in the shape of a question mark, clad in a beautiful gown bearing the trademark rosettes of Worth's Salon de Lumière. In a rustle of perfumed silk, she moved toward them, hand outstretched toward Rand.

"I've found you at last," the gorgeous blond woman said, her words an ironic echo of Lucy's.

Rand's pallor quickly changed to dull red as he bowed over her hand. "Miss Lucy Hathaway," he said, straightening up and stepping out of the way, "I'd like you to meet Diana Higgins." He slipped an arm around her slender waist. "My wife."

Two

For a few seconds, only the wailing of the night wind filled the silent void. Something, some bizarre state of nerves in those endless seconds, gave Rand a heightened sensitivity. The pads of his fingers, resting at the small of his wife's back, detected the smooth, taut silk over the armored shell of her corset. From a corner of his eye, he saw Diana's expression change from mild curiosity to keen nosiness. And although she probably did not mean to be audible, he heard Miss Lucy Hathaway breathe the words, "Oh. My."

Just that, coupled with an expression probably shared by Joan of Arc at the moment of her martyrdom. She looked as though she was about to vomit.

Foolish baggage, he thought. This was no less than she deserved for making outrageous proposals to strange men.

"How do you do, Miss Hathaway?" Diana said, unfailingly polite as she always was in social situations.

"Very well, thank you, Mrs. Higgins. It's a distinct pleasure to make your acquaintance." Lucy didn't shrink from Diana's probing gaze.

Despite his opinion of the radical young woman's views, Rand could not deny his interest. She was not only the most annoying creature he'd ever met, she was also the most compelling. Dark-haired and dark-eyed, she had a heart-shaped face. Her pointed chin, high brow and wide eyes gave her an expression of perpetual wonder. The passion and sensual awareness she'd spoken of so boldly seemed to reside in the depths of those velvety dark eyes, and in the fullness of her lips.

Yet as quickly as she'd shocked him with her outrageous proposal, she seemed to come to heel like a spaniel trained to obedience when thrust into a social situation. She dutifully exchanged pleasantries with Diana, who described their recent move from Philadelphia, and chatted about the unseasonable heat that plagued the city, robbing Chicago of the clear, chill days of autumn.

"Well, I must thank you for keeping my husband entertained," Diana remarked. "He was quite certain this would be a hopelessly dreary evening."

Rand shifted beneath a mixed burden of guilt and irritation. During the argument they'd had prior to his coming to the evening's event, he'd claimed she'd be bored by a bombastic evangelical reading, and that the only reason he was attending was to make the acquaintance of the prominent businessmen of Chicago.

The irony was, he'd really meant it.

Lucy Hathaway clasped her hands demurely in front of her. "I'm afraid I've failed, then," she said. "Your husband doesn't find me at all entertaining. Quite the contrary. I fear I've offended him with my . . . political opinions."

"You're not offensive, Miss Hathaway," Rand said smoothly. "Merely *wrong*."

"Isn't he charming?" Diana laughed. Only Rand, who knew her well, heard the contempt in her voice.

Miss Hathaway moved toward the door. "I really must be going. I don't like the look of the weather tonight." She curtsied in that curious trained-spaniel manner. "It was a pleasure to meet you both, and to welcome you to Chicago. I hope you'll be very happy here." In a swish of skirts and wounded dignity, she walked out of the salon.

"What an odd bird," Diana remarked in an undertone.

What a strangely charming bundle of contradictions, Rand thought. He was intrigued by women like Lucy. But he was also discomfited by a surprising and unwelcome lust for her. He'd engaged her in what he thought was a harmless flirtation, nothing more, but she had taken him seriously.

"How on earth did you get stuck with her?" asked his wife.

He'd seen her sitting alone at the back of the salon, and pure impulse had compelled him to sit down beside her. He thought about the way Lucy had taken his hand later, captured his gaze with her own and confessed her attraction to him. But to his wife, he said, "I have no idea."

"Anyway, you did well," Diana declared. "It's important to impress the right people, and the Hathaways are undoubtedly the right people."

"What are you doing here? Is Christine all right?" he asked.

"The child is fine," Diana said. "And I came because *I* am the one who is sick, not our daughter. I am positively ill with boredom, Randolph. All I've done all day long is sit by the window watching the boats on the river and the traffic going over the bridge to the North Division. I'm so tired of living like a gypsy in a hotel. Shouldn't you have started work on the house by now?"

"You're sure Christine's fine," he said, ignoring her diatribe. Their fifteen-month-old daughter was the bright and shining center of his life. Earlier in the evening she'd been fretful, a little feverish, and he'd convinced Diana to stay at Sterling House rather than leave Christine with the nurse.

"The baby was fast asleep when I left," Diana said. "Becky Damson was in the parlor, knitting. I thought you'd be delighted to see me, and here you are, flirting away with the most famous heiress in Chicago."

"Who? Lucy?"

"And on a first-name basis, no less. The Hathaways are an Old Settler family. Her father is a war hero, and her grandfather made a fortune in grain futures. If you hope to be a successful banker, you're supposed to know these things."

"Ah, but I have you to keep track of them for me."

"Apparently I need someone to keep track of you," she observed.

Already regretting the brief flirtation, he vowed to devote more attention to his increasingly unhappy wife. No matter what he did, it wasn't enough. She'd been dissatisfied with their life back in Philadelphia, so he'd moved her and their baby daughter to Chicago.

He was trying to launch a career in banking while Diana frantically shopped and planned for the grand house they intended to build on the fashionable north shore. But even the prospect of a palatial new residence failed to keep her discontent at bay.

"Come and meet Mr. Lamott," Rand suggested, knowing she would be impressed, and that Jasper Lamott — like every other man — would find his wife enchanting.

As he escorted her into the reception salon, Rand fought down a feeling of disappointment. When he and Diana had married, he'd been full of idealistic visions of what their life together would be like. He had pictured a comfortable home, a large, happy family putting down roots in the fertile ground of convention. They were things he used to dream about when he was very young, things he'd never had for himself. But as the early years of their marriage slipped by, Diana paid little attention to roots or family. She seemed more interested in shopping and travel than in devoting herself to her husband and child.

He kept hoping the move to Chicago would improve matters, but with each passing day, he was coming to understand that a change of venue was not the solution to a problem that stemmed from the complicated inner geography of his heart.

He caught himself brooding about Lucy Hathaway's bold contention that women were stifled by the unfair demands foisted upon them by men who shackled them with the duties of a wife and mother.

"Do you feel stifled?" he asked Diana.

She frowned, her pale, lovely face uncomprehending. "What on earth are you talking about, Randolph?"

"By Christine and me. Do you feel stifled, or shackled?"

She frowned more deeply. "What a very odd question."

"Do you?"

She took a step back. "I have no idea, Randolph." Then she fixed a bright, beautiful, artificial smile on her face and walked into the reception room.

Rand couldn't help himself. He kept trying to catch a glimpse of Lucy Hathaway, but apparently she and her friends had already left the hotel. For the past forty minutes, he'd wanted to do the same, anxious to get back to Sterling House and his daughter. She would be asleep by now, but that didn't matter. He loved to watch Christine sleep. The sight of her downy blond

51

curls upon a tiny pillow, her chubby hands opened like stars against the quilt, always filled him with a piercing tenderness and a sense that all was right with the world.

Diana had never been quite so well-entertained by their daughter, although she was proud of Christine's beauty and loved the admiring comments people made when they saw the baby. At the moment she was gossiping happily with the mayor's nieces and showed no sign of wanting to leave.

Restless, Rand went to the tall windows that framed a view of the city. Gaslight created blurry stars along the straight arteries of the main thoroughfares and the numerous tall buildings of the business district gathered around the impressive cupola of the massive courthouse.

"Quite a sight, isn't it?" asked a slender, vaguely sly-looking young man.

Philip Ascot, Rand recalled. Ascot, with some combination of Roman numerals after his name to prove to the world that the family hadn't come up with an original name in several generations.

It was a mean, petty thought, borne of impatience. Still, he had a low opinion of Ascot, who claimed to be in the publishing business but who, as far as Rand could tell, intended to make his fortune by marrying one of the debutantes of Miss Boylan's finishing school. Lucy? he wondered, recalling Diana's assessment that the Hathaways were stinking rich.

Rand stifled a grin. Lucy would make duck soup of a fellow like Philip Ascot.

"It is indeed," he said at last. Flipping open the gold top of his pocket watch with his thumb, he checked the time. "It's a bit late for sunset, though."

"Oh, that's another fire in the West Division," Ascot informed him. "Didn't you hear?"

A cold touch of alarm brushed the back of his neck. "I heard there was one last night, but that it had been brought under control."

"It's been a bad season for fires all around. But I can't say I'm sorry to see the West Division burn. It's a shantytown, full of immigrant poor. Could stand a good clearing out." Ascot tossed back a glass of whiskey. "Nothing to worry about, Higgins. It'll never get across the river."

Even as he spoke, an explosion split open the night. From his vantage point, Rand saw a distant flash of pure blue-white light followed by a roaring column of pale yellow flame.

"It's the gasworks," someone yelled. "The gasworks have blown!"

Rand crossed the reception room in three strides, grabbing his wife by the arm. "Let's go," he said.

"Randolph, you mustn't be rude —"

"We're leaving," he said. "We've got to get home to Christine."

Three

The big, blocky coach with the crest of Miss Boylan's school on the door lumbered through streets jammed with people. Every few feet, the driver was obliged to stop and make way for the firefighters' steam engines or hose carts.

"It's spreading so quickly." Phoebe Palmer pressed her gloved hands to the glass viewing window. "Who could imagine a fire could move so fast?"

She clearly expected no answer and didn't get one. Both Lucy and Kathleen O'Leary were lost in their own thoughts. Kathleen was particularly worried about her family.

"I knew I shouldn't have come," she said, her customary easy confidence shaken by the sight of the fleeing crowds. "I shall burn in hell entirely for pretending to be a great lady."

"If we don't start moving any faster," Phoebe said, "we shall burn right here in Chicago." She yanked at the end of the speaking tube and yelled at the driver to hurry. "There's an abandoned horsecar in the middle of the avenue," she reported, cupping her hands around her eyes to see through the fog of smoke and sparks. "Driver," she yelled again into the tube, "go around that horsecar. Quickly." With a neck-snapping jerk, the big coach surged forward. Phoebe scowled. "He's usually better at the reins," she commented peevishly. "I shall have to speak to Miss Boylan about him."

As the coach picked up speed, Lucy patted Kathleen's hand. "None of this is your fault, and you're surely not being punished for a silly prank." To distract her, she added, "And it went well, didn't it? Everyone at the reception believed you were a famous heiress from Baltimore."

Just for a moment, excitement flashed in Kathleen's eyes. How beautiful she was, Lucy thought. What would it be like to be that beautiful?

But then Kathleen sobered. "I lost my reticule. Miss Deborah's reticule, actually, for haven't I borrowed every stitch I have on except my bloomers? And I made a fool of myself altogether over Dylan Kennedy."

"So did half the female population of Chicago," Phoebe pointed out, sounding unusually conciliatory.

"All those worries seem so small now." Kathleen turned her face to the window.

"Blessed Mary, the whole West Division is in flames. What's become of my mam and da?"

"I'm sure they're fine," Lucy said. "You'll find them once everything is sorted out."

" 'Tis easy enough for the two of you to relax. Your families, bless them, are safe in the North Division. But mine . . ." She bit her lip and let her voice trail off.

Lucy's heart constricted. Inasmuch as she envied Kathleen's beauty, Kathleen coveted Lucy's wealth. How terrible it must be to worry and wonder about her parents and brothers and sisters, living in a little wood frame cottage, her mother's cow barn stuffed with mill shavings and hay.

Lucy thought of her own parents, and Phoebe's, secure in their mansions surrounded by lush lawns and wrought-iron gates. The fire would surely be stopped before it reached the fashionable north side.

She'd grown up insulated from the everyday concerns of a working family. She knew better now, and in a perverse way, she wanted to repent for her privileges, as if by being wealthy she was somehow responsible for the ills of the world. Phoebe thought her quite mad for staggering around beneath a burden of guilt. Phoebe just didn't understand. Because women of their station were complacent, ills befell those who had no power, women forced to endure drunken abuse from their husbands, giving birth year in and year out to children they could not afford to raise.

Lucy patted Kathleen's hand. "I'll help you find your family if you like."

Phoebe pointed out the window. "Not tonight you won't. Honestly, Lucy, I believe you would try to save the entire city if you could. You and your crusades."

"If we don't take the lead, then who will?" she asked. "The washerwoman bent over her ironing board? She doesn't have time to eat a proper meal much less lead a march for equal rights. We're the ones who have the time, Phoebe. We know the right people, for Lord's sake, we were just at a gathering with every person of influence in the city. And what did we talk about?" She flushed, thinking of her conversation with Randolph Higgins. "The weather. The opening of Crosby's Opera House tomorrow night. The contention that women are gates of the devil. It's absurd, I say. I, for one, intend to make some changes."

"Ah, Lucy." Phoebe sighed dramatically. "Why? It's so . . . so *comfortable* to be who we are."

Lucy felt a stab of envy. Phoebe was content to be a society fribble, to let her father hand her — and a huge dowry — in marriage to some impoverished European nobleman, simply for the status of it all. Phoebe actually seemed to be looking forward to it.

Lucy felt a stronger affinity with Kathleen, an Irish maid who felt certain she'd been born into the wrong sort of life and had other places to go.

As she looked out the window and saw well-dressed families in express wagons and carriages practically running over stragglers clad in rags, outrage took hold of her.

"There is plenty of room in this coach," she said, a little alarmed at the speed now. "We must stop and take on passengers."

"Oh, no, you don't." Phoebe grabbed the speaking tube. "You'll start a riot, the horses will balk and then no one will get where they're going."

Lucy spied a woman in a shawl, burdened with an infant in one arm and a toddler clinging to her other hand. Rolling up the leather flap covering the side window, she shot Phoebe a defiant look and leaned out the door. A flurry of sparks stung her face, and she blinked hard against a thick fog of smoke. "Driver," she called. "Driver, stop for a mo—"

Then she stopped cold. She was speaking to nothing but smoky air. The driver had fled. There was no one controlling the team of horses.

She drew herself back into the coach. "I don't suppose," she said as calmly as she could, "either of you know of a way to get the team under control."

Phoebe gave a little squeak and groped for her smelling salts.

Kathleen stuck her head outside the window. The coach swayed dangerously, and she clutched at the side. "Saints and crooked angels," she said. "There's no driver."

She said something else, but Lucy couldn't hear her because an explosion shook the night. Fueled by some forgotten store of kerosene or gas, a fireball roared down the street toward them. The coach jerked forward, narrowly evading the incendiary.

Lucy grabbed Kathleen's skirt and pulled her in. Kathleen's face was pale but firm. Phoebe moaned, looking dizzy and sick as buildings and people passed in a blur of speed. Then she pressed herself back against the tufted seat and shut her eyes, lips moving in desperate prayer.

Kathleen detached the stiff leather windshield of the coach, letting in a hot storm of sparks and smoke. Phoebe coughed and screamed, but Lucy made herself useful, helping Kathleen up to the driver's seat. Kathleen, who had learned to drive on her mother's milk wagon, tried to get hold of the reins, yelling "Ho!" at the top of her lungs.

The panicked team plunged down the street. The tallest structures in Chicago were burning, their high windows disgorging flames that lit the night sky. People were trapped in the upper stories, calling out the windows for help. Some of them dropped bundles of blankets containing valuables and breakables. Lucy was shocked to see that one of the bundles contained a live dog, which fought itself free of the bedding and ran off in a panic.

The horses churned along in confusion, knocking aside pedestrians and other vehicles as they headed straight for the heart of the fire. Phoebe screamed until Lucy grabbed her shoulders and shook her.

"That's not helping, you goose," she shouted, then prepared to climb up next to Kathleen, who had managed to catch hold of a flailing leather ribbon. Digging in her heels, she hauled back with all her might. Lucy grabbed the rein and added her strength to the tugging. The horses plunged and fought, but finally slowed.

Lucy let out a giddy laugh of relief. "Oh, thank —"

A second explosion crashed through the smoky night. The conflagration drew so much air that, for a moment, the flames around them died. The hot void left no air to breathe, then returned with a roaring vengeance. From the corner of her eye, Lucy saw Kathleen blown from her seat.

Lucy called to her, but the horses bolted again. Now she could do nothing but cling to the reins and pray.

Up ahead, the road veered sharply. The runaway team made the turn, but the coach teetered on two wheels, then went over. Lucy launched herself at Phoebe and they clung together. The coach landed on its side with teeth-jarring impact. The horses strained and whistled, trying to flee, but with the rockaway on its side, they could hardly move. The lead horse went up on its hind legs, raking the air with its hooves.

"Phoebe?" Lucy said, still holding her.

"Remind me to report the driver for negligence," Phoebe said shakily.

Good, thought Lucy. If she was well enough to complain, then she was well enough to climb out.

"I'm going to try to get the door open," she said. The door was now above her, and the latch had been torn away. She pounded with her fists, then put the strength of her back into it. Finally the small half door opened like a hatchway on the deck of a ship.

To her relief, Kathleen stood at the roadside, singed and disheveled, peering in.

"Are you all right?" the Irish girl asked.

"We are." Lucy took her proffered hand and pulled herself out of the fallen coach. The panicked horses created a menace with their rearing and shrill whinnies.

"Help me," Phoebe cried, her glass-beaded gown tearing.

Lucy and Kathleen pulled her out, and she began exhorting passersby for help. But the pedestrians had their own concerns and ignored her.

"It's every man — every woman — for herself," Lucy declared, feeling oddly liberated by the notion. "Let's try to get the horses loose."

"Loose?" Phoebe blew a lock of brown hair out of her face. "If we do that, they'll run off and we'll be stranded. We should try to get the coach upright again." She studied the ominous blazing sky in the west. "We can't outrun this fire on foot."

"Everyone else is." Lucy gestured at the bobbing heads of the crowd, borne along as if by a river current.

"Sir!" Phoebe shrieked at a man hurrying past.

He swung around to face her, and even Lucy felt intimidated. He was huge, clad in fringed buckskins, with long, wild hair. Even more terrifying was the large knife he took from the top of his boot. Phoebe's knees buckled and she shrank against Lucy. "Dear God, he's going to —"

The wild man cut the leather reins of the team. A second later, the horses galloped away, disappearing into a bank of smoke along with the stranger.

"He — he — the horses!" Phoebe said.

"At least they have a chance now." Lucy grabbed Phoebe's hand. "This way. We'll go on foot."

"I'll do nothing of the sort." Phoebe dug in her heels. "I won't get half a block in these shoes."

Lucy was losing patience, but the sight of bellowing flames, marching like an army toward them, kept her focused on escape. She spied a flatbed wagon and hailed the driver, yanking off a ruby brooch as he approached. "Can you give us a ride?" she asked.

He snatched the jewel, swept his gaze over her and jerked a thumb toward the rear of the cart. "Don't let anything fall off," he said.

The load of rolled carpets, gilt paintings and furnishings teetered precariously as the wagon lurched along the road. The sky burned so brightly that Lucy had to squint to look at it.

She was doing just that when Kathleen jumped off the back of the cart and ran toward a bridge to the West Division. Lucy screamed her name, but this time it was Phoebe who was the voice of reason. "Let her go." Phoebe coughed violently. "She won't rest until she gets home, and we must do the same. Our way is north, Lucy. You know it is."

Shaken, Lucy clutched her friend's hands and tried not to wonder if they would ever see Kathleen again.

The Chicago River cut a line from east to west across the city before turning south, where the conflagration had started. The howling windstorm had fanned an ordinary fire into a holocaust riding a gale, moving with voracious speed, devouring everything in sight.

Lucy had never seen such a powerful force of nature. The fire smashed through whole neighborhoods at a time, destroyed reputedly fireproof buildings and then did the unthinkable — it leaped across the south branch of the river.

The wind was the fire's greatest ally, driving the flames from rooftop to rooftop. Wooden shingles offered fuel for the blaze to feast upon. In the famous shopping district known as Booksellers Row, the buildings burned from the ground upward.

All those lovely books. Lucy winced at the thought of them being incinerated.

A towering dervish of flame reared at the end of the block, illuminating and then overtaking a throng of people.

Phoebe's face turned pale in the angry light. "Did you see that?" she asked Lucy.

"I did." As far as Lucy could tell, they were on Water Street, heading eastward toward the lake. She supposed that the driver would attempt to cross the river at the State or Rush Street Bridges into the North Division.

"The flames are moving faster than a person can run." Phoebe craned her neck and shouted over the stacked bundles in the wagon, "Driver, do hurry! The fire is closing in!"

"I can't go any faster than the crowd in front of me," he yelled in a hoarse voice, ragged from the smoke.

The closer they came to the lake, the denser the mob grew. The river was choked with boats and barges trying to get out onto the open water. The taller ones couldn't clear the bridges, and many caught fire as they waited for the bridges to rotate. As Lucy watched, a boy climbed the rigging of a sloop and scrambled up to the bridge, hoisted by someone in the crowd. But for the most part, people stampeded across in heedless terror, dropping things along the way, pushing strangers aside in ruthless terror.

Lucy's father, Colonel Hiram B. Hathaway, always said that a disaster brought out the best and worst in people, and she realized that she was witnessing the truth of it — timid men performing acts of heroism, pillars of society trampling the wounded in their haste to get to safety.

Her parents lived in the tree-shaded splendor of an elegant neighborhood to the north, but that didn't mean her family was safe. Aggressive, blustering and imperative, the Colonel, as he was known even though he was retired, had a public spirit that would not rest. If the city was burning, he was bound to launch himself into the thick of things.

A decorated war veteran, he was an expert in ammunition and explosives. This would make him particularly useful to those in charge of fighting the fire. The fire companies had resorted to blowing up the buildings in the path of the fire, robbing it of fuel. No doubt the Colonel would be directing the operations, his bewhiskered face ablaze with energy as he planned strategy to battle the flames.

In the midst of danger and mayhem, the thought of her father brought Lucy a needed measure of fortitude. Though he often grew exasperated with his outspoken daughter, the Colonel never treated her with anything less than respect. From a long line of old New England bluebloods, he was a gentleman to his core. He'd attended West Point, married the most socially prominent girl in Chicago and had distinguished himself in battle at Kenaha Falls, Bull Run and Vicksburg.

But as she grew up, Lucy came to realize that his love and devotion to her and her mother manifested itself in a protectiveness so fierce it was stifling. The Colonel tried to shield his daughter from everything — hunger, hurt, ugliness. He didn't understand that, in protecting her from what he considered life's ills, he was walling her off from life itself.

When she asked after the state of his business affairs, he would brush aside her queries, declaring that she needn't worry her pretty head about such vulgar matters. While her mother was ready enough to accept his patronizing ways, Lucy was indignant.

"For one thing," she once said to him, "my head is *not* pretty. For another, I can decide for myself what is worrisome and what is not."

Yet for all their differences, they shared a deep love and respect for each other, and Lucy said a silent prayer for her father's safety.

Reflecting on the evening at the Hotel Royale, she felt more foolish than ever. Of all the social outrages she had committed, tonight's faux pas had been the worst. When people looked back on this date, they would recall it as the night Chicago had burned to the ground.

But not Lucy. For the rest of her life, she would remember a far different disaster — this was the night she had brazenly propositioned a married man.

Four

"Did you *see* what Mrs. Pullman was wearing?" Diana asked as she and Rand left the Hotel Royale. Brushing impatiently at a flurry of sparks that flew around the hem of her gown, she added, "Her jewels were positively vulgar. She wasn't nearly as vulgar as that snippy little suffragist you were entertaining, though. If not for her family name, she'd be a pariah, wouldn't she, Randolph?"

Knowing she didn't expect a response, Rand tucked her hand more firmly into the crook of his arm and scanned the roadway. They had only been in Chicago for a short while, so he was unfamiliar with the city. But the streets were laid out in a neat grid, and he knew they had to head north to Water Street, where Sterling House was located.

An express wagon rattled by, but the driver ignored Rand's raised arm. A few hansom cabs, crammed with occupants, passed them without slowing. "We're wasting time trying to hire a ride," he said. "We'd best go on foot."

"Don't be ridiculous, Randolph. I never

walk anywhere." She drew her mouth into the sweetest of pouts. "Let's wait until something returns to the livery stables."

He clenched his teeth in frustration. On the one hand, he didn't want to alarm her about the fire. But on the other, he wanted her to understand the need to hurry. They had to get to their daughter and make sure she was all right.

The one option he never considered was leaving Diana. He'd sling his wife over his shoulder like a caveman if he had to, but he would never leave her. "We're walking," he finally said, pulling her along. "You can yell at me on the way."

Diana apparently decided that silence was a better punishment. She didn't speak to him, though she clutched his arm and leaned on him every few steps. Her fashionable, imported shoes were unsuited for walking any distance.

It was just as well she didn't speak, for he wasn't all that kindly disposed to his wife at the moment. He'd counted on her to stay with Christine. Instead, she'd grown bored and joined him at the lecture. Some men might have been flattered, but Rand knew Diana all too well. She hadn't come looking for him. She'd come seeking a diversion from her boredom and had left their daughter in the care of someone they barely knew. Becky Damson seemed a fine young woman, but he had learned long ago not to trust appearances.

After this night was over, Rand decided, he would find a way to turn Diana's attention and enthusiasm to the needs of her family. He wasn't certain how to go about it. Some women derived fulfillment from their duties as wives and mothers. He'd seen it himself, though not in his own mother.

The memory ignited a bitterness in Rand that never seemed to mellow. When he was ten years old, Pamela Higgins had walked away from her husband and young son, never to return. Rand had been raised by Grace Templeton Higgins, his paternal grandmother.

But his mother's departure had left a hidden wound in his soul that he'd carried around all his life. When he'd started a family of his own, he had sworn he would never have the sort of wife who would abandon her family.

A blast sounded in the next block, and a fountain of sparks mushroomed in the sky. Whipping off his frock coat, Rand covered Diana's head and shoulders with it. She huddled close against him, and despite their annoyance at each other, he felt a surge of tenderness toward her.

"We'll be home soon," he said. "I imagine it's only a few more blocks."

"That's what you said a few blocks ago."

Another blast ripped through the neighborhood, tearing the awnings from buildings and leaves from the few trees still standing. In the smoky distance, Rand made out a crew of militia men with a two-wheeled cart loaded with explosives.

"What on earth is happening?" Diana asked.

"They're blasting away buildings to create a firebreak."

In the road ahead, the fire spun and whirled across rooftops. His gut tightened, and he quickened his pace. His instincts screamed for him to run toward his baby daughter, but he couldn't leave Diana.

People jostled one another in a mad dash for the river or the lakefront. Family groups moved in tight clusters — men with their arms around their wives, women carrying babies or clutching toddlers by the hand. The sight of the children tore at him. He heard Christine's name in the hiss of the wind.

He thought about how casually he'd left her tonight, how casually he always left her, certain that he would return. Now, as he

73

fought and jostled his way through the packed street, he was haunted by images of his daughter.

On the day she was born, his heart had soared. At last he had what he'd always dreamed of — a family. He'd created something enduring and true. That very day he'd bought two cases of rare champagne, packing them away to bring out on the occasion of her wedding. It was a sentimental gesture, though he was not a sentimental man. But Christine had found a place in his heart where softness dwelled, and he cherished her for finding that part of him.

Tightening his grip on Diana's hand, he felt his wife's mounting fear, heard it in the little gulping breaths she took. As he forged ahead, Rand bargained with fate: He would devote more time to Christine. He'd work harder to please Diana, quit flirting with women no matter how provocative he found them and find a way to make Diana more content in her role as wife and mother. If only he could save his child.

Everything came to a standstill at a jammed intersection near Courthouse Square. Too many streets converged here, and chaos ruled. Disoriented, Rand wasn't sure of the way north.

"Which way to Water Street?" he bellowed at a passing drayman with a lurching, overloaded cart. The man didn't look at him but pointed. "You've got three blocks to cover and it'll be hard going. There's a bad flare-up ahead." A gap opened up and he drove his cart through it.

Rand pressed on. He noticed that Diana had fallen silent again, and he slipped his arm around her waist. "We'll get there," he promised, but a sudden explosion drowned his words.

"Look at the sky." She pointed at the wavering, burnished horizon ahead. "The whole city is on fire."

He led the way up a side street. In the middle of the roadway, a police paddy wagon had broken its axle. Swearing, the driver opened the wagon and fled while the conveyance disgorged a dozen convicts in striped shirts and trousers. Some of the prisoners swarmed into burning shops, but one of them advanced on Rand and Diana. Firelight flashed in his flat, dangerous eyes as his gaze traveled over Diana's gown and jewels.

He raised a rocklike fist. "Give me all your valuables. *Now.*"

Diana gave a squeal of alarm and buried her face in Rand's shoulder.

Rand pulled away from her. In an instant, his fear for Christine and frustration with the crowds crystallized into a pure and lethal rage. He didn't will himself to act, but the next thing he knew, he had the convict shoved up against a concrete wall, his hand clamped over the man's windpipe.

"Get the hell away from us," Rand said, his voice harsh with a deadly purpose.

The looter gagged, clawing at the hand on his neck. Rand let him go and backed off, sick at the thought of what he'd nearly done. The convict staggered away and disappeared into the crowd.

"Heavens, Randolph, I've never seen you like that," Diana said.

The breathless admiration in her voice did not please him. He took her hand again. "We're almost there. *Hurry.*"

"I can't see a thing through this smoke."

Rand pulled her along as fast as he could. Buildings burned from the roof down and others from the ground up. People dropped bundles from windows and exterior staircases. A ladder crew helped women trapped in a tall building, and the rescued ladies scattered like ants when they reached the street.

"Surely Sterling House has already been evacuated. Becky Damson would have fled to safety." Diana's eyes streamed as she spoke between panting breaths. "Yes,

Becky's got a good head on her shoulders. She is probably already at the lakeshore with Christine, waiting for us to find them. That is where we must go — to the lake."

Rand could think of no reply and she didn't seem to expect one. He prayed Diana was right about the nursemaid. Miss Damson had been recommended by the concierge of the hotel. But Rand had assumed she would be an adjunct to Diana, not a substitute.

He ground his teeth together, for he knew if he spoke they would be words of recrimination. And what was the point of that, especially here and now?

The wind picked up, and there was no way to stay ahead of the flames. He could hardly see his own wife in the thick curtain of smoke. For a few detached moments he felt adrift, his sense of direction unseated by a force too huge to control.

Rand didn't like things he couldn't control.

He drove himself harder, pulling insistently at Diana, who by now was so exhausted that she lacked the energy to complain. He focused on one thing and one thing only — getting to Christine.

They passed Ficelle's Paint and Varnish Factory, a long, low building that covered half a block. Firebrands rained down on the roof of the factory, and an ominous glow throbbed behind its small, square windows.

"I think we're almost there," Rand told his wife. "Only a block to go."

Diana coughed. "I can't see anything."

"It's just there, see?" His heart lifted as he spotted the distinctive dome of Sterling House.

Then a roaring gust of wind cleared the smoke like the parting of a curtain. It gave Rand a glimpse of hell. Sterling House, where he'd left his baby daughter, was engulfed in flames.

"*No!*" he bellowed, and for the first time, he let go of Diana's hand.

As he started to run, an unnatural and toxic burst of white heat flared inside the varnish factory. A flash, followed by an ear-splitting explosion, shattered the night. The detonation sucked the oxygen from the air, from his lungs, even.

The force of it picked him up off his feet and blasted him backward. The landing broke his arm; he could feel the dull snap of the bone, the stunning pain. Gritting his teeth, he dragged himself up and dove for Diana, who lay slumped on the pavement.

As he covered her body with his own, chunks of brick from the collapsing building rained over him. With his good arm, he tried to hold on to his wife and pull them both away, but the shower of bricks turned to a deluge. Rand could feel the breaking of his ribs, and then his shoulder was struck numb. The falling rubble kept coming in a thick, deadly avalanche, burying him and Diana.

No oh no oh please . . . The disjointed plea was drowned by the lethal crash of the building. Diana made a sound — his name, perhaps — and her hands clutched at him. Something hard and sharp struck his skull.

He had the sensation of floating, though he could not have moved amid all the falling bricks. There was no pain anymore. Only light. A hole in the sky, its edges burning, a white glow in the center.

And then there was nothing.

Five

"Look at that," Phoebe said, indicating a building by the river. "The hose crew has simply abandoned Sterling House."

The fashionable hotel's distinctive glass dome glowed bright yellow as flames licked up its walls. In the smoke-filled street in front of the residence, a cart was reeling in its hoses and moving on.

"I imagine they realized they could never control the fire," Lucy said. They'd seen so much destruction on the slow journey to the bridge that she began to feel as beaten down as the crew. "Let's pray the building was evacuated," she added. Most of the hotel's windows disgorged mouthfuls of flame. But on the second story, a single window stared at her like a blank, dark eye.

As they drew closer to the river, she spied an elderly man struggling along the roadside with painful slowness. When a woman bumped him in her rush to the bridge, he stumbled.

"Driver, stop for a moment!" Lucy jumped out of the cart. "I'm going to give my seat to that gentleman," she said.

Phoebe opened her mouth to deliver the expected protest, but Lucy held up her hand. "Don't waste time arguing," she said, pulling the shaken, wheezing man to the cart and tucking a saddle blanket around him. "You've got to get across the river before the bridge gets even more crowded."

"But if *you* do something noble, then *I* shall have to," Phoebe wailed.

"Dear, you must stay with the cart," Lucy said, accustomed to mollifying her friend. "The most noble thing you can do is hold fast to this gentleman and keep him in the cart. I'll follow on foot."

The elderly man shuddered and closed his eyes. Lucy put Phoebe's arm around his shoulders and signaled to the driver to move on. Just then an earsplitting explosion knocked her to her knees. Phoebe squealed and the cart lurched forward, disappearing into a wall of boiling smoke. Someone shouted that a varnish factory had just exploded.

Lucy stayed down on hands and knees, trying to recover the breath that had been knocked out of her. Her lungs seized up, unable to fill. She was suffocating. Light-headed, half-mad thoughts shot through her mind, but her air-starved brain couldn't grasp them.

The firelit images around her left a trail through the night sky, like the tails of bright comets. The wind had an eerie voice all its own, keening through the flaming row of doomed buildings. Flying debris — paper, clothing, sheets of metal — littered the air. Everyone else had disappeared. The last of the stragglers had gone to the bridge and there was no one in sight. Focus, she told herself. She stared at a burning building across the way. She'd gone to the very exclusive Sterling House for tea a time or two, her stomach in knots from the lecture her mother had given her on acting like a lady, sipping her tea demurely, nodding in agreement with anything a man cared to say, keeping her scandalous opinions to herself.

She wasn't sorry to see the last of that place.

What she saw next reinflated her lungs with a gasp of terror. The second-story window, the one she'd seen earlier, was now filled with flame — and a woman holding a bundle, screaming.

Without any conscious effort, Lucy propelled herself across the street.

The fire lashed out with a roar, its long tentacles of flame reaching for the hysterical woman trapped in the window, grasping her.

Lucy stood alone under the window, the heat singeing her eyebrows and lashes. She had no idea how to help the poor woman. The hotel entry was impassable, its doors blasted out by the flames, the marble lobby melting in the inferno. She looked around wildly for a ladder, a rope, anything.

The woman's screaming spiked to a shrill peal of hysteria. Her dress or nightgown had caught fire. A second later, the screaming stopped. Then something fell from the window.

Simple reflex caused Lucy to hold out her arms. The impact knocked her to the pavement, and once again the air rushed from her lungs. A cracking sound, like the report of a shotgun, split the air. The walls of the hotel shook, and the roof caved in, sucking down the big glass dome, and then the flaming rubble of the building itself. The woman disappeared, swallowed like a pagan sacrifice into the devouring flames.

Lucy sensed a movement in the bundle she held, but there was no time to check. She forced herself to scramble to her feet. Still clutching the bedding, she ran for her life, hearing the swish of raining glass and the boom of gas lines igniting. With a glance over her shoulder, she saw a geyser of smoke and sparks where the hotel used to be.

Racing to the river, she hurtled down the bank toward the water. She slipped in the mud, landed on her backside and slid downward into darkness. Firelight glimmered on the churning surface of the water, but the immediate area was sheltered from the flames.

Something buried within the bundle of bedding moved again.

Lucy shrieked and set it down. Planting her hands behind her, she crab-walked away.

Then she heard a sound, the mewing of a kitten.

"Oh, for heaven's sake," she said, disgusted with herself. "The poor woman was trying to save her cat." What a noble deed, she thought. The woman must have known she could not survive the fire, and as her last act on earth she'd bundled up her pet and tossed it to a stranger for safekeeping.

Hurrying now, Lucy knelt down beside the untidy parcel. The least she could do for the doomed woman was look after the cat. Firelight fell over her, and she felt a fresh stab of panic, knowing she'd best get over the bridge to safety.

The bulky parcel had been tied with satin ribbons of good quality, a man's leather belt and a long organdy sash. A lady's robe or peignoir formed the outer wrapping, and inside that were two pillows, a quilt and what appeared to be an infant's receiving blanket.

With more urgency than a child on Christmas morning, Lucy removed the wrappings, hoping the cat wouldn't bolt once she freed it.

It didn't bolt. It wasn't a cat.

Lucy shrieked again, this time with surprise, not fear.

Her shriek caused the little creature to wail in terror, round mouth open like the maw of a hatchling wanting to be fed.

Except it wasn't a hatchling, either. It was a *baby*. No, a toddler.

Lucy couldn't speak, couldn't even think. The firelight winked over the child, who kept wailing and pedaling chubby legs under a long pale gown.

"Oh, God," Lucy whispered. "Oh, Lord above." She could think of nothing more to say, and had no idea what to do. A baby. She'd saved somebody's baby.

She couldn't tell if it was male or female, though she saw with some relief that it was moving and bawling with great vigor. The fall from the window hadn't hurt it in the least. It must be hardier than it looked, then.

"Who . . . what on earth am I going to do with you?" Lucy asked, looking the child in the eye.

Something in her tone or her look must have caught the baby's attention, for it stopped crying and simply stared at her.

"Well?" she asked, encouraged.

The baby took a deep breath. Lucy actually thought it might speak to her, though she realized it was a very young child. Then it let loose with another wail. As she watched, it rolled over and crawled away, trailing the little blanket in the mud.

Lucy was completely at a loss. She'd never seen a baby up close before, but the sight of it, so helpless and lost, sparked a powerful instinct in her. She reached out and touched it, then tried to gather it up in her arms.

It was awkward, like trying to hold a wriggling litter of puppies, all waving limbs, surprisingly powerful.

"Come now," Lucy said. "There, there."

The baby quieted when she spoke, and stilled its flailing for a moment. The heated sky glowed ominously, and she knew she had to get them both to safety. When she stood, the child clung to her, its tiny hands clutching at her and its legs circling her waist.

"You poor thing," she said, eyeing the burning sky. "We have to go. Once you're safe, we'll find out who you belong to."

But in her heart of hearts, she already knew that the child's mother had perished in the collapsing hotel. Somehow she would have to find its surviving family. Not now, though. Now, her challenge was to make her way to her parents' home.

"Come along," she said. Her hand curved around the baby's head. The curly, fair hair was soft as down. "I'll take care of you." Keeping up a patter of encouraging words, she struggled with the ungainly burden of the child, climbing the riverbank toward the bridge. "You'll be safe with me."

"Oh, thank the Heavenly Father above, you're safe." Patience Gloriana Washington opened the door of the huge mansion on North Avenue to let Lucy in. Patience wore her plain preacher's garb, a habit she'd adopted when she'd embraced poverty, but no somber robe could mask her naturally regal air. Though she had never set foot outside Chicago, she resembled an African princess. Famous for her magnetic preaching in Chicago's largest Negro church, Patience was a close friend of the Hathaway family. Her older sister, Willa

Jean, had been the Hathaways' housekeeper since the war ended, and Lucy and Patience had practically grown up together.

"Land a-mercy, what you got there, girl?" she asked, regarding the muddy, bedraggled bundle in Lucy's arms.

Lucy sagged against the door, exhausted, her arms shaking from carrying the baby all the way from the bridge. About ten blocks ago, it had fallen dead asleep, its head heavy on her shoulder, and now it rested there, ungainly as a sack of potatoes.

"It's a baby," she whispered, pushing aside the blanket to reveal a head of wispy golden curls. "Its mother bundled it up and dropped it from a window while the building burned and I — I caught it." She took a long, shuddering breath. "Then the building collapsed, and I fear the woman died."

"I swear, that's a miracle for sure." A soft glow suffused Patience's face. "It purely is. Especially since —" She broke off. "Boy or girl?"

Lucy blinked. "I don't know. There wasn't time to check."

"Land sakes, let's take a look." With expert hands, Patience took the sleeping baby into the parlor and gently laid it on an ottoman. The child stirred and whimpered, but didn't fully awaken. She unpinned its diaper. "A girl," she said. "A precious baby girl. Looks to be about a year old, more or less."

Lucy stared in awe as Patience swaddled the child. A baby girl. She couldn't believe she'd rescued a baby girl. The child stretched and yawned, then blinked. When she saw Patience's face, she let out a thin wail.

"Oh, please," Lucy said. "Please don't cry, baby."

When she spoke, the baby turned to her, and an amazing thing happened. Something like recognition shone in the little round face, and she reached up with chubby hands. The deep, fierce instinct swept over Lucy again, and she picked the little girl up. "There now," she said. "There, there." Nonsense words, but they made the crying stop.

Patience watched them both, her eyes filled with a sad sort of knowing. "The Almighty is at work tonight," she murmured. "Sure enough, he is."

For the first time, Lucy noticed streaks of hastily dried tears on Patience's face. A chill slid through her, and she stood up, still holding the tiny girl. "What's happened?"

Patience touched her cheek, her warm,

dry hand trembling a little. "You best go see your mama, honey. Your daddy was bad hurt fighting the fire."

Lucy felt the rhythm of dread pounding in her chest like a dirge.

"I'll take the baby," Patience offered.

"I've got her." Lucy led the way up the stairs and rushed to her father's bedroom, adjoined by double doors to his wife's suite of rooms. Dr. Hauptmann was bent over the four-poster bed, and Viola Hathaway sat in a chair beside it. Patience's sister, Willa Jean, knelt on the floor, crooning a soft spiritual.

Lucy had never seen her mother in such a disheveled state. She wore a dressing gown and her hair hung loose around her face. Holding her arms clasped across her middle, she rocked rhythmically back and forth, taking in little sobs of air with the motion.

"Mama!" Lucy hurried over to her. "Are you all right? What happened to the Colonel?"

The doctor stood up, pinching the bridge of his nose as if trying to hold in emotion. "I'm so sorry," he murmured. "So very sorry."

"Lucy, my dear Lucy," her mother said, never taking her eyes off her husband. "He's gone. Our dear dear Colonel is gone."

Lucy's arms tightened around the child, who had stopped crying and was making soft cooing sounds. She pressed close to the bed.

Colonel Hiram Hathaway lay like a marble effigy, as handsome and commanding in death as he'd been in life. In flashes of remembrance, she saw that face lit with laughter, those big hands holding hers. How could he be gone? How could someone as strong and powerful as the Colonel be dead?

"He went out to fight the fire," Patience said. "You know your daddy. He'd never sit still while the whole city was on fire. He was with a crew of military men, knocking down buildings with dynamite. They brought him home an hour ago. Said he got hit on the head. He was unconscious, never even woke up, and right after we put him to bed he just . . . just went to glory."

A choking, devastating disbelief surged through Lucy as she sank to her knees. "Oh, Colonel." She used the name she'd called him since she was old enough to speak. "Why did you have to be a hero? Why couldn't you have stayed safe at home?" She freed one hand from the baby's blanket and gently touched the pale, cool cheek with its bushy side-whiskers. "Oh, Colonel. Were you scared?" she asked, her hand starting to shake. "Did it hurt?" She couldn't find any more words. What had they said to each other last time they were together?

She couldn't remember, she realized with rising panic. "Patience," she whispered. "I can't remember the last time I told my father I loved him."

"He knew, honey," Patience said. "Don't you worry about that. He just knew."

Lucy wanted to throw herself upon him, to weep out her heartbreak, but a curious calm took hold of her. Resolution settled like a rock in her chest. She would not cry. The Colonel had taught her never to weep for something that couldn't be changed. No tears, then, to dishonor his teachings.

"Good night, Colonel," she whispered, pressing a kiss to his cold hand. He still smelled of gunpowder.

Her mother sat devastated by shock, rocking in her chair. "What shall I do?" she said. "Whatever shall I do without him?"

"We'll manage," Lucy heard herself say. "We'll find a way."

"I shall die without him," her mother said as if she hadn't heard. "I shall simply lie down and die."

"Now, don't you take on like that, Miss

Viola," Willa Jean said. She had a deep voice, compelling as a song. But it was a small, bleating whimper from the baby that caught Viola's attention.

Lucy's mother stopped rocking and stared at the bundle in Lucy's arms. "What on earth — Who is that?" she asked.

Lucy turned so she could see. "It's a baby, Mama. A little lost girl. I rescued her from the fire."

"Heavenly days, so it is. Oh, Hiram," she said, addressing her dead husband while still staring at the child, who stared back. "Oh, Hiram, look. Our Lucy has brought us a baby."

Part Three

A woman's ability to earn money is better protection against the tyranny and brutality of men than her ability to vote.
— Victoria Claflin Woodhull

Six

Chicago
May 1876

"Where do babies come from, Mama? Really."

Lucy looked across the breakfast table at her daughter and smiled at the little face that greeted her each morning. Having breakfast together was part of their daily routine in the small apartment over the shop. Usually she read the *Chicago Tribune* while Maggie looked at a picture book, sounding out the words. But her daughter's question was much more intriguing than the daily report from the Board of Trade.

"I know where you came from," Lucy said. "You fell from the sky, right into my arms. Just like an angel from heaven." It was Maggie's favorite story, one she never tired of hearing — or repeating for anyone who would listen.

The little girl stirred her graham gems and frowned. She was stubbornly left-handed, a trait that often reminded Lucy of the mystery surrounding her. "Sally Saltonstall says

97

that's an old wives' tale."

"I'm not an old wife." Lucy gave a bemused chuckle. "I'm not even a young wife. I'm not anyone's wife."

"Sally says you can't be my mama if you're not nobody's wife."

"Anybody's wife. And Sally is full of duck fluff for telling you that."

Maggie passed Lucy the stereoscope she'd received for her birthday last fall. They didn't know her exact birthday, of course, so they had chosen October 8, the date of the Great Fire that had changed so many lives. Each year, Lucy gave a party for Margaret Sterling Hathaway, commemorating the night they had found each other.

"Look at the picture in there," Maggie said. "It shows a family, and the mama has a husband called the papa."

Lucy obliged her daughter by peering into the two lenses of the stereoscope. The shadowy, three-dimensional image depicted an idealized family — the mother in her demure dress, the upright, proper, bewhiskered father in boiled collar and cuffs and two perfectly groomed children, a boy and a girl.

"These are just strangers dressed up to look like a family," she said, ignoring a nameless chill that swept through her. "We *are* a proper family. I'm your mother, you are my daughter, forever and ever. Isn't that what a family is?"

"But the papa's missing." Maggie thoughtfully wiggled her top front tooth, which was very loose now and about to come out. "Could Willa Jean be the papa?"

Willa Jean Washington, the Hathaways' former maid, now worked as the bookkeeper of Lucy's shop.

Lucy shook her head. "Traditionally the papa is a man, darling."

"But you always say you're rearing me in a nontraditional way."

Lucy couldn't help laughing at the sound of such a sophisticated phrase coming from her young, precocious daughter. "You know, you're right. Maybe we'll ask Willa Jean if she'll be the papa."

"Do you think she knows how?" Maggie asked. "What does a papa *do*, anyway?"

With a gentle bruise of remembrance, Lucy thought of her own father. The Colonel had issued directives. He'd demanded obedience. Insisted upon excellence. And in his own commanding way, he'd loved her with every bit of his heart.

"I suppose," she said, "that a papa teaches things to his children, and loves and protects and provides for them."

"Just like you do," Maggie said.

Lucy felt a surge of pride. What had she ever done to deserve such a wonderful child? Maggie truly *was* an angel from heaven. Lucy set down the stereoscope. "Come here, you. I have to get down to the shop, and you and Grammy Vi have sums to do this morning."

"Sums!" Her face fell comically.

"Yes, sums. If you get them all correct, we can go riding on our bicycles later."

"Hurrah!" Maggie scrambled into her lap and wrapped her arms around Lucy's neck.

Lucy savored the sweet weight of her and inhaled the fragrance of her tousled hair, which had darkened from blond to brown as she grew. It was hard to imagine that there had been a time, five years before, when Lucy hadn't known how to hold a child in her arms. Now it was as natural to her as breathing.

The Great Fire had raged for days, though it had spared the block of elegant houses in the Hathaways' neighborhood. Hundreds of people had shown up for the Colonel's funeral, and Viola had received a telegram of condolence from President Grant. The day after they had buried the Colonel, Lucy had taken the baby to the Half-Orphan Asylum.

She shuddered, remembering the bilious smell of the institution, the pandemonium in the rickety old building, the cries of lost children and frantic parents searching for one another, the stern wardens taking charge of those without families. She'd hurried away from the asylum, vowing to find a more humane way to look after the child.

In the weeks following the fire, Lucy and her mother had been forced to flee the city to escape an epidemic of typhoid brought on by the lack of good drinking water. Even from a distance, Lucy kept sending out notices to find the child's family, to no avail. No trace was found of the woman who had perished after dropping her bundled child from the window. Despite advertisements Lucy had placed in the papers and frequent inquiries at the asylum and all the churches and hospitals in town, she'd found no clue to the orphaned baby's identity.

As she straightened the kitchen and took off her apron, she reflected on how much their lives had changed since the fire. Every aspect of their world was different. It was as if the hand of God had swept down and, with a fist of flame, wiped out their former lives.

After the smoke had finally cleared and a desultory, unreliable rain shower had spat out the last of the embers, Lucy, her mother and a fretful baby had gathered around a table with the bankers and lawyers, to learn that the Colonel had left them destitute. The fire had not only taken the Colonel, but his fortune as well, which had been invested in a Hersholt's Brewery and Liquor Warehouse. Uninsured, it had burned to the ground that hot, windy October night.

Her mother was lost without her beloved Colonel. As much as Lucy had loved her father and grieved for him, she'd also raged at him. His love for her and her mother had been as crippling as leg irons. He had willfully and deliberately kept them ignorant of finance, believing they were better off not knowing the precarious state of the family fortune. His smothering shield had walled them off from the truth.

For days after the devastating news had been delivered, Lucy and her mother, burdened with a demanding little stranger, had sat frozen in a state of dull shock while the estate liquidators had carted off the antiques, the furniture, the art treasures. Lucy and her mother had been forced to sell the house, their jewels, their good clothing — everything down to the last salt cellar had to go. By the time the estate managers and creditors had finished, they had nothing but the clothes on their backs and a box of tin utensils. Viola had taken ill; to this day Lucy was convinced that humiliation was more of a pestilence to her than the typhoid.

There was nothing quite so devastating as feeling helpless, she discovered. Like three bobbing corks in an endless sea, she and her mother and the baby had drifted from day to day.

Lucy had found temporary relief quarters in a shantytown by the river. She would have prevailed upon friends, but Viola claimed the shame was more than she could bear, so they huddled alone around a rusty stove and tried to bring their lives into some sort of order. Not an easy task when all Viola knew in the world was the pampering and sheltering of her strong, controlling husband; all Lucy knew was political rhetoric.

It was providence, Lucy always thought, that she'd been poking through rubbish for paper to start a fire, and had come across a copy of *Woodhull & Claflin's Weekly*, published by Tennessee Claflin and her sister, Victoria Woodhull, known in those days as The Firebrand of Wall Street. Since she'd appeared before Congress and run for president the year of the Great Fire, the flamboyant crusader had captivated Lucy's imagination and inflamed her sense of righteousness. But that cold winter day, while huddled over a miserable fire, Lucy had read the words that had changed the course of her life. *A woman's ability to earn money is better protection against the tyranny and brutality of men than her ability to vote.*

Suddenly Lucy knew what she must do — something she believed in with all her heart, something she'd loved since she was a tiny child.

Everything had fallen into place after that epiphany. In the fast-recovering city, Lucy had taken a bank loan, leased a shop in Gantry Street, occupied the small apartment above it and hung out her tradesman's shingle: The Firebrand — L. Hathaway, Bookseller.

Running a bookshop hadn't made her a wealthy woman, not in the financial sense, anyway. But the independence it afforded, and the knowledge that she purveyed books that made a difference in people's lives, brought her more fulfillment than a railroad fortune.

The trouble was, one could not dine upon spiritual satisfaction. One could not clothe one's fast-growing daughter with moral righteousness. Not during a Chicago winter, anyway.

Silky, the calico cat they had adopted a few years back, slunk into the room, sniffing the air in queenly fashion. Maggie jumped down from Lucy's lap and stroked the cat, which showed great tolerance for the little girl's zealous attentions.

"Run along, then," she said, kissing the top of Maggie's head. "Tell Grammy Vi that I've gone down to the shop."

"And bicycles later," Maggie reminded her.

"Bicycles later," said Lucy.

Tucking the paper under her arm, she took the back stairs down to the tiny court-yard behind the shop. A low concrete wall surrounded an anemic patch of grass. A single crabapple tree grew from the center, and just this year it had grown stout enough to support a rope swing for Maggie. The tiny garden bore no resemblance to the lush expanses of lawn that had surrounded the mansion where Lucy had grown up, but the shop was just across the way from Lloyd Park, where whitecapped nannies and black-gowned governesses brought their charges to play each day. When the weather was fine, Maggie spent hours there, racing around, heedless of the censorious glares of the governesses who were clearly scandal-ized by hoydenish behavior.

Lucy allowed herself a wicked smile as she thought of this. She was raising Maggie to be free and unfettered. No corsets and stays for her daughter. No eye-pulling braids or heat-induced ringlets. Maggie wore loose Turkish-style trousers, her hair cropped short and an exuberant grin on her face.

But sometimes, when she wondered about where she'd come from, she asked hard questions.

Lucy took a deep breath, squared her shoulders and walked into the shop. The bell over the door chimed, drawing the attention of Willa Jean.

"Good morning," Lucy said cheerfully. No matter what her troubles, the very sensation of being in the middle of the bookstore, *her* bookstore, lifted her heart. There was something about books. The smell of leather and ink. The neat, solid rows of volumes, carefully catalogued spine-out on the shelves. The lemony scent of furniture oil on the tables and the friendly creak of the pine plank floor. The gentle hiss of gaslight, the scratching of Willa Jean's pencil. Most of all, Lucy supposed, she loved the sense that she stood in the middle of something she'd built, all on her own. She'd spun it out of a dream, dug it out of disaster and lavished her love upon it the way many women did when building a home.

This was her home. And if, from time to time, she felt an ache of loneliness that not even Maggie could fill, she still told herself she had more than most women could expect in a lifetime, and she should be grateful. Those secret yearnings shamed her. She was supposed to be a New Woman, fulfilled by her own industry.

The one thing she couldn't figure out was how a New Woman dealt with needs as old as time. In certain quiet moments, the old loneliness stole over her. With veiled envy she watched young couples strolling together or stealing kisses when they thought no one was watching. Too often, she caught herself yearning to know a man's touch, his affectionate regard and his passion. The one drawback to free love, she'd discovered, was that with so many choices available, no man seemed likely to choose her.

" 'Bout time you got yourself down here." Willa Jean peered accusingly from beneath the green bill of her bookkeeper's cap. "We got to go over the figures for the bank."

A cold clutch of apprehension took hold of Lucy's gut. She'd had the entire weekend to prepare for this, but in fact she'd tried not to think about it. Perhaps that was a bit of her mother coming out in her. If she didn't think about troubles then they didn't exist.

But here was a problem she couldn't wish away.

"All right," she said. "Show me the books, and tell me exactly what I should say to the bank."

Willa Jean flopped open a tall ledger on the desk in front of her. Willa Jean was as clever with numbers as her sister Patience was with scripture. Willa Jean was gruff, blunt and usually right.

This morning, her bluntness was particularly apparent. "If you don't get an extension on your loan, you'll default and lose the shop," she concluded.

Lucy pushed her hand against her chest, trying to still the wing beats of panic there. "I don't expect the bank to cooperate. Our loan was sold to the Union Trust three months ago."

"All banks are the same, girl. They want to make money off you. Your job is to prove you're a good risk."

"Am I a good risk, Willa Jean?"

A bark of laughter escaped the older woman. "A bookseller? Honey, it ain't like you're selling grain futures here." She gestured around the shop. "These are books, see? People don't eat them, they don't manufacture furniture out of them, they don't keep them to increase in value. They *read* them. And who has time to read? Everyone's so all-fired busy trying to make a living, they don't read anymore."

"So my job is to convince a strange man that I can make a profit in a dying enterprise."

"Uh-huh."

"Remind me. Why did I get up this morning?"

Willa Jean held out an appointment card. "There's the name of the person you're to see. It's the bank president, girl. At least that's something."

Lucy glanced at the card, then froze in amazement. She was looking at a name she hadn't seen in a very long time, but one she had never forgotten. Mr. Randolph B. Higgins.

Seven

"Mr. Higgins?"

Rand glanced up from his desk to see his secretary in the doorway to the office. "Yes, Mr. Crowe?"

The earnest young man crossed the room and held out a small note. "A message from Mrs. Higgins, sir."

"Thank you, Mr. Crowe. Do I have any other appointments this afternoon?"

"One more, sir. It's about a loan extension." He set down a flat cardstock file, bound with a brown satin ribbon. "One of those loans in the batch you acquired from Commonwealth Securities."

"Thank you," Rand said again, keeping his expression impassive. He never betrayed his opinion about a professional matter, even to his secretary. It was this fierce discretion that had secured his reputation in the banking business, and he wasn't about to compromise that.

In the years since the fire, Rand had discovered within himself not just a talent for banking, but a passion for it. He welcomed the responsibility of looking after people's money and embraced the task of lending to those who demonstrated a brilliant idea, an acute need or a promising enterprise. Sometimes he thought his love of banking was the only reason he'd carried on following those shadowy, pain-filled months after the fire.

When Crowe left, Rand opened the note, written in a fine, spiderweb hand on cream stock imported from England. At the top was the Higgins crest, a pretentious little vanity created by his great-grandfather decades ago. The gold embossed emblem of an eagle winked in the strong sunlight of late afternoon. Rand stood by the window to read the note.

Another invitation, of course. She was constantly trying to broaden his social horizons, trolling the elite gatherings of the city like fishermen trolled Lake Michigan for pike, and setting her netted catch before Rand.

The trouble was, he thought wryly, that after a while the catch began to stink. It wasn't that he had no interest in social advancement — he knew as well as anyone that, in his business, connections mattered. It was just that he found them tedious and, deep down, hurtful.

This evening's soiree was a reception for a popular politician, arranged by Jasper

Lamott, who also happened to be on the board of the Union Trust. Lamott's group, a conservative organization called the Brethren of Orderly Righteousness, was raising funds to oppose a bill before the legislature giving women dangerously broad rights to file suit against their own husbands. Like all decent men, Rand was alarmed by the rapid spread of the women's suffrage movement, which was causing families to break apart all across the country. He believed women were best suited to their place as keepers of hearth and home, with men serving as providers and protectors. Perhaps he would attend the event after all. He would most certainly make a generous donation to the cause. The fact that women no longer knew or respected their place had brought him no end of trouble, and he supported those who labored to correct the situation for society in general.

Taking advantage of a rare lull in the day's activities, he turned to the picture window, with its leaded fanlights. Resting his hands on the cool marble windowsill, he looked out.

It was a dazzling spring afternoon, the sunlight shimmering across the lake and illuminating the neatly laid-out streets of the business district. Across from the bank was a park surrounded by a handsome wrought-iron fence. In the center, a larger-than-life statue of Colonel Hiram B. Hathaway commemorated his heroism in the War Between the States. Slender poplar and maple trees lined the walkways. The green of the grass was particularly intense. Newcomers to town often commented on the deep emerald shade of the grass in the rebuilt city. Some theorized that the Great Fire of '71 left the soil highly fertile, so that all the new growth was surpassingly healthy.

Rand looked down at his scarred hands and felt the ache of the old unhealed injury in his shoulder.

He started to turn away from the window to neaten his desk for the next appointment when he spied something that made him pivot back and stare. Out in the street, wobbling along like a pair of circus performers, were two bicyclists. It was a common enough sight of late. Bicycles were all the rage, and recent improvements in the design had made the new models slightly less hazardous than the extreme high-wheelers. In the lead rode a black-haired woman, followed by a scruffy little boy on a child-size bicycle of his own.

They looked absurd, yet he couldn't take his gaze away. Patently absurd. The woman's dress was all rucked up in the middle, bloomers bared to the knees for anyone to see. The boy resembled a beggar in patched knickers and a flat cap set askew atop his curly brown hair.

Yet even so, the sight of the child struck Rand in the only soft spot left inside him. The only place the fire hadn't burned to hard, numb scar tissue. The lad looked to be about the age Christine would have been, had she lived.

Briefly Rand shut his eyes, but the memories pursued him as they always did. The images from the past were inside him, and he could never shut them out. He was filled with bitter regrets, and they had made him a bitter man, the sort who resented the sight of a healthy young boy and an audacious woman riding bicycles.

Each morning when he woke up, he played a cruel and terrible game with himself. He imagined how old Christine would be. He imagined the little frock she would wear, and how the morning sunlight would look shining down on her bright curls. He imagined having breakfast with her; she would probably still favor graham gems with cream. And each day, before he left for the office, he would imagine the sweetness of his daughter's kiss upon his cheek.

Then he would force himself to open his eyes and face the harsh truth.

He opened his eyes now and studied the only picture he kept in his office. Gilt cherubs framed a photograph of Christine at fourteen months of age, clutching a favorite blanket in her left hand, startled by whatever antics the photographer had performed to get her attention. As soon as the flash had gone off in the pan, Rand recalled, she'd burst into tears of fright, but the picture showed the child who had brought him the ultimate joy with the simple fact of her existence.

He pulled in an unsteady breath. There were some moments when it was hard to resist wishing he'd lingered longer with his daughter each morning, watching the play of sunlight in her wispy curls.

He glared at the outrageous woman on the bicycle, resenting her for having the one thing he could never get back.

She wobbled to a halt in front of the bank building and dismounted gracelessly, launching herself off the bicycle like a cowboy being bucked from a horse. The lad was more nimble, landing on both feet with catlike lightness.

They leaned their bicycles against the brass-headed hitch post the bank had installed for the convenience of well-heeled customers. Then the black-haired woman shook out her skirts, straightened her ridiculous hat and marched up the marble steps to the bank. Her son came, too, clinging to her gloved hand.

Rand noticed something vaguely familiar about the woman. A chill of apprehension sped through him, and something made him pick up the file his secretary had delivered, containing the papers pertinent to his next appointment. He untied the brown satin ribbon and flipped open the file.

His next appointment was with someone he hadn't thought about in years, but whom he'd never quite forgotten: Lucy Hathaway.

What the devil was she doing, applying to him for a loan extension?

What the hell did she need a loan for, anyway?

And what was her name now that she was a wife and mother?

Some days, he thought, scowling down at Lucy Hathaway's file, banking offered unexpected challenges.

He stood behind his desk and waited for Crowe to show her in. She arrived like a small tempest, wrinkled skirts swinging, the feather on her hat bobbing over her brow and the little boy in tow. The lad stared openly at him, then whispered, "He's a *giant*, Mama, just like —"

"Hush," she said quickly. But her manner was all business as she held out her hand. "Mr. Higgins, how do you do?"

Oh, he remembered that husky, cultured voice from their first meeting that long-ago evening. He remembered that direct, dark-eyed stare, that challenging set to her chin. He remembered how provocative he had found her, how intrigued he'd been by her unconventional ways.

He remembered that she'd asked him to be her lover. And he remembered the look on her face when she learned he was married.

As he offered her a chair, he knew he would not have to worry about her being attracted to him now, scarred and dour creature that he had become. She gave his imperfect face, camouflaged with a mustache these days, a polite but cursory glance, nothing more.

"Very well, thank you," he said, then glanced pointedly at the boy, who boldly peered around the plain leather-and-wood office, looking like mischief waiting to happen. "And this is . . . ?"

"My daughter, Margaret," said Lucy.

Margaret stuck out a grubby hand. "How

do you do? My friends call me Maggie."

Rand was thoroughly confused now. She called her son Margaret? Then it struck him — the child in the rough knickers, short hair and flat bicycle cap was a little girl. He tried not to look too startled. "I'm very pleased to meet you, Maggie."

"I'm afraid I had no choice but to bring her along," Lucy said. "Ordinarily there's someone to look after her when I have meetings."

"But today is Grammy Vi's mahjong day," Maggie said.

She really was a rather pretty child beneath the bad haircut and shapeless clothing. He tried to picture her in a little pinafore done up in ribbons and bows, but she moved too fast for him to form a picture. She darted around the office, spinning the globe and lifting a paperweight so that a breeze from the open side window swept a sheaf of papers to the floor.

"Maggie, don't touch anything," Lucy said half a second too late.

"No harm done." Rand bent to retrieve the papers. At the same time, the little girl squatted down to help. Their hands touched, and she caught at his, rubbing her small thumb over the shiny scar tissue there.

"Did you hurt yourself?" she asked, her

118

face as open as a flower.

"Maggie —"

"It's all right," Rand said with rare patience. He was accustomed to people staring, and to youngsters who didn't know any better asking questions. Some children turned away in fright, but not this one. She regarded him with a matter-of-fact compassion that comforted rather than discomfited. He studied her small, perfect hand covering his large, damaged one. "I did hurt myself," he said, "a long time ago."

"Oh." She handed him the rest of the papers. "Does it still hurt?"

Every day.

He straightened up, put the papers back under the paperweight, then saw Crowe standing in the doorway.

"Is everything all right, sir?" Crowe asked.

"Everything's fine," Rand said.

"I wondered if the little b—"

"Miss Maggie would love to join you in the outer office," Rand said hastily, cutting him off. He winked at Maggie. "Mr. Crowe is known to keep a supply of peppermints in his desk, for special visitors."

"Can I, Mama?" Maggie's eyes sparkled like blue flames, and suddenly she didn't look at all like a boy.

"Run along," Lucy said. "Don't get into anything."

After the door closed, Rand said, "Congratulations. You have a very lively little girl."

"Thank you."

"You and your husband must be very proud of her."

"I'm afraid Maggie's father is deceased," she said soberly.

His heart lurched. "I'm terribly sorry."

"Thank you, but I never knew the man," she replied. Then she laughed at his astonished expression. "Forgive me, Mr. Higgins. I'm doing a poor job explaining myself. Maggie is my adopted daughter. She was orphaned in the fire of '71."

"Ah, now I see." What a singular woman she was, adopting an orphan on her own. Months after the fire, Rand had actually considered taking in an orphaned child or two, but discovered he had no heart for it. Losing Christine had taken away all he'd ever had to give to a child.

"I consider myself fortunate," Lucy went on, "for I never did encounter a man I wanted to spend my life with, and this way I simply have no need of one."

"Lucky you."

Her face colored with a vivid blush, like a

thermometer filling with mercury, and Rand knew he'd made his point. Clearly she now remembered the outrageous proposition she'd made to him at their last meeting.

Perhaps she recalled it as vividly as he did. No matter how hard he tried, he hadn't forgotten the forbidden attraction that had flared between them. She'd been the steel to his flint, two entirely different substances that struck sparks off each other.

"Tell me," he said, "do you often gallivant about town on bicycles?"

"I've never been accused of gallivanting before," she said with a little laugh. "I find it a useful means of transportation. Our bicycles are the most modern ever, built by an acquaintance of mine. Mr. Gianinni made them as prototypes for the Centennial Exhibition this July. The design still has a ways to go but at least the cycles are less ornery than horses."

"I see."

"They eat less, too, and I don't have to stable them."

He straightened the papers on his desk in preparation for getting down to business. He regarded Lucy Hathaway with a mixture of disapproval and interest, feeling drawn to her in spite of himself. She dressed her daughter in trousers and rode a bicycle. Yet she had the most fascinating dark eyes he'd ever seen, eyes that penetrated deep as she inspected him with unblinking curiosity.

It had taken him years to inure himself to the staring of strangers and acquaintances alike. Now Lucy's perusal made him freshly aware of the old wounds. "Is something the matter?" he asked.

"I was just wondering," she said, "if you knew you were missing a cuff link."

In spite of everything, Rand felt a short bark of laughter in his throat, but he swallowed it. Here she sat, looking at a monster, and her only observation was that he was missing a cuff link. "A habit of mine," he said. "Being left-handed, I tend to drag my cuff through the ink as I write, so I roll my sleeve back when I work."

"I see. It's unusual to be left-handed."

"Indeed so." It was the one habit Rand's father hadn't been able to break him of as a boy, though his father had tried extreme measures to get him to conform in all things. "But I assure you, I am a very ordinary man."

"I'm pleased to hear that, Mr. Higgins. Shall we get started?" She peeled off her gloves. He should have watched her without any particular interest, but instead he found the operation intriguing. With unhurried movements, she rolled the thin brown leather down the inside of her wrist over the palm of her hand. Then she neatly bit the tip of her middle finger, her small white teeth gently tugging at the leather.

Rand had the discomfiting feeling that he was watching a private ritual. The strange thing was, she never took her eyes off him as she worked the glove free, finger by finger, her red-lipped mouth forming a soft O as her little nipping teeth took hold of the leather. He found himself remembering her views on free love; she probably had a stable of lovers at her beck and call.

Feeling suddenly hostile, he picked up a steel-nibbed pen and noted the date and time on her loan file. "Indeed," he said. "Down to business. I confess I'm surprised to see you here, Miss Hathaway. You'll forgive me for saying so, but it's well-known that you come from a family with quite a noteworthy fortune."

She smiled, but there was no humor in the expression. "I come from a family better at preserving appearances than finances. I will be blunt, Mr. Higgins. My father was killed in the Great Fire, his fortune burned to nothing. My mother and I were left destitute. With what little I had, I established The Firebrand — that's my bookshop."

The name of her establishment didn't surprise him in the least. Neither, in fact, did her enterprising nature. The usual response for a woman who found herself in dire straits was to hunt down a husband with a worthy fortune. But Lucy Hathaway was an unusual woman.

"And that is your purpose today, to discuss the loan on your shop."

"Yes, sir, it is."

In the outer office, a thud sounded, followed by the patter of running feet and a gale of childish laughter.

Lucy looked over her shoulder. "Oh, dear —"

"Please, don't concern yourself. Mr. Crowe enjoys children. Occasionally."

"Thank you for understanding. I wouldn't ordinarily bring Maggie to a business meeting, but unfortunately, I find myself without a wife, so I have brought my daughter along. What luxury that would be, to have a wife. Perhaps a woman should aspire to *have* one rather than to *be* one." She touched the edge of the desk. "Have you any children, Mr. Higgins?"

"I —" He would never learn the proper way to answer that question. "No. I do not."

"But if you did, they would certainly be

left in the care of your wife while you attend to business," she said.

"Miss Hathaway —"

"I apologize. I sometimes get carried away with my own ideas."

He could not recall the last time he'd spoken to a woman who was so irritating — or so entertaining. But of course he could recall it, he reminded himself. It was the last time he'd met Lucy Hathaway.

The sooner he concluded his business with her, the better. Perusing the profit and loss statements, he tapped his pen on the file. "Please remember, it is my business to cultivate productive loans for this institution."

"I was never in any danger of forgetting it, Mr. Higgins."

Her comment assured him that she knew exactly what was coming.

Bluntly he said, "I don't believe a woman alone is capable of managing a business on the scale you envision for your bookshop."

"I have managed for three years."

"And you've fallen deeper into debt each year."

"That's not unusual in a new enterprise," she countered.

"I see no end in sight." He flipped to a recent balance sheet. "Your receipts show no sign of outpacing your expenditures. Eventually your credit will be cut off, artery by artery." He pressed his hands together, peering at her over his scarred fingers. "It sounds harsh, but that is the way of commerce. Businesses fail every day, Miss Hathaway. There is no shame in it."

He braced himself for tears, but she was as stoic as any young man pulling himself up by his bootstraps. "You are looking at columns of numbers, Mr. Higgins," she stated. "That's your mistake."

"I don't make mistakes in banking, Miss Hathaway." His arrogance was justified. Sound judgment, strict rules and a tireless capacity for work formed the cornerstones of his success. Banking was his life, the source of his greatest satisfaction. He knew nothing else.

"You should be looking at the heart of the matter, not just the numbers."

He tried not to seem patronizing as he leaned back in his chair to listen to her womanish ramblings.

"There is something that I bring to the table," she said, "that cannot be shown in any ledger. Something that will make the difference between success and failure."

"And what, pray, is that?"

She leaned forward, pressing her dainty

hands on the desk again. The angle of her pose proved the truth of what he had suspected the moment she'd walked into the room — she wasn't wearing a corset. "Passion," she said in her naturally husky voice.

Rand cleared his throat. "I beg your pardon."

"Passion," she repeated, pushing back from the desk. "That is what I have for my enterprise. You cannot put a value on it, but it is the most tangible of all my assets."

He tried not to stare at her uncorseted . . . assets. "And you contend that your passion for selling books will turn these figures around."

"Exactly."

"Have you any proof of that?"

"I do. You see, my shop is not merely a place where people come to buy books."

"That would be entirely too simple."

She sniffed. "The Firebrand is a meeting place where people exchange ideas. They talk about the books they've read, and of course buy them."

"Then why aren't you showing a profit?"

"Look at my balance sheet. The foreign tariffs on my imports are exorbitant."

"Then why import foreign publications? Sell American works."

"Spoken as a true chauvinist. I'll have you

know I am the only bookseller in the area who carries French periodicals. Everyone else thinks they're immoral, just as everyone else thinks the science tracts from Germany are ungodly and English periodicals are tedious. I proudly carry them all."

"And pay a small fortune in tariffs. Tell me more about these immoral French magazines. I'm fascinated."

She turned bright red but didn't shrink from replying. "The most recent issue is about techniques of physical love. If you like, I could send you a copy."

"No, thank you." He felt his face turning redder than hers. "We don't all share your views on free love."

She grinned, but her blush deepened. "So you do remember."

He took refuge in anger. "Tell me, did you ever manage to find what you were looking for the night we met? Did you find a lover, Miss Hathaway?"

"Of course," she said, her hands twisting in her lap. "Dozens of them! Mainly Frenchmen, for obvious reasons."

"In that case, you should qualify for a reduction of your tariffs. They're cutting into your profits."

"When it comes to the hearts and minds of my customers, sir, I can wait for profit."

The odd thing was, Rand realized, she did have a passion for what she was saying. She had built her shop out of idealistic dreams. A bookseller. What a perfect occupation for this woman. How she must love knowing what everyone was reading. How she must love telling people what they should read next.

The receipts from the shop were unusually high, which indicated that she was indeed selling books. He suspected it was quite impossible to get away from Lucy Hathaway without buying at least one book.

"An admirable sentiment," he said, not allowing his judgment to be swayed by the force of her personality. "But the trouble is, the bank won't wait. Your notes are due."

"I expect receipts to pick up," she said as if she hadn't heard him. "I've had lectures from some of the most respected leaders of our age — Miss Clementina Black, Mrs. Kate Chopin and Mrs. Lillian Paul in the past year alone."

"Radical activists are always a lucrative draw."

She dismissed his sarcasm with a wave of her hand. "I've been corresponding with Miss Harriet Beecher Stowe, who has agreed to present a lecture and sign books when she comes to Chicago."

"And this event is scheduled?"

"Not . . . exactly. Miss Stowe is currently in South America, observing the mating habits of the Andean llama."

"Fascinating."

"I also create events for my customers to draw them into the shop. Mrs. Victoria Woodhull is coming for the Centennial March this summer, and last year, I set up a registry for voters."

He removed a newspaper clipping from the file. His predecessor had been thorough in keeping records on this particular client. "It says here you were arrested for encouraging women to register illegally to vote."

"And does it say that I protested the arrest on the grounds that I was simply exercising my constitutional rights?"

"It says you created a public scandal."

She crossed her arms over her chest. "A public scandal occurs with every election in which women are denied the right to vote."

"According to this report, you had a mob of radical suffragists in your shop trying to corrupt decent women."

She laughed, looking genuinely incredulous. "I had a group of voting registrars, assisting American citizens in registering to vote."

"You were arrested."

"My constitutional rights were trodden upon."

"You were made to pay a fine."

"By a twisted, unfair, corrupt judge. And I never did pay."

He slapped the file shut. "So this shop is where you advocate free love and divorce on demand? Where you meet your lovers?"

"So what if I do?" she retorted.

"My point, Miss Hathaway, is that the loan committee is bound to view your so-called passion in quite a different light. To them, your actions will seem a sign of irresponsibility and immaturity, making you a bad risk." He wondered why he was taking the time to explain all this when it should be a foregone conclusion. "I'm sorry, Miss Hathaway. The loan is due, and there can be no extension."

She sat very, very still. Her absolute stillness discomfited him. As did her direct stare. Finally she spoke. "I love my bookshop with a passion you will never understand. I don't know why I've tried to explain it to you. Sir, you have a heart of stone. You have never loved a thing."

Her bald statement seared into him like a brand, igniting a rage and resentment he hadn't known he possessed. "Love has nothing to do with it," he snapped. "But I wouldn't expect a woman to understand that. Like all of your sex, you are a creature governed by sentiment, not sense. You belong at home rather than struggling through a morass of crass commerce. Look to your duties as a mother, and leave the commerce to men."

"I have heard such views voiced before," Lucy said, unaware of the absurd bobbing motion of the feather in her hat. "I have heard such views from Southerners who favor slavery. They claim slaves are incapable of looking after themselves and need to belong in bondage to men who will 'care' for them. Tell me, Mr. Higgins, do you favor slavery?"

"Don't be ridiculous. No thinking man approves of slavery. It took a war to settle that, but it's settled."

"Then perhaps it will take a war to settle rights for women."

"I don't doubt that you shall do your part." In spite of his outrage, he felt a reluctant compassion for her. "Look, Miss Hathaway. You seem a genuinely determined woman. Perhaps, given time, you might be able to eke out a living as a bookseller. But I'll never convince my associates of that. They are a conservative lot, as intractable as they come."

She leaned forward again, her eyes bright with optimism. "You must be my advocate, then, Mr. Higgins. You must convince them that I am a good risk."

"You're $486 in arrears, Miss Hathaway. I cannot tell them it is light when it's dark, or it's Wednesday when it's Friday."

"I see. I'm sorry to have wasted your time." She shoved herself back from the desk. With the motion, her fingers pushed at the leather-and-felt ink blotter, and the single framed picture on his desk fell facedown.

They both reached for it at the same time.

"I didn't mean to —"

"No harm done —"

They both spoke at the same time.

Their hands touched. And just for an instant, a current of recognition sizzled between them. Rand felt it all the way through him, hand and heart and body, and it astonished him. He hadn't felt anything remotely like this in years.

Lucy glanced down at the sepia-toned photographic portrait, but looked immediately back at him, eyes wide as if she, too, felt the bright heat of their connection. "I thought you said you had no children."

"I . . ." Clumsily he propped the picture up, facing him. "My daughter, Christine, was killed in the fire."

"Oh, good heavens." She captured his hands in both of hers. "Oh, Mr. Higgins, I am so terribly sorry."

He sensed the questions she was too polite to ask aloud, the questions so many had asked with their suspicious stares. *Where were you when your child was in danger? Why didn't you save her?*

He'd asked himself the same questions every single day.

He extracted his hands from hers, expecting her to take her leave. Instead she snatched up the portrait of Christine and stared at the picture as if she'd never seen a baby before. Her cheeks drained to a sick pallor, and she sank back down into her chair. "Mr. Higgins," she said, "is it terribly painful to speak of your loss?"

"Of course it is."

She shut her eyes, and her chin trembled. He was amazed at how moved she was. She'd never known Christine — she barely knew him — yet she looked devastated. "Sir, may I ask . . . what were the circumstances of your baby's, uh, accident?"

Rand knew he had every right to dismiss her question and order her from his office. But she seemed so genuinely distressed that he found himself, perversely, willing to speak of that night.

"My wife — we left Christine in the care of a nurse at Sterling House. As you might recall, we attended a meeting at the Hotel Royale and stayed until it grew quite late."

"Yes," she said faintly. "Yes, I did the same."

"By the time we realized the fire was heading our way, it was almost impossible to get through the city. Diana and I went on foot, and we nearly made it to Sterling House. But there was an explosion, a varnish factory." Rand took another deep breath as nightmare images streaked through his mind. "I knew nothing until I awakened weeks later in a hospital. No one expected me to survive. But I . . . I did. I survived."

"And your wife?"

"Diana recovered sooner than I. It was she who first heard about the disaster at Sterling House. The damage to the area was so great that very few . . . remains were recovered." He and Diana had been strangers in the middle of the burnt-out city struggling to rebuild itself. No one came forward to comfort them in their loss, and those few who had probably didn't recognize Rand, mummified by layers of bandages.

Lucy got to her feet and took an awkward

step backward. "I really must be going. I'm sorry we could not come to an accord. I'm sorry . . . for everything. Good day, Mr. Higgins."

Before he could even rise to see her out, she was gone. He turned to the window in time to see her and the little girl called Maggie wobbling down the street on their bicycles.

Eight

"I was transported by the book," declared Mrs. Dottie Frey, bustling into the shop. "Utterly transported. I swan, I haven't been so entertained since Mr. Frey decided to take up golf. Thank you for recommending it to me, Miss Hathaway."

"My pleasure, of course," Lucy told her customer. "I'm delighted to hear you liked it."

"I count on your recommendations, dear." Mrs. Frey, who hailed from Buffalo, was one of her favorite customers, always ready with a lively, insightful review of a book she'd just read.

When she'd first come to the shop, Mrs. Frey had never read a novel. Her devoutly Baptist husband disapproved of secular entertainment. Lucy had invited her to join a discussion group of *Hope Leslie* by Catharine Maria Sedgwick, and the lady had been a devotee of reading ever since. Her husband, who loved his wife better than he loved conservative dogma, wisely held his tongue.

"Tell me, has the author ever written any others?"

On any normal day, Lucy would have taken great pleasure in leading Mrs. Frey to the fiction shelves. But today her smile felt stiff and forced as she went through the motions. "Mrs. Frey, you are in luck. Barbara Dodd is a very prolific writer, and we have several more of her titles in stock."

"Oh, I must have them."

All day long, Lucy had been battling a persistent feeling of dread. She tried to deny what she knew in her heart to be true, but her conscience wouldn't leave her alone. Preoccupied, she led the way to the fiction shelves and climbed halfway up the wheeled brass ladder to reach the books.

"Here you are. *Fire on the Wind* and *Candle in the Window*. Two of my favorites."

The bright, cherubic older lady took the books and hugged them to her chest. "Mr. Frey won't be back from St. Louis for a week, and it's wretchedly lonely without him. I don't know what I'd do without a good book to read." She flipped through the new volumes she'd chosen and sighed. "Ah, to be young again, as Beatrice was in the Stokely Hall series. I was such a hopeless twit when I was young, and I had such a wonderful time. There is something to be said for being a twit at times."

As Lucy wrapped the parcel, she held her

smile in place with an effort.

"So how have you been, dear?" Mrs. Frey inquired as she paid for her purchase. A mischievous gleam twinkled in her eye. "Any suitors come to call?" Mrs. Frey was an incurable romantic who believed in the happy endings of the novels she read.

"Not this week," Lucy said. They traded the exchange on a regular basis. It was well-known in the neighborhood that Lucy Hathaway, avowed crusader for free love, had no suitors. For years she'd been telling herself she didn't need a man. She didn't know what devilish impulse had possessed her to blithely lie to Mr. Higgins about her legions of French lovers. The truth was, men preferred women who were quiet and demure, not outspoken and ambitious. They liked women who were dainty and fair, not sharp-featured and dark.

But Mrs. Frey had never been one to give up hope. "Look at me, dear," she said, spreading her arms. "Plain as biscuit dough, I am, and always have been, but Mr. Frey saw something in me no one else saw. There's someone out there for everyone. Look at Jane Eyre and poor Mr. Rochester, for heaven's sake. They were both so troubled, yet so perfect for each other. And so shall you find someone —"

"Mrs. Frey, you're very kind, but I don't need anyone."

"Nonsense. Every woman does. Every man does, too, so don't go spouting your ideas about independent womanhood. Men and women need each other equally. That's what equality is."

In spite of the huge matter weighing on her mind, Lucy laughed. "I give up, Mrs. Frey. You are right. You always are. Enjoy the books."

As her customer left, Lucy released the sigh she'd been holding in. Then she impulsively turned over the sign in the door, indicating that the shop was closed. It was only an hour to closing time anyway, and she hadn't been busy. Some days, she needed quiet time for herself.

Like today.

She rushed over to the counter, where a little corner formed a work area. Snatching up a framed photograph, she stared at it with all her might. Her heart lurched, for there was no denying what she'd discovered.

Her Maggie was not an orphan after all.

She was the daughter of Randolph Higgins.

There could be no mistake, though Lucy

had prayed for one. The picture on Higgins's desk constituted incontrovertible evidence. She was undeniably the baby Lucy had rescued from the fire.

Soon after the disaster, Lucy had a picture made for circulating to the papers and posting at the local orphanages and churches. Each day, she'd waited for someone to claim the little girl, but as the days stretched to weeks and then months, she'd concluded that Maggie's family had perished in the fire.

Lucy had greeted the notion with a certain guilty relief. She'd come to love the baby. As time went on, she stopped thinking about the missing parents, though every so often she would wonder at some unique aspect of Maggie. Where did she get her blue eyes, and why was she left-handed? Was her pert way of cocking her head an echo of her lost mother?

A passerby peered in the shop window. Ordinarily Lucy would get up to greet a prospective customer with a smile and perhaps a tidbit about a new book, but today she couldn't think about business. She couldn't think about anything but the stunning discovery she'd made at the bank.

She sank down into a chair behind the counter and buried her face in her hands.

She could barely remember the bicycle ride home from the bank. While Maggie had chattered blithely away, Lucy's entire being had been awash with fearful amazement. Upon returning to the shop, she'd sent Maggie off to play in the narrow row garden behind the house until Lucy's mother returned from her mahjong game. Then Lucy had racked her brain, trying to decide what to do.

Still undecided, she sat for a long time, her mind sluggish with shock. She felt a dull horror at her own thoughts.

She was the only one who knew the truth about Maggie. The only one. And if she never told a soul . . .

She heard the shop door open and shut. A swift instinct, driven by a sharp protectiveness, made her slap the photograph facedown on the desk.

"I didn't mean to startle you," said Viola Hathaway, setting a big wicker basket on the library table. "It's just me."

"Where is Maggie?" Lucy asked. Wing beats of panic rose in her chest. "Mother, where is she?"

"Don't get your bloomers in a bunch, dear. She and Silky have had their lunch, and they are fast asleep on the parlor sofa." Viola had a peculiar gift — under any circumstances whatsoever, she was able to conjure up a pot of tea, complete with cream and sugar. From her basket, she took the chipped old Wedgwood pot, a linen napkin and a stack of cups and saucers, laying the table with the finesse of a duchess. "I declare, letting that child ride around town on that monstrous bicycle is a hazard. She is always so exhausted after such an outing."

Lucy chose not to bicker with her mother, not today. Despite all that had befallen her since the death of the Colonel, Viola still clung to antiquated ideas about what a girl should and should not do. Bicycling was definitely a "should-not" in her code of etiquette. Lucy wanted to sink behind the counter and disappear. She wanted to take Maggie and run away, and never come back.

No, she thought, that was the coward's way out.

The little brass bell over the door chimed again. Lucy wanted to scream with frustration, but Viola hastened to open the door. "Come in, come in," she said in a bright chirp. "I'm so glad you could join us."

Lucy was surprised to see Patience Gloriana Washington along with two women she'd known since finishing school

— Deborah Silver and Kathleen Kennedy. Deborah, now five years married and the mother of two, was as blond and beautiful as ever. Flame-haired Kathleen had produced a set of twins and two others during her four-year marriage to the roguish Dylan Kennedy. Only Phoebe Palmer was missing from the alumni of Miss Boylan's. Years earlier, she'd set her sights on marrying an English lord, and she'd held out for the real thing. Finally her wish had come true. She had wed Lord de Grey, heir to a British duke. She now lived in his ancestral home on a windswept moor in the north of England.

"I thought you might need a bit of tea and sympathy," Viola explained as Lucy greeted her friends, "after what happened at the bank this morning."

Lucy blanched. "What do you know about that?"

Her mother waved a hand, then offered everyone a seat around the scrubbed oak display table. With practiced grace, she poured the tea. "I am not as ignorant as you think I am, Lucy. And besides that, I am your mother. I took one look at your face at lunchtime and knew things had gone ill for you at the bank. So I sent a message 'round to Patience, Kathleen and Deborah.

Friends are so essential in times of trouble."

Patience added three lumps from the sugar loaf to her tea. "What happened at the bank, girl?"

"Tell them, dear," Viola said gently. "Unburden yourself."

Lucy was speechless. She had no idea how her mother had learned about Randolph Higgins.

When she said nothing, Viola spoke for her. "I'm very much afraid," she announced, "that Lucy's request for the loan extension was refused by the bank. The Firebrand will have to close."

"Oh, sweet Lord in heaven, no," Kathleen said. "This is your dream, Lucy. You can't give it up."

"Closing down is a terrible idea," Deborah added, "not to mention unnecessary. I shall personally lend you —"

"Never mind." Lucy held up a hand, not knowing whether to laugh or weep. Of course her mother couldn't have guessed. "Something *did* happen at the bank, but it wasn't about the loan." Her financial concerns seemed so petty, given the issue that weighed on her mind now.

"Then why the long face?" Patience asked.

Lucy took a deep breath. For a few moments, she'd actually entertained the thought of keeping silent on the matter, but she could not. It was not only cowardly but dishonorable. No matter how much she loved Maggie, no matter how fiercely she wanted to protect her, she would never be able to live with such a deception.

"Something extraordinary has occurred." She looked around the table at each of her friends and then at her mother. "I have found Maggie's parents."

The silence was as absolute as eternal damnation. Everyone sat completely still. Lucy fancied she could hear her own heart beating.

Then, with a clacking of cups and saucers set down in astonishment, everyone began talking at once. "How can you be sure?" "Who are they?" "Why didn't they find her after the fire?" "What will you do now?"

Lucy waited for the noise to subside. A thick heat filled her throat and she feared she might cry. But Lucy never cried. She was the Colonel's daughter, and she would keep control.

"I realized the truth," she explained, "when I was in Mr. Randolph Higgins's office at the bank." Her listeners sat stone-still, staring in amazement. After five years, Lucy had discovered the solution to a haunting mystery.

All of them had wondered from time to time where Maggie had come from, and now they were about to find out.

"As we were discussing the loan, I learned that he and his wife had lost a child in the fire." She flushed, remembering her blunt questions and how callous they had seemed in light of what she'd learned about Mr. Higgins. She thought of his scars, his rigid self-control as he'd spoken to her of the tragedy. "I offered my condolences, but thought no more of it until I saw, on his desk, a five-year-old photograph of his child." With a shaking hand, she held up her own baby picture of Maggie. "It was my Maggie. He said the baby in the photograph was his daughter, Christine, who was killed along with her nursemaid in the collapse of the Sterling House Hotel."

Another long, shocked silence greeted the revelation.

"That's astounding," said Deborah. "Extraordinary."

"Did you tell him straightaway?" her mother asked.

"Of course not. Good God, I've not even recovered from the shock myself."

"But Maggie went to the bank with you. He saw her. Didn't he recognize his own child?"

Lucy gave a pained smile. "He mistook her for a boy until I introduced them. Then he —" She considered his gentle, indulgent manner with Maggie. "He was lovely to her. Sent her off to beg candy from his assistant. It's been almost five years. Maggie's changed from a towheaded baby into a young girl. Can any of us say for sure we'd recognize her, under the circumstances?"

"And you're certain she's the one?" Kathleen asked after a pause.

"Completely. The photograph was more than enough to convince me. It was Maggie, down to the last eyelash, and she was even clutching the baby blanket she had when I saved her. Add to that the Sterling House connection, and the scene is com . . . complete." She stumbled over the word and was ashamed to feel tears burning in her eyes. Determinedly she blinked until they went away.

In contrast, Viola was an unrepentant leaky spigot. She saturated both her handkerchiefs as she wept. "This is a disaster."

"Or a miracle," Patience said.

"What if this encounter was supposed to happen?" Kathleen asked. "It could be an act of fate, or a preordained event."

"What if it's a blessing in disguise?" Deborah ventured.

"The Lord's work," Patience murmured.

"How can it be?" Viola asked. "What possible good can come of this?"

Lucy stared down at the table. "I have no idea. I am trying to keep an open mind."

"Maggie is ours. It's too late for anyone else to claim her. Isn't there a statute of limitations on this sort of thing?"

"I doubt it, Mother."

"Those people are strangers to her."

"They are her parents, who gave her life," Patience pointed out.

"Why the devil didn't they move heaven and earth to find the poor mite?" Kathleen asked. "Lord knows you posted notices in every paper, and registered the baby with every church and orphanage in the region."

"You did everything in your power to find the baby's parents," Deborah assured her. "Yet they never contacted you."

"Why?" Viola asked.

"I wondered the same thing myself," Lucy said. "Mr. Higgins . . . bears quite a few scars. He spoke very little of the fire and I hesitated to pry, but I gather he lay senseless with his injuries for weeks afterward. And by that time, you'll recall, Mother and I had taken the baby out of Chicago because of the typhoid epidemic."

"But you still sent notices to the papers," Viola said.

"What about Mrs. Higgins?" asked Kathleen. "Was *she* senseless with her injuries, too?"

"She was injured, though I didn't dare ask how badly," Lucy explained. "As you can imagine, I didn't quite have my wits about me. He would have grown suspicious if I'd kept probing." She ran a hand through her hair, finding it even more curly and unkempt than usual. "Now I must decide what to do," she added quietly.

"First off," said Deborah, "you must engage a solicitor to look out for your interests."

"Barry Lynch would do nicely," Kathleen suggested. "He's an old friend. I've known him since he was a dockyard clerk."

Lucy guessed he had been one of her many suitors from years past. With her looks and charm, Kathleen had attracted men from every walk of life.

"He studied the law after he married," Kathleen explained, "and now he has a busy practice."

"I would guess that he's never seen a case quite like this," Deborah murmured.

Viola put a hand on her daughter's arm. "Lucy, please don't be hasty. If you do nothing, we could go on as before."

"Mother —"

"Hear me out. Years have passed. Mr. Higgins has become a successful banker. Surely he's moved on from a terrible tragedy."

Lucy wasn't so certain. He wasn't a raving lunatic, of course. His sadness was . . . deeper. It seemed to pervade every cell of his body.

"Mr. Higgins has come to terms with the loss of his daughter, and no doubt his wife has done the same," Viola argued. "If they never learn she survived, you won't be hurting them anymore than they've already suffered."

The same cold-blooded thought had occurred to Lucy. "But Mother, I can *end* their suffering by telling them about Maggie."

"Oh, really?" Viola drew herself up. "What about Maggie's suffering if you're forced to give her back? You would make a sacrificial lamb of my granddaughter. She is the one who would be hurt the most. We're the only family she's ever known. What would she think if we suddenly thrust her into the arms of strangers?"

"Don't you think I've been agonizing over this?" Lucy asked.

"If you tell them about Maggie, what do

you predict will happen? Put yourself in their shoes. They've been grieving for a baby five years gone, and suddenly a miracle occurs. Do you think they're going to pat the child on the head, wish her well in life and then go on as before? Of course not. They will take her away."

Lucy's blood chilled. "I am her mother. They are strangers to her."

"My point precisely."

Deborah covered Lucy's hands with her own. "Mr. and Mrs. Higgins brought her into the world. They lost her in the most horrible way imaginable. They're going to want her back."

Kathleen nodded. "They might canonize you for a blessed saint, but they'll fight you to kingdom come for that child."

Lucy pushed up her chin. "I'll fight back."

"What if you lose?" Patience asked. "Are you prepared to accept that?"

The air rushed out of Lucy as though someone had punched her in the gut. In the hollow silence, Viola said, "This is all so unnecessary. Mr. and Mrs. Higgins have settled this in their hearts. Surely they have all they could want."

"Perhaps they've had more children," Deborah suggested.

"No." Lucy found her voice again. "I asked."

She could still feel the solemn resignation that had pervaded the office when Randolph Higgins had denied having any children. She wondered why he and his wife hadn't had more. Perhaps it was a health issue with Mrs. Higgins. She thought about the woman she'd met ever so briefly the night of the fire. Blond hair, alabaster skin, eyes the color of Delft china. The color of Maggie's eyes.

What sort of mother would Diana Higgins have been to Maggie?

What sort of person would Maggie have been, raised by the Higgins family?

The questions and uncertainties built up in her head until she thought she would explode.

Patience's warm hand settled on her shoulder. Lucy turned to her old friend. "Help me," she said in an agonized whisper. "Tell me what to do, Patience. Tell me what is right."

"Child, you'll figure it out. Just listen to your heart."

"My heart tells me that I have a beautiful, healthy, exuberant daughter," Lucy said. "A daughter I would die for."

Deborah dabbed at her eyes and

Kathleen blew her nose.

"And what does your heart tell you about Mr. and Mrs. Higgins?" Patience asked quietly.

The doorbell jangled yet again. "Mama?"

At the sound of Maggie's voice, Lucy shot to her feet, feeling inexplicably guilty. Her mother, Kathleen and Deborah busied themselves adding sugar and cream to their tea and dabbing their faces with napkins.

"Hello, sweetheart." Lucy crossed the shop to her daughter. How could she shatter this child's world? "Did you have a good sleep?"

"I did! I did! And I dreamed I could fly like a bird. Do you think I will one day, Mama?"

Lucy opened her arms, familiar with the routine. "I think you already can."

Maggie raced toward her and launched herself, springing up into Lucy's arms with the agility of a monkey. She clung there, laughing, her soft brown curls fragrant with soap and the faint, evocative essence that was Maggie and Maggie alone. Lucy swung her around while the little girl sang out with pure joy, leaning her head back to watch the ceiling spin.

The next day, when Mr. Higgins's assistant told her to wait in the outer office, Lucy concentrated on her firm purpose. She'd returned to find out more about Mr. Higgins. She and her mother had decided, in a whispered conversation late the night before, that she needed to investigate him further before deciding what to do. Perversely, she wanted to believe the straitlaced banker was a bad man. A man who didn't deserve to know what had become of his child. But she kept remembering the scars he bore and the pain buried in his eyes. How different he was from the cocky, flirtatious young rogue she had met the night of the fire.

"How much longer must I wait?" she asked Mr. Crowe.

He peered at her from beneath his green celluloid visor. "You didn't have an appointment, ma'am."

"But if you'd just tell him I'm —"

"He's in an important meeting and cannot be interrupted."

She leaned back against the leather chair and drummed her fingers on the arm. Mr. Crowe glared at her, but she didn't stop. "Is he in his office?" she persisted.

"I told you, Miss Hathaway. He is in a meeting."

"But *where* is this meeting?"

Mr. Crowe dabbed at his forehead with a

folded handkerchief. "It's in the conference room down the hall, ma'am. You might be pleased to know that your request is their main topic of discussion. I can't say how long he will be, but I assure you, the moment he has concluded his business, you'll be the first to know."

She kept drumming her fingers, then she jiggled her foot. Perhaps she would annoy him to the point where he left his desk just to escape her, and then she could snoop around at will.

Anxiety tingled along her nerves. She'd lain awake half the night, trying to figure out what to do, but she wasn't the least bit tired. First thing in the morning, she'd gone to visit Barry Lynch, the solicitor Kathleen had recommended. He'd listened with growing astonishment to her story, and like her mother and her friends, had declared it entirely unique. Unprecedented. It would take a judge's ruling to untangle the mess.

That was where she'd balked. In her experience, judges on any level were a conservative, reactionary lot. Old-fashioned and superior, they made their pronouncements with little compassion, particularly for women. The judges of Cook County seemed bound and determined to halt all forward social progress.

She could hardly expect a judge to rule in favor of an adoptive mother who had no husband, no fortune and a failing book-store.

Lynch had told her, obliquely but in no uncertain terms, the same thing her mother had. A little girl's future was at stake. She had to do what was best for Maggie.

That was all she'd ever done. It was all she'd ever wanted to do. Lucy was not a particularly spiritual woman, but she believed with all her heart that she'd been put upon the earth for the sole purpose of being at Sterling House the moment Maggie had been dropped from a window.

Surely she was meant to keep and protect the child forever.

All night long she'd wavered back and forth, back and forth, wishing for an answer that was simple, that wouldn't change anything or hurt anyone.

That was when she had remembered her father. Oh, she remembered the Colonel every day, to be sure, because dead or alive, he was not a man to be forgotten or dismissed. But he had a way of coming to her when she was quiet in her mind, and reminding her of certain important matters. True, he'd been an aggravating traditionalist; he had wanted nothing more for his daughter than the shackles and servitude of marriage and family, but he'd loved her. And in his blustering way, he'd been wise.

She recalled a time when she'd been about twelve years old, and her father had posed her a riddle. *A barking dog awakens the sleeping household of an Egyptian palace. Antony and Cleopatra lie dead on the floor. Shards of a broken bowl are scattered over the wet floor. There is no mark on either body, and they were not poisoned. How did they die?*

The Colonel often did this, taking a fierce pleasure in pushing Lucy to tackle difficult, seemingly impossible puzzles.

She recalled pacing the schoolroom floor in a fury, certain the Colonel hadn't given her enough information to solve the problem. The Colonel had sat with her and examined the question from all angles, and finally the correct answer came to her.

She'd savored the look on her father's face when it dawned on her: *Antony and Cleopatra are goldfish, and the dog knocked over their bowl.*

"All the information you needed was there, right before your eyes," the Colonel had said, stroking his sidewhiskers. "You simply had to devise a new way of looking at it."

There had been many more puzzles, and

many more days like that. Yet only when she grew older did Lucy realize the true meaning of the seemingly frivolous riddles. Her father was more than a good man. He was a wise man who had loved his daughter. And he had taught her to think, to do what was right.

That thought had troubled her through the night. It had brought her back to the bank this morning to learn more about Randolph Higgins. Because she wasn't sure she had the right to deprive Maggie of a father.

Or, for that matter, her natural mother. Perhaps, as Kathleen had suggested, this was meant to be.

"Can I bring you something to drink, Miss Hathaway?" Mr. Crowe asked. "You look a bit pale."

"No," she said, "I — Yes. I've changed my mind. I believe I'd like a cup of tea." He rose from his desk. "With cream," she added, "and a barley sugar on the side. And please be sure the tea is quite hot, because I can't abide lukewarm tea."

"Of course." Mr. Crowe pasted on an accommodating smile and left the outer office.

Praying the task would keep him occupied for several minutes, Lucy went off in search of Mr. Higgins. Several doors flanked a high-ceilinged hallway. The windows were covered in slatted blinds, and each office was empty, save the last.

Edging along the wall so she wouldn't be seen, she peered into the room. A group of men sat around a long, gleaming table. She recognized Randolph Higgins instantly. He was a large man, tall and broad-shouldered, with that head of thick, russet-colored hair. From this angle, he looked exactly the same as he had the night they had met, except for the mustache — aggressively handsome, almost haughty. But she knew from their encounter the day before that the years had changed him more profoundly than she could imagine.

Pausing in the deserted corridor, she heard strains of their conversation and clenched her fist in apprehension. If she caught him off guard, she would learn his true character. Now she would discover the sort of man he truly was. Perhaps he was evicting poor people from their homes. Foreclosing on the mortgages of widows or ex-slaves from the South. Lending money to a wealthy industrialist so he could tear down schools and hospitals to make way for heavy commerce.

That was what bankers did. If Mr. Higgins proved to be a heartless beast, she could keep her secret with a clear conscience.

". . . Miss Hathaway's request," said a man's voice. "That is what we are discussing, is it not?"

Lucy stiffened as if someone had poked her in the backside. She clapped her hand over her mouth just in time to stifle a gasp. They were discussing her! It was too perfect. Now she would hear the real Mr. Higgins, denigrating her on the basis of her gender alone. It would be easy to dismiss such a man.

"There is nothing more to discuss," said another man. "I read the assessment of the loan committee. She's a losing proposition. She'll default, there'll be nothing for us to repossess and we'll lose everything we've lent her."

"Did you even look at the figures, Mr. Crabtree?" Higgins said, sounding annoyed.

"She's losing money each month. The woman's a bleeding artery. That's all I need to see."

Lucy's throat ached with the need to defend herself. The Firebrand had only been in operation for three years. Cyrus McCormick had taken longer than that to show a profit but she doubted he had trouble obtaining a loan.

"We're wasting time, gentlemen," someone objected. "This is a matter for the loan committee, anyway. They've rendered their decision. No extension. No increase. No one should have lent that woman money in the first place." A general shuffling of papers followed.

It was business, Lucy told herself even as her heart plummeted to her shoes. A business decision should not hurt her to the core of her being, and yet it did. Her worth as a person had somehow become all tangled up in her business dealings.

Shaken, she gazed at the paintings along the walls, focusing on an idyllic scene of a prosperous-looking family strolling through a pastoral landscape. Something was happening to Lucy. Ordinarily a sentimental picture would not make her want to weep, but there were times when she felt so empty and lost. She just wanted, for once, to have someone to turn to, because ever since the fire, everyone had been turning to her. She would never admit to being lonely, but oh, how she ached with it.

Damn Randolph Higgins for making her feel these maudlin sentiments. She was about to barge into the meeting when he spoke sharply to his associates.

"I advise that we reconsider Miss Hathaway's request," Mr. Higgins said with an excess of patience. "Her revenues are increasing every month. The reason she's not showing a profit yet is that she's driving all the monies back into her shop."

She froze. Was he justifying her position?

"She's probably driving them all into new hats and gowns," someone grumbled. "It's what women do."

Lucy scowled, resisting the urge to pace in agitation. Did they speak of loans to men in his manner? No, of course not.

"Don't judge her by her gender, Mr. Lamott."

Jasper Lamott, she realized. Archenemy of the Women's Suffrage Movement. Her cause was as good as dead.

"Judge her by her actions in the past," Mr. Higgins temporized, "and her vision of the future. Did you read her proposal?"

"It's entirely preposterous. No bookstore can be a gathering place for people without turning into a mob scene. The sooner we close her down, the better."

"Isn't that the idea for any retailer? To attract a crowd?" Mr. Higgins asked.

Noncommittal murmurs rippled around the table.

"I suggest you take these materials and reread them," he said, shuffling papers. "If we lose Miss Hathaway as a client, she'll take her business to First National and we'll regret it."

Lucy pressed herself back against the wall, dropped her hand and shut her eyes. Pride and wonder filled the places that had felt so empty only moments ago. Her lips curved into a smile. This must be how Guinevere felt when Lancelot had fought for her honor. It was a magical feeling, to have someone stand up for her, and she pressed her hands to her chest, cherishing a rare, tingling warmth.

"Are you ill?" asked a familiar voice.

Her eyes flew open. "Mr. Higgins!"

"I take it you've been eavesdropping long enough to hear that there is no news with regard to your application." He spoke impersonally, almost brusquely. "We have tabled our discussion until Thursday."

Hot color flooded her face, but Lucy was used to being humiliated. She embarrassed herself all the time in the name of the cause she supported. She pursued him down the hallway. "Mr. Higgins, I'd like to thank you for speaking up for me."

"I spoke up for a loan I consider an acceptable risk." He seemed put off by her gratitude, uncomfortable with it.

She was unexpectedly moved by this gruff, scarred man. The trouble was, he wouldn't show her enough of himself for her to understand him. "No one has ever believed in me before."

He stopped walking and glared down at her from his prodigious height. "I don't believe in you, Miss Hathaway. Your radical politics are harmful, your shop a blight upon the neighborhood and your morals questionable."

Her jaw dropped. For once she was speechless. Why, oh why had she invented that story about the French lovers?

"However," he continued, "I believe you are capable of turning your shop into a profitable enterprise. Since earning money for the bank is my business, it makes sense to support you."

Mr. Crowe returned with a cup of tea. Assuming it was for him, Mr. Higgins helped himself to it and stepped into his office. "Good day, Miss Hathaway."

He shut the door with the toe of his expensive shoe. She considered pursuing him, but she had more thinking to do. Perhaps the next step was to inspect his home. Meet his wife.

Suppressing a nervous shudder, she bade

Mr. Crowe good day.

As she was exiting the bank building, she encountered quite possibly the last person she wanted to see.

Jasper Lamott was a tidy little man who hardly resembled the bane of anyone's existence. His assistant, the obsequious Guy Smollett, was as unobtrusive as a shadow as he followed his employer through the door. Lucy knew Lamott all too well. His Brethren of Orderly Righteousness worked tirelessly to derail all the efforts of the Suffrage Movement. With the money and political power of his cartel of businessmen, he advanced candidates and judges who subscribed to his dogma. More than once he and his black-clad cronies had disrupted peaceful rallies and voting registration efforts.

"It's a good thing you're leaving, Miss Hathaway," he said in a voice that stung like a lash. "You'll spare me the trouble of having you thrown out."

She glared at him. "Do you treat all the bank's clients with such courtesy?"

"This institution doesn't need your patronage. Come along, Smollett. This is a waste of time." The assistant glared at her and held the door for Lamott. The older man turned for a parting shot. "You are a disgrace to womanhood, Miss Hathaway, you and the whorish radicals who congregate in your bookstore. It's a pestilence, spreading sedition, and no decent Christian will be sorry to see it wiped out."

"I am leaving," she stated, trying not to show how rattled she was by his virulent hatred. "But I assure you, The Firebrand is not going anywhere."

Nine

"Maggie," said Lucy as they sat together at the beach, "remember how you asked what it would be like to have a papa?"

The little girl was playing in the sand at the shore of Lake Michigan. It was one of those crystal-clear Sundays of late spring, with weather so perfect it created an ache in the heart. The unrelieved blue of the sky met the deep azure of the lake in a sharp, straight seam. Mayflowers and buttercups painted the verges and parkways with sunny color.

Maggie didn't look up from digging her roadways and trenches as she answered, "You said Willa Jean could be the papa. I asked her if she would, and she gave me a hug and said she'd be anything I wanted her to be."

Lucy grinned. How typical of Willa Jean. And how accepting Maggie was.

"Suppose you had a father like the man in the stereoscope picture," Lucy suggested cautiously.

Maggie shrugged and balanced two sticks to make a bridge. "Everybody's father looks like that," she observed. "Those side-whiskers look enormously bristly."

Randolph Higgins didn't have side-whiskers.

The image of his trim mustache and un-smiling mouth flashed through Lucy's mind. The first night they'd met, she'd thought him the handsomest man she'd ever seen. She'd been foolish about him, not to mention quite mad, asking him to be her lover. Married or not, a man with looks like that would never be interested in a plain, gawky creature like Lucy Hathaway.

Now he bore the scars of suffering and loss. His looks had changed, yet, when she was with him, she still felt the unreasoning, sharp-edged attraction that had consumed her that long-ago night. He was married, she kept telling herself. She had no right to feel this way. Besides, he was about to become the enemy, and she could see no way to keep that from happening.

Idly brushing grains of sand from the blanket she sat on, she looked out across the lake. Catboats and little day sailors plied back and forth between the shore and Government Pier. The white wings of the sails flew along like birds about to take flight.

Lucy had delayed long enough. Her chest

pounded with apprehension at the thought of risking her child. But she'd always been truthful with Maggie. She had to follow her conscience.

"Time to go," she said to Maggie.

"But my village —"

"We'll come back to see if it's still here tomorrow."

"It never is. Someone always ruins it."

"And you always build it back up."

Maggie stood and brushed off her trousers. "Where are we going?"

Lucy shook out the blanket, lifting it high to hide the anguish in her face. "We are going visiting."

After the fire, Bellevue Avenue had been transformed into a fashionable enclave of the comfortably well-off. As Lucy and Maggie passed through the soaring wrought-iron gates of the district and rode their bicycles up the paved lane, they passed formal gardens that looked too verdant, too perfectly groomed, to be real. It was like riding directly into a Watteau painting; they expected at any moment to see people in powdered wigs strolling the grounds.

Yet as she counted off the house numbers, Lucy felt like a condemned prisoner crossing the final mile to the executioner's block: 362, 366, 372 . . . her destination. Taking a deep breath, she turned her bicycle into the curved driveway of the Higgins house.

"Look, Mama, a statue!" Maggie veered off the driveway, wobbling along a footpath flanked by box hedge trimmed as precisely as cut stone.

Lucy was going to call her back. Trespassing and snooping was not their purpose today. But she shared Maggie's curiosity. Built after the fire, the homes and estates were even grander than they had been in her father's day. The home in which she'd been raised now housed a relative of the railroad car magnate, Mr. George Pullman. She hadn't been back in years.

The fact was, the people of the affluent enclaves shunned her. They were shocked by her radical politics and considered her a bohemian. She'd trained herself not to feel stung by their disregard, but her mother cared deeply. Sometimes Lucy felt guilty for being an embarrassment to the woman who had once dreamed of her daughter making her debut at a White Ball in New York City. The once-proud Colonel's wife had been one of Chicago's leading hostesses. Viola had lost more than her husband in the fire,

171

she had lost a way of life.

Maggie dismounted in her usual spring-loaded fashion, leaping from the seat and landing on the grass while the cycle toppled behind her.

She scampered over to the small statue, an alabaster angel with a cherubic face and blank eyes turned to heaven. A small fountain burbled at her feet, the stream spilling into a little lily pond. "See how pretty it is, Mama." Skirting the pond, Maggie dropped to her knees at the edge, parted the reeds with both hands and leaned over to peer into the water. "I wonder if there are fish in here."

She didn't wonder long — Maggie didn't do anything for long — but jumped up and went to inspect the statue.

"She's all bare-naked," Maggie announced loudly, using one of her favorite words. "Naked as a jaybird. Naked! Naked!" She ran in circles, startling a few robins from a nearby tree.

"That will do," Lucy said, biting her lip to stifle a laugh. "We had better go to the door before we're arrested for trespassing."

"Like you got arrested for voting that time," Maggie declared. She traced a grubby finger around the base of the statue. "There are words carved in the stone." She brushed away some old leaves. "Ch-Chris — Does it say Christmas, Mama?"

Lucy peered over her shoulder and nearly choked on her own breath.

"Does it, Mama? Does it say Christmas?"

"It says 'In loving memory of Christine Grace Higgins. June 24, 1870 to October 8, 1871.' And there's a phrase. 'All hopes and dreams lie buried here.' "

"Your voice sounds funny, Mama. Why does your voice sound funny?"

Lucy kept staring at the date. *That's your birthday, Maggie. I know your real birthday now.* She knew the true date Maggie had been born, and the name she'd been given.

"Come on, sweetheart," she said, holding out her hand. "We really should —"

A deep, malevolent growl bit the air.

Lucy whirled around to see a massive creature bounding toward them, jaws opened wide to reveal rows of sharp, dripping teeth.

"Look, Mama." Maggie clapped her hands. "A doggie."

She rushed forward before Lucy could snatch her up. Child and hellhound met and clashed on the lawn. Lucy dived for her daughter but stumbled and missed, falling to the ground. The dog tackled the child. Lucy dragged herself up, horrified to see

Maggie pinned to the ground by the marauding beast.

But instead of screaming, Maggie giggled. The huge dog licked her, then lay belly up in the grass as she scratched its chest.

"Maggie, be careful," Lucy said.

"He's harmless," said a deep voice. "Though I can't vouch for the child."

Lucy picked herself up, plucking bits of grass off her cycling dress. Randolph Higgins strode across the lawn toward her. In the verdant setting, he looked even more imposing than he had at the bank. The perfection of the spring day highlighted his rugged appeal. He wore dungarees and a loose blue shirt, the morning breeze lightly toying with his rich brown hair. The informal garb suited him, somehow.

Her heart skipped a beat. It didn't seem to matter that years had passed since she'd first felt this wild attraction to him. It didn't seem to matter that he was married and that extraordinary circumstances had brought her here today. He simply made her light-headed with a feeling only he could inspire.

"I apologize for Ivan," he said, indicating the dog. "His appearance is startling, but I assure you, he is as gentle as a spring lamb."

"Look, Mama," Maggie crowed. "He

likes me." The dog stretched and quivered in ecstasy when she petted it. Maggie had always wanted a dog. She'd begged for a puppy for years, but in their tiny quarters over the shop, they had no room for one. Silky the cat was a beloved pet, yet Maggie still longed for a dog.

"He gave me quite a scare," Lucy said. "He's a great brute of a thing."

"Ivan is an English mastiff," Mr. Higgins said. "Though I believe his dam dallied with some sort of retriever or bird dog. He can sniff out anything."

She couldn't keep her gaze from Mr. Higgins. His sleeves were rolled back to bare his forearms, and sweat glistened on his neck and in the open V of the shirt collar.

"We weren't expecting visitors," said Mr. Higgins, mistaking her stare for disapproval. "I was just doing some gardening. I like . . . to grow things." He seemed to regret revealing something personal, so he turned gruff again. "Tell me, is showing up unannounced a habit of yours?"

"He *is too* a giant," Maggie whispered. "A real live giant, just like in the story."

Ignoring her, Lucy checked to see that her small satchel was still secure in the basket of her bicycle. She brushed at her wrinkled skirts, trying to compose herself. "I realize we're intruding, sir." Heavens, how was she ever going to do this? "But I have a matter of some importance to discuss."

"Your loan is still under consideration, I assure you," he said. "Nothing's changed from yesterday, so there is no need to —"

"May we come in?" Lucy blurted.

His lips thinned in an expression of displeasure.

"Please," she added. "It's important. I assure you, I have something monumental to tell you."

"I want to hear the monumental thing, too," Maggie said, trying out the new word.

"Very well," he said, helping Maggie pick up her bicycle and wheel it along. "I suppose I can offer you a glass of lemonade. This way."

Behind him, Lucy watched the small child next to the large man, and she felt a chill that had nothing to do with the breeze gusting in off the lake. Rolling the bicycle between them, Maggie and Mr. Higgins walked side by side with no notion whatever of their relationship.

She followed him to the house. For Lucy, an eerie familiarity haunted the wide sandstone steps leading to the entranceway. She'd grown up in a house like this; she recognized its staid formality and hushed halls gleaming with beeswax polish. A gauntlet of servants used to assemble in the vestibule in preparation for the Colonel's daily inspection. Mr. Higgins's home was much the same in formality and perfection of order, she observed. His wife must be an expert household manager.

"Look, Mama." Maggie's voice rang through the paneled halls as she raced into the foyer and skidded to a stop in front of a statue set in a niche at the base of the stairs. "That boy is peeing." She dissolved into gales of laughter as she regarded a small fountain fashioned to replicate the famous Mannequin Pis of Brussels.

Lucy's lips twitched with the urge to laugh or at least smile, but then she glanced at Mr. Higgins. He appeared baffled, as if Maggie were a life form he'd never encountered before. Lucy had been watching him for a single spark of recognition, but there was none. Too much time had passed.

But still, this man had known her as a baby. He'd held her, surely, touched her hair and smelled her smell. How could he fail to recognize his own child?

Perhaps, thought Lucy, the moth— Mrs. Higgins would respond to Maggie. A woman knew her baby more intimately than a man, particularly in a tradition-bound family. Mr. Higgins had probably stayed well away from the nursery, seeing his child for only a few moments each day.

"What in heaven's name is all this ruckus?" demanded a stern, female voice from the top of the stairs. The tip of a walking cane punctuated each descending step, stabbing at the carpeted stair. Lucy heard a thunk and then a shuffle, the eerie, measured rhythm filling the cavernous space of the foyer.

Never one to possess any patience, Maggie bounded up the stairs, shouting, "I want to see the ruckus, too!"

Lucy could find no voice to call her daughter back. She stood stiffly, as if taken by a sudden frost. The hem of a dark dress appeared, belled out by layers of petticoats and followed by a gloved hand grasping the head of the cane. Lucy didn't dare move as she waited to see the lovely, fair face of Mr. Higgins's wife.

"I'm Maggie," the child said, meeting her halfway up the stairs at the turn of the landing.

"You are loud," the woman said.

"What's your name?" Maggie inquired.

"You may call me Mrs. Higgins."

Lucy could find no air to breathe as she waited.

Maggie grabbed the woman's free hand and they descended the stairs together. When the two of them emerged from the shadows, Lucy stared in shock.

Dear God, Randolph Higgins's wife had turned into a crone.

Lucy forced herself to close her gaping mouth. The terrible ordeal had changed the coolly beautiful Mrs. Higgins into this wretched old —

"Grandmother," Rand said when she reached the vestibule, "I'd like you to meet Miss Lucy Hathaway. Miss Hathaway, this is my grandmother, Grace Templeton Higgins."

Lucy thawed out so quickly that her knees felt like water. Holding in a sigh of relief, she extended her hand. "How do you do, ma'am?"

"I cannot shake hands with you," the old lady said imperiously. "Both of mine are occupied. One with my cane, and one with this . . . this . . ."

"Maggie," Maggie repeated. "I *told* you, that's my name. Here. You can have your hand back."

"Thank you."

"Why do you wear those black things?" Maggie demanded.

"These are lace mitts made in Belgium.

179

They are considered fashionable, and they also keep my grip from slipping on my cane."

"Oh. When I want to grip my baseball bat, I just spit on my hands, like this —"

"Maggie, please don't spit in the house," Lucy said.

"I was going to spit in my hands."

"What sort of creature *is* this?" Mrs. Higgins demanded. "Where on earth did she get such atrocious manners?"

"Mama keeps meaning to order me some from the mail catalogue, but she hasn't done it yet." Maggie had always thought the reply enormously clever and delighted in using it. But Mrs. Higgins looked so severe that Maggie flushed. "I thought you might want some help getting down the stairs, on account of you're crippled with that cane."

"I am crippled *without* the cane. With it, I can get around quite well, thank you very much."

"You're welcome." Maggie seemed determined to make up for her manners now.

Lucy simply held her silence. Maggie was . . . Maggie. She always had been. Her exuberance often burgeoned into mischievous behavior or cheeky remarks, though she didn't have a malicious bone in her body. Sooner or later, the Higginses were going to learn her true nature, and it might as well be sooner.

Lucy was surprised by the expression on Mr. Higgins's face. His lips strained taut as if he were holding in a cough . . . or laughter.

"What is that you're wearing, child?" the old woman demanded. "Trousers?"

Maggie plucked at the rough fabric. "I always wear trousers. Mama and I believe in equal rights for women, and she lets me dress as comfortably as any boy."

"Hmph. So you think boys' clothes are more comfortable."

"Yes, and I can ride my bicycle easier, too."

"Bicycle."

"I have a two-wheeler and I can ride all the way down State Street to the river, faster than the horsecar."

"Boys wear neckties," Mrs. Higgins pointed out. She put an imperious hand on Maggie's shoulder and steered her down a hallway toward the back of the house. "Why aren't you wearing a necktie?"

"Neckties are dumb," Maggie said, gamely going along with her. "No one should ever wear one, boy or girl."

"Where are they going?" Lucy whispered to Mr. Higgins.

"I imagine Grandmother will take her on

her daily walk, if that's all right with you."

"Of course," she said, relieved that Maggie wouldn't be around when she made her announcement.

"Don't worry about a thing. Grandmother isn't any more vicious than Ivan. But she can be just as frightening to those who don't know her."

"Maggie isn't afraid."

"True. Your daughter seems quite fearless."

"Thank you. I take that as a compliment."

"It's meant as one."

She shifted the leather case in her arms. "Mr. Higgins, do you suppose we could sit down somewhere?"

He brushed at his grass-stained shirt. "As I told you earlier, I wasn't expecting company."

"I realize that. But as you might guess, Maggie and I are rather informal."

"Very well." He pressed a small bell in the vestibule. A moment later, a maid appeared and he requested a pitcher of lemonade. "On the side porch," he added, then led the way through a parlor, opening a set of French doors.

The parlor was silent and spotless, with an ormolu clock, fringed drapes and furniture, tufted silk carpets and cut crystal chimneys on the gaslights. Lucy paused to study the portrait that hung over the mantel. The hairs on the back of her neck lifted. The painting depicted Diana Higgins seated upon a draped stool, holding a beautiful baby in her arms. Rendered in rich, shadowy oils the style of a Dutch master, the picture captured the cool perfection of Diana's features, the precise grooming of her fingernails and hair, the dreamy, soft innocence of the baby.

The baby had Maggie's face. The resemblance was so uncanny that Lucy couldn't believe Mr. Higgins didn't see it. I can't do this, Lucy thought, panic knocking in her chest.

"It's a very beautiful portrait," she said, clutching her bag a bit closer.

"Thank you."

She tried to imagine what he and his wife thought about each day when they saw the picture of their child. Swallowing hard, she went through the French doors to a porch that faced the lake. A velvety green swath of lawn, sectioned by tree-lined walkways, connected the elegant neighborhood to the beach, crossing over Lakeside Drive. The crisp beauty and intense light of the view filled her with nostalgic memories of long walks along the shore with her father.

Lucy cleared her throat. "I would like for Mrs. Higgins to join us."

"My grandmother is quite content to entertain your daughter, I think."

The maid arrived with a tray of lemonade in a crystal pitcher.

"I was speaking of the other Mrs. Higgins," Lucy said, smiling anxiously at the mixup. "Your wife."

Crystal clinked nervously, and the maid's hand trembled as she poured. Cutting quick glances at Lucy, she finished her task and scuttled away.

Randolph Higgins seemed to grow even taller. "What the hell is this all about?" he demanded.

She blinked, then thrust up her chin, defensive at his bluster. "It's a simple request. I would like to speak to you about a matter of importance, and your wife should be present."

A strange stillness gripped him. He tilted his head slightly, as if she'd spoken in a foreign tongue.

Discomfited, Lucy shifted in the wicker chair, causing it to creak in the unnatural silence. Out on the broad side lawn, three figures appeared — Maggie racing along with Ivan the dog, followed by Grace Higgins, looking like a large black crow in a dark bonnet and shawl, holding her cane in one hand and a fringed black parasol in the other.

"Well," she prodded Mr. Higgins. "Will you send for your wife?"

"Miss Hathaway, your attempt to gain my sympathy in the matter of your loan has gone too far —"

"This is not about the cursed loan," she snapped, nervousness sharpening her tone.

"Then what other business could we possibly have?" His brows lowered in suspicion. "Let me guess. You're hoping to convert one more bitter, frustrated woman to your cause of social chaos and French paramours."

She planted her hands on her hips. "Is your wife bitter and frustrated, sir?"

"Not anymore," he said softly, his lips thin with a fury she didn't understand.

Lucy wasn't certain she'd heard correctly. "I beg your pardon?"

"Nothing," he said.

"Why are you being so disagreeable and difficult?"

"Why are you being so meddlesome and annoying?"

"Because I have every right to be." Lucy grabbed a chilled glass of lemonade with a mint leaf garnish and took a long drink, letting the cool liquid soothe her throat. Clearly this was going to take all the patience she possessed. "Now," she said, setting down the glass. "Please send for your wife. I want to discuss this with both of you."

"I'm afraid that's not possible." His icy hostility leached the warmth from the bright spring day. "I do not have a wife, Miss Hathaway."

This man had the unique ability to render her speechless. He was the only one capable of it. Her heart ached for him and her hand heated with the uncanny urge to touch him. It was not enough that he'd lost a daughter. His wife was dead, too.

When she found her voice, she could only manage to say, "I'm so sorry. I didn't know. You have my condolences, Mr. Higgins."

He hissed a breath through his teeth. "You don't understand. My wife is not dead. She has divorced me."

Divorce.

The word hung almost visibly in the air between them. To Lucy's ears, the term possessed the energy of something rare and bold. As a member of the Women's Suffrage Movement, she lent her support to the option of divorce. No woman should be forced to endure a man who mistreated or abandoned her. But she'd never imagined that a divorce would happen to the handsome, golden Higginses who had glowed so brightly that long-ago night.

Her first thought was that tragedy had torn them apart. The laughing, clever young man she'd met that night had been transformed by loss; perhaps his beautiful wife could not abide the changes. "I don't know what to say," she finally blurted out.

"You needn't say anything. My private life is none of your affair. It is something that happened in the past, and it is over."

Was it? Although Diana was no longer his wife, she would always be the woman who had given birth to Maggie. How powerful was the bond of sharing blood and breath and food? Lucy was terrified of finding out the answer, yet she knew she had to. "This complicates things, then," she forced herself to say, "for I feel I should speak to your w— your former wife as well."

"Believe me, she subscribes lock, stock and barrel to your infernal cause. However, you won't be able to enlist her." He glared out at the elegant expanse of lawn. "She lives in San Francisco now."

"I see." Lucy sipped her drink, trying to reorganize her thoughts. What if the former

Mrs. Higgins decided to take Maggie off to California?

"Let me be plain, Miss Hathaway," Mr. Higgins said. "For reasons you refuse to disclose, you are prying into my private affairs. Would I not be well within my rights to show you the door? To make you put your sweet little backside on that bicycle and leave the premises?"

She nearly choked on a mint leaf. How dare he comment on her backside? How dare he call it sweet? She tried to summon indignation, but mingling with her worry about Maggie was a fierce interest in this man. With inappropriate, shameful curiosity, she wanted to know every last detail of the divorce. She deserved to know, she assured herself. What had become of Maggie's natural mother? Why had she left? Could she hand Maggie over to a broken family?

Impulsively she reached out and covered his hand with hers. His skin was taut and waxy with scars. "Believe me, Mr. Higgins," she said, "you do not want to send me away."

He reacted swiftly, yanking his hand away. "Yes, I do," he stated.

What if the divorce was his fault? Lucy wondered, hearing hostility in his voice.

Was he cruel? Neglectful? Autocratic?

"Please. I know it's painful to speak of, but I must learn more about your — Mrs. — Why you divorced."

"Since you have taken such an inexplicable interest in the matter, you should be able to guess what happened," he said with a clipped detachment that chilled her. "Thanks to radical groups like your Suffrage Movement, the laws of Illinois are particularly favorable to divorce. Chicago is crammed with lawyers who make it easy."

"Was it?" Lucy asked softly. "Was it easy for you?"

He looked at her for a long time, and she lost herself in the vivid clarity of his eyes. A thousand stories lurked inside him, and she found herself wanting to know them all. At last he spoke. "No one's ever asked me that before."

"Maybe someone should have."

Another pause. He took a gulp of his lemonade and stared into the blue distance. "We were very young when we wed. Full of dreams." He cleared his throat. "Full of . . . a terrible hope. We had a good life in Philadelphia, but Diana wanted more."

"More what?" asked Lucy.

His eyes flickered. "No one's ever asked me that, either. She always seemed to be looking for something that lay just beyond the horizon. I thought once the baby came along, she would be content."

Lucy was struck by the idea that he'd come halfway across the country to find a better life for Diana. Was it a blessing or a burden, she wondered, to have one's happiness matter so much to a man?

A humorless half smile lifted his mouth. "But here's the irony of that. I was the one who found contentment when Christine was born, not Diana. They say it is the woman whose nesting instincts are aroused. In my case it was being a father. It seemed to fulfill every dream I ever had."

His candor amazed her. The blunt, probing questions she'd asked had opened a floodgate of confessions. Perhaps he'd never had anyone to tell this to before. Lucy didn't dare speak, hoping he'd continue. She felt torn, admiring his honesty even as a part of her wished he'd prove himself an unfit father so she could keep her secret.

"We came west because I thought Diana might enjoy the excitement of a new city and the challenge of building a new home for our family. I intended to establish myself at the bank, and she would build a grand new house. The one thing we never could have anticipated was the fire." He leaned forward, resting his lanky wrists on his knees and staring at the ground, seeing things Lucy didn't dare to imagine.

She suddenly wanted him to stop talking, for she didn't wish to share his pain. Yet for Maggie's sake, Lucy knew she had to hear everything.

"This will sound odd to you, Mr. Higgins, but I truly do wish to know what your life has been like."

"Why?" he demanded. "Why would you care? Have you another sexual proposition?"

She chose not to dignify him with an answer, but responded with another question, one she hoped would shift the mood from bitterness to honesty. "What happened after the fire?" She pictured them that night, handsome and golden, standing in the glow of everyone's admiration. After her idiotic blunder, she'd stood back and watched, thinking them the most romantic, luckiest couple in the world.

And an unholy envy had burned in her heart.

"After we lost Christine, I couldn't even be present to comfort Diana," he admitted. "I lay unconscious while she made a full recovery. Her wounds were fortunately superficial — or so I was told. But something broke the night we lost Christina. In the worst moment of our lives I failed to console her. Perhaps that is why she left." His face flushed. "Though on the legal decree she gave quite a different reason."

Lucy couldn't bring herself to ask what that reason was. Not yet. His former wife had a side to this story, too, Lucy reminded herself. "A great tragedy can change the very fabric of life," she said, thinking of her mother.

He steepled his fingers together and held her gaze with his. "I had this house built for her, but it was an act of futility. With Christine gone, Diana and I had nothing to hold us together."

Lucy didn't comprehend how love could simply stop in the face of adversity, yet she held her tongue, troubled by the idea that he had no wife. She'd come here today thinking to find a loving family. If she made her great revelation now, she would be making it to a bitter, wounded man who had lost the ability to love.

Without a mother in the picture, she must proceed with care. Perhaps, she thought, this was a test of her true convictions. She had always claimed women and men to be equal. She had to believe a man could be every bit as good a parent as a woman.

Agitated, she stood and went to the porch rail, standing with her back to him. It wasn't too late to change her mind. He still didn't know. He might never know. Oh, how she wanted to run away and never tell him.

Silence hung between them as the moments passed, the lemonade glasses sweating and forgotten, the breeze scented with the blue freshness of the lake. Lucy tried to imagine how he'd felt, having lost his daughter and then his wife as he lay wounded.

In the distance, Maggie and the dog skipped along the beach. The little girl waved at them, then ran in circles around Grace Higgins, who sat on a painted bench, watching Maggie's antics from beneath the fringed parasol.

Turning, Lucy contemplated Mr. Higgins and wondered why his sadness hurt her.

He was too damaged, she thought in apprehension. Even learning the truth about Maggie would not banish the pain in his eyes.

Then a thought struck her. Perhaps he and his former wife would reconcile if they realized they hadn't lost their daughter after all.

"She is quite a lively child," he said at length, and she realized he'd been watching Maggie, too.

Gathering her courage, she asked, "Do you disapprove of liveliness in a child?"

His face closed. "It is not for me to approve or disapprove. My knowledge of child rearing is extremely limited."

"Maggie is the greatest blessing of my life." In anguish, Lucy sat down and braced her hands on the arms of the chair. "Do you understand that? The greatest and most precious part of me. She is all my heart and soul."

He looked startled, then his expression softened. "Actually, Miss Hathaway, I do understand."

She caught her lower lip in her teeth, trying to keep in the request she knew she must make. And then she made herself say it. "Tell me about your child. Not how you lost her, but . . . how you loved her."

He fell still, and she sensed his hesitation. He turned his glass around and around in his hand. "Did you really come here to ask me these things? Surely you have better things to do with your time than to poke around in my past."

Lucy took a chance. "Can it make you feel any worse to speak of it?"

He glared at her, and she feared she'd lost him. But then he began to speak. "The day Christine was born, I bought two dozen bottles of Sire de Gaucourt champagne. I drank an entire bottle myself in celebration, but I put the rest aside. I thought what a fine thing it would be to serve that champagne on the day she married."

Lucy felt the depth of his loss in each softly spoken word. "Do you still have the champagne?"

He nodded. "After the fire, it was shipped from Philadelphia with the rest of our household goods. Now each year on the date of her birth, I make a fire in the study hearth, prop up a photograph of the two of us together and drink a bottle of that champagne." His eyes, now dull with grief, didn't even seem to see her. "I'm not sure why I do it. I suppose because the taste of the champagne always brings back the joy of that first day I held my tiny baby in my arms."

Lucy nearly reeled with his dizzying anguish. It seemed to pulse in the long silence. Until today, she'd never known her daughter's true birthday. But this man had always kept the day in his heart.

When she looked up at him, his image blurred within a shimmering veil of tears. But she did not shed them, and her chest hurt with the effort.

Birds warbled in the trees as the breeze sifted through the chestnut leaves. Down on the lawn, Maggie brought Mrs. Higgins an offering in her cupped hands. They bent their heads together, Maggie's brown curls a bright contrast with the old lady's somber black bonnet. Maggie opened her hands and a frog popped out with a frantic leap. Maggie went bounding after the frog while Grace snapped open a fan and fanned herself as she sagged back against the bench.

Lucy stole a glance at Mr. Higgins, and his expression shocked her. Far from the stern disapproval she'd expected, he was grinning from ear to ear, shoulders shaking with quiet laughter. "Now there's something we don't often see around here. How old is your daughter, Miss Hathaway?"

"She is five years old." Lucy paused and swallowed hard, plucking courage out of abject terror. Her next words would change all their lives forever. "She will turn six on . . . June 24."

She held her breath and watched his reaction. The smile that had lit his face froze until it was no longer a smile but a hostile grimace.

"There's no simple way to put this," Lucy said, plunging ahead, afraid to stop. "So I must be blunt. Mr. Higgins, your daughter did not die in the fire."

Ten

There was a sort of pain so deep and intense that for a moment it was indistinguishable from ecstasy. Rand knew this anguish with the same familiarity as others knew the sound of their own voices. Unlike ecstasy, the agony that came after the first shock had the power to crush his soul.

Nothing changed outwardly at first. He still sat on the porch in the white wicker chair, watching the sunlight filtering through the trees. He still smelled the light peppery scent of the daisies that bordered the verge surrounding the porch. He was still aware of the woman sitting just a few feet away, watching him intently.

Who the hell was this creature? She'd made him bare his soul to her. She'd drawn from him things he'd never told anyone, and when she'd excavated the weakest, most damaged part of him, she had moved in for the kill.

With an iron control clamping down on the howling grief inside him, he set aside his glass. "Why —" His voice broke over the word. He had to clear his throat and swallow before starting over. "Why in God's name would you lie like this?"

Her jaw dropped. A small explosive sound of disbelief came from her. "I would never lie about such a thing, Mr. Higgins. What do you take me for?"

Icy heat crawled over his skin, awakening vivid and searing memories of the dark, lost time after the fire. Upon learning of Christine's death and of Diana's divorce suit, he'd wished with unholy fervor for death. Only the propitious arrival of his grandmother, demanding in her imperious way that he look after her in her old age, had persuaded him to rise from his sickbed.

But he had still wanted to die.

"I take you," he said slowly, "for a sadistic little radical who would go to any lengths to save The Firebrand. Get the hell out of my house."

She made her hands into fists on the arms of the chair. "You think I'm telling you this in order to get you to approve my loan?"

He didn't trust himself to reply.

"Sweet, sweet heaven," she whispered. Her eyes drifted halfway closed as if she might faint. It was a stunning performance; she looked appalled and devastated by his accusation, even as she hid her disappointment that the trick had failed.

"Or perhaps —" He thought for a moment. "Perhaps you're more clever than I give you credit for. It's significant that you would broach the topic upon learning I'm no longer married. Could it be that you're trying to trap me into marrying you?"

"M . . . marry?" Her voice was little more than a squeak. *"You?"*

He was well aware that he was considered hideous by women. His ruined looks, combined with the gossip in the wake of his divorce, had effectively driven off any prospects. It was just as well. He didn't want to remarry. Ever. Why would he risk himself like that again?

"I understand most decent ladies wouldn't consider marrying a monster like me," he said, "but I imagine at your advanced stage of spinsterhood, you cannot afford to be too particular."

"How dare you —"

"Your bastard needs a rich father, no respectable man will have you, and so you've come to me with this cock-and-bull story. I have only one precious thing, Miss Hathaway — the memory of my daughter. Clearly you have no respect for that."

Her face was very white, a stark contrast to her dark hair and rosy lips. "How did you ever get such a low opinion of me?"

"You earned it, Miss Hathaway." He felt weary, drained, as if he'd been in a fight and lost. "Now take the little hoyden and leave. Please."

"Believe me, I'm tempted. If only you knew how hard it was for me to come here, to bring you the truth when it would have been so much easier to hide it from you forever."

He glared stonily out at the lake, where water and sky met in a hard, flat blue line. Lucy Hathaway rose from her seat and opened the leather bag she'd been dragging along. A small, soft parcel wrapped in tissue paper landed in his lap.

"Take that away," he snapped.

"You'd best see what it is first."

He wanted to fling the thing aside, whatever it was, but when he grabbed it, the tissue fell away, leaving behind the faint scent of dried lavender and bergamot. The tissue wrapping drifted to the porch, and his big rough hands were suddenly filled with the softness of a woven blanket.

Soft yellow lambswool fibers. A one-inch fringe all around. A carefully hand-stitched border —

His head snapped up. "Where the devil did you get this?"

She held up a sepia-toned photograph in a

small oval frame and turned it toward him. "Your baby was lost that night, but by a miracle she did not die. That blanket was wrapped around her when she was dropped from a window of the Sterling House Hotel."

Rand studied the picture. His heart plunged, and for a moment he couldn't breathe. A terrible heat burned in his chest.

Christine.

It was his baby, holding the familiar blanket, wearing an unfamiliar little gown and a pair of tiny shoes.

"I had it taken," Lucy Hathaway explained with incredible gentleness, "a week after the fire. So I could circulate her picture to the papers."

Christine.

He looked from the photograph in Lucy's hand to the child laughing and playing on the lawn. Deep inside his head, he heard a roar, gathering strength as it spilled like a storm through him. During the explosion that had almost killed him, the all-encompassing light had imparted the sense that he existed somewhere outside of himself. That same sensation burst through him now, and it was almost like another kind of pain.

And then he did the unthinkable. He pressed the woven blanket to his face and nearly exploded as he tried to take in the revelation. His baby had survived after all. He felt a searing regret for all the years he'd missed with her, yet sheer wonder shone through. She was alive.

Lowering the blanket, he stared at the child in the yard, trying to reconcile her with the image he'd carried in his heart for nearly five years. But he was looking at a little stranger. How could he fail to recognize his daughter?

He felt a tentative touch, like a bird alighting on his shoulder. Lucy Hathaway's hand patted him awkwardly as she spoke in low tones. "Oh, Mr. Higgins. I can't imagine the shock of this. I didn't know how else to tell you."

"How long have you known?" he asked. "Goddammit, how long have you kept this from me?"

She bridled, taking a step back. "I can't believe you'd think me capable of carrying on a deception."

"I have no idea what you are capable of. Why would you come forward now?"

"I only just found out myself. My first inkling was at our meeting in your office. Until I saw the picture of your child, I believed Maggie to be an orphan. The photograph proves she is not."

"It does," he whispered, his gaze riveted on the child. Then he unfroze from his shock and leaped to his feet, striding across the lawn. Christine. Christine was alive! He could think of nothing but taking her in his arms, claiming her as his own.

"Wait," cried Lucy, racing to catch up with him. "What the devil do you think you're doing?"

"I am going to my daughter," he said, the words tasting as sweet as young wine.

She planted herself in front of him and grabbed his arms. He had no choice but to stop short or bowl the determined creature over. "What?" he asked, annoyed by the delay. Yet at the same time, her proximity was as profoundly unsettling as ever.

"You will do nothing of the sort," she said in a low voice so deadly serious that it cut through his agitation. "I've said nothing to Maggie. It would be cruel to deliver this shocking news with no preparation and no plan for what will happen next."

"There is no need for a plan," he said. "Christine will return to the family where she belongs."

Lucy's face turned paper-white. "No —"

"Get out of my way," he said.

"Maggie is mine, too," she said with a voice of steel. "You're a stranger to her."

The blunt words hammered through his single-minded determination, and suddenly he understood what was at stake. She'd raised his child as her own. She'd been Christine's mother.

Like a slap, the realization cleared his mind. He couldn't simply grab the child and claim her like a portmanteau left at the hatcheck. He forced himself to subdue the instincts screaming at him to seize the child skipping along the lakeshore walk.

"You must think me a complete ass," he said.

"Well," she said, "not *completely*." She pulled him over to a granite garden bench, motioning for him to sit beside her. "If I thought that, I would never have brought Maggie to you. But I'm counting on you to be reasonable." He started to say something, but she held up her hand, stern as a schoolmarm. "No, you will listen. I'll tell you when it's your turn to speak."

He forced himself to wait, conceding to her logic. This was too new; he didn't want to frighten Christine. He took a deep, shuddering breath, catching the scent of the blanket again. He'd never lost control like this before, not even in private. He wondered why he didn't feel more humiliated by his show of emotion, his rash behavior. Perhaps it was because Lucy was being so matter-of-fact about it all.

He forced himself to stay seated. "Tell me how you found Christine."

"I was making my way home through the fire," she said. "I headed for the bridge in front of the Sterling House. The hotel was burning out of control, and I found myself quite alone." A distant horror shone in her eyes.

Rand remembered the young idealist she had been, and he could easily picture her standing alone before the inferno. Any other woman would have run. But not Lucy.

"There was a movement in a window," she continued. "I think it was two floors up."

"Our suite of rooms was on the second story." He tightened his fists in the blanket. He kept staring at the little girl on the lawn across the way, expecting some magical shimmer to bond them instantly. But even to his searching, hungry eyes, she resembled any child of nearly six, not one special child in particular.

"There was a woman holding a bundle of bedding," she said.

"That would have been Miss Damson, the nurse Diana had engaged to look after

Christine." He shut his eyes, imagining the scene. Becky, frantic, the baby wrapped up to cushion the fall. He remembered his annoyance at Diana for leaving Christine that night. But if Diana had stayed home, then she might have died, too, as poor Becky Damson had.

"Earlier in the evening, I had seen stranded people dropping pets and belongings from windows when there was no other way to leave the building," Lucy explained. "So when I saw the bundle, I didn't even really think. I held out my arms to catch it. Immediately afterward, the building —" She paused and blinked fast, and he realized the fire had been traumatic for her, too. "The building collapsed. In seconds it went from a tower of fire to a pile of burning rubble. I ran to get clear of the flames, and then I —" She took a deep breath. "Then I discovered what — who I was holding. She was frightened but unharmed.

"My only thought was to reach a place of safety. My parents' home was spared by the fire. I brought the baby there." She bit her lip. "When I arrived home, I learned that my father had been injured battling the flames. He died moments before I got there."

"I'm sorry, Miss Hathaway," Rand said.

The night had held its terrors for her, too, then. Only hours before the fire, she had boldly aired her views for a well-heeled crowd and brazenly propositioned Rand, never flinching as she tilted back her head and regarded him with a sparkling defiance. It was hard to imagine anything bad happening to such a woman, yet she'd lost someone dear to her that night. And she'd found someone dear to him. She'd saved his baby's life. He wanted to fall to his knees, kiss her feet, call her a miracle worker.

"I made every effort to find the baby's family," she said. "We posted bills at every camp, published the photograph in the papers, registered with churches and orphanages, tracked down people who had fled from Sterling House. But there was no response."

All the while, Rand thought, he'd lain senseless and half-dead in the hospital. Later, he'd hired a private insurance investigator just to be certain, but that had only confirmed his worst fears — there were no survivors.

Now here was this miracle of a woman, telling him Christine was alive and well. Again, his gaze sought out the child on the beach. She raced at a flock of gulls, scattering the white birds into flight.

A pair of hands cradled his cheeks, startling him. With her usual forthright lack of manners, Lucy turned his face to her. "Mr. Higgins," she commanded. "I want your full attention."

She was touching his scars.

She was touching his scars, and she didn't even seem disgusted.

There were things he hadn't experienced since the night of the fire — joy, elation, hope. They were coming back to him now, rushing through him like fast liquor. "All right," he said. Carefully, self-consciously, he took her hands and set them away from him.

Her small, pointed face softened. "I knew this would be a shock, but I also knew you would have the sense not to rush off half-cocked and upset Maggie." She inhaled deeply and began to speak in a way that made him suspect she'd been rehearsing the words. "It is a physical certainty that you and your wife — ex-wife — are her parents. But it is equally certain that I am the only mother Maggie knows. I am the one who nursed her through fevers and comforted her after nightmares. I'm the one who laughed with her and tickled her. I taught her to whistle and swim and ride a bicycle. She's beginning to read and write. All that

208

she knows, all that she *is*, comes from having me as a mother for the past five years."

Each word thudded into him, reminding him of all he had missed. He started to speak, but she shushed him again.

"I'm not saying this to aggrandize myself or to exaggerate my own importance. To tell you the truth, I spent the first six months with Maggie trying to give her away." She caught the look on his face and said, "I was searching high and low for her family, not trying to abandon her like an unwanted kitten. Though Lord knows, I was the last woman on earth who needed a child. I had no husband, my father had died and my mother had gone bankrupt. The three of us had no means of getting on in the world. But something unexpected, almost magical, occurred. Maggie saved *me*. She forced me to be stronger, better than I ever thought I could be." Her face glowed when she spoke, and she was beautiful in the way all mothers were when speaking of their children. "Her needs gave me the power to move mountains. Because she needed me, I started the bookstore, invested all I had in it. I'm convinced I wouldn't have done it if Maggie hadn't been depending on me."

She reached into the voluminous satchel

and drew out a packet of papers tied with string. "That is what being a mother is. That, and being as protective as a she-dog. Maggie looks quite sturdy, but I know her. There is a part of her that is a fragile, glass thread. I won't allow her to be hurt."

"I never thought I would find myself agreeing with you, Miss Hathaway, but I do." For the first time since grasping the news, he felt more like himself. Competent. Decisive. Firm in his convictions. "Christine must be protected."

He was grateful she'd held him back from seizing his daughter straightaway. With his scarred face and large size, with such a fierce joy and amazement spurring him on, he might have frightened the life out of the poor child. He nodded at the papers in Lucy's hand. "What have you there?"

"I thought you might like to get a glimpse of Maggie's life."

The part he had missed.

"Of course," he said, forgetting to breathe as she untied the string and produced several photographs mounted on card stock.

"I dated each picture on the back. Since I never knew Maggie's true date of birth, I could only guess at her age, but now we'll know how old she really is in each photograph."

She handed him a picture of herself holding Christine as a toddler, and standing beside a handsome older women. The three of them posed in front of an elegant house that looked vaguely familiar to him. "This is the house in which I grew up. My mother was forced to sell it after the death of my father. She used the proceeds to pay off his debts, and there was nothing left for us. She sold it at a fraction of its actual value."

"Why would she do that?"

"Because she was cheated."

"Why did she allow it?"

"It wasn't a matter of her allowing it so much as her being entirely unaware that she was grossly undervaluing the property. I will be frank with you, Mr. Higgins. My mother is a very traditional woman. She never challenged the assumption that a woman is incapable of managing property and finance. My father believed in keeping her in happy ignorance. Upon his death, she was as innocent as a child in the ways of the world. When a speculator came along with an offer, she was only too happy to put her trust in him. By the time I realized what was going on, he'd taken possession of all she had." She handed him another photograph. "We were left virtually destitute."

He studied the picture of the three of

them on a boardwalk in front of a building he didn't recognize. "What did you do?"

"We took refuge in this temporary shanty village by the river." She touched his sleeve. "Now, don't look like that."

"Like what?"

"Like you pity us for suffering the fires of hell."

"But look at you —"

"Dressed in old clothes, living in a shack — Yes, yes, I've heard it all before. Some of my dearest friends discovered our circumstances and insisted on helping, but do you know, in all the years of tutors and governesses and finishing school, I never had so fine an education as I had in that shantytown right there."

"I don't know what you mean."

"Nor did I, so long as I was some idealistic debutante with no knowledge of the real world. Here, among the lowliest poor, I discovered the true evils of injustice. And the true strength of a determined woman. I saw women abandoned to raise seven children on their own, and they managed, sometimes through sheer faith alone. I discovered that at the heart of their deprivation was a desperate ignorance. They had a need I believed I could fill. I would create a place where women could read and learn. One evening a week, I hold a reading class for those who never learned, and women of all ages come. So I don't regret the months we spent there, Mr. Higgins, and Lord knows neither does Maggie. She was always warm and had plenty to eat, and more than enough children to play with. When a child feels loved and secure, she has no notion that she is deprived."

Looking at the picture, he had to admit that Christine appeared perfectly content, plump and clear-eyed in Lucy's arms.

The next picture showed them in yet another unfamiliar place, this one a wild, rocky shoreline with a backdrop of towering pine trees.

"That is Isle Royale, in northern Lake Superior. Our friends, Deborah and Tom Silver, kindly provided hospitality over the summer of 1872." Her dark eyes grew dreamy with memories Rand could not share. "How Maggie loved it there, running free and barefoot, eating fish roasted on an outdoor fire and sleeping under handmade quilts."

Rand couldn't even imagine it. His daughter. Barefoot and free as a savage.

The next picture showed a much older Christine in a little cloth coat, standing on a sidewalk and holding Lucy's hand. Behind them was a shop window and overhead hung a carefully lettered tradesman's shingle: The Firebrand — L. Hathaway, Bookseller.

Both Lucy and the child were grinning broadly, as if being dignified for the camera was too much of an effort.

"I'm afraid we hadn't the time or the means for frequent photographs," Lucy confessed. "Honestly, the years just flew by." She pointed to a spot in the corner of the picture. "Our apartment is here, on the second floor. That's our cat Silky in the window. And beyond that low wall is the garden."

Rand couldn't sit still anymore. He handed back the photographs and stood to pace, agitated, trying to take everything in. His gaze kept wandering to the green belt across the esplanade. His grandmother sat with her hands folded around the head of her cane; she had a habit of nodding off and was probably napping. In contrast, Christine's tireless energy matched that of the dog. She'd found a stick and kept flinging it out into the water. Ivan obligingly fetched it each time, making her collapse with laughter as he shook off water in all directions. Rand ached with the need to go to her, to grab her and hold her against his heart.

"So," he said, suppressing the urge, "you have raised my daughter over a shop with a calico cat and a concrete garden."

"Indeed I have."

"She's had no nurse, nanny nor governess. No formal education."

"She is five years old," Lucy pointed out.

"Nearly six," he said. "Five years, ten months and four days." As soon as he saw the pity in her eyes, he regretted revealing so much of himself. She'd raised his daughter, yes, but she was a stranger. She didn't need to know that he measured the days and weeks and years of his life by the age Christine would be, had she lived.

"You disapprove," she said, sounding defensive.

"Do you blame me?" he asked. "Christine is my child. When she was born, I had such dreams for her. I had great aspirations as to how she would be raised, and you'll excuse me for saying so, but I never did imagine her as a shopkeeper's child."

She laughed again, that incredulous burst of sound she employed when she wanted to make him seem ridiculous. "Are you saying Maggie would have fared better here?" She encompassed the property with a sweep of her arm. "Imagine my happy, active daughter living in this chilly mausoleum."

The way she spoke made him wonder about her own childhood in her father's palatial house.

"Mama, look, Mama, Mama!" The little girl came crashing toward her with heedless abandon. Grinning from ear to ear, she held a twig in her grubby hand. "Look very hard, Mama, and you'll see it."

Lucy went down on one knee, as lacking in dignity as a washerwoman to inspect the stick. "What am I supposed to see?"

Christine pursed her lips. "Look *harder*." Losing patience, she thrust the twig at Rand, startling him. "*You* look. Do you see what I've got?"

Rand was completely taken in by the appeal in those wide eyes. He squatted down close to her. "A praying mantis."

She frowned adorably, and his heart melted. She said, "A what?"

"It's an insect." He pointed without touching. "There's its head, and its hind legs are all bent. The forelegs seem like they're clasped together, praying."

She beamed at Lucy. "I found a praying mantis, Mama!"

Lucy cut a suspicious glance at Rand. "So you have. The female bites the head off the male after mating."

"*Eeuw.*" Christine held the twig at arm's

length. "Mating is revolting."

Rand felt himself redden, but he didn't want to lose this moment of connection with his daughter. His Christine. "More revolting than biting a head off?"

She thought for a moment, then nodded. "I think it probably is."

She looked so grave and earnest that he had to swallow a laugh. At that moment, Ivan came trotting over. He raked at the ground with his giant paws like a bull gearing up to charge.

"I think he wants you to throw that stick," Rand said.

"Not with the praying mantel on it!" She handed it to Lucy.

Stretching his mouth into the unfamiliar expression of a smile, he found a larger stick. "Let's see how far he can go."

Christine laughed and clapped her hands. "Throw it far! Throw it as far as ever you can!"

Rand drew back his arm and flung the stick. It rotated high in the bright sky, and the foolish dog took off after it with no notion as to where it would land. Rand's arm ached with the motion. He hadn't had occasion to throw anything since cricket matches at university. But at a single command from his daughter, he would move mountains if bidden.

Christine scurried off after the dog. Lucy regarded Rand with a wary expression.

"What?" he asked.

"She likes you."

An aching warmth flooded his chest. "Do you think so?"

"Yes. Yes, I do."

He watched her putting the photographs away, and surprised both her and himself by saying, "As long as you are here, Miss Hathaway, I should tell you that you'll have the loan extension you requested for your shop. I'll see to it personally."

She froze, and her expressive face drained to white. Then, despite her size, she seemed to swell and grow. "Mr. Higgins." His name exploded from her like an oath. "My child is not for sale."

Her emphasis on the word *my* ignited his temper. "No," he informed her, "I have a legal right to keep my daughter, and to tell you the truth, I'm not obliged to offer you so much as a by-your-leave."

She made a choking sound, then managed a voiceless *"What?"*

"I will concede that you have raised a healthy child, and for that you have my gratitude. The fact that you came forward with Christine once you solved the puzzle proves you do have the integrity to be trusted with the loan."

"You're making me sorry I came forward," she said in a low, threatening voice.

He forced himself to calm down. She was right, of course. He needed to be measured in response to this. "Look, Diana and I never could have imagined our baby was dropped into a stranger's arms. Our worst fears were confirmed by the Board of Fire and a private investigator. They assured us Christine and her nurse could not have survived. We never saw the announcements you claim you sent out. Even months later, when I was well enough to read, I never could abide all those melodramatic tales of survival that were so popular in the press at the time. Damn it, I was too busy grieving for Christine and struggling with —" He almost said losing Diana. He remembered lying in bed, staring at the pockmarked ceiling of St. Elspeth's Hospital, pondering his idea of what a family should be and wondering why such a simple thing had eluded him. He had built this house in his mind long before he'd built it in fact; he'd actually believed if it was big enough, beautiful enough, Diana would come back to him.

"I never paused to consider that a miracle

had occurred," he concluded.

"Well, now we must decide how best to proceed."

"I'll send a wire to Diana straightaway." As he spoke, he tracked the little girl with his gaze. Christine. He could scarcely believe it was her.

"Agreed," she said.

The strain in her voice caught his attention. "I'm sorry. This must be difficult for you."

"I confess my first instinct was to keep Maggie for myself."

"So why did you come forward?"

"Because . . . it would be morally wrong to hide the truth from Maggie. It would make me no better than the unenlightened patriarchs who keep women in ignorance and deny them their rights. I will still be Maggie's mother and fiercest protector, but I won't hide the identity of her natural parents from her. Therefore, my coming forward to you has certain conditions attached."

Amazing. She managed to be high-minded and annoying in the same breath.

"My first condition is that we must keep Maggie and her needs in mind. We must do what is best for her, first and foremost."

"I agree."

"Good. I was hoping you would."

He prepared to get up. "So shall we go and tell her?"

She grabbed his sleeve and yanked at it. "Tell her what?"

"That she is my daughter and henceforth will be living here with me."

She kept a stranglehold on his sleeve. "Wait."

"I see no reason to delay." He stood up.

"Here is your reason, Mr. Higgins." She slapped a parchment document into his hand.

He unfolded the paper and his blood chilled. "This is —"

"Yes," she said, "it is. A legal adoption. Maggie is my daughter in the eyes of the law."

Eleven

Lucy held her breath until her chest hurt and a pulse hammered in her ears. Then slowly, half afraid she would deflate like a spent balloon, she let out the air and stepped away so he could read every word of the adoption papers.

Almighty heaven, what had she been thinking?

She should have listened to her mother, whose occasional bursts of wisdom were too often ignored. Lucy had always been one for opening doors and poking her nose into places she shouldn't. When most would leave well enough alone, she tended to dig and pick at things until she exposed them. This was no great virtue, her mother had pointed out, particularly in the current situation. Her campaign for justice was about to cost her the one thing she could not give up — her daughter.

And all because she could not keep her mouth shut.

It had always been that way with her. From the time she was small, she'd always spoken up when she perceived an injustice.

And that, of course, was what had befallen Randolph and Diana Higgins. A tragic injustice of the cruelest sort. And she, in her usual crusading manner, had felt compelled to rectify it.

But Lord, why? Why couldn't she, for once in her life, have kept her own counsel and maintained the status quo?

She was still not even certain he was the sort of person she would want in Maggie's life.

He stood like an oak tree on the lawn, solid and quietly powerful-looking as he perused the long legal document she'd handed him. He was tall indeed, but she knew his strength was a deceptive thing. In certain places in his heart, he was as fragile as spun glass. He'd nearly been killed in the fire and had awakened to find that his baby was gone, his wife divorcing him. He lived alone in this large house with a sour old woman. His strength was the strength of endurance, of forbearance.

Lucy got up from the garden bench and paced, waiting for him to finish inspecting the document. Her gaze automatically turned to Maggie, and an unbidden smile softened her mouth. She never tired of watching her daughter. The child possessed an uncanny ability to become completely absorbed in her world, whether she was telling stories to Silky, building cities in the sand or simply staring out the window. At the moment, she was making some sort of game only she understood, which involved overturning certain rocks on the pathway and arranging them in a crooked line. Lucy found the mind of her daughter endlessly fascinating, and she never questioned Maggie or expected her to justify her imaginative forays.

When Lucy was small, the Colonel had subscribed to the traditional notion that a child not visibly occupied in a productive pursuit — study, prayer or domestic arts — was a sinner waiting for opportunity. He'd scheduled her day to the last minute, so much so that from the moment she awakened until the moment she fell asleep — with her hair twisted into ringlet rags, her hands tied on top of the covers so she wouldn't interfere with herself — her hours were filled with lessons deemed important to the development of a proper young lady.

Lucy had rebelled every chance she got, and she'd sworn that if she ever became a mother, she would not put her children through such a regimen, restricting them and binding them up as if they were espaliered vines. She'd never forgotten that vow, and Maggie was free to play however she pleased.

The breeze blew through the birches and chestnuts, and the leaves shimmered, making a chiming sound. She pictured the childhood a little girl might experience in this elegant, shaded house, with a stern great-grandmama and unsmiling servants moving through the halls.

She could never let Maggie live here, only come for visits.

Mr. Higgins finished reading and approached Lucy. He walked with a slight limp, and she guessed that it was another injury from the fire.

But the deepest wounds were hidden inside him.

What was it like, she wondered, to be divorced? To have pledged love and devotion for a lifetime, only to have his wife recant her vows? Lucy was all in favor of divorce, naturally. Too many women were shackled to horrible men through the institution called marriage, and they deserved a way to extricate themselves. But in the case of Mr. Higgins, she hardly thought he was a drunk or a bully. He was just . . . too sad and too scarred to bring his wife joy.

He held out the papers to her, and she took them and put them away.

"I suppose," he said, "you think this means you have the same rights as Christine's mother."

Her hackles rose at his choice of words. "Christine's natural mother has suffered a great loss, but that doesn't give her more rights than I have. My child's name is Maggie now, and *I* am her mother. In the eyes of the State of Illinois, and most particularly, in the eyes of Maggie herself."

"This adoption is based on the assumption that she was orphaned in the fire. That assumption is erroneous. Therefore, the adoption is invalid."

Lucy forced herself to remain very still and calm. Her solicitor had declared that her situation was unique. It would take a skilled and sensitive judge to sort it all out, and Mr. Lynch's advice had echoed her mother's: Let sleeping dogs lie.

Too late, she thought, eyeing Mr. Higgins.

"I will dispute that," she said, "to my dying breath."

"There's no need for histrionics, Miss Hathaway. The situation is simple. My lost daughter has been found. She will come and live with me as nature intended. I'll see to it you're adequately compensated for your —"

"Oh, stop it," she said, covering her rising

panic with bravado. "Who's being melodramatic now? From my point of view, the situation is equally simple. When Maggie thinks of her mother, she thinks of me."

The lake breeze lifted his thick dark hair. The untended locks curled at the nape of his neck in a way Lucy recognized. Maggie's hair curled in that precise fashion. Lucy knew then that she would never look at her daughter in the same way again.

"Miss Hathaway, if you're so set on fighting me," Mr. Higgins said, "what were you thinking by bringing her here, telling me your story?"

"How ironic to hear you ask that." She stood and followed him in his pacing, taking two steps to each one of his. "I was wondering the same thing myself. I certainly didn't intend for you to steal my child," she said fiercely. "I only thought it my moral duty to come forward with the truth. Once I saw the photograph in your office, I felt obligated to do the right thing. But that does not mean you can rip Maggie from my arms."

"Nor does it mean you can keep a child who wasn't yours in the first place," he snapped.

"She'd be dead if not for me." She could feel the air crackle between them.

"Standing here and arguing about it won't accomplish a thing."

"Then what do you propose we do?"

"We have to come to an arrangement we can all accept. One that keeps Maggie's needs and her happiness in mind. Will you at least agree to that?"

"It is precisely her needs that I am thinking of."

Lucy willed herself to be patient and calm. For Maggie's sake, she had to be civil to this man. "It's time to take my daughter home now," she stated. "You'll want to send for your — for Diana. Then we will determine the best way to proceed." She could not resist adding, "And make no mistake, I never shared breath or blood with Maggie, or nourished her with the milk of my breast. But I am her mother in every sense that matters."

"Your love for Christine is genuine and admirable," he said with obvious reluctance. "But we do have much to discuss."

"Indeed we do. We mustn't tell her yet. She'll be too frightened and confused. Promise me."

"All right. For now." He seemed calm and resolute as he offered her his arm. To seal their truce, she put her hand into the crook of his elbow and they strolled along the walkway. She found that she enjoyed the connection, which was strange, since this man posed such a threat to her. Yet his solidity and warmth appealed to her in a deeply physical way.

She gave a little wordless laugh.

"If you've found something amusing," he said, "I wish you'd share it."

"I was just thinking — last time I walked arm in arm with a man, I was in handcuffs." She remembered hiding her terror behind a mask of bravado.

"The voting incident," he said.

"Yes."

"And where was my daughter while you were being thrown in jail?"

Lucy yanked her hand away from him. "She was perfectly safe, I assure you. What are you trying to say, Mr. Higgins?"

He gestured at Maggie with his free hand. "She's very young yet, and unschooled. Before long, it will be time for her to get on in the world, and she'll need —" He paused.

"You can say it, Mr. Higgins. It won't be the first time I've borne criticism. She will need more than I can give her." Saying the words herself somehow numbed the sting. "I used to lie awake at night wondering if I was doing right by Maggie, raising her in the only manner I am able. But I don't worry anymore, and do you know why?"

"Why?"

"Because Maggie herself gives me the answer every day. She is a bright, joyful child with a heart full of love, an adventurous spirit and a great curiosity about the world. So I must be doing something right."

"Of course you are," he conceded readily as he escorted her across the esplanade. "But as she gets older, her needs will grow more complex. Think about it, Miss Hathaway. You want a good education for her. You no doubt want safety and stability and complete freedom from deprivation."

"Of course. Every mother wants that for her child."

"Look around you." With a gentle pressure, he turned her to face the staid elegance of the lakefront neighborhood. Well-dressed gentlemen drove buggies toward the bridge, and nannies in crisp white aprons pushed prams along the neatly laid out sidewalks. Uniformed maids swept porches and women sat watching the boats and barges on the lake. "All that is here," said Mr. Higgins. "Just waiting for her."

Lucy couldn't answer as she pictured the cramped flat over the shop, the noise and dust of Gantry Street and her worries about making the food budget stretch to the end of the month. She moved away from him and walked toward her daughter.

Maggie stood by the line of stones she'd laid out near the bench where the old lady sat. Waving her arms in circles, she screeched like a seagull. Mrs. Higgins awakened with a snort and a scowl. "Child, what in the world are you doing?"

"I'm a bird!" Maggie cried, angling her arms and racing toward the old woman. "I can fly!"

"Nonsense, you are a girl, and girls don't fly."

"We do, too," Maggie insisted. "Well, I do, at leas— Yikes!" She clapped her hand over her mouth.

Lucy and Mr. Higgins hurried over, but Grace Templeton Higgins was more spry than she looked. Using her cane for leverage, she sprang up and went to the child. "What is it? Are you hurt?"

"Mmmmmm." Maggie kept her hand in place and spoke in a muffled voice. "My tooth ith very looth."

"Let me see." Putting aside Maggie's hands, Grace tilted up her chin and said, "Open."

"Grandmother —" Mr. Higgins began.

Lucy touched his sleeve, holding him back. As her fingers brushed his bare arm, that peculiar sensation rolled through her again. "It's all right," she said, amazed to see the severe old lady getting along so well with Maggie.

"Wider," Grace said, and untucked a dainty handkerchief from her sash. "Let me see which tooth it is. Could it be . . . this one?"

She held the handkerchief flat on her palm.

"It's out!" Maggie cried, dancing a little jig. "It's out out out!" She paused to spit upon the ground.

Grace looked aghast, but when Maggie grabbed her hand and said thank you, she quickly recovered from her disgust.

"Mama, Mr. Higgins, look at this!" Maggie said, wrenching a finger into the side of her mouth to give them a wide view. "My tooth came out."

"Congratulations," said Mr. Higgins, looking suitably impressed.

Lucy realized that it was a milestone he'd not yet witnessed. What a wonder this must be to him, seeing his baby suddenly transformed into a little girl.

Maggie wadded up the handkerchief with the tooth and handed it to Mrs. Higgins. "You can keep it if you like."

The old lady blinked behind her steel-rimmed spectacles. "Thank you," she said, tucking the handkerchief in her sash. "I think perhaps I shall."

"Honestly, I have no idea why you sell such drivel." Mrs. Mackey held a dime novel between thumb and forefinger, letting it dangle there like a dormouse. "Waste of shelf space, if you ask me."

Lucy was in no mood to spar with one of her least pleasant customers, but it was hard to let the remark pass. She took the slim booklet, printed on foolscap, from Mrs. Mackey. "Actually there are several reasons," she said. "I am a bookseller, ma'am. These are books, and so I sell them. Dime novels sell briskly and in great numbers. I would be a poor businesswoman indeed if I ignored them."

Mrs. Mackey, splendidly dressed as always in a mustard-colored morning dress and matching bonnet, sucked her tongue in disapproval. "But they are such . . . such awful little stories. Sentimental and simplistic. Don't you see it as your mission to uplift and enlighten the hearts and minds of readers?"

"Of course," Lucy said. "And that's why I would never presume to determine what a woman should or shouldn't read." Some booksellers considered themselves too high-minded to stock such popular offerings; they saw themselves as gatekeepers of literary taste and roundly censored books of which they did not approve. But not Lucy. She understood all too well the dangers of censorship, banning books or sitting in judgment of someone's reading choices.

Smiling in her most professional manner, she took one of the small books from the shelf and held it out to Mrs. Mackey. This one was called *The Hostage,* or *Isle Royale Paradise* by a lady author no one had ever heard of. "Have you ever read one?"

The bird feathers on her bonnet trembled indignantly. "Certainly not. Nor have I read anything remotely like it."

"Then," Lucy said with a wry smile, "you are well-qualified to criticize them."

"Well, I — it's just that they are just so . . . so *preposterous,*" Mrs. Mackey insisted. "Why would I waste my time reading something so preposterous?"

Lucy pressed the book into her hand. "There's a reason these books are so popular. People like them. They like the drama and the sentiment. Take this book, Mrs. Mackey. If you don't like it, bring it back."

She hesitated, then accepted the garishly

illustrated paperbound volume. "Very well. I suppose there's no harm in taking a peek."

Lucy caught Willa Jean's eye and gave her a wink. Perhaps Mrs. Mackey would turn into a loyal devotee of the genre, which meant more frequent visits to the bookstore.

Though she enthusiastically sold the cheap, popular novels, Lucy didn't understand them herself. Who on earth could believe such an outlandish plot as a bride taken hostage to an island paradise, and who could admire a woman who spent a whole book pining away for a man? But she had to admit, no matter what trials and perils the perfect blond beauty went through, she always reached a moment of blissful triumph in the end. Perhaps that was the appeal, the notion that out of the ashes of despair could come a grand passion and a shining new hope.

Lucy spent the rest of the day tending shop as usual, trying to convince herself that all would be well. She normally joined in the weekly reading circle, particularly when the theme was as compelling as this week's topic of the upcoming Centennial March, to be led by Victoria Woodhull herself. Mrs. McNelis came in to purchase her monthly copy of *The Voting Woman*, but when she wanted to discuss the July Fourth event, Lucy was too preoccupied to give it her full energies. Today, it was all she could do to remember how to add a column of sums. After lunch, she simply gave up, letting Willa Jean handle the trade while she tried not to go absolutely mad with worry and apprehension.

Maggie was still oblivious to the turmoil surrounding her. Lucy's mother had promised to go on as if everything was normal, helping the little girl through her morning lessons and taking her to play in the park after lunch. Soon, however, Lucy would have to break the news to Maggie.

Standing behind the tradesman's counter, Lucy pretended to organize a stack of papers. In reality, she brooded upon her most recent meeting with Barry Lynch. On her behalf, he'd consulted a judge, and the news hadn't been good. The law preferred the rights of the natural parents over the adoptive ones, and of course it favored the rights of a man over a woman. That was no surprise. The fact that Lucy had saved a helpless child and provided a safe and happy home for Maggie would arouse the court's sympathy and admiration, but a ruling in Lucy's favor was a longshot. Her best hope was to negotiate privately with the parents.

The notion daunted Lucy. She couldn't even negotiate a bank loan with Randolph Higgins.

Near closing time, Patience Washington bustled in, her robes billowing with the summer wind and her face sober and fierce with concern. She greeted her sister, then turned her attention to Lucy. "I just got your message, child, and came right over," she said.

Lucy motioned her into the tiny office cubicle behind the desk. Publishers' broadsheets and book review journals lay scattered in untidy but well-organized heaps. On the wall was a newfangled bell system for calling up to the apartment. There was just enough room for Lucy and Patience to sit together.

"I went to see him," she said without preamble. "I told Mr. Higgins about his daughter."

"Oh, blessed day." Patience beamed. "I knew you would."

Lucy told her about Mr. Higgins's stunned reaction, the furious suspicion followed by such wonder and gratitude that even recounting the tale, she felt an uncomfortable prickle in her throat. She described the rolling lawns of the neighborhood, the lake beach, the sad stone angel monument to Christine, the stern grandmama who had kept Maggie's tooth, and most of all her concern about the absent wife, the former Mrs. Higgins.

"She divorced him," Lucy said in a scandalized voice. "Left him when he could barely rise from his bed."

"I thought you believed a woman is entitled to divorce her husband at will."

"Of course I do, but not when it involves my child's parents." She stopped, wondering at the irony of her own child having other parents.

"Do you think he treated her bad, maybe beat her?"

Lucy considered the tall, brooding man who was master of the cold, tree-shaded mansion. "I cannot imagine him mistreating anyone. He is so . . . careful and controlled. So very gentle with Maggie. He was gardening when we arrived. I showed him the photographs of her growing up and he —" She remembered the reverent way he'd held the blanket to his face and handled the pictures. Even in his frustration over missing his daughter's life, he had never given way to rage.

"Mr. Higgins thinks Maggie's life is unsettled and strange. She lacks a proper nurse or governess, she lives over a shop . . ." His words haunted Lucy and undermined her confidence. She pulled in a long, apprehensive breath of air. "Patience, it is just as I feared. Simply knowing Maggie is alive and well is not enough for Mr. Higgins. He wants her back."

Patience folded her hands and stared down at the desk. "We didn't expect anything else, honey."

"It's more than that." Lucy felt a fresh wave of panic. Every instinct a mother could have leaped up in denial inside her. "He wants more than the occasional visit. He intends to take her away."

Patience's head snapped up. "Land of mercy. Child, I don't know what to say."

"Please." Lucy reached across the desk and grasped the hard-knuckled dark hands that had always touched her with kindness. She gazed pleadingly into eyes that had looked upon her with wisdom and affection since they were girls together. "You have to know what to do."

"Nobody knows that."

"Mr. Lynch consulted Judge Roth on my behalf to see if I have any legal recourse whatsoever."

"And do you?"

"Not likely." Lucy nearly choked on the words. "He thought perhaps I might be entitled to some manner of compensation for my troubles, but that is all." She let loose with a sharp, humorless laugh. "How much is a mother to be paid for loving a child? A thousand dollars? Ten thousand? Six million? How can you put a price on such a thing?"

"What does your heart tell you to do?" asked Patience.

"Run," Lucy answered instantly. "As fast and as far as I can, to a place where he will never find us."

"Girl, that's not your heart speaking. That's instinct. You got to ask yourself what your life would be like, always running, always looking over your shoulder. You'd never feel safe. Is that any sort of a life for a child?"

"I know you're right, Patience. I can't flee. My whole world is here. The Firebrand, my mother, our customers." She gave the preacher's hands a squeeze before letting them go. "My friends and my church. Without that, life would not be worth a copper penny."

"So . . . ?"

"So I suppose I must fight Randolph Higgins on any grounds possible." She shut her burning eyes; she hadn't slept a wink the night before. "I would fight to the death to keep Maggie."

Patience was silent for so long that Lucy dragged her eyes open. Patience had a tender, thoughtful expression on her handsome face; she waited with an abiding forbearance that made her name so fitting.

"What?" Lucy demanded.

"You better think about what Maggie's going to go through during this here fight of yours." She stood slowly, her lumbering movements a distant echo of the toil and abuse she'd endured growing up poorer than poor until the Hathaways had taken her and her sister in.

"Is that all you have to say?" Lucy asked.

"Good Book's got something to say. First Book of Kings, chapter three, girl. See if the Lord will show you the way."

The moment she was gone, Lucy raced to the bookcase in the shop containing religious and spiritual titles and took out a heavy King James. Ignoring Willa Jean's probing stare, Lucy opened the book to the chapter and verse Patience had cited.

She was painfully familiar with the story. Two women laid claim to the same infant. To figure out the identity of the true mother, King Solomon commanded that the baby be cut in half and distributed in equal parts to the two mothers. One woman instantly shrieked out a protest and begged the king to give the child to her rival. In that moment, the king knew the protesting woman was the infant's mother because no true mother would sacrifice her child for the sake of her own selfish needs.

Lucy replaced the Bible on the shelf. The message was clear. If she chose to put up a fight, the casualty would be Maggie.

She walked to the shop window, her footsteps clicking on the scrubbed plank floor. Standing at the window, she viewed the park across the way, where her mother sat with her knitting in her lap and Maggie played a disorganized round of baseball with a group of neighborhood boys. A powerful wave of love nearly sent Lucy to her knees, but she stood firm.

She knew what she had to do.

Twelve

Based on the scandalous reputation of The Firebrand, Rand half expected to encounter chanting, wild-eyed Amazons on the sidewalk outside the establishment. Instead the little shop appeared to be a rather ordinary, even pleasant-looking place. Situated amid a row of merchants' shops on the west side of Gantry Street, it faced a stand of sycamores on the opposite verge, which bordered a small city park. The brick front facade framed a picture window he knew had been wildly expensive. But in her loan papers, Lucy Hathaway had written that the outward appearance of her establishment was a critical factor in its success, and in building its false front she'd spared no expense.

Typical woman, he thought. More concerned with appearance than substance. And clearly, judging by the cryptic message he'd received from her, enamored of high drama.

She had summoned him by telegraph messenger. Everyone, even the janitor at the bank, knew Randolph Higgins did not enjoy correspondence by telegraph, yet apparently Miss Hathaway was a dedicated user of the newfangled system, sending young men dressed like organ grinders' monkeys out to deliver her messages.

Miss Hathaway desires that you call at her shop at ten o'clock in the morning. . . .

It had the tone of a royal summons. From anyone else in the world, Rand would ignore it as the self-important imperative of a bank client, but this was different. This was Lucy. This was the person Christine called "Mama."

He forced himself to sit still while his driver fitted the brake blocks in front of the wheels of the coach, though he did crane his neck around, looking for his daughter.

His daughter. Alive and well. To a man who had never before dared to believe in miracles, this had made a believer of him.

The hard part was the waiting, the holding back. Only minutes after Lucy and Christine had left his house, he'd summoned a team of solicitors from the best law firm in the city. Since it was a Sunday, he'd gathered them from their family dinners and rounds of golf. After recovering from their initial amazement, the lawyers had advised him to progress methodically through the steps of reclaiming his child. One legal misstep, and he could lose her again. They did assure him, however, that he would get her back. What judge in the city would dare to question the rights of a natural parent, particularly a man of Randolph Higgins's status?

What about the fact that his wife had divorced him? He'd been forced to ask it.

The lawyers were not worried about that. Besides, they pointed out, when she learned of Christine's survival, Diana would surely come rushing back to him.

And surely, thought Rand morosely, the moon would fall out of the sky.

Still, miracles did happen, and Christine was proof of that. The task ahead was to find the best and fairest way to bring her back into his life. That imperative, more than any lawyer's advice, governed his impulses now. The child was about to undergo a big change in her way of life, and he wanted to make the transition as smooth as possible.

But as he thought of Lucy Hathaway, he could not imagine anything going smoothly. The woman was a human cyclone, ripping through his life and leaving chaos in her wake. But she'd saved Christine. She'd raised a happy, healthy child. For that, he owed her a debt beyond counting.

Holding a black leather case stuffed with

hastily prepared legal briefs, he took out his pocket watch, thumbing open the gold dome of the cover. He was five minutes early. He flipped the watch shut and put it into the shallow pocket of his waistcoat, remembering the day he'd received it. His father, Bradwell Higgins, had given it to him on the occasion of his engagement to Diana Layton, the most sought-after debutante in Philadelphia. Rand remembered his father's approval and his own feeling that for once he'd done something right.

His father was notoriously difficult to please. Grandmother Higgins had always said it was because of Rand's mother. Her name hadn't been spoken aloud by any Higgins since Rand was ten years old.

His memories of her were few and vague. He remembered Pamela Byrd Higgins as a gentle, soft-eyed woman who rarely spoke or smiled. He recalled the soothing tenderness of a woman's hand upon his brow when he was sick. Sometimes, if he closed his eyes, he could still summon the faint, haunting fragrance of lily of the valley, with which she scented her handkerchiefs. Rand kept his memories of her secreted away, like things kept in a trunk he never looked in but could not bear to part with.

His father had destroyed all traces of

Pamela when she had left, offering no explanation and disappearing like a melting snowflake, never to return.

Only the intervention of Grandmother Higgins had soothed Bradwell's savage temper. She'd pointed out that Pamela had always been unstable and unpredictable. Hadn't she slid into a deep depression after Rand's birth, refusing to speak for nearly a year? Didn't she spend hours hunched over her writing desk, churning out Lord knew what?

Rand paced back and forth on the sidewalk, trying unsuccessfully to shake off the memories. He knew why they had been haunting him. He was a man who had met with success in every area of his life except the only one that truly mattered, and that was family. His mother had left his father, Diana had left him and his daughter had been raised by a stranger.

He wondered if he'd done a terrible thing in a past life, to be so cursed. And truly, the only thing he wanted was a happiness most men acquired without a great deal of trouble. Was it so much to ask for a contented wife and family?

At precisely ten o'clock, Rand opened the door of the shop, setting off a high-pitched brass bell as he stepped inside. A small

Negro woman looked up from her post behind a plank counter.

"You must be Mr. Higgins," she said.

Her unsmiling scrutiny made him conscious of his scars, yet she seemed to be taking his measure, not wondering about his wounds. This woman probably knew more than his name. Lucy Hathaway had likely told her associates that he meant to steal "her" daughter. He inclined his head in slightly formal fashion. "I'm here to see Miss Hathaway," he said needlessly.

"I'll let her know you're here." The woman kept her eyes on him as she left the counter and stepped through a glass-paned door behind her.

His nerves alive with anticipation, Rand turned his attention to the small shop. He was curious about the establishment, so adamantly opposed by the men associated with his bank. Near the front window was a comfortable rocker, and the walls and aisles were lined and sectioned by shelves. A brass ladder on rollers was positioned at the end of one aisle, and several customers browsed through books of varying quality. The shoppers wore dresses with prominent bustles; they hardly resembled the suffrage-minded viragos depicted by the satirists in the *Chicago Tribune.* They appeared as ordinary

248

and proper as the wives of his banking clients. These ladies did not seem the sort to beat their breasts or breathe fire with passion for their cause. Yet somehow, their very ordinariness made them all the more powerful. They sent sideways glances his way, no doubt wondering what a man was doing in their midst. He nodded briefly to acknowledge the ladies and turned away.

Contrary to the picture he'd formed in his mind of an unkempt and lawless environment, he found the shop to be surprisingly orderly. The books were organized by subjects indicated by hand-lettered signs. A long table surrounded by battered yellow maple chairs dominated the room. Stacks of books and pamphlets covered the table. He picked one up, glanced at the title: "The Science of Preventing Conception." He dropped the pamphlet as if it had stung him.

Propped at the end of the shelves was a slate board with a message in chalk: "No state shall make or enforce any law which shall abridge the privileges or immunities of citizens of the United States. — Fourteenth Amendment of the United States Constitution. Patrons are kindly reminded to vote . . ." He recognized Lucy Hathaway's handwriting and her egalitarian spirit. Below that, in a scrawl of block letters, was a sketch of a cat and the word "Silky."

Christine's work, no doubt. A sense of wonder touched him. When he'd lost her, she'd barely been able to talk. Now she was writing words on a chalkboard. Clearly Miss Hathaway had done her best, but Christine needed a complete education, not just the haphazard schooling of a political radical.

He strolled over to a window that framed a view of the tiny concrete garden at the rear of the shop. There was Christine, playing with a cat while an older lady sat nearby, knitting.

His daughter was alive and well. More than well, she seemed filled with a special energy as she dangled a ball of yarn in front of the cat, which tracked the loose end with intense, predatory purpose. The older lady, a softer, more mellow version of Lucy, smiled indulgently and didn't seem to mind that a cat was attacking her yarn.

When Christine jammed her foot into the crotch of the old apple tree and hoisted herself up, his instincts told him to rush outside and stop her. But Mrs. Hathaway simply tilted up her head, spoke briefly and then returned to her knitting. Christine climbed like a monkey through the branches, paying out the yarn as she went. The cat shot after the dangling end, and the child laughed as the inept hunter kept missing its mark.

Despite being raised in unorthodox circumstances, Christine appeared happy. Of course, he assured himself, she'd never known a conventional way of life. Once she made the transition, she would find an even deeper, safer happiness, he was certain of it.

"Don't worry about the tree climbing," Lucy said, suddenly standing behind him. "She is an expert."

He swung around, startled even though he was expecting her. "I have a natural apprehension about children behaving in risky ways."

Lucy studied the little girl out the window. A peculiar softness suffused her face, making her look almost pretty. "All of life is a risk, Mr. Higgins."

She led the way into a cluttered office little bigger than a closet. "Here you have it," she said, seating herself behind a desk littered with correspondence and invoices. "The heart of my enterprise."

Pulling the door shut, he sat on a narrow bench and set down his case with a thud. They had an uncomfortable discussion to get through. Lucy Hathaway was no fool, and had probably made certain preparations of her own. He braced himself to do battle for his child. How far would he have to go? His lawyers had warned him that he might have to discredit her, even if it meant attacking her character. Her lovers from France, her precarious finances, her activism in the suffrage movement — all were fair game in the fight to keep Christine.

"Thank you for coming so promptly," she began, folding her small hands upon the desk. They were rather nice hands, he observed, unassuming and prone to nervous flutters if she didn't keep them clasped and in view.

"I am as eager to get this settled as you are," he assured her.

"Yes, well, yes. Settled. Let me begin by saying that I see this situation from one point of view only — the point of view of someone who cares about Maggie above all else. My decision has been made with her well-being in mind, even when that is at odds with my own desires."

So far, she sounded bloody reasonable. He wasn't quite sure what to do with a reasonable woman.

"Naturally, that is my paramount concern as well. Christine's future is the most important work I have ever undertaken."

Her breath caught with a barely audible hitch. "I see," she said. "Then I must ask you to consider letting Maggie stay with me. You will be welcome to visit anytime you wish, but she belongs here."

He gritted his teeth. "Out of the question. My child will not be raised over a shop. By a woman who boasts of her sexual exploits with French lovers."

Her cheeks burned scarlet. "Sir, you seem preoccupied with my private life. Don't tell me *you* have been celibate all these years."

Her comment darted into him, unexpected as a sneak attack. "Very well, I won't tell you that."

She narrowed her eyes. "That tells me nothing."

Exactly as he'd intended. He pressed his hands on the edge of the desk. "I know where my bitterness comes from, Miss Hathaway. What is the source of yours?"

She glared at him. "Perhaps your accusations make me edgy —"

He raised a hand to silence her before she continued. "We should cease this arguing. For Christine's sake, we must be rational in our approach to this dilemma. My position is clear. My daughter will live with me."

She swallowed hard. "I feared you'd say that. But you understand, I had to try. Now, since you refuse to yield to my judgment, I've devised an alternative arrangement."

She pushed a long document across the desk to him. "Here are my terms."

His instinct was to crush the papers into a ball. Who the devil did she think she was, dictating the terms of his reunification with his own flesh-and-blood daughter? Still, he reminded himself, this was Christine's foster mother, and he would grant her the courtesy of reading her agreement.

"May I have a moment?" he asked.

"Of course." Her skin was very white, her lips taut. "Take as long as you need."

But he didn't need much time at all. By the time he finished the first page, he understood the gist of it. His heart thumped wildly and a chill passed over his skin.

"You are surrendering her to my custody."

"Yes." Her face was a mask he could not read.

He swallowed past the dryness in his throat. "Forgive me for sitting here like an idiot, but I didn't expect this."

"You expected me to fight like a wet cat in a corner."

The accuracy of her prediction amused him a little. "Well, actually —"

"Believe me, Mr. Higgins, I considered it." She clasped and unclasped her hands. "I considered many possibilities, including disappearing to a place where you would never find us. But I discounted that. I will not live in exile."

He was amazed she was giving the child up so easily. Perhaps, like many radical suffragists, she'd felt shackled by the responsibility of raising a child. Perhaps she felt liberated by the notion of giving Christine up.

As soon as the thought crossed his mind, he dismissed it. Lucy Hathaway was a stranger in many ways, but one thing had been clear from the start. She adored the little girl and was devoted to her. "I have to ask why," he said.

"Of course. You probably think I feel oppressed by the burden of motherhood and wish to be rid of it as soon as possible."

A rueful smile tightened his lips. "You see right through me, Miss Hathaway. I confess, the notion did cross my mind. But I rejected the thought. I may disagree with your politics, but I'll not deny your love for my daughter."

She was quiet for a moment, and he sensed her struggling with something. It was strange, this affinity he had for her, this way of knowing she was in pain.

Then she nodded. "I kept coming back to one matter — what is best for Maggie. I don't want to force her to endure the life of a fugitive just because of my own selfishness. Nor do I want her to feel like a piece of disputed property. She would be hurt by a protracted battle, so I've chosen not to fight."

Rand leaned back against the wall, trying to sort out his feelings. He'd been prepared for every possible resistance from her and had prepared every possible justification for reclaiming his daughter. His attorneys had drafted arguments in support of his claim, proving him the superior parent by virtue not only of the nature and law but of his stature in the community. He'd drawn up reams of proof of his financial and social viability. He would have dragged Lucy's reputation through the mud, publicly, in order to win a favorable ruling from a judge. But thanks to Lucy, he hadn't needed to fight.

Elation soared through him, yes, and triumph and joy sweetened the victory. But he could not quell a vague twinge of regret. He hadn't wanted to do battle with this woman. However, he also didn't want her to make herself a martyr over this.

"You've made a wonderfully wise and generous choice," he said at last. "I do admire you greatly for this, Miss Hathaway."

"I didn't do it to gain your admiration,"

she assured him. "I did it to make this as easy for Maggie as possible." Her voice sounded cold and flat, and he suspected she was trying hard to stay calm. "Look over the rest of the document, Mr. Higgins. I expect you'll find it agreeable."

Her terms were far more liberal than those in the restrictive documents in his briefcase, but he was willing to make concessions because she'd taken the high road herself. Although the child's chief domicile would be with Rand, Lucy had assigned herself generous rights to visit. The document spelled out the terms of the custodial arrangement, from visitation to maintaining membership in a church Maggie had attended since 1872. One condition, he noticed, was that the child was not to be taken from Chicago without Lucy's approval.

"May I take this?" he asked, holding up the agreement.

"Of course." She pressed her palms carefully on the blotter. "But I warn you, I will not change a word of it."

He opened his briefcase. "I brought a document of my own, but it was drawn up with a contest in mind."

"My daughter is not a prize to be won. That's why I gave her up without a fight. I'm doing this the only way I know how."

He'd expected tears and hysterics. Instead she seemed as steady as a marble icon.

"What have you heard from your former wife?"

As always, Lucy Hathaway aimed straight for the heart of the matter. "I had a wire last night from San Francisco." Over the past years, his feelings for Diana had run the gamut, from an abiding commitment to blind hatred to a profound indifference.

"When will she return?" Lucy asked. "Did she say?"

"Actually," Rand said, hating the admission, "she did not. She declared her surprise and joy to learn that our daughter is alive and well, but there was no mention of her coming back for a reunion." He didn't reveal that the wire had been filled with suspicions even darker than the ones Rand had entertained when Lucy had first come to him. Diana believed the claim to be fraudulent. She accused Lucy of being a blackmailer and manipulator.

Wishful thinking will not bring Christine back, Diana had concluded. *Take care you're not duped by an opportunist.*

"There is something we must consider," Lucy said, leaning across the desk. As he so often did, he felt drawn to her. She was a thin woman with busy hands and probing eyes, intense in a way that captured his interest and held it riveted.

"What is that, Miss Hathaway?"

"I assume she could arrive at any moment — for heaven's sake, how could she stay away?"

"Indeed." Yet Diana had given no indication of further interest in the subject. He settled back, waiting for her to make her point.

"And when she comes, what if she —" Lucy broke off, trouble furrowing her brow.

"Go on," he said. Christ, did she expect him to read her mind? "What were you going to say?"

She looked him square in the eye. "I mean you no insult whatever, and I beg you not to take this wrong."

"Just say it, Miss Hathaway. Now is the time for complete candor."

"Suppose your ex-wife is unwilling to renew her marriage vows with you?"

He let out an explosive sound that was not quite a laugh. "Do you think I was expecting that?"

"Actually, yes. I assumed that the impact of the tragedy broke you apart, and now that you have found your child again, you would come back together."

Rand used to hope for a reconciliation.

He'd built his house — a grand behemoth he could ill afford — in the hopes that it would lure her back to him. Finally he'd concluded that whatever bonds he and Diana had shared had been broken long before the tragedy. It took the drama and agony of the accident to sever the ties completely.

But Lucy couldn't know that. All she knew was that his scars had made him a monster no woman could possibly want, not even the mother of his child.

"Diana is not likely to want a reconciliation," he said.

"That is why I stated in the agreement that Maggie is to be raised in Chicago. Mr. Higgins, I beg you to support me in this."

"Diana will not take my daughter from Chicago," Rand promised her. "But for now, there's no point in speculating about her plans. The next task is to share the news with Christine."

"Christine." The name came from her on a whisper, as if she were almost afraid to utter it. She shut her eyes, and the expression on her face was so taut with uncertainty and yearning that he had a sudden urge to touch her, to rub his thumb along the tense line of her jaw and tell her everything was going to be all right. He didn't, of course.

He didn't touch anyone anymore.

"When shall we tell her?" he asked.

"Not yet," she said, her eyes flying open. "You'll want time to look over my terms. We must sign the agreement and have it notarized. Everything must be in place before she —" Lucy broke off. "Everything must be in place."

"Miss Hathaway, I have barely slept three hours since you gave me this miracle. What do you suppose I've been doing in that time?"

"I don't know you, Mr. Higgins. You'll have to tell me."

"I've been getting the house ready. A crew of workmen has been laboring 'round the clock, preparing a suite of rooms for her. Christine will live like a princess in a fairy tale."

"I'll want to inspect the premises myself."

"Of course." He stood up, briefcase in hand. He'd come here expecting the worst. Instead he was getting his child back. He wanted to laugh, to smile. To shout with joy.

"And I want for us to tell her together."

"Of course," he said again, and felt a blessed relief. He was not too proud to admit that the prospect was daunting. In taking his place as Christine's father once again, he would need all the help he could get.

The knowledge that Randolph Higgins would be taking Maggie away sat like a stone on Lucy's chest. She devoted the remaining week to her daughter, knowing she would have to live the rest of her life on the precious memories they made in their final days together. Mr. Higgins would permit her to visit, of course, and she would always be a part of Maggie's life, but it wouldn't be the same as living together, day in and day out.

But she would never forget, never. And if there was a benevolent God — Patience swore there was — Lucy would remember even the small moments that seemed to pass in the blink of an eye. She would always savor the simple joy of bathing Maggie's healthy body, the sound of the child's unrestrained laughter, the patter of her feet as she and Lucy danced and whirled, pretending they were princesses. She would remember standing over Maggie's little spool-spindle bedstead and watching her daughter sleep with her hand clutched around Amelia, her rag doll. She would never let herself forget the little-girl smell of her, equal parts grass and fruit and something uniquely Maggie. She'd have to learn to close her eyes and conjure up cherished images to banish her loneliness — the expression on Maggie's face when she spied a nest of ducklings by the pond in the park, her round-eyed look of wonder on Christmas morning, the way her little hand fit so perfectly into Lucy's and the way that hand always seemed to be there, right when Lucy needed it most.

Being a mother had taught Lucy that a child gave as much as she took. More, even, for she was completely unaware of the importance of her gift as she held up a scrawled drawing of a sailboat, plucked a daisy for her grandmother or kept Willa Jean company by singing "You Are My Sunshine." These were all things Maggie gave without calculation or purpose. She gave selflessly simply because she was a child with a loving heart.

For Maggie's sake, everyone kept up a cheerful facade. Viola still supervised baking day and washing day with a song on her lips, though her gaze lingered extra long on Maggie as the little girl folded the tea towels with clumsy diligence.

Willa Jean entered figures in the account books, and as she worked, her attention kept wandering to the wall calendar. Everyone knew time was short, but no one spoke of it.

On the appointed day, Deborah and Kathleen came to visit, finding Lucy in the kitchen with a large spoon and an old bucket.

"Wait a minute." Kathleen tilted her head at a comical angle. "Has hell frozen over?"

Lucy laughed; her aversion to cooking was well known. "Don't worry," she said, "it's not lunch. I'm getting ready to do an art project with Maggie."

Deborah touched her arm. "How are you?"

"Wretched," Lucy admitted. "I feel as though —" she peered out the window, making sure Maggie was out of earshot "— we're waiting around for someone to die."

"Don't be morbid," Kathleen said. "Maggie will be fine. I told my husband to find out everything he could about the man."

Dylan Kennedy had always had a fine nose for uncovering information. "And?"

"Dylan says he's a hardworking, decent man. Smart in business, though he associates with that ee-jit, Jasper Lamott. Outside of banking, your Mr. Higgins has had a share of troubles."

"Does Dylan know anything about the

former Mrs. Higgins?" Lucy asked.

Kathleen and Deborah exchanged a glance heavy with apprehension.

"Tell me," Lucy insisted. "You absolutely must. This is Maggie's future we're talking about."

"They say Diana Higgins divorced him with indecent haste and claimed nearly all he had."

Deborah smoothed her skirts in her lap. "People say all sorts of things in a divorce suit. I don't think her getting the fortune means a thing. It certainly doesn't mean he's an unfit father. Perhaps it means he's . . . overly decent."

"A man?" Kathleen snorted. Then she sobered and took Lucy's hands. "The night of the Great Fire was a turning point for all of us, wasn't it? Deborah was taken hostage and fell in love with her captor."

"You make it sound so easy," Deborah said.

"And I got married, of all things, though I didn't learn to love Dylan until later."

"We all found someone to love that night," Lucy said brokenly. "But now I'm losing my Maggie."

"You mustn't think of it that way," Kathleen said, her clear green eyes deep with an abiding and very Irish belief in magic. "Something good will come of this, you'll see. That was the night that shaped our lives."

"Of the three of us, you were the bravest of all," Deborah said. "Kathleen's right. You were meant to bring Maggie back to Mr. Higgins, and you won't be abandoned for it."

"He's very suspicious of me," Lucy confessed, thinking of the modifications he'd made to their agreement.

"Most men don't trust a woman with a mind of her own."

A dull red heat crept up Lucy's cheeks. "I'm afraid I once said a foolish thing to him. He was mocking the free love movement, so I happened to mention all my lovers from France. He believes I have a whole raft of them."

Kathleen laughed and slapped her knee. "I wish you did."

"Sometimes I wish that, too," Lucy admitted. "But men don't like me."

"You just haven't met the right man yet. Or perhaps you have and you don't know it. The gas man, the postman, the printer, the Harper Brothers sales representative."

In spite of herself, Lucy laughed as she measured water into the bucket, then bade her friends goodbye.

"You'll be all right, Lucy," Deborah promised her. "You always are."

Kathleen hugged her hard. "Remember what I said, girleen. Something good will come of this."

After they left, Maggie came in, her cheeks bright from being out in the crisp spring day. "What is this stuff, Mama?" she asked, peering into the battered bucket.

"Plaster of Paris," Lucy said. "You'll love it."

Maggie stuck a finger into the thick mixture and brought it to her mouth.

"It's not to eat," Lucy said quickly. "It's for making things."

"Like what?"

"Just watch." Lucy poured the wet plaster into three cardboard trays on the worktable.

"Look, Grammy Vi," Maggie shouted as Viola joined them. "Plaster apparent!"

Lucy's mother looked intrigued. "What on earth are you making?"

Silky the cat slipped in, leaping silently to the table to inspect the mixture.

"It's a surprise," said Lucy, trying in vain to shoo the cat away. "But we mustn't waste time. It hardens quickly. Give me your hand, Maggie."

The child eagerly complied. Lucy kissed the little hand, eliciting a giggle from

Maggie. "Hold your fingers apart, like so," Lucy instructed, demonstrating. "We're going to bring your hand straight down."

Maggie grinned as her hand sank into the white plaster. "It's warm," she exclaimed. "Feels like mud."

"I knew you'd love it. Now, lift it straight out, don't wiggle around."

Maggie raised her hand, leaving a detailed impression in the plaster. "It's my hand," she crowed. "My wonderful bunderful hand! My hand!"

"Yes, my sweet, your wonderful hand. Now Grammy Vi and I are going to do the same. We're going to make impressions of our hands."

"I'll just take my rings off and put them in a safe place." Viola left the room.

"We must put your name and the date in the plaster," Lucy said. "I'll get a stick to use for writing."

She was only gone a moment, but a moment was all it took. An angry feline yowl filled the kitchen. Maggie had decided to use the leftover plaster in the bucket to make an impression of Silky. With plaster clinging to her paws, the protesting cat raced straight up the front of Maggie and crawled over her head before leaping across the table and disappearing. Maggie had plaster on her cheeks, in her hair, on her clothing — everywhere.

The little girl's face grew red, and her chin trembled. "I'm sorry, Mama. I didn't mean —"

Lucy burst out laughing, knowing she was close to shedding tears the child wouldn't understand. She opened her arms and sat down, folding Maggie in an embrace. "Don't you worry, brat. Don't you worry about a thing."

Maggie snuggled happily against her.

"Take this stylus and print your name right here," Lucy said, indicating the impression of her hand. "Just scratch it into the plaster."

With deep concentration, Maggie wrote her name, carefully drawing each letter. Lucy felt dizzy, trying to conceal her grief as she wrote the date.

"Why, Mama?" Maggie set aside the stylus and admired her work. "Why are we making our hands in plaster?"

Lucy felt as if everything vital had been sucked out of her. Somehow, she found her voice and said, "So that, no matter where you go, I'll always have your little hand to hold."

Part Four

No one can say of his house, "There is no Trouble here."

— Oriental proverb

Thirteen

Maggie knew Mama wasn't really mad at her about the plaster, because she gave her a big hug and a kiss, and when she pulled back, there was plaster in Mama's hair, too. Grammy Vi came into the kitchen and looked at them both in that Grammy way of hers, shaking her head. And when Silky ran out from behind the stove, still covered in plaster, they all started giggling.

That was when Maggie heard heavy footsteps on the stair and then a sharp knock.

"I'll get it!" she yelled, and ran for the door. She loved visitors. You never knew who was coming to call. Important People came for long, serious talks with Mama about Politics and The Movement. Maggie found such discussions boring, but the Important People usually had a sweet or two in their pockets and when company came, Grammy Vi would make jam tarts for tea.

Silky always got excited when Maggie ran, and chased after her. Snatching up the plaster-covered cat, she held her draped over one arm and hauled open the door with the other. A huge shadow loomed in the hallway.

It was the giant! The giant had come to call!

Silky leaped out of her arms and jumped high as ever she could, landing smack in the middle of the visitor's chest.

He made a grumbly sound and grabbed for the cat. Silky let out a yowl and ran down him as if he were the trunk of a tree. Then she streaked down the stairs, leaving white footprints all over the carpet runner.

Maggie stared up at him with very big eyes. She tried to remember his name but all she could think of was the giant in "Jack and the Beanstalk" who wanted to grind Jack's bones to make his bread. All she could manage was a "Yikes!" and then she ran to get her mama.

But Mama was there already, coming through the kitchen door. She had plaster smudges and a funny look on her face as she said, "Hello, Mr. Higgins. Welcome to our home."

Now Maggie remembered. The giant's name was Mr. Higgins. He really wasn't scary, just *big*. He looked confused about the plaster. She wondered if he knew he had white cat feet prints all over his black coat.

"Thank you," he said, not "Fee fie fo

fum," as he stepped into the parlor.

Grammy Vi came in, looking terrifically proper. Mama introduced them, and the giant called her Mrs. Hathaway in a respectful way and gave a bow like a gentleman in a stage play. Standing in the middle of the parlor, on the faded flowery carpet, he made everything around him look tiny — the horsehair sofa, the glass lamp, the shelves of books against the wall. Even the tall case clock, which Maggie was learning to read, seemed little beside Mr. Higgins.

"We didn't expect you so soon," Mama said in her Polite but Firm voice. "May I take your coat?"

He set down his case. It looked like a leather carpetbag, only it was black. He took off his coat and handed it to Mama. She brushed at the white cat prints as she hung the coat on the hall tree.

"Thank you," he said.

The way he stared at Mama reminded Maggie of something Sally Saltonstall had once told her. Some ladies had what were known as Gentleman Callers. Gentleman Callers usually brought gifts of lemon drops and fresh flowers. Mr. Higgins didn't seem the sort at all, and his black bag appeared too Important to contain lemon drops.

Maggie thought about his enormous house and lovely garden and Ivan the dog, who never got tired of chasing sticks and rocks. She thought about his old, gray grandmother, who seemed as fierce as the Bad Queen in Maggie's favorite fairy story.

"Let's all sit down, shall we?" Mama said.

Maggie heard that funny note in Mama's voice again — the one she'd been hearing for a few days. Mama was the same as usual, but Maggie was the sort of girl who noticed everything. She'd noticed that her mother's voice got a bit higher and a little strained when she was Upset. Usually it was Injustice that upset her, but when Maggie asked her about it this week, Mama would simply say something like "I'm just thinking about how much I love you."

The words made Maggie feel all warm and Important inside but a little nervous, too. Because she noticed everything, she noticed that lately Mama's hugs lasted a few seconds longer. Her bedtime stories were softer and not so scary. And when she thought Maggie was fast asleep — Maggie was *very* good at pretending to sleep — Mama stood by the bed an extralong time.

Grammy Vi sat perfectly straight on the sofa, patting the seat next to her for Maggie, who clambered up. She was delighted to escape a scolding about the plaster, even though it was drying to a white powder and making little clouds in the room. Maggie swung her legs, watching the plaster dry on her bare feet, while Mama and Mr. Higgins sat down in the straight-back wooden chairs on each side of the squatty parlor stove. Mr. Higgins's knees came up high in front of him.

"I bet you have a very tall bicycle," Maggie said admiringly. "The ones with the biggest wheels go the fastest."

"Actually I've never ridden on a bicycle," he said. His voice was very deep. "I don't know how."

"It's the best thing ever," Maggie said.

"Is it?" He made an expression with his mouth that might have been a smile, but Maggie didn't know him well enough to tell. "Better than strawberry ice cream?"

Now she was sure it was a smile. And his watchful eyes had a nice twinkle in them. "Maybe the same as strawberry ice cream," she admitted.

Grammy Vi patted her hand, making a tiny puff of white powder on the sofa.

"This is a very special meeting," Mama said.

Maggie stopped swinging her feet. A Meeting? She was at a Meeting? Mama had lots of those, but Maggie had never been invited to one. Suddenly she felt very grown-up.

"Will we have a March?" she asked excitedly. "Will we have a Protest? Will Patience come and teach us hymns of solid— solid—" She looked at Grammy Vi and whispered, "I forgot the word."

"Solidarity," Grammy Vi said. "And no, it's not that sort of meeting."

"Maggie," said Mama, "Mr. Higgins is here because he is part of the most wonderful story in the whole wide world. You know which story I mean, don't you?"

Maggie wiggled up and down on the sofa. "The baby from heaven story?"

"Yes."

"But that is *our* story," Maggie said. "There was a great, terrible fire, and I fell from the sky, and you caught me, and that is how I came to be your daughter." She looked from the strange, big man to her mama. "Right?"

"That's our part of the story. But there's another part, too. Mr. Higgins can tell you about it."

She stopped wiggling and regarded him with new interest. "Really?"

"Yes," he said in his giant's voice. "Before the fire, you had a mother and father who loved you very much."

"I know that. My mama has always told me so."

He lifted one eyebrow, an expression that made him seem extremely interested. "Has she?"

"Of course," Mama said, speaking to Mr. Higgins. "I never wanted her to feel she'd been abandoned, ever."

Maggie wasn't sure what abandoned meant.

"Now a very surprising thing has occurred," Mama continued.

"A miraculous thing," Mr. Higgins said, and the way he regarded Maggie made her feel like the most Important girl in the world. She got a funny prickle in her chest, like the feeling she got on Christmas morning as she lay in her bed, waiting for Grammy Vi to call her into the parlor to see her presents.

"What is the miraculous thing, Mama?" she demanded, unable to contain her excitement. The rusty springs of the sofa creaked as she bounced up and down. "I want to know the miraculous thing!"

"Well, now there is something new to add to our story." Mama was quiet for a second as she took a deep breath of air. "We always thought — It was always assumed that the loving mother and father had died trying to save their little girl from the fire."

"Because they were too big to be wrapped up in blankets and mattresses," Maggie said. She didn't like to think about it, but her mama had said it was a tragical part of the story. She caught Mr. Higgins's eye. "Last October on my birthday, Mama let me pick out two stars in the night sky. She said those two stars were the lost mother and father, who would always watch over me."

"That's a nice story," he said. "But we have some good news for you. Those people didn't die after all."

Maggie took a moment to think about this. "The mother and father?" She had always pictured them like people in a stereo-scope photograph — frozen strangers posed side by side, wearing the same clothes and the same statue expressions every time she peered through the scope at them.

"That's exactly what I mean," he said. He kept catching Mama's eye, and each time he did, she would nod in a nervous way. "Your mother and father were hurt in the fire, and for weeks and weeks, they had to stay in the hospital. They were asleep almost the whole time."

"Like Rip van Winkle," Maggie observed.

"A little. But bit by bit, they got better. It took a long time. They went to the hotel building where they had last seen their daughter, and it was gone. The city officials told them everyone in the building had died."

Maggie heard a rough break in his voice. He splayed his big hands on his knees, and she could see shiny scars on his knuckles and fingers.

"They were the saddest people in the world when they heard this news," Mr. Higgins went on. "For all the years since the fire, they have been missing their little daughter." His hands squeezed his knees as if looking for something to hang on to. "They never knew she was safe and sound, living with a foster mother and a grandmother up over a bookshop."

The Christmas-morning feeling in Maggie turned to something different. She began to feel a shy, odd cramping inside. Mr. Higgins kept staring at her in a way that was funny and sad and hungry all at once.

"Maggie, sweetheart," Mama said in her softest voice. "A most remarkable thing has happened. Mr. Higgins is your papa, who lost you in the fire."

Maggie pulled her knees up to her chest, trying to make herself very small. Looping her arms around her knees, she said nothing.

"You always wanted a papa of your own," Mama pointed out.

"But Willa Jean is the papa," Maggie objected, her voice very loud. "You *said*."

"That was just pretend," Mama said. "This is for real."

Everyone was very, very quiet for a long time. They all seemed to be waiting for Maggie to say something. Finally she set her chin on her knees and said, "I already have a mama." She couldn't imagine any other, except as a faraway star in the night sky.

Mama's eyes turned enormously bright as she said, "Now you have two who love you. Isn't that lucky?"

Maggie didn't feel lucky at all. She lowered her eyelashes and peeked at the man sitting in the chair with his hands on his knees. He didn't really look like the papa in the stereoscope pictures. He didn't even have side-whiskers like Sally's father or a bristly beard like Mr. Kennedy, whose red-haired wife had a new baby every year.

And that made her realize why Mr. Higgins didn't look like a father — he had no children with him, none crawling in his lap or whispering in his ear or bringing him treasures from the lakeshore.

Maggie stood up, raining bits of plaster on the floor, and walked over to Mr. Higgins. If he really was her papa then she wanted to look at him up close.

He put out both of his hands and held them palms up. There were some whitish scars on his fingers; she'd noticed them that first day at the bank. Maggie stared at his face and saw the scars there, too.

"Did it hurt very much?" she asked.

"Yes," he said. "It did."

Sometimes grown-ups didn't answer questions directly. She was glad Mr. Higgins did.

"Can I touch them?" she asked.

"Of course you can."

She put her hands into his. They fit together nicely, and his hands were dry and warm and smooth. Just for a second, he shut his eyes, and when he opened them, she thought they looked extra shiny.

"Where's the —" Maggie stopped herself from asking the question. She didn't know what to call the other mama, even though they told her she was so lucky for having two.

"Your mother?" he asked, guessing her thoughts.

"The — my *other* mother." She hoped he knew it was an important distinction.

"She lives far away in a place called California. Do you know where that is?"

"Of course I know," she said with an excess of patience. "It's in San Francisco."

"Actually your . . . other mother does live in San Francisco. It's a big city by the sea."

"Why does she live there? Isn't she your wife?"

"No," he said. His voice was flat, but he didn't seem cross at all. "She's not my wife anymore because we had something called a divorce."

"Is that anything like the mumps? Sally Saltonstall had mumps and we couldn't be together for days and days."

He made a rusty sound, and it took her a moment to realize it was a laugh. "Being divorced means we're not married anymore. But Diana will always be your mother."

She's never been my mother, thought Maggie, but she didn't dare to say that aloud. She knew somehow that it would be bad manners.

She smiled to let him know she liked him. "Thank you for coming, Mr. Higgins. Maybe you'll come and visit again."

As she turned away, he said a funny thing. He said, "Christine."

The tone of his voice made her turn back to face him. "Who is Christine?"

He smiled. It was a nice smile but it was stiff around the edges, as though his mouth wasn't used to smiling. "You are," he said. "That's your name — Christine Grace Higgins."

She jumped back as if he'd breathed fire like a dragon. In her mind, she saw the stone angel with the name *Christine* on it. "My name is Maggie," she said stoutly. "Margaret Sterling Hathaway. Maggie Maggie Maggie." She stamped her bare foot each time for emphasis, raining specks of plaster on the floor.

He didn't get mad, but smiled again, just a little. "Maggie's a very nice name. We'll call you Maggie if you like."

She'd been expecting an argument. She folded her arms and said, "Very well."

"Very well," he said back at her. They stared at each other for quite a long time, until a funny feeling came over Maggie and she couldn't help herself. She giggled. And then Mr. Higgins laughed, too, and Mama and Grammy Vi smiled and whispered something between them.

But after a while, Mama started to look serious, as she had when she was telling the story. "Maggie, darling, there's something else we have to tell you."

"What?"

"We've talked about what's best for you now that we know where you came from. We talked to important judges and lawyers trying to figure out how to arrange this so that all of your parents have a chance to love you. You're going to be living with Mr. — with your papa. Won't that be nice?"

There was a silence in the room as big as Lake Michigan. She pictured Mr. Higgins's giant house and his old grandmother.

Maggie thought maybe she had bees in her belly, because something was buzzing around in there. Then she realized it wasn't bees at all, but a scream. When she opened her mouth, out it came — the loudest, longest, most desperate scream she'd ever screamed.

Fourteen

Rand had known that starting Maggie on her new life was not going to be easy. He'd expected it to bother him when she clung to Lucy and begged, "Please don't make me go!" He understood that, blood ties notwithstanding, his daughter was bound by the heart to Lucy Hathaway.

He thought he'd braced himself for a wrenching transition. But he wasn't prepared for how helpless he felt.

He was, by nature, a problem solver. He was the sort to fix things, find remedies. But as he regarded the wailing little girl who clutched at her mother's skirts, he had no idea what to do.

Miss Lowell, the governess he had engaged to look after Christine, had admonished him to be firm with the girl, to ignore any childish objections and get on with the business of bringing her back where she belonged. Miss Lowell, who had twenty-five years' experience managing children, had made it sound so simple. But how could it be simple to tear a child away from the only mother she knew?

He caught Lucy Hathaway's eye over the head of the weeping child. Lucy appeared pale but calm as she held Maggie and kissed the top of her head and made soothing sounds. But Rand knew that inside she must be breaking apart.

He imagined that, in this moment, Lucy was like a shipwreck in a storm — her destruction slow and violent, inexorable, sinking into coldness. He knew, because that was how he'd felt when he'd lost Christine.

She is Maggie now, he told himself. With all the other upheaval, he would not try to force a strange name on her.

Viola Hathaway sat very still, the only motion a steady stream of tears down her cheeks.

He still could not believe how easily Lucy had ceded custody of Maggie. Now, as he watched her holding the little girl, he understood why. It wasn't that Lucy had something to hide, or that she wished to shed herself of the cumbersome inconvenience of a child. Quite the opposite. She lived and breathed for Maggie. Lucy had known that any resistance to Rand's suit would hurt Maggie, and so she'd surrendered quickly and completely.

She must have understood from the very

start that it would come to this. So why had she come forward, when she could have let him go on believing his daughter dead? Why wouldn't she let him go on year after year, sitting with an old photograph and drinking a single bottle of champagne on Christine's birthday?

He knew now, and the understanding humbled him.

After what seemed like a long time, Lucy put Maggie on the floor, held her by the shoulders and gazed solemnly into the miserable little face. "This is the way it has to be," she said. "Before there was me, there was your papa, and he needs you now."

Maggie shot him a look over her shoulder. "He doesn't need me. He's got Ivan and his old grandmama and that great big house."

Rand held her gaze. "You're wrong, Maggie. I need you very much."

She blinked, her eyelashes spiky with tears. "Why?"

"Because you are the most precious thing in my life, and I thought I'd lost you forever. Now that you're back, you're all I think about."

"Could you maybe think about me while I stay here?" she suggested. "And I could come and visit you sometimes?"

She spoke with such adult logic that she nearly did him in, but Lucy took charge. "Come, sweetheart. Grammy Vi and I got all your favorite things ready. I want you to be all settled in your new room so that when I come to visit you, I'll know you feel right at home."

Rand stood out of politeness, but he had no idea what to do with himself.

"I'll never feel at home there. Never!" Maggie stomped her foot. "I'll hate it there. I'll hate it forever!"

Remarkably, Lucy pretended not to hear, and even more remarkably, the tantrum subsided. Maggie followed Lucy out of the parlor down a narrow hallway.

"A tantrum is only a tantrum if there's someone watching," Viola Hathaway murmured to him, dabbing at her cheeks with a lace-edged handkerchief. "Remember that technique. I suspect you'll need it."

He nodded. "I feel like a monster."

She didn't try to soothe or placate or deny it. "Perhaps now you understand my daughter," she said with a touch of pride. "Justice and honor are everything to her. She puts them before everything, even her personal desires."

"There is no humane way to do this." He wanted to pace the room, but it was so tiny and cramped he feared he might break something.

A knock sounded at the door, and it opened before anyone could respond. Into the room burst a large, handsome black woman dressed in a dark dress. "Oh, good," she said in a rich, almost musical voice, "he's still here." With the attention of a cow buyer at the Union Stockyards, she inspected Rand from head to toe. She nearly matched him in height, and her regard was filled with the special authority of a person who knew exactly what she was about.

"Patience," said Viola, "this is Mr. Higgins."

"I know." Her hand was large and smooth, her grip strong. "How do you do?"

"Mr. Higgins," Viola continued, "this is the Reverend Patience Gloriana Washington."

"I'm honored, ma'am," he said.

"Patience!" Maggie raced out of her room and flung herself at the tall woman. "Patience, help! This man is my papa and he's taking me away!"

"I know that, child." As if Maggie weighed nothing, Patience lifted her up to one hip and held her there. "It's a blessed miracle. Your mama told me all about it."

"Don't let him take me, Patience! Don't!"

Maggie pushed her head into Patience's shoulder and peered at Rand.

"Land sakes, girl. I never knew you to be such a baby," Patience said. "Here the good Lord gives you back your daddy, and you act like you don't even want him."

"I *do* want him, Patience, but I —" She pushed back and looked directly at him. "I do want you, Mr. Higgins." Her voice was curiously controlled, reminding him sharply of Lucy. "I just don't want to leave my mama."

"Honey child," Patience said, "everything's going to be just fine, you'll see. The Lord fixes things in ways we don't understand."

"Why? Why would he do that?"

"To test the strength of our faith."

"Well, I failed the test."

"Almighty, but you got a mouth on you, girl. This is a chance to see if we'll trust the Lord's wisdom and obey his law." She had a magnetic way of speaking. Even the little girl seemed drawn in. "You're going to find a brand-new way of life with your daddy, but you'll always have this life, too," Patience said. "You must learn to call him Papa, and you'll learn to love him as much as he loves you."

"Aw, Patience, I can't."

"Sure you can, honey. Sure you can." As she spoke, the preacher brought Maggie over to Rand and handed her to him.

Maggie stiffened, but Patience made a clucking noise and the little girl relaxed against him. Rand was nearly overwhelmed by the sensation of holding his daughter in his arms once again.

"You know," he said, "when you were a baby, I used to hold you every night and walk around the room until you fell asleep."

"Really?" she whispered.

"Yes. You had a nurse who used to scold me for spoiling you, but I did it anyway."

"Why was there a nurse? Was I sick?"

"No, not that sort of nurse. Someone to help your mother take care of you."

"My mama never needs help taking care of me. Why did my — the other one need help?"

"I'm not sure." He patted her on the back. "You were a lot smaller then."

Lucy arrived with a carpet bag in each hand. Her face was ashen, her smile false and strained. "Hello, Patience," she said. "Thank you for coming." Her heart was in those words; Rand could hear it. For all her steely reserve, Lucy Hathaway was inches from crumbling.

"Let's all go down together," Patience said.

Maggie strained toward her mother, fingers splayed so that her hands resembled tiny starfish, but Lucy pretended not to see and headed down the narrow stairway with the valises. Over her shoulder, she spoke to Rand. "Did you have time to go over that list I gave you?"

The list had been a mile long. "You mean the one that says Maggie likes to fall asleep with a lamp on, with the flame set very low?"

"Yes, that's the one."

He could feel the little girl's interest pique. She expressed herself with her whole body, limbs stiffening and hands clenching when something caught her attention.

"And she dislikes a creaky bed, her favorite story is Cinderella, pork disagrees with her, she prefers to take her bath on Wednesday and Saturday night and she uses Dr. Denmark's tooth powder. Oh, and she attends the Calvary Baptist Church." He quickly rattled off the rest of the list — where she was in her sums and penmanship, the names of her friends, the title of the book Lucy was reading to her at night.

Lucy reached the bottom of the stairs and turned to gape at him. She set down the valises and patted Maggie's back. "You *did* look over the list."

He had memorized every word.

Rand had worked tirelessly to prepare for the arrival of his daughter. He wanted her to have the life he'd always envisioned for her. He wanted her days filled with sunshine and nights filled with pleasant dreams. He wanted to hear her laughter ringing through the halls and to see her busy at her sewing or dancing lessons. He wanted her dressed up pretty as a picture for supper each night, smiling across the table from him as she dined on fruit compote and buttered biscuits.

The only thing missing from the picture was a woman. His dreams and visions of the perfect family were incomplete. He couldn't help wondering about Diana. Her first reply to his ecstatic wire had been suspicious. Her second had been cautious and oddly congratulatory, as if he'd reported getting a new coach horse or an important client at the bank. This morning he'd wired her that Christine was returning home. As soon as possible, he would have a photograph made of Maggie, and mail it to Diana. If that didn't get her to Chicago, he didn't know what would.

From the moment his coach lurched away from the curb, Rand realized that nothing was going to proceed as planned. Like a fool, he always mapped things out according to some idealized vision in his head, not according to the way things were.

Instead of sunshine, a storm rolled in off the lake. It was a typical lake squall — swift and vicious, dark and drenching. In minutes, the sky seemed to disappear and a high wind, laced by slanting rain, lashed through the streets. Lightning cracked close by. Maggie winced, then drew herself into a tight ball on the leather seat.

He put his arm around her, but the gesture felt awkward and forced. Touching people was a habit he would have to relearn. She didn't move away, but tightened her posture like a turtle pulling itself into a hard shell. Rain slapped at the glass windscreen of the coach hood.

"Storms have always scared me," he said over the wail of the wind and the drumming rain.

"You?" She lifted her head from her tucked arms. "But you're a grown-up."

"Being a grown-up doesn't mean you never get scared."

"My mama's not afraid of anything. Ever."

He smiled. "That doesn't surprise me. But storms are scary. All that noise, crashing down when we don't expect it."

"What do you do when you're scared?" she asked.

"I used to shut my eyes and hold my hands over my ears, like this." He demonstrated, exaggerating his expression of sheer terror. When he opened his eyes again, she was laughing, though she stopped abruptly when he grinned at her. "Now that I have you," he said, "it's not so scary."

"Because you're not so all alone."

"Right."

The coach lurched and splashed through the streets of Chicago, heading north along the lakeshore. The strong wind caused the vehicle to sway. Maggie turned her face to the window, peering through a blur of raindrops at the lake. The choppy, gray waters were frosted with white wave crests, churning restlessly with the force of the storm.

The coach halted under the portico at the side of the house, well out of the rain. Rand opened the door and stepped down, reaching for his daughter. As he held her by her tiny waist, he was filled with such a feeling of joy that he laughed aloud, swinging her high in the air so that her little legs flew out. She looked startled, and then she laughed, too.

The driver, with hooded oilskins dripping and streaming water, leaped down and gaped at them.

"Is something wrong, Bowen?" asked Rand, still swinging her up and down.

"No, sir. You sounded as though you were choking, is all."

"I was laughing," Rand said.

"So I see, sir."

He realized that Bowen, who had been his driver since he'd been wheeled out of St. Elspeth's, had never heard him laugh.

Still holding Maggie, Rand headed for the entryway. She pushed her hand at his arm. "You're very strong."

"Am I?"

"The only one who's ever picked me up that high before is Bull."

"Bull?"

"I'm supposed to call him Mr. Waxman, but he lets me call him Bull." She cupped her hands around his ear, seeming not to notice the burns. "He's courting Willa Jean."

The brass-and-glass double doors both opened at once as if they worked automatically. Glaring light flooded the foyer. Rand had ordered it so — all the lights on, all the help assembled to greet his daughter, and Grandmother in the center at the foot of the grand staircase.

Yet the effect was not what he'd planned. The white gaslight struck like lightning, abrupt and dazzling. Their footsteps echoed on the gleaming floor, the sound tomb-like and intimidating. The servants and domestics and even Grandmother were garbed in funereal black and stark white.

Maggie dropped her chin to her chest and studied the floor.

Rand cleared his throat, preparing to make the best of it. "Look, sweetheart. Everyone has come to welcome you."

Like a little squall-battered boat, she clung to him. Any port in a storm, he thought, but felt gratified by her tight grip.

Her silver-tipped cane measuring a slow rhythm, Grandmother came forward. "Christine," she said, her voice as strong as ever. "What a miracle to find you again, after all these years."

Rand patted her back. "We're going to call her Maggie from now on."

Grandmother's mouth puckered like a prune. "Her name is Christine."

"Maggie!" shouted Maggie, her entire body going stiff and hard in a combative stance.

Grandmother tapped her cane meaningfully. "We'll see about that."

Rand had spoken to his grandmother at length about the importance of making Maggie feel at home. But he hadn't even thought about the name. Stupid, he thought. What else had he failed to foresee?

Everything, it seemed. The staff stared at him, waiting. So did Maggie.

"Let's see if we can play a game," he suggested.

Maggie relaxed again. "What sort of game?"

"A remembering game." He took her hand. "I'll introduce you to everyone here, and you see if you can remember their names." He brought her to meet a petite, pale-haired woman with nervous hands and darting eyes. "Miss Lowell is new. She has come to live with us so she can be with you every day, helping you with your lessons. She is called a governess."

"Hello, Maggie. Aren't you a fine, big girl?" Miss Lowell asked in a well-modulated voice. Rand felt relieved. She'd come highly recommended by a member of the bank board, whose own daughter had been raised by her. "I'm new here, too. Did you know that? You and I shall get to know this place together, won't we?"

"All right," Maggie said in a tiny voice.

"Let's meet everyone else, shall we?" Miss Lowell said.

"You ask a lot of questions," Maggie pointed out.

"I suppose I do, don't I, though it's a bit rude of you to point it out. I ask questions because I'm curious about everything, aren't you?"

"Yes." Maggie's cheeks turned bright red, and Rand felt sorry for her. She clearly didn't understand why Miss Lowell considered her comment rude.

He stepped forward, resting his hand on her shoulder. "Here is Mr. Nichol, who looks after everyone in the house and sees that everything is run properly."

"Hello, Miss Chr— Miss Maggie. Welcome." Chilly and impeccable as always, the butler offered a proper bow.

Rand guided Maggie down the line, introducing the maids, the gardener, the kitchen help and Grandmother's personal companion, Miss Benson. He knew the child would never remember everyone's name, but with time, she would eventually learn. So he was startled when the introductions were over, and she said, "What about the remembering game?"

"Do you think you're ready?"

She planted her hands on her hips. "You

said I was supposed to remember everyone's name."

"Indeed I did."

"Well?"

"Well, what?"

"Ask me. Ask me someone's name."

He decided to pick out a few easy names, for he didn't want to embarrass her. "What is the butler's name?"

"Mr. Nichol," she said without hesitation.

"And the cook?"

"Mrs. Meeks."

He was impressed by her quickness, and some of the servants began smiling cautiously. "The upstairs maid."

"Miss Fulsom."

He decided to challenge her. "All right, what about the gardener?"

In the end, the little girl was able to name every last member of the staff.

"That's quite remarkable," Miss Lowell said. "Isn't it, Mr. Higgins?"

"It certainly is. Maggie, how did you remember everyone so perfectly?"

"My mama taught me a game for remembering people in a hurry." Her face glowed with pride as she explained, "My mama goes to a lot of important meetings and has to meet a lot of people involved in the

Cause. She says people respect you if you learn their names right off."

"She's right, isn't she?" Miss Lowell said. "What is the game, then? Can you show us?"

"I just remember a rhyme for everyone."

Even Grandmother shuffled forward in curiosity. "What sort of rhyme, child?"

"A rhyme that matches the person to the name. Like Mr. Nichol." She indicated the butler. "Nose like a pickle. And the cook is Mrs. Meeks, bright red cheeks." She pointed out the maid. "Miss Fulsom, great big bosom."

It wasn't just shock that held all mouths silent. Everyone, furtively, was noticing that Nichol's nose *did* seem to resemble a large, bumpy pickle, and the maid's bosom was indeed prodigious. There was a general clearing of throats and a shuffling of feet.

"Did I do a naughty thing?" Maggie asked, cutting a fearful glance at Miss Lowell.

"No —" Rand began.

"Yes," said the governess, then quickly added, "but you did a good job learning everyone's name, didn't you? Come. We had best show you to your room. Shall we?"

She held out her hand.

Maggie pretended not to see the outstretched hand. "What's through here?" she asked, running down a passageway to a back door. Before anyone could stop her, she pulled it open.

In bounded Ivan, all one hundred soaking wet pounds of him. Toenails skittering on the marble floor, he galloped into the foyer and paused to shake himself vigorously, showering everything in a six-foot radius with rainwater. Then he headed straight for Maggie, knocking her down in his enthusiasm and licking her face while she laughed uproariously. For the second time in as many minutes, everyone simply gaped in surprise, until the cook's helper, a tall girl of about thirteen, started to giggle. The cook scowled and hissed at her, and she struggled to sober herself.

Nichol yelled, "Bad dog," and strode forward, reaching for Ivan's collar. The dog shied away, but Nichol seized him and dragged him back the way he came.

"Can't he stay?" Maggie asked. "I want Ivan to stay!"

"That is an outdoor dog, isn't it, Mr. Higgins?" said Miss Lowell, patting her face with a handkerchief. "It belongs outside, doesn't it?"

"But —" Maggie caught one freezing look from the governess and snapped her mouth shut. She looked crestfallen, a stark contrast to her untrammeled delight a moment earlier.

"Let him stay," Rand ordered. "Dry him off, and he can stay in the house with Maggie."

Fifteen

Miss Lowell was nothing less than a miracle worker. By suppertime that night, she'd transformed Maggie from a hoyden in trousers to a vision in blue silk. Standing formally beside his grandmother in the dining room, Rand heard the old lady gasp with admiration when Maggie and Miss Lowell joined them.

The patched knickers and loose shirt had been replaced by a dress with lace at the collar and cuffs, shiny little shoes peeping out from under the scalloped hem. Maggie's short curls had been crimped, lacquered and anchored in place by steel combs.

But her bright, direct regard had turned guarded and tentative.

"And who," Rand asked, "can this enchanting creature be?"

She favored him with a brief smile.

"I think it must be an angel from heaven," he said. "Don't you, Grandmother?"

"She certainly looks like one," his grandmother agreed.

"It's me," Maggie burst out, spreading

her arms. "Maggie! Don't you recognize me, silly?"

Miss Lowell cleared her throat, and Maggie sobered. Like a bird shot from the sky, she sank into a deep curtsey.

"Good evening, Grandmother Grace," she said with a precision of elocution that hinted at much practice. "Good evening, Mr. — Father."

"And a very good evening to you," he said. He held a chair for his grandmother, then for Miss Lowell, and finally Maggie.

"You should sit down, too, Cora," Maggie said to the maid waiting by the green baize door to the kitchen. "Your foot's bothering you."

Cora flushed scarlet beneath her starched cap. Furtively she drew a battered leather brogan into the shadow of her skirt, but not before Rand saw the livid ulcer near her heel.

He felt a peculiar annoyance — at himself. How long had the poor girl been limping around in pain? Why hadn't anyone noticed, and why hadn't the girl dared to speak up?

"Go home, Cora," he said quietly. "See to that foot."

"But, sir, I can work, I swear I can."

He pushed open the double-hinged door.

She shrank from him, her fear piercing him like a small dart. "I'm not giving you the sack, Cora. You can come back when you're better," he said. "That's a promise."

"Thank you, sir," the girl said, then ducked out.

"Well," his grandmother said, "I hope Mrs. Meeks can manage on her own." She scowled down at her place setting. "I've mislaid my spectacles again."

"No, you haven't," Maggie said. "They're right here." She jumped up and found the glasses half hidden under a napkin.

"Ah." Grandmother perched the spectacles on her nose, looking as jolly as Rand had ever seen her. "Thank you, my dear."

Maggie sat down and jammed her hand into the bodice of her dress.

"You mustn't fidget," Miss Lowell murmured.

"I don't like this corset. It's stiff and it itches."

Rand lifted an eyebrow in inquiry. "You put her in a corset?"

"A posture corset, sir. All young ladies must wear one."

The watery distress in Maggie's eyes tore at him. "Only on special occasions," he said, gratified by his daughter's relieved smile.

He put his hands together. "Shall I ask the blessing?" They all inclined their heads. "Thank you for the bounty of thy goodness," he said. "Dear Lord, for the miracle of my beautiful daughter there can be no gratitude deeper than the thanks in my heart. May we be eternally humbled by the glory of this blessing, which you have brought. Amen."

"A-*men*," Maggie said so loudly that Grace jumped. Maggie caught a censorious look from Miss Lowell. "Well," she explained, "Patience always says a prayer ain't finished until you give it a good a-*men*."

"A friend of hers," Rand explained. "Patience Gloriana Washington."

"She's a preacher at my church," Maggie said.

"Oh? And what church is that?" Grandmother asked. Everyone important attended First Congregational, the choice of Chicago's Old Settlers.

"It's the Calvary Church."

Miss Lowell lifted her napkin and coughed spasmodically. "The church on Kearns Street?"

"Yes," Maggie said brightly. "That's the very one."

"But — that's a Negro church."

"No it isn't, silly," Maggie said with exaggerated patience. "It's a *Baptist* church."

"A-*men*," Maggie said firmly, concluding her bedtime prayer. Kneeling beside the pink-and-white bed, she looked up at Rand. "Did I remember everybody in the blessing?"

"I think so." He held out his hand and drew her to her feet.

"I have a lot more people to bless nowadays, don't I?"

"You do, and you remembered every single one. Even Ivan."

At the sound of his name, the big dog thumped his tail against the expensive new carpet.

"I'm glad you're letting him sleep in my room," Maggie said. "Silky always sleeps right next to me on the bed." She cast her eyes down. "She used to, anyway."

"When I was a boy, I slept by myself, but I would have liked a cat."

"Did your mama read you stories every night?"

His stomach clenched. He hadn't prepared himself for this, either, but he should have realized she'd be curious about his background. When it came to questions about his mother, he could think of no answer Maggie would understand. How

310

could he explain to a child that everything he was, all of his convictions, had been formed by the fact that his mother had walked away from him? A young boy's heartbreak and yearning had gradually hardened into the man he had become.

"I don't remember much about my mother," he said.

"I remember every single-ingle thing about my mama," she declared.

He was relieved that she'd changed the subject. "Of course you do. She's right across town, and she's coming to see you on Saturday."

She bounced up and down on the bed. "How many days until Saturday?"

"Seven."

She counted the days off on her fingers. Her lower lip quivered. "Can I write her a letter?"

"Of course. We'll post it by special delivery."

"Can I send her a wire?"

"She'd probably like that."

"I want to send her a wire." The lip quivered ominously again. "I want to ask her why she gave me away."

"Ah, Maggie." He picked her up and held her close. "Remember how I said I used to walk with you until you fell asleep?"

"Uh-huh." She yawned and leaned her cheek on his shoulder.

"I didn't really walk," he whispered.

"You didn't?"

"I danced. I hummed the Emperor's Waltz."

"Show me," she said. "Do it again."

He cradled her head in one hand, moved in a slow, rhythmic circle and hummed the old, familiar tune. He danced for a long time, until the last of twilight disappeared and the only light in the room was the faint glow of the lamp. At some point he felt her shudder into sleep, slumping heavily against him. His arms and shoulders strained and went numb with the weight of her, but he welcomed the burden with his whole heart. "We were happy together once," he whispered, though he knew she didn't hear, "and we will be again."

Then, with painstaking care, he laid her on the bed and covered her up. "Maggie," he whispered. "My Maggie. Your mother didn't give you away. She gave you to *me*."

Each day, Rand left the bank early and hurried home to see Maggie. He usually found her in her suite of rooms, diligently bent over a practice book while Miss Lowell supervised, occasionally reaching down to correct her posture or adjust her grip on the pen. Maggie accepted instruction with admirable aplomb. In all that she did, her bright spirit shone through. Even when a wave of longing for Lucy swept over her, she would struggle through the moment with dogged determination, no doubt clinging to thoughts of Saturday.

One afternoon Rand stood watching her from the doorway, telling himself she would be fine. She needed more time to adjust to the enormous changes in her life. He'd done his best to create the life he'd always envisioned for his daughter. She had servants and a governess to attend to all her needs and an ambitious schedule of special lessons in music, fancywork and deportment. Thus far, she seemed to regard her new life with curiosity and a good bit of humor.

Her room, flounced and fringed in pink and white, was filled with toys — a miniature house furnished with fragile figurines, an army of dolls, their porcelain faces staring out from a glass-fronted display shelf, a little pram for pushing them around.

Ivan sprawled on a braided rug with pink fringe, looking as out of place as a bull in a china shop. When Rand walked in, he lifted his big head in friendly expectancy.

"Am I interrupting?" Rand asked.

"Hello, there — oh." Crestfallen, Maggie looked down at her paper. "I've blotted it again."

"Then you shall have to do it over, shan't you?" Miss Lowell said gently.

Rand picked up the copybook. "It's not a bad blot. The clerks at my bank often do much worse."

"They do?" Maggie brightened.

"Your father's only trying to be polite, isn't he?" Miss Lowell said.

"No, this is very good work." He held up the book and read, " 'An obedient child is a joy to her sire.' See? I can read this just fine." He grinned down at Maggie. "But I don't know what 'obedient' means. It's a big word." Turning back a page or two, he found a sketch of a boat on the lake, then a drawing of Silky the cat. On the page before that, he found the start of a letter: Dear Mama, Pleas come —

Maggie saw what he was looking at, and her eyes grew bright with tears. She blinked fast and hard, as stoic as Lucy when it came to holding them back. Miss Lowell took the copybook and set it aside. "I'm sure we'll do better next time, won't we?"

Maggie's little hand crept out and covered her knee. The furtive movement caught the governess's eye.

"Sir," said Miss Lowell, "I believe your daughter has something to tell you, don't you, Maggie?"

Maggie took a deep, nervous breath. "I'm sorry."

"Sorry for what?"

She moved her hand to reveal a grass-stained tear in her dress.

"I caught her climbing a tree in the garden, can you imagine?" Miss Lowell sounded incredulous.

"If you would let me wear dungarees instead of dresses, it wouldn't catch on things," Maggie said.

"She has the most inexcusable habit of answering back, doesn't she?" Miss Lowell said. "We shall work on it, won't we, Maggie?"

"Yes, Miss Lowell."

Rand said, "Take some time for yourself, Miss Lowell. I shall visit with my daughter." When the governess hesitated, he said, "Please, I insist."

"I really am sorry about my dress," Maggie said earnestly, once Miss Lowell was gone.

He sat on an upholstered bench beside her, feeling as out of place as the mastiff. He had an urge to take Maggie into his lap, but despite their nightly Emperor's Waltz, he still felt awkward around her. He patted her on the head. "Don't give it a thought."

"Miss Lowell said it is a sign of disrespect to destroy something given to me."

"You haven't destroyed a thing. It's just a little tear." Rand didn't like to see her fret over such a trivial matter. He handed her a packet wrapped in parchment and tied with string. "I've brought you something to look at."

Her eyes lit up. "What is it?"

"See for yourself."

With eager fingers she untied the string and pulled away the parchment. "Oh!" she said. "Photographs. I love looking at photographs."

"I thought you'd like to see some pictures of yourself when you were tiny. And your family."

"I would! I surely would!" She studied the first picture. "This is me, isn't it? What a funny little baby I was." She laughed at the wide eyes and fat checks.

"We were very proud of you," Rand said.

She took out another picture. He could see her tongue poking thoughtfully at the gap in her mouth where she'd lost her tooth.

"Who do you think that could be?"

"A beautiful bride and groom."

Rand had been deeply proud on his wedding day. All his life, his father had aimed him toward this event. The time had come for him to shoulder the mantle of tradition and responsibility. He'd been filled with a feeling of solemn purpose — to offer the world the next Higgins generation.

"That's your mother," he said.

Maggie studied the image of Diana, who looked as perfect as a marble icon, her cheeks flawless, her hair lacquered beneath a jeweled tiara holding a ghostly veil in place. She looked eerily like one of the painted dolls lined up on the shelf.

"She's pretty," Maggie said. "That's a fancy dress, isn't it?"

"Yes. There was a great fuss over it. She and her mother went to Paris, France, to buy her entire trousseau."

"What's a trousseau?"

"A lot of ladies' clothes and things. I'm not exactly sure. No one has ever explained it to me. The man just gets to pay for it all."

"They went all the way to France to buy clothes?" Maggie's eyebrows shot up. "Didn't they know you can buy ready-to-wear at Haver Brothers over on Mercer Street?"

"I suppose they wanted certain special clothes. It was a fancy wedding."

"I've never been to a wedding."

"You'd probably find it boring, sitting still and listening to a lot of reading and vows, but you might like it when the bride and groom kiss, and the music plays, and the bride carries a fine bouquet of flowers."

"I'd like to see that. Can we have a wedding, Papa? Can we?"

"I don't think so."

"Why not?"

"There's no bride. No groom. No one who wants to get married."

She sat quietly for a few seconds. "What's a bastard, Papa?" she asked suddenly, the question popping out of her like a champagne cork.

"Where did you learn a word like that?"

"Sally Saltonstall — she's my best friend on account of I play with her every Wednesday — says I'm a bastard because my mama and papa ain't married."

"Aren't married. And your friend is full of sh— succotash." He rubbed his jaw, silently resolving to have a word with the Saltonstalls.

Maggie mouthed the word "succotash," and seemed satisfied. Then she went back to studying the picture. He watched her face to see if she had any reaction at all to the image of her mother.

She poked a finger at the image. "Who is that man?"

For a moment, Rand froze. He could not even take the next breath as he stared at the picture, trying to see what she saw. A clear-eyed young man with very little character stamped on his face. Sculpted features, a firm mouth, his hair groomed to the last strand.

"That's —" He cleared his throat. "That was me."

She pulled back to look from him to the photograph. "Oh! It doesn't look at all like you."

In a single night he'd changed from a promising young man with the world at his feet to a desperate, grieving monster scarred inside and out. He tried to remember what it had been like to look into a mirror and see that face. What did that handsome, arrogant man used to think about, dream about? What were his hopes and his fears? He'd wanted a storybook life — a wife and child, a prosperous career, the admiration of society. He'd thought that having such things would fulfill him. But he'd been wrong. He'd achieved all that and he had not been happy. Satisfied, perhaps. Proud, even. But happy? Had he ever really known what that was? After the fire he'd known only its lack, a loneliness so acute that he felt hollowed out by a sharp object. Now, with Maggie, he glimpsed occasional flashes of happiness, like sunlight filtering down through a dark forest. She *was* the sunlight . . . but the darkness was still there.

He mentally shook himself and gave his attention back to her. "I've changed," he said. "I'm older, and in the fire, the night I lost you, I was burned. The scars make me look different."

"They do."

"Does that bother you?"

"Bother me?"

"Does it worry you or . . . frighten you?" He forced out the words. He had learned to pretend not to notice that women averted their eyes from him or that neighborhood children played a game of running from "the beast," diving for cover when they saw him coming.

Maggie did something most unexpected. She laughed. "No, silly. *Spiders* frighten me." Still laughing, she jumped up and went to the door. "Hello, Mr. Nichol. Do you want to come and play?"

The usually unflappable butler stood in the doorway, his cheeks red with pleasure. "Perhaps later, miss, and thank you for the invitation. Mr. Mosher is waiting for you both in the garden."

"Who's Mr. Mosher?"

"A photographer." Rand took her hand and led her downstairs. "I asked him to come and make a picture of us."

"Hurrah!"

Charles Mosher and his assistant had set up their camera and tented darkroom. The photographer grinned when he saw Maggie. "No one told me I'd be photographing a real live princess," he said.

"And my papa," she said, looking at the lone stool. "You must put him in the photograph, too."

Rand clenched his jaw. He had not been photographed since before the fire and never intended to again. "Sweetheart, I was planning on a picture of you all by yourself."

She folded her arms across her chest. "I won't. I won't. I won't." Her voice crescendoed with each *won't*.

Rand remembered what Viola had said about tantrums. He turned from his daughter, pretending great interest in the assistant's strong-smelling chemical brews of collodion and nitrate of silver.

Mosher pulled on a pair of white gloves for handling the plates. "Sir, if I may say so, she might sit more still in your lap."

Rand wanted to object, but the truth was,

his looks didn't matter. The whole point of today's exercise was to produce a photograph to send to Diana. "All right," he said. "Tell me where to sit."

A few minutes later, he held Maggie in his lap. She squirmed, still cross with him. Mosher positioned himself behind the camera. "You have to sit still for the count of three," he said.

"That goopy stuff smells," Maggie complained.

"It's a mixture of ether and alcohol," Mosher explained. "And guncotton. I use it to keep the plates wet." He framed his view. "You don't have to smile, miss."

"Good. I don't feel like smiling."

"Suit yourself."

He exposed a few plates, then promised to bring the prints first thing in the morning. Maggie sat on the grass, her knees drawn up to her chin. When the photographer left, Rand squatted down beside her. "Maybe you'll smile for the camera next time."

She lifted her shoulders in a shrug.

Though he knew the answer, he felt compelled to ask, "What's the matter, sweetheart?"

"I want my mama," she stated. "And Silky. And Grammy Vi."

"I know you miss them, but —"

"Why can't we all be together? Isn't that what a family is?"

Simple questions, but they made him feel as though he had dived into deep water and couldn't find the surface. "Sometimes, yes. But there are different types of families. In this one, the parents live in separate houses."

"I wish my mama was right here at the house, all the time. You have lots and lots of room."

The thought of Lucy, living in his house, seized him with unexpected heat. "She would never agree to live here. She likes being on her own, independent." All those lovers she boasted of so shamelessly would miss her if she moved to a respectable household, he reflected peevishly. "Even if she did, people would think it . . . strange."

"What people?"

"Neighbors. Clients at the bank. People at church."

"Mama says if you worry too much about other people's opinions you'll forget to think for yourself."

Lucy's wisdom, coming from this little girl, always surprised him. "I know what I think," he said.

"What?"

"That I would like to take Ivan to the

beach and throw sticks for him. Want to come?"

"Hurrah!" Jumping up, she kissed him on the nose. "I love Ivan, and I love you." She scampered toward the esplanade.

He couldn't get over the wonder of her. She was as capricious as the lake wind, and totally nonjudgmental. Totally accepting of him.

It struck him then that someone had taught her to be this way — open-minded and bighearted, unconcerned with appearances and more concerned with the things that matter, like a maid's sore foot, his grandmother's misplaced spectacles, a blooming rosebush in the garden.

He knew exactly who had taught his daughter to be like this, full of love, free of pretensions or unreasonable fears.

Lucy Hathaway.

Sixteen

Lucy clutched the summons from Randolph Higgins to her bosom and shut her eyes in an ecstasy of relief. "I knew it," she whispered. "I knew he couldn't manage without me."

"Are you sure that's what this means, dear?" Viola Hathaway held the rail of the horse trolley as it lurched up the avenue.

Lucy opened the note and read the words again. *Mrs. Hathaway and Miss Hathaway are cordially invited to call* . . . When the message had arrived at the shop an hour earlier, she'd sent for her mother and rushed to catch the horsecar.

"I can't imagine what else," she said with her first genuine smile since Maggie had left. She tried not to think about how empty her life felt, how lonely and meaningless without Maggie around. Without her daughter's lively chatter, her constant presence, Lucy had felt half alive.

Before Maggie had come into her life, Lucy had held an idealized notion of independence. She thought a woman should be self-sufficient and not dependent on anyone for anything. Maggie had proven her wrong.

There were some things even a modern, independent woman could not live without, such as the abiding love of a child. Maggie had taught her more about the nature of justice and independence than all her readings and rallies.

And just like that, with the stroke of a pen, she'd lost her.

Self-pity was never a pleasant sensation, and Lucy battled it with a will. She stayed busy with the shop and planning the upcoming Centennial March. But a part of her lived each moment with Maggie. What was she doing right now? Was she eating right, remembering to clean her teeth and say her prayers?

"Such a cryptic message could mean several things," her mother said. "Your official visiting days are Saturday and Sunday, isn't that so?"

"I've already ruled out some emergency with Maggie. I made him promise to summon me by wire for that." Lucy eyed a prosperous-looking family walking along State Street, a lively little boy clutching his parents' hands and swinging between them. "The sudden appearance of a child was bound to be a disruption in Mr. Higgins's well-ordered life. I believe he's found the rigors and challenges of fatherhood unexpectedly harsh. Men think child rearing is such a simple matter — which it is, so long as they have wives to do the real work."

"Don't be smug, dear. You could be wrong, just this once."

Lucy noticed that her mother had put on her best blue serge dress and matching bonnet, the gloves she usually saved for church and an expression of almost heart-breaking eagerness. Viola loved visiting; when the Colonel was alive it had been the center of her life. After the fire, widowhood and poverty had taken their toll, robbing her of the privileges she used to enjoy. Invitations to the polished drawing rooms of Chicago's fashionable neighborhoods had evaporated with cruel swiftness.

Viola's eyes shone as they entered the gentrified area of turreted mansions, splendid greystones and trim esplanades between Bellevue and Burton Place. Stepping out of the trolley on the corner, they walked along the lakeside promenade, their steps quickening as they neared the Higgins's house.

The massive door opened and Lucy stepped inside. Immediately she heard a squeal of delight followed by the patter of running feet. Shrieking "Mama! Mama!" Maggie raced along the railed upper gallery and down the stairs. Behind her, the large dog galloped. Lucy opened her arms and scooped up her daughter. The thin wiry legs wrapped around Lucy as she inhaled the little-girl smell and rubbed her chin on the top of Maggie's head. Emotion overwhelmed Lucy. She lived and breathed for this child. How in heaven's name could she abide being apart from her? Finally she found her voice. "Hello, sweetheart. I've missed you so."

"I missed you, too, Mama. I was waiting and waiting until Saturday and it never ever came."

Lucy set her down. "Look at you," she said, careful not to voice her true thoughts. Maggie had been trussed into a child-size corset and laced into a dress with a stiff bodice and bustle, and leg-o'-mutton sleeves that gave her the look of a dressmaker's doll. Her hair had been heated and curled into sausage ringlets, which looked absurd, given the short length of Maggie's locks. She even smelled different, of gardenia eau de toilette. "You look very grown-up," Lucy said.

"I don't like to wear dresses and petticoats and combs in my hair," Maggie said.

Lucy didn't blame her, but stilled her tongue to keep from objecting. She tried not to feel shocked and disturbed but she was. Ever since she'd found Maggie, all decisions regarding the child had been hers alone to make. Suddenly there was someone else involved. Someone entitled to teach and guide Maggie. To determine what she wore, what she ate, what she learned. Maggie had only been away a short time and already Lucy had the dreaded sense that her daughter was becoming a stranger.

Stepping aside, Lucy said, "I have a surprise for you."

"Grammy Vi!" Maggie hugged her hard around the waist. A moment later, Randolph Higgins arrived, looking very much the lord of the manor as he strode into the foyer.

Lucy greeted him with cautious reserve. Maggie gave him a bright grin and took his hand without hesitation. Lucy was startled. Something was happening between the two of them, some affinity that hadn't been there only a few days ago.

A shadow from above fell over them. Lucy looked up to see a very buttoned-down and proper Miss Lowell in the gallery. Lucy had met the woman only once. Before sending Maggie to live here, Lucy had come to meet the governess and the household staff. Though tempted, Lucy had refrained from commenting that Mr. Higgins had hired an entire staff to do the job Lucy had been doing by herself for the past five years.

"Hello, Miss Hathaway," the governess said. "Miss Maggie has not finished her penmanship practice today. We were just in the middle of our lesson, weren't we?"

Maggie clung to Mr. Higgins's hand and ducked behind him. Lucy bit her tongue. Under this roof, it wasn't her place to make decisions for Maggie.

"The day is much too fine to stay indoors," Mr. Higgins said easily. "And Miss Hathaway and her mother have come to visit. I think we might take a stroll out to the lake."

"As you wish, sir." Miss Lowell bowed and withdrew. Somehow, in her nod of acquiescence, Miss Lowell managed to convey a note of disapproval. It was very subtle and Lucy couldn't tell if Mr. Higgins had noticed at all. She would have to think about that — should she protest a governess who disapproved of letting a child play out of doors on a beautiful day?

"Hurrah!" Maggie yelled, running to the door. "Come on, Grammy! It's marvelous at the lake!"

Lucy decided to discuss the governess

later. For now, she was simply grateful to see Maggie once again. Holding her grand-mother's hand, the little girl skipped and twirled along the path that wound through the parklike neighborhood. How vast this must seem to Maggie, who was used to the cramped garden behind the shop. Already, she seemed at home in her new world, Lucy realized with a jolt. She resembled a fairy, dancing along the pathway in her new silken skirts, with lace-edged bloomers showing beneath the hem.

As a knot tightened in her stomach, Lucy followed Maggie and Viola to the avenue, heading toward the beach.

"Can I take Grammy to see the otters?" Maggie looked to Lucy for approval, then seemed to remember, and turned to Mr. Higgins. Confusion dimmed the eagerness in her eyes.

Lucy's heart ached for her. Everything had changed so fast.

"I would love to see the otters," Viola de-clared, taking control of the situation. She indicated a row of wrought-iron benches. "Why don't the two of you wait here?"

Her mother, Lucy reflected, was wise in ways she was only beginning to understand. She and Maggie made a perfect picture as they walked away, blithely chattering, the lake and summer sky creating a rich blue background.

As she took a seat on the bench, Lucy sent a tentative glance at Mr. Higgins and was surprised, as she always was, to feel a lurch of . . . something. She could not think why he moved her, but he did and had from the first moment she'd set eyes on him. He was so very different now from that handsome, teasing young man who had caused her to humiliate herself so completely. Yet in a way, he was much the same. Scarred, yes. And sobered by unimaginable pain and loss, yet . . . his eyes were still as clear and deep as leaves with the sun behind them.

Heavens. She'd come about the matter of her daughter and here she was indulging in all manner of speculation about Randolph Higgins. Clearing her throat, she said, "I must admit, I was surprised to receive your message. I didn't expect to be permitted to visit Maggie until Saturday."

"That was the original arrangement," he said.

"Is there a problem?"

"I wouldn't call it a problem."

Then it struck her. She turned to him on the bench. "Your wife is coming back, isn't she?"

"It's nothing to do with that," he said.

"Diana has declared herself unable to travel from California. Frankly she claims the fire was such a traumatic time of her life that re-visiting Chicago even to see her daughter might not be possible. I had a photograph made of Maggie and me, and sent it to her."

Lucy was struck dumb. Floored. The woman had been informed that the child she believed dead had actually survived, and she wouldn't even come for a reunion. What could it mean?

Lucy took a deep breath. "Is she — Your wife —"

"Ex-wife," he reminded her.

"Is she — You said she recovered from her injuries after the fire. But was she — is she —"

His face, stamped with anguish and for-bearance, deepened with color. "You mean is Diana as grotesquely disfigured as I am?"

"I —" Lucy stopped. She did mean that. And he wasn't disfigured. Why on earth did he think a few scars could disfigure a man like him? Mr. Higgins had learned to live with his infirmities. In a way, the scars only seemed to add to his aura of quiet strength. But a woman of Diana's beauty might never adjust to the changes.

"She looks the same now, or so I imagine, as she did the night you met her," he said.

"Diana's reaction to the news of Christine's survival is unexpected, I admit, but it has nothing to do with my asking you to come today."

"Then perhaps you'd best tell me the reason."

"This whole matter, miracle that it is, has proved to be more . . . complicated than I ever could have imagined."

She had every right to gloat. For all his money and power, Randolph Higgins had found something he could not buy or influence. For all his cold competence in matters of commerce, he'd encountered a challenge beyond his skills. He'd discovered something Lucy had known all along. That being a parent was hard. In his arrogance he'd thought that simply creating a fairy tale chamber for Maggie and hiring an army of servants would magically transform him into a father.

He had quickly figured out that there was no luxury he could buy or expert he could hire to create a bond that took years to form.

But Lucy couldn't gloat. His bafflement and his candor were somehow endearing and sincere.

"I will be direct," he said. "I don't know any other way to be. Maggie is wonderful. More wonderful than I ever dreamed."

"I knew you'd think so. I'm very proud of her."

"You should be." He stared out at the lake as he spoke. "At first, I pretended that all would be well. Both Maggie and I are trying hard, but I can't deny the obvious. She loves my dog but misses her cat. She would rather play baseball in the service alley than have a tea party in the summer parlor. She's more at home climbing a tree than practicing dance steps, and prefers dungarees to dresses. She befriends the servants. She's so delightful, so bright and inquisitive that I kept thinking everything would be all right."

"And it's not?"

He turned to her on the bench. "She's desperately lonely for you. At night she cries for you, and she's been counting the hours until your visit."

She tried not to flinch at the thought of her daughter, crying and alone in her big new bed. "We all knew this would be an enormous adjustment." Lucy tried to sound reasonable even as she burned with the need to know what he was leading up to.

"My aim was to live with the daughter I'd lost, not torture her."

Oh, she wanted to hug him for his honesty, for not pretending all was well. Instead she stayed quiet, holding herself stiffly in check on the bench. Though accustomed to speaking her mind, she found it easy to listen to Randolph Higgins. "Go on," she said.

"I was wrong to believe this arrangement was the best possible step for Maggie."

Lucy gasped. Men didn't admit being wrong, did they? She'd never met one who did. "You want to give her back?" she blurted out.

"No — nothing like that," he said. "The thing is, Maggie needs you. I think, in time, she will come to need me as she once did. I want her to need us both." He ran his splayed fingers through his hair. "I'm not saying this well. I want — that is, I think it would be best for Maggie if you were to live here."

Shock stole her breath. She wasn't sure she'd heard correctly. "Here," she echoed. "At your house?"

"Yes. My sole concern is Maggie, her happiness and her welfare. And with each hour that passes, I understand even more clearly that her happiness depends on having you near. I must have you here, Miss Hathaway. Maggie and I both need you to live here."

She stood up and turned, holding the

railing. Her glance swept across the vast lawn, the pristine waterfront and the neat square house that looked as though it had sat there for centuries rather than years. And it looked . . . magical. For years she'd worked to convince herself that she had everything she needed at the little flat in Gantry Street and was perfectly content. But the truth was, she sometimes had a secret wish for a place of splendor and luxury — a place like Mr. Higgins's home, the home he'd built for a woman who didn't want him.

Lucy was instantly ashamed of her yearnings, for they violated her egalitarian principles and — She stopped herself. Mr. Higgins was not interested in her ethical dilemmas. He simply wanted her to come and make things easy for him and Maggie.

Bitterness filled her throat. She would be his employee. A servant to do his bidding, to be hired or sacked at his whim. Could she, for Maggie's sake? Could she humble and subject herself to this man for the sole purpose of being close to her daughter?

"That would be impossible," she said through stiff lips.

"You miss her. I know you do. If you lived here —"

"Maggie would never understand why her

mother had suddenly become her servant."

"You don't understand." He stood with a restless energy that made her nervous. "Hear me out. A child needs a mother, and Maggie regards you as her mother."

"So you're saying if I agreed to live here, that would solve the problem?"

He paused in his pacing and shot her a rueful look. "In truth, Miss Hathaway, I think it will introduce a whole new set of problems. But with you here, Maggie will have both parents in her life and that is the most important thing —"

"And once I get everything running smoothly, then what is my position?"

"You haven't let me finish, Miss Hathaway." He walked toward her to stand only inches away. "I'm offering you a permanent arrangement." He put his hand over hers.

She caught her breath. He'd never voluntarily touched her before. Except the night they had met, the night she'd made her scandalous proposition.

"Miss Hathaway, I've thought long and hard about making you this offer. It's the best possible solution."

When he finished speaking, a peculiar stillness seized him. She thought he might be holding his breath. She found herself drawn into the complicated facets of his eyes, wishing she could decipher the mysteries there. Her heart pounded so loudly in her ears that she saw his lips move but couldn't hear his words.

Ah, but she did hear him.

She heard exactly what he said: "Will you be my wife?"

Lucy had heard that the human heart could soar, but until this moment she'd never believed such sentimental nonsense. Now her own heart took wing, launched by Mr. Higgins's proposal. Oh, she understood that he would never have asked her if not for Maggie, but still . . . For the first time in her life, she craved that most feminine of accoutrements, a fan. Her face and chest felt hot.

Kiss me, she thought. Oh, God, if you would kiss me, I would have only one possible answer for you.

He didn't kiss her. They stood together staring at each other. She could not imagine what he was thinking, though she knew very well what she was feeling. Giddiness. Longing. Confusion. Shame. All her life she'd scorned the institution of marriage as a form of bondage for women. Yet in the most secret place inside her, she'd yearned to know the consuming magic of romantic love. Over the years she'd idealized it, fusing the concept of free love with a sort of medieval notion of what true devotion should be.

But she was a modern woman. She was not supposed to feel this way about Randolph Higgins, or any man.

Dragging herself to her senses, she snatched her hand away. "No!"

"What?"

"I will not dignify your outrageous proposal with any further discussion." She prepared to march down the beach and collect her mother and daughter.

"Before you leave," he said coldly, "at least listen to what it is you're turning down."

"I know what I'm turning down," she retorted, pacing in agitation as he'd done a few moments ago. "I am turning down a life of servitude. I am turning down an invitation to surrender my right to property, liberty and prosperity for the dubious honor of subjugating my will to your needs."

"As to those needs," he interrupted. "If you would stop ranting for a minute you might learn something."

"I'm not ranting, I —" But she was. In this, at least, he was right. She snapped her mouth shut and folded her arms.

"This is an arrangement for the sake of Maggie, not for you or me. We'd be marrying for love. Not for each other, but for a child. People have started with far less than that."

"Wars have started with far less than that," she countered.

His eyes narrowed dangerously. "I propose a marriage of mutual convenience. As to my 'needs,' which you seem so obsessed with, you won't be bothered by them. Believe me, my 'needs' do not include bedding a cranky, disagreeable suffragist who talks too much and says too little."

There was no other way to describe the sensation: her cheeks flamed. "Well," she said in a huff.

"You're not getting any younger, Lucy, and I'm not getting any better looking. I don't see prospects lining up to court you. I might just be your last chance at marrying."

"You're assuming I even *want* that chance. I don't have to stay and listen to this." She turned on her heel.

"Not," he snapped, "unless you want to be with Maggie."

She stopped cold, spinning back to face him. *Maggie.* How dare he use the child as a tool of manipulation? Yet now she had no choice. "I'm listening."

He eyed her warily. "Then don't interrupt."

"But I —"

"I said, don't interrupt. This is getting tedious."

Without a word, she sat back down on the bench and scowled at him as he took a seat beside her. "Have you ever contemplated the meaning of the wedding vows, Miss Hathaway? For better for worse . . ."

"For richer for poorer . . ."

"In sickness and in health . . ."

"Until death do us part," she concluded. "I consider it the most solemn of vows. It implies an abiding commitment I have always felt ill prepared to give. That's one reason I never married." She shifted her gaze away, loath to admit that the other reason was that no man had ever wanted her.

"Perhaps you're wiser than I credit you for."

"Or perhaps," she admitted, "I'm merely saying so because I am a complete failure in the marriage market. I was a sore trial to my parents. All they ever wanted was for me to marry well. I've done a good many other things, but never that."

"Now you have a chance," he said. "I'll be frank, Miss Hathaway. I didn't want to make you this offer. For obvious reasons, I am dubious about the reality of marital bliss. I looked at every possible option. I considered asking you to live here without marrying me, but that would subject Maggie to derision and scorn for living with unwed parents."

"Public opinion has never bothered me, nor does it bother my daughter."

"Oh, Lucy," he said, surprising her by using her given name. "It does, though you try so hard to pretend otherwise. And when Maggie's older, she'll care, too."

She fell silent, resenting him for his insight, resenting him because he was correct.

"The point is, I'm not making this offer lightly. Nor do I expect you to accept a conventional arrangement. Here is what I propose. We'll be married in a quiet ceremony. You will move into the house. Naturally, I would hope your mother would come, too. Maggie loves her very much."

Mother. Lucy's gaze sought her out on the beach, where she stood watching for otters with Maggie. How she would adore this place in all its elegance and splendor. Now Lucy understood why Mr. Higgins had included Viola in the summons today. He must have known she would be enchanted by the beauty of his home. Despite her acceptance of their reduced circumstances, she'd always missed the way of life she'd enjoyed when the Colonel was alive, and Mr. Higgins was smart enough to sense that.

"Have you considered precisely *how* things will be if I were to move into your house?" she asked him. She couldn't believe she was actually considering this, and yet she was intrigued.

"We shall live like any proper couple in separate chambers, only in our case the door adjoining our rooms will remain shut."

How she must repulse him. Her pride wanted her to walk away. Then she thought of Maggie and her mother, and her selfishness retreated.

"Of course," he said, "you'll have to give up all your lovers."

She gave a brittle laugh. "Even the French ones? But they were my favorites." Studying his face, she realized he was serious. He'd actually believed her when she'd spouted off about her liaisons. This man had no idea what equality for women was really about. "Very well," she said, "You won't find any man near me. You have my guarantee on that."

"As to guarantees, I've drawn up a written agreement, securing each party's rights."

She clutched her hands into her skirts,

trying to keep her temper in check. How smugly certain he'd been that she would accept his offer. Yet such a measure seemed . . . reasonable. For decades, advocates of women's rights had extolled the virtues of such agreements before marriage. But Mr. Higgins opposed equality for women — he'd said so many times. He was probably worried about her laying claim to his fortune as the first Mrs. Higgins had. Narrowing her eyes in suspicion, she said, "I would have to study this agreement very closely."

"I'm sure you'll see that the terms favor Maggie, if anyone."

"When a woman marries in the state of Illinois, her property is surrendered to the husband. If I were to consider your offer, I'd expect a special exemption for my shop. I want the right to earn and keep my own money."

"I assumed you'd want to sell The Firebrand. The struggle to make your way in the world would be over, Miss Hathaway."

"That proves you don't know me at all. If I had a million dollars ten times over, I would not give up my shop. Would you forfeit your position at the bank if you suddenly found some other means of support?"

"Don't be absurd. I love the bank. Until

you brought me Maggie, it was my life."

"So you'll advance your career at the bank, and I shall devote myself to Maggie."

"Exactly." He looked supremely satisfied.

"When she's grown, you'll still have your career, but I shall have an empty nest. Don't you see this is the dilemma of all women? They are obliged to put aside their own dreams and ambitions until all opportunities have passed them by. I shall be like a cart horse used during its prime strength and then sold to the knacker when it's too feeble to work anymore."

"That's a bit dramatic."

A seagull hovered like a kite in a gust of wind, its plaintive cry sharp in the silence between them. She focused on the mundane sight of the bird. On such an ordinary afternoon, she couldn't believe they were having this extraordinary conversation. She couldn't believe that she, plain Lucy Hathaway, whom no man had ever looked at with anything but scorn, might suddenly have a husband.

In the back of her mind, she had always kept a slender possibility tucked away, the possibility that she would fall in love. If she married this man, based on a cold contract, all possibility would die.

But she would be Maggie's mother.

"Say you'll do it, Miss Hathaway," he urged her. "Do it for Maggie."

She couldn't speak, but backed against the hard iron rail, holding it with both hands as Maggie and her mother came hand in hand along the esplanade looking like figures in a Renoir painting, surrounded by sunshine filtered through green leaves and glancing off blue water. They looked so perfect and happy in this setting, as if they belonged here and here alone.

She felt as though she stood on a high, sharp precipice, with a forest fire burning behind her and a yawning canyon below. She went through her options, tried to find some other way out of the dilemma. But Mr. Higgins had already enumerated and discarded all the possibilities until she had no choice. No choice but one.

Seventeen

On Lucy's wedding day, the lake generated a storm of stiff winds, swirling rain and seething clouds.

Imprisoned by a whalebone and buckram corset, she stood in the apartment over the shop, which had been closed in honor of the occasion. Her mother, Patience and Willa Jean hovered around her, preparing her as if she were a princess bride.

At her mother's insistence, Lucy wore her best gown of watered silk adorned with satin ribbons in a pale green color that made her look as sick and pallid as she felt. Each sumptuous layer of the costume represented another bar in the cell to which she'd consigned herself. She wanted to approach this with cool determination and her eyes wide open. But the truth was, she felt as fearful as a virgin bride — which, ironically, she was.

Her mother tugged and twisted and pinned her hair into a painfully neat arrangement that pulled at Lucy's eyes. The thick, coiled braid was crowned with a veil and anchored by combs. When Viola

348

stepped back, tears shone in her eyes. "Imagine," she said, leaning on Willa Jean for support. "My daughter, a bride at last."

"Oh, Mother." Lucy's patience strained to its limit. "This isn't a love match to get all sentimental over."

"Marriages have started out for lesser reasons than the love of a child," her mother said.

"Take joy where you find it, girl," Patience admonished. "Don't be looking away from the gifts of the Lord."

Lucy rubbed her temples, resisting the urge to tear out the combs stabbing at her scalp. "Remind me, Patience. What gift would that be?"

"A daddy for that sweet baby of yours," Patience said, her powerful affection for the child shining in her smile. As the cleric who would officiate, she looked splendid in a stiff collar and somber robe, her hair done neatly in a bun at the nape of her neck. "A fine new home for you and your mama. The good Lord arranged it all, and you got no business asking why." Patience had that special look on her face, the one she always got when she was doing the Lord's work. "Now, just you wait here, honey. Willa Jean and I'll go down and wait for the coach."

Lucy paced the small room. Since Mr.

Higgins's shocking proposition, she'd been as nervous as Silky the cat when Mrs. McNelis brought her obnoxious pug dog into the shop. Once Lucy had agreed to the marriage, she felt as though she'd stepped into a storm from which there was no escape, swept up in a whirlwind of preparation that left no time to think or reflect. That was probably a good thing, since if she thought about it she would know how foolhardy it was to sacrifice her freedom to a man.

Still, Mr. Lynch had approved the marriage agreement with only minor alterations. Mr. Higgins claimed he had no interest in seizing her property. He simply wanted Maggie to live with two loving parents — and he wanted protection for his own property should Lucy decide to undo the arrangement.

Painful experience had taught him that sort of caution.

Lucy scowled away the thought. How awful of her, already thinking of Diana as the wicked First Wife. Like every woman alive, Mrs. Higgins deserved the right to escape her marriage if she wished it. But a part of Lucy — a part she was not proud of — had already tarred and feathered the woman who had left her wounded, grieving husband lying in a hospital. Still, Lucy had only this one side of the story. One of her favorite customers, Sarah Boggs, was married to a man everyone respected, but Sarah bore his private abuses. Yet Lucy could not imagine Mr. Higgins raising his hand to a woman.

"What is this frown?" her mother asked, neatening Lucy's sash. "This is a day for joy, not for scowling and regrets."

Turning to her mother, she said, "Everything's happening so fast. All my life I've devoted myself to proving a woman can survive without a man. And here I am violating everything I believe in."

"Oh, Lucy." Her mother fluffed out the ridiculous veil. "Such talk and carrying on. For years I've stood by and watched with pride while you rescued us from poverty, started your bookstore and raised a happy, healthy daughter."

Unexpected warmth filled Lucy's heart. "Thank you, Mother."

"Let me finish. I've listened to the speeches at your suffrage rallies, and I admire your devotion to women's rights, but the truth is, my darling daughter, as smart as you are, you have peculiar ideas about love and marriage."

The warmth cooled considerably. "I

never claimed any special expertise in that area."

"That's why you're so afraid." Viola picked up her summer lace gloves from the hall tree and carefully put them on, finger by finger. "Oh, yes, I know you're afraid, though you've done your best to hide it. But you needn't be. There is great power and beauty in a good and loving marriage."

Driven by the lake winds, the summer rain lashed at the windowpanes, blowing the curtains inward. Agitated, Lucy went to latch all the windows. Then she checked the gas jets to make sure they were all turned off, and tightened the lid on the kerosene can; they wouldn't be returning to their little abode over the shop for a long time. Maybe never.

"I've done fine on my own," she said. "For that matter, Mother, so have you. We've been free to make our own way in the world any way we please. I'm not looking forward to the prison of marriage."

"Dear, this is your doing," her mother reminded her. "Even if you won't admit it, you want this. You want to make a family for Maggie." Viola deftly pushed a hatpin through the crown of her bonnet. "My love for the Colonel and his for me was not a prison but a place of sanctuary and growth, a place where I brought forth a daughter in joy and where my happiness was complete."

Moving away from the rain-blurred window, Lucy stared at her mother. She'd never heard her speak with such vehemence. She'd assumed Viola lacked passion and conviction but that wasn't the case at all. It was simply that Lucy's mother had reserved her passion for her marriage and family rather than a social cause.

"Here," Viola said, flushed from her outburst, "come over to the looking glass and see what a lovely bride you are."

Taking Lucy by the hand, she led her to the tall, oval cheval glass that stood in a hinged frame in the corner. It was a mistake. She looked absurd, a sad and cynical parody of a bride. She was too old, too tall, too dark, too skinny, too . . . everything.

She looked like one of Cinderella's ugly stepsisters.

A terrible shame heated her throat. For all her fierce convictions and impassioned politics, she hadn't been able to rid herself of a disgraceful, private yearning that had plagued her all of her life.

"Lucy, please," her mother pleaded softly, kindly. "What's bothering you now?"

Lucy closed her eyes, then opened them. The loving regard in her mother's face proved to be her undoing, drawing from her a candor she could not stifle.

"Couldn't I just for one day be pretty?" she asked in an aching whisper. There. She had done it. She'd finally revealed how shallow and superficial she was. And how pathetic, wishing for something that could never come true.

"Oh, Lucy." Pure, maternal understanding shone in Viola's eyes. "You're so much more than pre—"

"Please." Lucy held up a hand. "You'll only make it worse. I know what I am, and what I am not, and wishing for anything different is a waste of time." She hugged her mother and stepped back, forcing a smile. "There. My moment of doubt is over."

She avoided the looking glass after that and concentrated on her purpose. For the sake of Maggie, she'd agreed to bind her life to Randolph Higgins. In the contract, she followed the example of Dr. Lucy Stone, who had kept her maiden name after marriage. There wasn't a thing wrong with the name Hathaway, and she didn't intend to give it up. In claiming her rights in the marriage contract she'd struck a blow for women everywhere.

But even that failed to calm her racing heart. Only one woman had to marry

Randolph Higgins today.

Squaring her shoulders, she led the way down the stairs to the small, tiled foyer where Patience and Willa Jean stood looking out at the dreary day.

A giant holding an umbrella came to the door and pulled it open. Willa Jean gave a cry of delight when she saw him. Eugene Waxman, nicknamed Bull, had been courting her for several months. He was the largest man Lucy had ever seen. His skin was the color of buffed ebony, and when he grinned, the day grew brighter. In a tailored suit, new spats buttoned around his ankles and a round derby hat crowning his head, he made an impressive sight.

Bull was a powerful reminder that people were capable of changing for the better. The night of the Great Fire, he had been among dozens of convicts released in a panic as the city burned. He'd made the mistake of trying to rob Kathleen O'Leary, who had not only foiled the attempt, but befriended him. Now he was employed by Dylan Kennedy, and his dream was to build a bungalow and marry a strong woman with a ready laugh — a woman like Willa Jean Washington. She had asked him to accompany them aboard the coach to city hall.

"Ready?" Lucy quelled a flutter of foolish

excitement in her chest and herded everyone out the door. Sheltered by the wide umbrella, they moved in a little knot to the curb.

Holding another umbrella high, the smartly dressed driver waited to help them into the coach. Lucy could feel the press of attention emanating from the nearby shops. All the merchants, tradesmen and shopkeepers who shared her little section of Gantry Street watched from doorways and windows. It had been impossible to keep the news of her hasty marriage quiet.

"I have only one daughter," her mother had declared. "I have only one chance to spread the news of her engagement." She'd even published a formal announcement in *The Firebrand*, Lucy's newsletter devoted to women's suffrage. Each time someone congratulated her, Lucy had to bite her tongue to keep from pointing out that becoming the bride of Randolph Higgins was no special achievement but a business arrangement.

Even so, she felt swept up by the rising excitement, too. And the terror.

She and the others settled into the rain-battered coach. Chicago passed in a wet smear of gloomy low clouds, dripping eaves and pavement pocked with puddles. Arriving at the city hall at precisely eleven o'clock, they walked up the broad cut granite stairs to the chambers of the Honorable Judge Roth. In the outer lobby waited Mrs. Grace Higgins, Mr. Higgins and Maggie.

"Mama!" She rushed across the room and threw her arms around Lucy. "Mama, you look so pretty in your fancy dress. Did someone put rouge on your cheeks?"

Despite her blush, Lucy couldn't help smiling. This was one of the blessings of having a child. Maggie thought her mama was pretty no matter what.

"Have you been waiting long?" She held Maggie by the shoulders to look at her. She'd missed that adorable little face.

"For ever and ever. Miss Lowell said it's a special day and I must look my best. Is this my best, Mama?" Maggie stared dubiously down at the froth of pink satin and lace that draped her from neck to ankle. A giant pink bow adorned her profusion of short ringlets.

"You're always beautiful, no matter what," Lucy said, privately vowing to have a word with Miss Lowell. It wasn't healthy to dwell on appearances. Lucy was proof of that. Even as an adult, she was plagued by self-consciousness. "And it's very special that you dressed up for today."

"It's the best day ever." Her face shone as

she pulled Lucy across the room. With careful solemnity, she took Mr. Higgins's hand and then Lucy's, bringing their two hands together. "Now we'll always be together."

This marriage meant the world to Maggie. To her, it was no cold business arrangement, but a lifelong commitment. For Maggie's sake, Lucy would make this work. She tried to be discreet as she unhitched her hand from her future husband's. He wore a bemused expression, but his fingers were chilly and slightly damp with sweat.

Dylan and Kathleen Kennedy arrived, followed by Tom and Deborah Silver. "Look at our dear Lucy," Deborah said, moist-eyed and beaming.

"A bride at last," Kathleen added.

Lucy made hasty introductions, growing more nervous by the second. "The three of us met at finishing school — Deborah and I have known each other since we were Maggie's age," she explained.

Her friends studied him as though he were on exhibit in a zoo. Kathleen was the more brazen of the two, putting her hands on her hips and strolling in a circle around him. "My, Lucy dear. For such a hasty wedding, you made out rather well, I'd say. Big shoulders and a snappy dresser besides."

"Oh, for mercy's sake, Kathleen," Deborah scolded, blushing furiously. She caught Rand's eye. "Forgive her terrible manners. And please accept our congratulations, both on being reunited with your daughter, and on your marriage."

"Isn't it too wonderful?" Maggie jumped up and down. "I shall have a mama and a papa both!"

"You're a lucky girl," Dylan told her. He turned to Mr. Higgins, speaking as though he'd known him for years. "How is your golf game?"

"Close to par, when I find the time to play," Mr. Higgins replied.

Lucy had no idea he played golf.

"I prefer fishing, myself," Tom said.

"I can't believe you're discussing sports during this momentous occasion," Kathleen burst out.

"We'd best behave," Dylan said. "I don't trust my wife when she uses that fishwifey tone of voice."

"Shall we go?" Mr. Higgins stepped aside to let the ladies pass.

Drawing a deep breath, Lucy followed everyone into the judge's chambers. "It's Judge Roth," Kathleen exclaimed. "The very one who married us the night of the fire. Surely you remember us, Judge Roth?"

Black-robed and white-haired, he put on his spectacles, nodding vigorously. "How could I forget?"

"It's a sign of luck for sure," Kathleen whispered as the judge motioned them to a long table with a lamp, pens and inkwells and the heavy tome of the registry.

"Who are the bride and groom?" asked Judge Roth.

Maggie proudly pointed at Lucy and Mr. Higgins. "My mama and papa are," she announced.

The judge's thick white eyebrows descended in thunderous disapproval.

"You see, Your Honor," Lucy began, "We —"

"Do you really want to explain?" Mr. Higgins leaned down to whisper it in her ear, and she pulled away, startled by the warmth of his breath.

"We're anxious to get started, Your Honor," she said simply, conceding his point. And anxious to finish, she thought. On stiff legs, she forced herself to walk over to the table.

Patience cleared her throat and the judge nodded, signaling for her to begin. In her rolling tones, she said, "We are gathered here today in the sight of the Almighty to witness the marriage of Lucille Dorcas

360

Hathaway and Randolph Birch Higgins, and to ask God to bless them."

Maggie bounced up and down on the balls of her feet. Viola put a gloved hand on her shoulder, and she slowed down.

" 'It is written —' " Patience continued, " 'Unless the Lord builds the house, those who build it labor in vain.' It is also written — 'In all your ways acknowledge God, and he will make straight your paths.' Lucille and Randolph, if either of you know of any lawful impediment why you may not be married, I charge you now, before the Lord, the Searcher of all hearts, to declare it . . ."

Lucy pressed her lips together to keep from shrieking a protest. What she was doing was completely within the law, yet everything about it felt false. She sensed Mr. Higgins beside her, and his shadow felt heavy, oppressive. She must have made some sign or motion of distress, for he put a discreet hand beneath her elbow, steadying her. Even that, the slightest of touches, set off a reaction. Sensations she didn't want to feel darted through her, compounding her confusion.

"I will," Mr. Higgins replied to something the judge had said.

Delicate snuffles rose from Viola, Deborah, Kathleen and Willa Jean, and out came the handkerchiefs.

Then the judge turned to her. "Lucille, will you take Randolph to be your husband, to live together in the holy estate of matrimony? Will you love him, comfort him, honor him and keep him, in sickness and in health, forsaking all others as long as you both shall live?"

Love him? Comfort him? Honor him?

She forgot how to speak. She could not force one word past her lips. Then Maggie tugged at her skirt, and in a terrible, broken voice, Lucy said, "I will."

"Almighty and everlasting God," Patience prayed, "in whom we live and move, grant unto us purity of heart, so that no selfish passion may hinder us from knowing your will. Grant that what is said and done in this place may be blessed, both now and forevermore. Amen."

"A-*men,*" Maggie echoed in her strongest voice.

The judge pronounced them man and wife. *Wife.* Lucille Dorcas Hathaway had ceased to be a woman of independent identity.

Maggie looked from Lucy to Rand to the judge. "Is it over?" Her blunt, childish question rang loudly in the stillness of the judge's chambers.

"It's over," Lucy said quietly.

Mr. Higgins surprised everyone by sweeping Maggie up in his arms. "It's just beginning," he declared.

Dear God, thought Lucy, trying wildly to catch Patience's eye. What have I done? But Patience was busy signing her name to the register. The other women dabbed at their eyes; the men checked their watches.

Surrounded by friends and family, Lucy had never felt more alone. For once in her life, she wanted someone to pat her on the hand and tell her everything would be fine, even if it was a lie. How she longed to be the sort of bride who set off on her journey to love with a heart full of joy. But Lucy felt only dread and uncertainty.

"What about the wedding?" Maggie said, the corners of her mouth turning down. "There's supposed to be music and a bouquet. You're supposed to kiss the bride. You *told* me, Papa. You said there would be music and flowers and kissing."

For a moment, no one spoke or moved.

"How could I forget?" asked Rand. After setting Maggie down, he held Lucy lightly by the shoulders and bent close to her.

"No, please," Lucy murmured, for his ears only. She'd had enough of lies and pretenses.

Equally softly, he whispered, "Let's give her something to remember."

Before she could escape, he set his lips upon hers, firmly imprinting the warmth and unfamiliar flavor of his mouth on her. It was a simple gesture, yet Lucy feared she might burst into flame. She wanted to fall into this kiss, to expand and deepen it until she was totally consumed. At the same time, she wanted to run away and hide forever.

With casual ease, Mr. Higgins pulled back. He took the little carnation boutonniere from his lapel and held it out to Lucy, his little finger crooked with exaggerated daintiness. Maggie giggled, and Lucy, blushing furiously, had no choice but to accept the flower. Taking Maggie's hand, he turned and walked toward the door, a distinct swagger in his step, whistling the wedding march between his teeth.

Eighteen

An unearthly yowl, followed by a crash, brought Lucy bucking up out of the bed. Fumbling through the dark, unfamiliar room, she went to the nearest door and yanked it open.

A feline bolt of lightning streaked into the room. A moment later, a large, hairy beast knocked her off her feet in pursuit of the cat.

Lucy hit the floor, the wind knocked out of her. Dazed, she watched her husband's dog tree her cat atop the canopy of her bed.

The door connecting her room to her husband's opened with dramatic swiftness. Mr. Higgins stood there in a pale flood of gaslight, looking mysterious and imposing in his long robe.

"Ivan," he yelled. "Ivan, to heel."

The giant dog snapped to attention, then slunk to his master's side.

Lucy sat up, rubbing her elbow, which rang with numbness. She felt totally disoriented in the spacious chamber with its soaring ceilings and tall windows, its ornate furniture and sumptuous draperies and rugs. The paneled door led into the shadowy cave of her husband's room.

This was the first time the door had been opened.

Mr. Higgins pointed to a rug in front of the massive hearth in his own room, a lair of heavy masculine furnishings and mysterious accoutrements. "Go lie down, you big oaf," he ordered sharply. As the dog obeyed, her husband returned to Lucy's room and twisted a knob on the lamp. The gaslight hissed high and bright, chasing the gloom into the corners. The casualty of the pursuit was a Meissen vase that had been displayed on a hall table outside Lucy's room. He collected the broken pieces onto a lace doily and piled them on the table.

Then he returned to Lucy, who sat, stunned, on the floor. The whole incident had taken place in the span of seconds, and part of her brain was still half asleep. When Mr. Higgins held out his hand, she groggily took it and pulled herself up.

Squinting around her new room, she blinked and rubbed her eyes to clear her vision — and immediately wished she hadn't.

Mr. Higgins's dressing gown, hastily donned, gaped open to reveal his chest. Though he couldn't know it, this was the first time she'd ever seen a man's chest. It was broad and banded by muscle, with a fascinating pattern of dark hair. Slanting across the area just over his heart was a smooth, livid scar.

He yanked the robe closed. His was the self-protective anger of a wounded beast, and she felt an unbidden surge of compassion.

"I'll bet," he said, "you weren't expecting so much excitement on your wedding night."

She forced herself to stop staring at him. In his dark silk robe, with his hair tousled and his feet bare, he appeared so . . . so decadent. Hurrying over to the bed, she said, "Silky, do come down. It's safe now. That nasty dog won't hurt you." Rising on tiptoe, she reached for the canopy that arched over the bed.

The calico cat peeked over the top, its slanted eyes flickering nervously around the room.

"It's all right," Lucy coaxed. "He's just a dumb dog, all brawn and no brains. Come, Silky."

The wary cat crept down into her waiting arms. Hugging the cat to her chest, Lucy turned to find Mr. Higgins watching her. The moment of compassion vanished. He looked large and threatening, painted by lamplight and shadow.

"So this is your idea of excitement?" she asked tartly, feeling as though her entire body had caught fire. What *had* she been dreaming about when she'd been so rudely awakened? Whatever it was, it left her feeling warm and lethargic.

His gaze took her in with slow-paced deliberation, from her long unbound hair to her bare feet, lingering at the places where the light shone through the thin organdy of her nightgown.

"It's a start," he said. He must have sensed her fascination with him, for he studied her minutely, his clear-eyed gaze taking her in, bit by bit. The interest she couldn't quite hide sparked an answering interest in him. In the space of moments, he seemed to transform himself into the arrogant rogue she had encountered so long ago.

She clutched the cat closer until the poor creature let out a mew of protest. At a loss, Lucy stared at the floor, her gown brushing the rich carpet. She waited, expecting him to leave.

When showing her around the house, Mr. Higgins had gestured offhandedly at the door between their chambers. "My room is through there," he'd said.

"Is it locked?" she'd asked.

"Does it need to be?" he'd fired back.

And that, Lucy thought, had been that.

She'd spent the remainder of her wedding day with Maggie, who was giddy with excitement as she helped her mother and grandmother settle into the new house. Lucy had gone to bed exhausted from all the unpacking, and until now she hadn't given the closed door another thought.

"Who was it," she wondered aloud, "who coined the term 'marriage of convenience'? I am not finding this very convenient at all."

"Neither is my dog," said Mr. Higgins.

"He shall have to get used to having a cat around," Lucy said firmly. "It wasn't poor Silky's idea to uproot herself and move to a strange house ruled by a great hairy beast." Realizing she was staring at her husband's bare feet, she shifted her gaze up to his face.

"It's not Ivan's fault, either," he said. "The old boy was perfectly content to mind his own business until his domain was invaded by a peculiar female with a nasty temper and no discernible purpose on earth."

"Silky has a purpose."

"Murdering small birds?" he asked. "Sneaking around in the dark when civilized creatures are asleep?"

"Keeping me company. Curling up to sleep in my lap."

"Then she'd better learn to get along with Ivan."

"He had better learn to get along with her." Curiosity got the better of Lucy. Still cradling the nervous cat, she went and opened the door a crack. Ivan lay on the hearth rug with his chin planted sullenly between his front paws and a mournful look on his heavily jowled face. The dog glowered when Lucy stepped into the room. The cat dug her claws into Lucy's shoulder. She looked around, experiencing her first real glimpse into the inner sanctum of her husband.

The dog growled, but fell silent when Mr. Higgins shushed him.

Her gaze took in the massive fireplace, the tall bookshelves crowded with well-thumbed books, a large globe and skeletal brass telescope, the huge bed. The scale of everything was massive. Intimidating. Much like its inhabitant.

The cat shifted skittishly in her arms and nearly bolted. Stroking Silky to calm her, Lucy was drawn to the French doors, which framed a view of the lake. She knew she was trespassing but that had never stopped her before.

"It's beautiful," she said softly. "I've never seen such a sunrise."

Without being asked, he opened the glass-paned doors for her. The impatient cat fled immediately, shooting from her arms, vaulting over the balustrade and then melting into the shadows of the yard below. Though knowing she, too, ought to bolt for cover, Lucy stepped out onto the balcony into the moist chill of the morning air. Clusters of lilacs hung from the tall hedge plants, heavy with dew, filling the air with the fragrance of early summer. The sky burned bright pink; the lake mirrored and intensified the glow, casting up the light so that the entire yard and quiet roadway were bathed in eerie radiance. As Lucy watched, a raft of waterfowl took wing, skimming along the surface before arrowing cleanly across the sky.

She turned to Mr. Higgins. "It's the most beautiful thing I've ever seen," she said.

"I agree," he said. But he wasn't looking at the sunrise. He seemed amused, although he didn't smile. She could somehow detect a subtle humor dancing in his eyes, those mesmeric eyes that had first drawn her attention so long ago.

An unsettling chill slithered over her, yet at the same time, she felt the fire of the sunrise, only now it burned inside her. She thought about what he'd said, about him being her last chance.

She lifted a hand involuntarily to her throat, holding her gown closed. She wished she'd thought to put on her robe, but she hadn't counted on being so abruptly awakened. She found her voice and said stiffly, "That's a wonderful view of the lake, Mr. Higgins."

She moved toward the tall mahogany door, eager to reach the empty safety of her own room.

He stepped in her way to block her exit. "You shouldn't keep calling me Mr. Higgins."

"Why not?"

"It's too formal after a kiss like that."

Was he referring to that absurd, mocking embrace at their wedding? She frowned in confusion. "What kiss?"

"This one." Taking her by the shoulders, he tugged her against him and slid his arm behind her back. With the same motion, he pressed his lips down onto hers. Lucy found herself at a loss, for she couldn't seem to govern her reaction to him. She wanted to feel the texture of his mouth upon hers, to know what he tasted like, to experience the dizzying sensation of desire lifting her up and sweeping her away. She wanted to stay, yet at the same time, the longing to linger and explore the desire he ignited shamed her.

She pushed against his chest, but her own hands betrayed her and the defensive motion turned into a searching caress. His chest was broad — hard-muscled, warm beneath her chilled fingers. Her betraying hands explored upward, spreading over his big shoulders, feeling the ridge of a scar across the top of his arm. His muscles contracted, and she sensed his self-consciousness returning. She moved her hand to let him know it didn't matter.

The old, old longing fell over her like sunlight through the window. Past and present fused into this single moment. More than five years had passed since she'd first looked into his challenging eyes. So much had changed in those eventful years, but one thing stayed constant — there was still a seductive magic that bound them together.

She caught her breath and said, "No more —"

He touched his finger to her lips and then put his mouth there, brushing lightly back and forth in a motion she felt all the way to her toes.

Her hands tightened into fists on his

shoulders and once again, instead of pushing him away, she clutched him closer. The brushing motion changed and softened into a tender pressure. She was shocked to discover that he'd parted her lips with his own and touched her with his tongue. She shocked herself even further by opening to him and letting him fill her with the forbidden taste of passion.

She felt him everywhere, even in the places he wasn't touching. She burned with a fever so intense that she felt disoriented, not herself at all.

Then, slowly, he lifted his mouth from hers. She could neither move nor speak. Since her days at finishing school she'd imagined what kissing was like, but this embrace, so long in coming that she'd nearly given up on it, surpassed any imagining.

"It's morning," she stated, wishing her voice didn't have that odd tremor in it. She took a step back. "I must go."

"You could stay." He ran his hand down her arm and maybe she imagined it, but she felt his thumb briefly outline the curve of her unbound breast. "You take me out of myself, Lucy. You make me forget —" He stopped abruptly and drew his finger along her jawline, the proprietary touch nearly as intimate as his kiss. "We didn't marry because of this," he said, then bent and touched her mouth with his, searing her briefly with a reminder of the intimacy and heat they'd just shared. Then he pulled back. "But that doesn't mean —"

"Mr. Higgins —"

"Rand."

He was right. As his wife, she must learn to use his given name. But she couldn't just yet. Everything was too new and . . . disturbing. He seemed so different, an unsettling combination of the former, flirtatious rogue and the wounded, withdrawn man who still had a man's desires and still remembered his seductive ways.

"I must go," she repeated, speaking with stronger conviction now. She hurried away, rushing through the door between their rooms and pulling it shut with desperate haste.

Nineteen

His sleep hopelessly disrupted and his nerves rattled by the encounter with Lucy, Rand dressed in the growing light of early morning. He hadn't employed a valet in many years, though it was the fashion for men of his class. Since the accident, he was reluctant to expose his scars and imperfections to anyone, even to a servant. A petty vanity, he knew, but he didn't want to bare the old wounds.

Five years after the tragedy, he could still hear the whisper of those hovering around his hospital bed, when they didn't think he would ever regain consciousness.

They had been wrong. The first part of him to awaken had been his sense of hearing.

"He may never come around," a man, probably a doctor, had said. "The head injury is severe. I'm surprised he hung on this long."

"Perhaps it's for the best," said another voice. "Who could live like . . . this?"

Despite the chilling words, he'd struggled to come back, for he couldn't die without knowing what had become of Christine.

Swimming through a fog of pain, he became aware of hospital smells — overcooked food, boric acid and body waste — and knew he was beginning his journey back. Unable to make a sound or movement, he'd pleaded with frantic eyes, peering out through the web of gauze around his head. No one had noticed, not the doctors who marveled at his stamina, not the nurses who cleaned him and patiently fed him liquids through a hollow tube. And especially not Diana, who finally arrived, pale and thin, at his bedside.

He waited for her to speak, desperate to hear his wife's voice.

Her image came into focus between the diffuse threads of the wrapping. Finally she spoke. "What is that awful smell?"

A doctor cleared his throat. "I fear the burns are quite extensive, Mrs. Higgins."

She drew away, and he could see the shudder pass through her like a bitter wind. She didn't come back until summoned by his doctors, days later.

"Really," she protested, "you are the doctor, not I. I don't see how my presence could possibly make a diff—"

"He spoke, Mrs. Higgins. Your husband said something. That's why I called you here today."

"Well, what did he say?"

"Ma'am, is your name Christine?"

She went to Rand's bedside with utmost reluctance. He could see resistance in the set of her shoulders and the way she avoided looking at him.

"Randolph?" she said.

He had marshaled all his strength in order to ask his question. *"Chris-tine?"* He hissed his baby's name through damaged lips.

Diana had shut her eyes while tears escaped and rolled down her hollow, white cheeks. "She's gone, Randolph. The hotel collapsed and burned. She and Miss Damson were both . . . killed."

The denial that had roared through him had more healing force than all the efforts of the doctors of St. Elspeth's and the specialists from Rush Medical College combined. He couldn't accept that his baby was gone. He had to get up, get out of there. He had to find her. Perhaps the mindless refusal to believe what he heard had given him the strength to do what he did next.

He'd sat up in bed, startling everyone. And then he'd pulled the bandages off his head. The doctor and nurses were used to him from weeks of changing his dressings, but this was Diana's first glimpse of him since the fire. He didn't know at the time that it would be her last.

He would never forget the expression on her face or the involuntary sound that escaped her when she looked at her husband.

He hadn't seen her again after that day. His next visitor had been a hired lawyer informing Rand that Diana was suing him for divorce.

Buttoning a waistcoat over a crisp white shirt, Rand pulled himself back to the present. He cursed under his breath, furious that the encounter with Lucy this morning had sparked memories of his tormented past.

Perhaps Diana's stated grounds for divorce still haunted him. Never mind that he'd been confined to a hospital bed, recuperating from saving her life. He could have argued that point, but in his wounded state after the fire, he could do nothing to disprove her claim. When he saw the official papers, he'd finally admitted something that had lurked like poison in the back of his mind for weeks. He didn't want to be Diana's husband anymore.

He'd signed his capitulation with a shaky, bandaged hand.

This morning Lucy had disproved the humiliating claim unequivocally. He'd wanted her with a reckless need he hadn't felt since he was a lad of seventeen, seducing scullery maids in the linen closet. Exuding the careless charm of a young man of privilege, he'd been spoiled by those who were easily swayed by good looks and a glib tongue. Thoughtless, impulsive and ever looking to fill the void left by his absent mother, he'd used his looks and status to full advantage. On his graduation from university, his father had directed him to marry Miss Diana Layton, and he'd readily obliged, certain that trading in his wild ways for marital bliss would finally bring him the soul-settling contentment he'd always craved. He'd been so stupid. And so damned eager.

Finding his daughter again was a miracle in itself, but having Lucy in his life was a separate issue altogether. He didn't trust the way she made him feel, because long ago, he'd felt the same enthusiasm for Diana. That had turned out to be false, a chimera, shimmering and then disappearing like a shadow at dawn. Still, he had wanted to seduce Lucy. She'd reawakened his self-assurance along with his passion.

As he made his way down to the breakfast room, he caught himself whistling tunelessly between his teeth — something he hadn't done in years. Ordinarily breakfast was a cursory affair — he drank his coffee, read the morning paper and bade his grandmother a good day before going to the bank.

This morning the breakfast room was a hive of activity. In addition to his grandmother and Miss Lowell, he encountered Lucy, Maggie and Viola Hathaway, sipping tea and all talking at once.

"Good morning," he said, disoriented by the intimidating profusion of females sitting in the bright, sun-drenched room.

"Hello, Papa, did you sleep well?" Maggie said, all in a rush. "Miss Lowell says I have to ask you if it's all right to play baseball this afternoon. Mama says I can play baseball anytime, but Miss Lowell says I need your permission, too, on account of I got two parents now, so can I?"

"May I?" the governess corrected her.

"And may I, too?" Maggie asked. Her gap-toothed grin let him know the reply she expected.

"On one condition," he said.

The grin disappeared, and she eyed him warily.

"You have to promise to play a game of catch with me when I get home today."

She bounced up and down in her chair. "Now! I want to play catch now!"

"After work," Lucy said. "You heard . . . your father."

How strange to hear himself referred to in that fashion. He couldn't quite figure out what he was feeling, but it was something rare and new.

"What do you *do* at the bank, anyway?" Maggie asked, swirling her spoon in a cup of tea diluted with milk.

"Customers bring me their money," he said, "and I keep it safe for them."

"Are you very good at it?" she asked. "Are you good at keeping it safe?"

"He is," his grandmother said grandly. "In three years, there hasn't been a run on deposits, while every other bank in town suffers from regular panics."

Maggie clearly had no idea what his grandmother was saying, but Viola looked impressed. "That's wonderful," she said, spooning sugar into her tea.

"Some customers *borrow* money," Lucy pointed out, aiming a meaningful glance at him. "The bank makes a lot of money off such customers."

"*Do* you make a lot of money?" Maggie asked.

Miss Lowell set down her coffee cup. "Child, that is a vulgar ques—"

"The bank does," Rand said. They might as well understand that, although comfortable, he was not endlessly wealthy. "I'm paid a salary for what I do. If I do a bad job, they'll give me the sack."

"What kind of sack?"

"They'll stop paying me and tell me not to work at the bank anymore."

"Then we could play catch all day long."

"True, but it wouldn't seem as much fun if we did that. I do love the bank, Maggie. I wouldn't ever want to get the sack." Giving her a wink, he took his usual seat at the head of the table, but instead of reading the paper, he drank his coffee while watching the ladies of the house. Viola, Miss Lowell and his grandmother seemed content to visit pleasantly while Maggie and Lucy slathered their biscuits with butter and jam.

He caught Lucy's eye, and again was struck by the swift heat of attraction. What the devil was it about her? She kissed like a girl, her mouth soft and her hands tentative as if she did not know where to put them. He assumed that she'd had much practice when it came to the act of love. Perhaps, in the amorous adventures she boasted about, she'd learned that hesitation had a certain charm.

He might be deluding himself entirely, though. He knew exactly why she'd married him. Somehow, he would make it be enough.

★ ★ ★

A nervous Mr. Crowe informed Rand that the Board of Directors had convened a special meeting. As he stepped into the plush boardroom of the Union Trust, the subtle, monied smells of old leather and ink filled the air. Like a panel of distinguished jurors, the directors lined both sides of the table.

As usual, Lamott's personal assistant was in attendance. Guy Smollett was a mild-faced young fellow who dressed well and said little. Rand knew him only slightly, but he had a bad feeling about the fellow. For no particular reason, he sensed a subtle cruelty masked by Smollett's choirboy face.

"Higgins," said Jasper Lamott after a round of cursory greetings, "until recently you've never given us cause to question your judgment."

"I assume this means you've finally found cause." Rand kept his voice quiet, neutral. Jasper had been his friend and mentor since his arrival in Chicago. When Rand had left the hospital after the fire, broken and alone, Jasper Lamott had been the first to call on him — and to remind him that finding a purpose could make life bearable, if not filling it with joy.

"When you began your term at this institution," Lamott continued, "we overlooked the fact that you were a man with a troublesome personal background."

He'd been the first employee of the bank to be involved in a divorce. But he'd quickly found a way to deflect moral outrage and skepticism. He made money for the bank, lots of money. His lodged deposits were sound, his loans productive and his instincts unerring. The banking world forgave a multitude of faults in men who made money.

"We were not disappointed," Mr. Crabtree said. "But this latest gossip is spreading faster than a financial panic." Expressions of disapproval darkened the room.

Rand faced them with a steely, inborn calm. The directors were known to have reduced grown men to tears, but after all Rand had been through, there were few things that intimidated him.

"I assume," he said, "you are referring to the recent changes in my personal life." He'd informed them of his plans in a cursory letter. Clearly, they expected a fuller explanation. "I've found my young daughter, years after giving her up for dead in the Great Fire. Maggie is nearly six now, and very attached to the woman who raised her. For Maggie's sake, I have married her foster mother."

"You don't say," Mr. McClean said. "That's extraordinary. Purely extraordinary."

"It was all over the papers," Crabtree pointed out.

"I don't read the gossip rags."

"I haven't read the accounts, either," Rand said. "The tale is probably embellished, but the fact is, I have clear evidence that Maggie is my daughter, including photographs."

"What a pity the rescuer turned out to be *her*." Lamott took out a fresh cigar and Guy Smollett handed him a clip. He snipped the end, cleanly and precisely.

"Who?" asked Crabtree.

"The Hathaway woman. Runs that radical bookstore and engages in spreading sedition. Same damned female who came to us about a loan —"

"There you are," McClean said in exasperation. "She's snookered you, Higgins."

"Why did you have to *marry* her?" Mr. Crabtree wanted to know. "Surely it wasn't necessary to go that far."

"Lucy has raised Maggie from the night she rescued her," Rand said. "They are very, very close, and Maggie needs her. Rather than engage in a lengthy legal battle over custody of the child, we decided her needs would best be served by becoming a family."

Smollett struck a match and carried the flame to Lamott's cigar. Jasper fogged the room with bluish smoke. Smollett laid the match in the brass ashtray, staring intently at the flame until it went out.

"Probably filled the poor child's head with claptrap and blasphemy." Crabtree steepled his fingers atop a stack of printed forms. "Equal rights. Free love. Women who vote."

Rand forced himself to ignore the comment.

"She's not a bookseller anymore," Lamott pointed out. "She's your wife."

Something inside Rand froze. This was it, then. Here was the flaw in his plan.

"Actually, sir, Lucy will be keeping her interest in the bookstore."

"Don't be absurd, Higgins. You're the president of the Union Trust. Your wife does not work at a bookstore."

"There's no law that prohibits a married woman from employing herself." The words sounded strange coming from him. He'd believed with every fiber of his being that a proper wife and mother stayed home to mind the business of the family. Yet Lucy had been looking after both Maggie and her shop with no adverse consequences, and she had no intention of giving up now.

"I don't like it," Crabtree said, thumping the tip of his umbrella on the floor. "Don't like it in the least. It's ungodly and immoral, the goings-on in that place."

Smollett leaned toward Jasper and murmured something.

"What'll our clients think?" Lamott asked. "They are men of principle, mindful about whom they do business with."

Jasper Lamott's arch-conservative religious group had mounted a fierce and well-organized opposition to the Suffrage Movement. Clannish and distrustful, Lamott's associates in the Brotherhood lodged their deposits at the bank.

"They're interested in good business and fair dealings," Rand said, holding his temper in check. "My having married a woman engaged in commerce won't change that."

"We've a reputation to uphold." Lamott puffed aggressively on his cigar. "Men are fastidious about their money. They're particular about who they deal with when it comes to banking. You understand that, Higgins. Don't pretend you don't."

"Trust me," Rand assured them, "my

wife's conduct and her business will be discreet. People will take no more note of Lucy than they do of a matron at a church social."

When he arrived home that afternoon, he was greeted by a huge political banner spread across the driveway, a pack of mismatched children racing around the lawn and his nosiest neighbor lying in wait.

"Good afternoon, Mrs. Wallace," he said, pretending not to notice the red-and-white banner with the paint still wet. The slogan Votes For Women shouted in bright block letters. "And how are y—"

"What in heaven's name is going on, Mr. Higgins?" Mrs. Wallace demanded, gesturing at the carriages parked at the curb. "It's practically a mob scene, and I heard them singing the most dreadful protest songs. I was about to send for the police."

"I'm sure there's no need," he said. The barefoot children stampeded across the yard with Maggie in the lead, whooping like a wild Indian. "If you'll excuse me, Mrs. Wallace, I must be going."

He left her sputtering in outrage on the sidewalk, pretending to be unperturbed by the uncontrolled mayhem. As he walked up to the front door, his daughter ambushed him.

"You're a prisoner," Maggie screamed, tightening a rope around his middle. In addition to loose dungarees, she wore streaks of warpaint on her face and a crooked feather in her hair. "You'll never get out of here alive!" A few other children leaped from the gooseberry bushes flanking the front walk and ran in circles around Rand. Barking his foolish head off, Ivan added to the noise. Rand counted at least eight youngsters, ranging from about Maggie's age to toddlers with sagging drawers. And in spite of his irritation, he couldn't help laughing.

"I surrender." He turned his hands up in capitulation. "Here, I'll pay you a ransom." Reaching into his pocket, he took out a handful of peppermint drops. Having learned that first day that Maggie loved peppermints, he always carried a supply.

Instantly diverted, they ran off with their booty, leaving Rand to make his way into the house. Stepping over buckets and brushes in the foyer, he recalled leaving an orderly household that morning. What greeted him this afternoon was chaos.

Placards and banners in various stages of completion covered every surface of the downstairs. They bore slogans like All Men And Women Are Created Equal, I Will

Vote, and Give The Vote To The Woman Who Gave You Life.

"How do you spell despot?" someone asked from the parlor.

"L-a-m-o-t-t," another woman answered. "Chief of the Brethren of Orderly Righteousness. Have you ever noticed the initials of that moniker? BOOR."

"Highly appropriate. Did you see in the paper where his group wants to revive coverture restrictions for women?"

"Oh, for Pete's sake, really?" Lucy's voice was sharp with annoyance. "I thought such restrictions ended in the Middle Ages. I shall have to register myself as a femme sole trader so I can conduct business on my own. Honestly, I think men who make the laws must leave their brains at the hatcheck."

"Actually," someone said, "a man's brains are —" Her voice dropped to a whisper and was followed by a chorus of female laughter.

Rand took a deep breath and headed for the parlor.

Miss Lowell waylaid him in the vestibule, her carpetbag in one hand and a piece of paper in the other.

"What's this?" he asked.

"My letter of resignation." Her mouth was so pinched he was surprised she could speak. "My services are clearly not appreciated here. Your wife has excused Maggie from needlework and deportment. She allows the child to chase balls in the alley with the children of laborers, and now the little hoyden is racing around out of control with her visitors."

"I believe that's called playing," he said politely, thinking how agreeable it had been to return home to a yard full of laughing children. "At Maggie's age, it's permissible."

"At the expense of learning?" She sniffed. "And good manners? I cannot abide the disorder. Good day, Mr. Higgins."

She was gone before he had a chance to respond. Out in the yard, two women he'd never seen before shooed the children away from Miss Lowell as she marched down the gravel driveway, veering around the painted banner.

It was just as well. Judging by the noise from the parlor, Rand had other matters to worry about. Unnoticed, he stood in the doorway. Viola sat in a draped window seat, contentedly sewing a sash in patriotic colors. Wearing a paint-smeared smock and her hair pulled away from her face, Lucy discussed the design of the placards with Deborah and Kathleen.

Pushing aside a curl that strayed over her brow, she said, "Perhaps the banner should read, 'All men are despots.' "

"But all of them are not," said Mrs. Silver.

"Just most of them," Mrs. Kennedy pointed out.

"Our claim is —" Lucy spied Rand and stopped abruptly. "Oh, hello," she said. "You're home."

He had an instant and unexpected reaction to seeing her again. She was disheveled, her face flushed, eyes bright and hair in charming disarray, and he found her appearance uniquely unsettling. There was a peculiar quality to the lust she inspired in him. It had a way of undermining his every thought and intention. He meant to yell at her for running off the governess, but instead he simply stood there, the letter forgotten in his hand.

Wiping her fingers on her smock, she gestured at her friends. "Deborah and Kathleen have come to help. You met them at the wedding, remember? Miss Landauer and Mrs. Boggs are working on the banners in the yard and keeping an eye on the children."

Pretending the circumstances were not completely absurd, he said the usual how-do-you-dos. He wondered why a woman like Deborah Silver would involve herself in politics. She was well-known as the wealthiest heiress in the city. After losing her father in a scandal-laden tragedy, she'd married Tom Silver, turned her efforts to philanthropy and was much in demand by the leading hostesses of Chicago. He knew less about Mrs. Kennedy, though like everyone else he'd heard the gossip: She was the daughter of Mrs. O'Leary, in whose barn the Great Fire had started.

He glanced at the sign Deborah was lettering. "I am no man's chattel." Odd that such a seemingly agreeable, refined woman could be a radical.

"Thank you," said Mrs. Kennedy, "for the use of your home for our work. It's ever so much more spacious than Lucy's apartment over the shop."

"To be honest, I had no idea any 'work' would be taking place here."

"We meet once a month to work on the campaign for the vote," Lucy said, not even pretending to be contrite. "We shall have to meet more often to prepare for the Centennial on July Fourth."

Something in his expression must have alerted Mrs. Silver, for she stood quickly. "Kathleen, we really must be going. The children will be as wild as coyotes if we don't round them up soon."

"But —"

"Now, Kathleen." Mrs. Silver spoke sweetly, but eyed the other with steely determination.

"I'll see you ladies out," Viola said.

After the four women had left with their children in tow, Rand surveyed the house. "I don't suppose you'd be interested in explaining yourself to me."

"I explain myself to no one," Lucy said.

"As my wife, you have a duty to —"

"I *told* you I wouldn't be good at being a wife."

"Suppose I were to ask out of simple, polite interest?"

"In that case, I would be happy to enlighten you."

"I'm interested," he said.

"But you're not very polite. You practically ran my friends off. It was rude."

"I'm not accustomed to coming home to chaos." Stalking to the window, he glared out to see the four women herding the children into the waiting coaches. "Who the devil are they?"

"I told you —"

"Their names." He turned back to face her. "But that's not what I'm asking."

She planted her hands on her hips and thrust up her chin. On her, the defiant stance merely looked charming. "Deborah and Kathleen are two of my dearest friends. Lila Landauer came to the shop, hoping to improve her English, which I'm happy to say she has. Sarah Boggs and her two children visited the shop, too, when she —"

He didn't like the way she hesitated. "When she what?"

"She never learned to read, and her husband forbade her to pursue it. So she comes in secret." Lucy dropped her hands and clenched them into fists at her side. "She tried to divorce him once, but her suit was denied. All she got for her troubles was a beating from her husband and another baby on the way. This is the sort of injustice I'm fighting. Don't try to stop me."

"Is painting provocative slogans on banners going to change things for the woman?" he asked.

"Yes," she said. "Perhaps not today or tomorrow, but one day it will. Not just for her, but for all women." Agitated, she began tidying up the room, stacking pamphlets and closing the lids on the paint jars. "There is to be a significant march on the Fourth of July," she announced, "and we intend to be prepared."

"A march," he said, picturing a line of wild-eyed, chanting women surging through the streets of Chicago.

"Indeed. The Centennial of our nation's birth provides the perfect occasion to make a plea for our cause. A hundred years ago, Americans protested taxation without representation and declared that all men were created equal."

"I'm well aware of that."

"Women pay taxes," she explained. "Yet we are not permitted to vote for representation. It's a travesty, and I will not rest until it changes."

Her pale face lit with determination, Rand realized then that, in arranging to marry her, he'd overlooked a key element. Simply marrying Lucy Hathaway was not going to make her a biddable wife.

He had a sudden thought of his mother, lurking deep in the shadows of memory. She hadn't been biddable, either. Her independent spirit had left the broken wreckage of her family in its wake, and years later, he was still finding jagged shards of betrayal in his heart.

"You're not to do any more of your organizing under my roof," he snapped. "I won't tolerate it."

Her brown eyes widened with amazement. "I beg your pardon?"

"I said —"

"I heard what you said. I simply can't imagine why you'd think I would do as you say."

"Because this is my house. Maggie is my daughter, and you are my wife."

"I'm not an idiot, Mr. Higgins. Was I foolish to believe you're not, either? Because truly, only an idiot would oppose equal rights and universal suffrage."

He clenched his teeth, holding in his anger. "I don't give a damn who gets the vote. But if equality means women will turn their backs on their families, then I have a problem with that."

"I haven't turned my back on my family," she said heatedly. "If anything, I've been even more attentive to the needs of my daughter."

"So attentive that you've driven away the governess."

She formed her mouth into a round O of surprise. "Really? What a pity." She made a bouquet of paintbrushes in a jar of water.

"Miss Lowell is one of the most reputable educators in Chicago." He took out the letter, which he'd stuffed into his pocket. "She has resigned, citing your lack of cooperation with her educational program."

"Her educational program consisted of trussing my child into a corset and forcing her to recite meaningless phrases, memorize pointless rules of etiquette and stay inside on a perfectly beautiful day."

"She has worked for some of the best families in Chicago. Clearly she knows what she's about."

"As I know what I am about." Lucy rolled up a large banner and aligned it on the table with several others. "I'm about justice and commitment and change for the better."

"You are about ineffective carping and agitation. If marches and demonstrations worked, then you'd already have the vote. What you're doing isn't just foolhardy, it's dangerous."

She planted her hands on the tabletop and leaned forward. He knew he shouldn't be staring at her breasts, but he did, nearly forgetting the thread of their argument until she said, "You're wrong. What could be dangerous about fighting for freedom?"

"Next time you see Robert Todd Lincoln, you could ask him," Rand bit out.

She narrowed her eyes. "Your point is well taken. But if the people who fought to make this country free had accepted tyranny, we'd still be singing 'Rule Brittania.'"

"You think I'm being an alarmist. You think I'm overreacting."

"For once we agree."

"A public demonstration is tempting fate. You know as well as I do that there are those who will resort to violence in order to silence you."

"Are you one of those?" she demanded.

"Of course not."

"Then I have nothing to worry about, do I?"

God, but she was naive. Frustratingly so. He could see he was getting nowhere arguing with her, but he couldn't seem to stop himself. He wondered why keeping her safe mattered so greatly. It was because he cared about her. As the woman Maggie called mother, of course, but there was something more. To his amazement, he realized he cared about Lucy as his wife.

"You have nothing to worry about," he stated, shaken by the realization, "because there will be no more of your organizing under my roof."

"We'll just see about that." Holding her rolled-up banners like a stack of battle lances, she spun around and marched out of the room.

Twenty

Lucy was a prisoner, trapped like a rodent. There was no other way to look at it. On the table in her bedroom lay a newspaper opened to an account of her wedding in the *Chicago Tribune.* "Mr. Randolph Higgins, President of the Union Trust Bank, was married to Miss Lucille Hathaway, daughter of the late Colonel Hiram and Viola Sherman Hathaway . . ." The article went on, but she could barely bring herself to read it.

She was accustomed to committing social blunders and inspiring gossip. And in a perverse way, she enjoyed being the subject of scandal. When she shocked people by hosting a rally or by getting arrested for voting, that meant she was pushing aside antiquated ways. Her reputation and her career depended on stepping outside the social norm. But deep down, it had always bothered her when people scorned her.

After the fiasco today, she realized that her husband's career depended upon his avoiding scandal and exhibiting unimpeachable behavior.

Lucy put aside the paper and pressed her

fingers to her temples. Dear Lord, she thought, what have I done? Rand had accomplished the one thing she'd dedicated her life to avoiding. He'd taken her freedom from her. She couldn't stay here another instant.

As she paced her room, her gaze fell on a pair of carpetbags, and panic seized her. Could she simply walk away, as the governess had? She thought of Maggie and her heart constricted, but what sort of mother would she be if she were a miserable prisoner under the thumb of an autocratic husband?

This was all her own doing. She was the one who had insisted on taking the path of honor, bringing Maggie together with the father she didn't know. Lucy had known there would be consequences, and she should have been better prepared for them.

Now she must do what she should have done in the first place. She must take her fight to the courts, even though she'd been advised that her cause was hopeless. If it took every last penny she had, she would win Maggie back again.

With chin held high, she began to pack the carpetbags.

"I very much doubt," said a stern voice from the doorway, "that he explained the reason for his reluctance to allow subversive activities in his home."

Lucy froze. Taking a deep breath, she turned to face Rand's grandmother.

"I won't pretend ignorance," Grace said. "It's quite clear that you're leaving because Randolph has forbidden you to do your organizing here."

"It's unreasonable. I cannot live like this."

Leaning on her cane, Grace crossed the room and sat in a gilt chair upholstered in rose-colored damask. "Why do you suppose he disapproves of your suffrage work?"

Lucy tightened her grip on the handle of the bag. "Like all men, he's uncomfortable admitting a woman can be his equal."

"You're oversimplifying the situation."

"What do you mean?"

"You might claim your rights as an individual, but you have a blind spot when it comes to your husband. It's not your fault, you married in haste, but now you must ask yourself, what do you really know about him?"

Lucy had picked up the box containing her favorite pen and inkwell, but the question made her pause. This was her husband's grandmother, someone who had known him all his life. She rubbed her thumb over the lid of the olivewood box. "Only what little he's chosen to share."

"I thought so." Behind the round, steel-rimmed spectacles, Grace's eyes clouded with nostalgia. "He was a beautiful boy, always the best at sports and his studies. His father was so proud of him. He grew into a man whose looks exceeded his fortune, and believe you me, he used those looks to advantage."

Recalling their first meeting five years ago, Lucy pictured the arrogant, flirtatious ladies' man, so handsome that when he had walked through the salon of the hotel, people had stopped their conversations simply to stare. She was forced to remember her helpless attraction to him. "He did," she said quietly.

"As you might imagine, he had his choice of brides, and was smart enough to choose one with a handsome dowry. I believe they would have settled into quite a conventional and pleasant life, except that a disaster occurred."

"The fire." Lucy would forever recall that night with mixed emotions. "I lost my beloved father that night, Grace. But I gained a precious daughter."

"Until recently, your husband knew only loss. Now he has regained his daughter and found a new wife." Her bulb-knuckled hands, in their lace mitts, closed over the head of her cane. "But there is one thing he can never recover."

Diana, thought Lucy. The beauty he'd picked from the dozens who wanted him.

"His looks," Grace stated, taking Lucy completely by surprise.

"I don't understand. Are you saying the change in his appearance has caused him to disapprove of suffrage work?"

"Don't pretend to be daft — I know you're not." The cane thumped the floor with impatience. "He disapproves because he fears it will break apart his family — again. My grandson used to have all the self-confidence in the world, but that changed after the fire. A man can be as vain as a woman. In this I agree with your equality talk. And Randolph certainly did have his pride. I arrived in Chicago eight months after the fire. This house was nearly finished, and Diana wouldn't even step inside, even though he'd built it for her. There was not a single mirror in the place, and all the curtains remained shut. He lived like a beast in a cave, hating the sunlight, hating the stares, hating everything. But most of all, hating himself." The old lady's voice broke, but she held Lucy's gaze. "In time, he rejoined the world again, finding his place at the bank. He uses gruffness to cover his true sentiments. That creature in the dark is still there, inside him, I think."

Lucy stood riveted in place. She'd never considered this aspect of Rand, but she should have. What must it be like, to awaken with the face of a stranger? "His looks have changed somewhat," she conceded, "but he's certainly no monster. He has character and depth, and there is an expressiveness in his face that wasn't there when I met him before the fire."

"You and I know that, but we don't see him the way he sees himself."

Despite the stirrings of sympathy Grace's explanation evoked, Lucy could not yield. She couldn't forget his anger, his dictatorial manner, his furious opposition to her cause.

"I wish he'd been spared the agony of his wounds," she said, putting the small box in her valise, "but he should know that his success did not come about as a result of his looks, of all things. He's strong and principled, a brilliant banker, a generous father to Mag—" Seeing the smug expression on Grace's face, she broke off and grabbed the handle of the bag. "Still, I haven't changed my mind. Where I'm concerned, he's an unenlightened, autocratic —"

"Did you know his mother abandoned him when he was a little boy?"

Lucy's heart lurched. "What?"

"Sit down, dear. Set down that carpetbag. You're not going anywhere."

Grace's words haunted Lucy all through the day. During dinner, she cast furtive glances at Rand, trying to picture him as a small boy, needing his mother, being told that she'd left, never to return. That had been the first of three terrible losses he'd suffered in his life — first his mother, then his child, then his wife. Each loss had probably made him more guarded of his own heart and less tolerant of any change, and that included a wife who wanted to change the world.

Now Lucy had to decide if it was possible for the two of them to build a life together. For the sake of Maggie, she smiled and chatted at supper, making believe nothing was amiss. Watching her daughter's delight in her new family filled Lucy with renewed conviction. She had to make this work. And Grace, though it might not have been her intent, had given her the key.

According to Grace, Pamela Byrd Higgins had been a difficult, uninvolved wife and mother, given to fits of melancholy and periodic, unexplained disappearances. She had a habit of writing obsessively in private. Grace hinted that her daughter-in-law had an unhealthy attachment to medicinal laudanum — and to the doctor who dispensed it.

Pamela had brought a son into the world, but she hadn't stayed to raise him in the comfort of her love. Instead, she had left a small boy grieving and alone. No wonder he had grown into the sort of man who espoused such rigidly traditional values. He wanted the sort of life for Maggie that his own mother had deprived him of — a stable family to love and protect and support, to provide shelter from the storm and a haven for happiness.

Yet Lucy knew there was another side to the story — Pamela's side. From the first mention of her name, Lucy had sensed a haunting familiarity, and this afternoon it had come to her. Long ago, she'd heard of a talented poet and essayist named Pamela Byrd, and she wondered if she might actually be Rand's mother.

Lucy had always believed that she had been put on this earth to rescue Maggie from the fire. Now, perhaps for the first time, she sensed that there was more to her destiny. Who else but a dedicated bookseller would remember the name of an obscure lady author? Her friend Kathleen would call it fate, pure and simple. Magic or not, Lucy intended to use all her expertise as a bookseller in order to unearth the writings of Pamela Byrd.

After supper, she tucked Maggie in, the familiar routine a comfort in this unfamiliar place. The house was painstakingly orderly, the furniture buffed to a high sheen, the carpets swept and the windows gleaming. The antechamber, which joined Maggie's room to Viola's, had a small sitting area and writing desk, the bastion of a proper woman of quality. It reminded Lucy of her childhood, when her mother had been busy organizing the Colonel's social life. No wonder her mother seemed so content here. As did Maggie. Even Silky was getting used to Rand's dog. The only malcontent was Lucy.

Seated on the edge of the ornate little pink-and-white bed, she read through a favorite story.

" '. . . when he saw that the glass slipper fit,' " she recited aloud from a book of fairy tales, " 'the prince realized Cinderella was indeed the princess he sought.' "

She sneaked a glance at Maggie, who had solemnly vowed she would go to sleep after her bedtime story. The child lay upon the lace-edged pillows, as wideawake as a sunflower at high noon.

Pretending not to notice, Lucy turned the page. " 'The prince sank down on one knee and begged her to marry him and be his queen.' " Long ago, Lucy had devised her own ending for the tale. " 'Cinderella laughed and told him to get up off his knees. *I will not marry you or anyone else,* she said. *I never liked those glass slippers anyway. I am going off to have adventures of my own!* ' "

Maggie sat up in bed and plumped the pillows behind her. "How many adventures?"

"Six, and you're procrastinating. You're supposed to be asleep," Lucy said.

"After my story."

"The story's over."

"No," Maggie said with exaggerated patience, "the *next* story."

"My dear, we agreed a long time ago that you would only get one story at night."

"From you," said Maggie.

Rand stepped into the room. Lucy stood quickly, clutching the book to her chest. She could tell, from the bemused expression on his face, that he'd heard her revision of *Cinderella.*

"It appears she's taking full advantage of having two parents," he said.

"Two stories!" Maggie patted the edge of the bed. "Sit right here, Papa. It's still warm from Mama."

Lucy hoped her blush didn't show as she gave Maggie a good-night kiss and retreated from the room. Standing in the hallway outside, she heard him begin reading. " 'Once upon a time, there was a good little girl who wanted to grow up to become the best wife and mother in the world . . .' "

Twenty-One

Maggie had so much excitement building up inside her that she thought she might pop like a soap bubble. It was June the 24th, her real true birthday, and she knew suppertime was going to be special.

"Happy birthday, darling," her mama said, waiting in the dining room. "How do you like having your birthday in the summertime?"

"It's the best," Maggie declared happily as she sat in the chair Papa held out for her. "Thank you," she said, and that got the smile of approval from both grammies, because the grammies liked nice manners. "All my friends came today," she continued, fluffing out her linen napkin. "Did you know that Nancy Boggs's papa went to work camp?"

"No, I didn't," Mama said.

"Nancy says it's quieter around her house these days." Maggie twisted around in her chair. "You won't ever go away to work camp, will you, Papa?"

"Never," he vowed.

Maggie grinned from ear to ear, showing

off the stub of her new tooth growing in. "Sally Saltonstall was cross because I turned six before she did, and she used to be the oldest. Now I'm the older one, aren't I?"

"Indeed you are," Grammy Vi said.

Jiggling her foot against the table leg, Maggie quivered with excitement as she eyed the stack of presents on the buffet. She only picked at her food, pausing every few minutes to examine her gifts, wrapped in brown paper and tied with satin bows.

Mrs. Meeks brought out a tray of petits fours for dessert, and Maggie dutifully ate one. It was sort of dry and crumbly, but she didn't complain. "Is it time yet?" she whispered.

"No," said Mama.

"Yes," said Papa at the same time.

"Hurrah!" Maggie jumped up from her seat. Mama tried to look stern, but she couldn't help smiling as Maggie brought the packages to the table, balancing her chin on the top of the stack. Ripping into the first one, she gasped. "A hat!" she cried. "A beautiful hat!"

"That's from me." Grammy Vi beamed as Maggie tried on the straw bowler, decked with birds and butterflies made of dyed feathers. "You look wonderful, and so grown up."

"Thank you, Grammy Vi." Maggie hugged her grandmother so hard the hat was knocked crooked. Straightening it, she opened a package from Grammy Grace, which contained an embroidery hoop and colorful skeins of floss. "Thank you, Grammy Grace," Maggie said, even though she didn't think embroidering would be much fun.

Grammy Grace pruned her lips, but Maggie saw a gleam in her eye. "Keep looking in the box, child. That's not all there is."

"Oh!" Her smile broadened as she discovered a pincushion in the shape of a frog. She hugged Grammy Grace, too, and set the frog on the table for everyone to admire.

"Open this next." Papa handed her a big box. "Happy birthday, sweetheart."

Mama leaned forward. She seemed terribly interested in what Papa had bought.

The box was filled with fluffy tissue, and inside that nestled a tiny china tea set. Maggie carefully lifted out the pieces, each cup and saucer painted with small pink flowers. "This is the most wonderful thing ever." She had a warm feeling inside as she climbed into his lap and kissed him on the cheek. Oh, she did love having a papa. Even though she'd only had him a short time, she didn't ever want to be without him.

She wasn't sure if Mama liked it yet. She had Disagreements with Papa — sometimes Maggie could hear them talking in quiet, cross voices about the Cause. Other times, like now, Mama smiled at Papa, and there was something soft in her eyes that made Maggie feel hopeful.

Maggie picked up the remaining box. "This must be from you, Mama."

"It is." Mama winked mysteriously.

"Marbles," Maggie cried, looking into the box. "These are the best marbles in the world!" She picked up a large cat's-eye. "Look at this shooter. I'll be able to win all of Willie Sanger's marbles." Willie was visiting from New York City, and had all the children in the neighborhood shooting marbles. "Thank you, Mama."

Papa slid another parcel across the table, and Mama blinked as if she was very surprised. The grammies looked from Papa to Mama, but even Grammy Grace kept quiet.

"A book," Maggie said, opening the leather cover. Pointing to the title, she sounded out, "*Little Women,* by Miss L-Lucy?"

"Louisa May Alcott." Mama gave Papa a different sort of Look. Then she handed Maggie a small parcel.

"Another book!" Maggie said, opening the second one. "This one's called *Little Men*."

"Heavens be," Grammy Grace exclaimed. "Viola, would you like to join me for a cup of tea in the parlor?"

"Yes, please," Grammy Vi said. "This is all entirely too much for me." They both wished Maggie many happy returns of the day and left the room.

"This book is inscribed with Miss Alcott's signature." Mama showed Maggie a page with handwriting on it.

"There is one more surprise for you outside," Papa said, pushing back from the table. Now he gave Mama a Look.

"Hurrah!" Maggie raced for the door. Hand in hand, she and her papa headed for the carriage house while Mama hurried after them. The carriage house was filled with the nice smells of the horse and molasses oats. Behind the buggy was a small, two-wheeled cart, painted red. Papa picked her up and showed her the stall next to Jake, the horse.

A shaggy pony stood amid the wood shavings, switching his tail and looking at her with beautiful velvety eyes.

"His name is Roy," Papa said, "and he's all yours."

Maggie pressed her hands to her cheeks. For a few seconds, she couldn't say a word. She felt like one of those church ladies on baptism day, when the Spirit moved them. She hugged her papa around the neck as hard as ever she could, and finally she found a whisper in her throat. "Thank you, Papa. Thank you ever so much."

He kissed her and helped her lean over to stroke Roy's buttery-yellow mane. "A pony and cart, Mama!" Maggie yelled over her shoulder. "Come see!"

Mama made sounds of admiration as she inspected Roy, petting him and asking Papa if Roy was tame and gentle enough for a little girl. Then, with a secret smile that made Maggie's heart race, Mama lifted a canvas tarp from a corner of the storage area. "Hmm," she said, "what could this be?"

Maggie went to investigate, and she couldn't believe her eyes. With a whoop of joy, she leaped into her mama's arms and hugged her. "A new bicycle! It's much bigger than my old one. Papa, look. When are *you* going to learn to ride a bicycle?"

"I suppose I must," he said. "Very soon."

Grabbing both their hands, she swung her feet up in the air and declared, "I'm the luckiest girl ever."

Exhausted by her big day, Maggie finally fell asleep at nine o'clock, when the peepers came out, chirping from the deep shadowy places at the edge of the lawn. Lucy stood at the landing, looking out at the lake and thinking back on the day. The gift-giving had turned into a rivalry, and Lucy wasn't proud of that. Yet Maggie had been so happy and excited that her mood had buoyed them all.

Lucy wondered if Rand had picked out the tea set himself. She had no idea, for ever since their disagreement, the tension between them had grown tighter, while the distance gaped wider. Had he picked it deliberately, a symbol of female servitude?

Deep in thought, Lucy jumped violently when a loud *pop* startled her. She rushed down to the dining room, where the sound had come from.

"What was that?" she asked. "I heard a gunshot."

"Relax," said Rand, pouring champagne into a crystal flute. "I've not been tempted to shoot you . . . yet." He handed her the glass and poured a second for himself. Touching the rim of hers with his own, he said, "To Maggie?"

"To Maggie."

She took a sip of the champagne and shut her eyes. "Heavens to Betsy."

"Is something wrong?"

"I haven't had champagne since before the fire. This could be one of the few things I've missed about being well off."

They drank in silence, and Lucy savored the exotic taste, then looked at her glass in surprise. It was empty.

Without a word, he refilled hers and then his own. She sensed the tension between them, but it had a different quality. It was heavy with an expectant heat that hadn't been there a few minutes earlier. Her gaze wandered to his strong hands and his wonderful, unsmiling mouth. She thought about the revelations from Grace. How could he believe his looks were gone? Then she thought about that morning he had kissed her, and in spite of everything, she wanted that moment back.

How could she be so foolish? She used to believe in the value of pure honesty, yet here she was, a willing partner in a dishonest marriage. Telling herself it was for Maggie's sake did little to help, particularly at this moment. Flustered, she took a deep drink of champagne. He watched her with an expression she couldn't quite read. His intense regard caused a phantom warmth to rush over her skin.

"It's absolutely delicious," she said.

"Is it?" He moved in close, then hesitated as if he might change his mind.

She didn't want him to. His proximity heightened the pleasure of the champagne. "Yes," she whispered.

"Let me taste." He took the glass from her. Totally unprepared, Lucy felt liquid slosh over the rim as he set the flute aside. Bending low, he kissed her, his tongue searching for the flavor of the champagne she had just drunk. Lucy gave a small, involuntary moan, giddy with a surge of wicked sensuality.

He lifted his mouth from hers and she instantly felt bereft. He had some uncanny power over her, forcing her into an unwinnable war between desire and reason. There was so much she wanted from him, but she knew the price would be her free will.

"You're right," he said. "It's delicious." He handed her the glass again, and drank from his own. He seemed perfectly calm, but she could see the pulse leaping in his neck. Perhaps Grace was right after all, and he was not so self-possessed as he seemed.

Trying to regain some sort of balance, she glanced at the bottle. The label read Sire de

Gaucourt Grand Cuvée, 1870. Lucy gasped. "This is it, isn't it?" she asked.

"This is what?"

"The rare champagne you bought when Maggie was born. The one you drink on each of her birthdays." What had this day been like for him, six years ago? she wondered. Had he paced the halls, wrung his hands, stayed up all night listening for the sound of a newborn infant's cry? Had he held the baby while his heart filled up with love? Had he kissed his wife and told her he was proud of her, that he loved her?

He picked up the bottle. "You can't imagine what I'm feeling right now, Lucy."

The way he stared at her as he spoke made her whole body tingle. "I cannot," she admitted. "Why don't you tell me."

"I'm not used to this," he said with rough-voiced candor. "I've grown accustomed to being alone."

"As have I," she said. She understood all the things he would not say — he wasn't used to closeness, to having a daughter who adored him, to having a wife again. Discomfited, she lifted her glass. "Here's to you. You'll drink this on your daughter's wedding day after all —"

He didn't give her time to finish, but took away her glass and kissed her again, hard, pulling her up against him so that she felt his shape against her thighs. He was impulsive, aggressive, yet curiously unsure of himself, and for some reason that complicated her feelings for him. She had the sensation of drowning in some viscous substance — honey, perhaps — and a sudden panic shot through her. She was sinking, disappearing, turning into a slave to this man.

Pushing her hands against his chest, she leaned back and studied his face, the scarred cheek and the trim moustache, the eyes with their unknowable depths.

"Is something the matter?" he asked.

"I have no idea." She moved away and tried to organize her scattered thoughts. The moment of connection had disturbed her deeply, and she didn't like feeling so vulnerable. To distract him, she asked, "Did you have something to do with Sarah Boggs's husband being sent to work camp?"

"He was owing on some debts," Rand said. "He was sent up for failure to pay."

"I see." She clung to a familiar thread of righteous resentment. "So a man may beat his wife and walk free, but when he defaults on a loan, he's a criminal."

"You said he was a menace to his wife." With a sharp movement, Rand tossed back his champagne. "I merely found an expedient way to separate him from her."

"I'm sure that's appreciated," she said grudgingly, "but it only helps one woman. Liberalizing the divorce laws would help ten thousand women like Sarah Boggs."

"And ten thousand who are nothing like her," he said, his voice taking on the chilly, quiet tones of suppressed anger. He poured himself more champagne and took a drink. She felt both his anger and his desire rippling over her.

Lucy stepped back, wanting to scream in frustration. Her body hungered for this man with a need that burned like wildfire, but he had the politics of a troglodyte. "We can't seem to have a single conversation that doesn't turn into a quarrel," she said.

He stepped closer, and dear Lord, he smelled like heaven, of the summer air and champagne and . . . just him. "Then we probably shouldn't talk at all."

It took every shred of her willpower to duck down and step away before he could pull her against him. "I can't do this," she whispered, wanting him so badly she shook with it. "It's not right. We'd be no better than animals, ruled by blind instinct rather than a true meeting of the heart and soul."

"Blind instinct is agreeable to me."

"Well, not to me."

"Then what is it your heart and soul need?"

She ignored his sarcasm. "I suppose you could start by telling me about your mother."

A flash of fury banished the passion from his gaze and his fist tightened on the champagne flute. "You've been gossiping with my grandmother, then."

"Not gossiping. She was trying to help me understand why you're so bitter, so rigid in your opinions about a woman's place."

He finished his second glass of champagne and set it down too hard on the table. The delicate stem snapped, and Lucy winced at the sound. Rand scowled down at his cut hand, then negligently wrapped a handkerchief around it. "She had no idea of commitment, of permanence, of obedience —"

"Obedience," Lucy said. "She was a woman, not a hunting dog."

"She left like a prize bitch abandoning her litter," he shot back. "A woman who becomes a mother is bound by every law of man and nature to serve her family."

"It's frightening," Lucy whispered, "how much you oppose freedom for women. Will you oppose it for your daughter one day, too?"

"I'll raise Maggie to accept herself as a woman rather than try to imitate a man," he said, unwinding the handkerchief to check the cut. "What is it you find so fascinating about a man, Lucy, that you aspire to be one?"

"I aspire to equality," she said.

"You want equality?" he demanded. "Fine, then I can give you equality." He took a fat cigar from the inner pocket of his waistcoat. "You should learn to smoke. All men do."

"I choose not to adopt your bad habits." Watching him rewrap his cut hand, she was reminded of a wild, wounded animal that would attack even someone trying to help. She amazed herself by wanting to help. He was angry, intractable and insulting. He showed no comprehension of her needs, her desires. His manhandling had the most peculiar, unsettling effect on her, and her reluctant fascination was growing harder and harder to deny.

She forced herself to meet his challenging stare, but when she saw the anger burning in his eyes, she did something she rarely resorted to. She retreated from the argument.

"Thank you for the champagne," she said, then turned and hurried out of the room.

Twenty-Two

"I did it, Papa," Maggie called, seated proudly in her pony cart. "I drove Roy all the way down to the esplanade and back, all by myself."

Rand beamed at her. "You're an expert driver already. Bring him 'round to the carriage house, now, and we'll give him some water and a rest."

She clucked at the pony and concentrated on guiding him to the head of the drive, where Rand waited. It was a perfect Saturday afternoon of sailing clouds and dazzling sunshine, the lake a shifting, crystal mirror of the summer sky. Maggie helped him put up the pony and cart, laughing as Roy dipped his muzzle into the watering trough.

As they worked, Rand watched Ivan and Silky from the corner of his eye. The dog lolled on the lawn, seemingly unaware of the cat slinking toward him through the shadows. The sneaky feline had lost all fear of her nemesis. She crouched, her emerald eyes held in a trance by the mastiff's swishing tail. Then she pounced, sinking her claws into the tail.

Ivan leaped up and spun around in a clumsy counterattack. Rand noted that the dog took soft-mouthed care not to injure the cat, even when she batted at his nose and sidled away, far enough to be out of reach but close enough to hold his interest.

"I want to ride my bicycle now," Maggie announced. "I want you to ride with me."

Rand scowled. He'd been dreading the request. Maggie had wheedled him into borrowing a large bicycle from Dylan Kennedy, and he had made a few attempts on it, but he regarded the contraption as a bone-crushing menace.

"Maybe another time," he said.

"Now!" She grabbed his hand and sank to her knees. "Please, Papa. Mama's busy with her old march, and you were so busy at the bank this week, you didn't play with me *one time*."

"How about a game of catch?"

"Bicycles," she said. "Please."

He knew there was no point in arguing. Maggie could be as intractable as her mother when it came to getting her way. The fact was, he'd idly promised Maggie he would learn to ride, and he'd run out of excuses.

"Only for you," he muttered.

"Hurrah!"

Within minutes, Maggie was rolling happily along the broad pathway while Rand stood holding his machine by the tiller-bar, regarding it like a matador with a mad bull. "Get on get on get on!" Maggie yelled.

Gritting his teeth, he rolled the cycle forward, resting one foot on the mounting-peg and propelling himself along with the other, but he resisted getting on.

"Swing your leg over," Maggie called, turning and gliding back toward him. "It's easy. Mama says it's easier than mounting a horse."

"Mama says, Mama says," he grumbled. But the thought of Lucy provoked him into swinging his other leg up and over the saddle. He promptly fell off on the other side, banging his elbow on the hard ground. A strolling couple at the lakeside paused to watch.

Maggie rode in a wide circle, roaring with laughter. "Try again, Papa. Try hard!"

On the third humiliating attempt, he landed on the skinny seat. He was drenched in sweat and out of patience, but Maggie was so thrilled that he forced himself to press at the pedals. Every wobble and movement of the cycle went against all nature and instinct. When the thing leaned one way, he wanted to steer the wheel in the opposite direction, but each time, it resulted in a spill. Only his laughing daughter prevented him from wheeling the contraption down to the lake and pitching it to the depths.

He managed a few wavering rotations of the wheel, but had no control over his direction. "Faster, Papa, it's easier if you turn fast," Maggie advised.

He discovered that he had no choice. He had to speed up, or topple. As he rode boldly forward, he was glad Maggie was out of earshot, for he had nothing good to say about wheeled contraptions, staring pedestrians, hot summer days or women who bought bicycles for their daughters.

"Look at you, Papa," Maggie said. "You're riding! You're riding fast!"

He was. Somehow, he had gained his balance and was actually rolling along at a good clip. Even the merest pebble or rise in the terrain intimidated him, but before long he learned to control the steering. He found a smooth rhythm, and laughed aloud with his success. Now he understood the appeal of this bizarre sport. It felt like flying.

"All the way to the end of the lane," Maggie directed, rolling past him. "Let's dismount on the grass there."

"I'm an expert at dismounting," he assured her, and demonstrated with a loud crash. Maggie followed suit and tumbled across the grass to him in a fit of giggles.

As he watched his little girl, dappled by sunshine as she lay in the soft grass, he felt himself approaching that shining state of happiness that had always eluded him. This was the way things should be, he reflected. There was only one thing missing from the picture. But Lucy wasn't likely to join them, not after their spat on Maggie's birthday. He'd been on fire for her that night. He'd dared to touch and kiss her with the seductive command that had been so easy for him before the fire. The moment hadn't lasted. His wife's quicksilver temper and his own stony reserve had doused the brief passion.

"You did wonderfully well," Maggie declared.

"Did I?" He inspected his shirt, torn at the elbow.

"You have a scrape," she said with grave concern. "When we get home, tell Mama to put Pond's Extract on it."

Lucy would probably delight in telling *him* where to put the Pond's Extract, he thought.

"I came to say goodbye." Dressed in a white gown decked with red and blue rosettes and ribbons, Lucy entered her husband's room through the door that divided it from hers. That door had remained shut since the morning after their wedding, but today she felt brazen and self-assured.

He hadn't finished dressing, and his robe gaped open. She focused on the flash of bare chest, but he tugged the robe closed and turned his back on her. There was something almost furtive about the movement, and her confidence faltered a little.

"Goodbye," he said, and walked over to the washstand as if she weren't there. While he stirred shaving soap into a lather, she glanced down at the book in her hand.

At last, at long last, she'd found a copy of the works of the late Pamela Byrd. Lucy had stayed up past midnight reading the book. In searingly honest prose and poetry, Pamela Byrd had told her story. She had written of her ordeal as the object of an arranged marriage, likening herself to a bartered bale of wool, submerged and boiled in toxic dye in order to change her character, twisted into taut threads and woven into an unrecognizable pattern. It was a painful portrait of a fragile woman wed to a rigid, autocratic man who controlled her with threats only hinted at in the yellowed pages of the book. Lucy felt as though she'd unlocked an ancient and baffling puzzle.

Rand would have been too young to understand his mother's turmoil; all he knew was that she had left. She had spilled agony, fear and outrage into her writing, taking refuge in doses of ether and laudanum. According to a biographical note in the book, she'd died less than a year after leaving her family. Lucy had wept for her, and now she was bringing the truth to Pamela's son. Lucy knew what she was risking by giving him the book. He would either thank her for it, or condemn her for stirring up bitter memories and exposing his late father's cruelty. But she had to try. She couldn't bear another day of this icy truce.

"Aren't you even going to ask me about my plans?" she asked.

He picked up his razor strop. "I know what day it is." He sharpened his straight razor with long, rhythmic strokes on the leather.

Lucy's palms began to sweat. She had never seen a man at his ablutions before. He was giving her an unsettling and intimate glimpse of himself and she wondered why. Was it because he felt comfortable in her presence, or because he simply didn't care?

"It's the Fourth of July," she said, deciding to tackle the easier matter first.

After a moment, he stopped. "Stay

432

home," he said. "A banker gets few enough holidays. Spend this one with Maggie and me."

"You know I can't. We've spent weeks preparing for the Centennial March." They had argued for days about her participation in the controversial event. "Come with me," she said, knowing what his answer would be. "You and Maggie are welcome to join the march."

He leaned into the mirror, drawing the straight razor along one cheek. "Maggie's not going anywhere near State Street this morning."

"How did you know it's on State Street?"

He paused in his shaving. "All parades follow that route. For those who oppose you, it'll be like shooting fish in a barrel. This whole business is absurd. You have no need to go crusading through the streets. Don't I keep a roof over your head, clothes on your back, food in your belly?"

"This is not about being comfortable." Lucy tightened her grip on the small, cloth-bound book. Ah, Pamela, she thought. Why did you have to die? He needed you so.

"Our nation has only one Centennial," she said. "One hundred years ago today, we declared ourselves a free and independent nation. Will you deny your own daughter the opportunity to partake of that freedom? Deprive her of a chance to witness a moment of history?"

"I'm depriving her of an opportunity to see rotten fruit and stones pelted at her mother."

"Let the fools do their worst," Lucy retorted. She'd received a few anonymous threats at the bookstore, but she'd concealed them from Rand. "They don't scare me."

He finished shaving and stalked into his dressing room. "Maybe they should."

The ominous note in his low tone struck her. "Why would you say such a thing?"

"Because you refuse to." Wearing dark trousers and a blue shirt, he emerged from the dressing room. "Damn it, Lucy." He grabbed her by the shoulders. "Your cause endangers you."

His touch disturbed her, yet at the same time made her want to touch him back, to feel the contours of his body, the texture of his skin, his hair. How could she want him so much, even now?

"If my cause dies because I'm too timid to support it, then all women will be in danger."

He dropped his hands. She could feel his disappointment, harsh as a spoken censure.

"For the last time, Lucy. I'm asking you not to go."

She squared her shoulders. "And for the last time, I'm asking you to come with me."

He took a step back. "You know my answer to that."

She took a step back, too. "Then there's nothing more to say."

"Just remember what's at risk."

"I'll be safe," she vowed. "I promise."

"You can't keep yourself safe from things flung at you in a rage. Damn it, there are consequences I can't even begin to —" He shoved his fingers in long furrows through his hair.

"What consequences?"

He regarded her with a dull flat stare. "Ever since I married you, I've faced daily threats from our depositors."

So, she thought, he had his secrets, too. "What sort of threats?"

"To pull deposits from the bank."

She burst out laughing, then realized this was no joke. "That's ridiculous."

"Men don't like leaving their money with a banker who can't control his own wife."

"I am no man's to control."

"Exactly. If I can't keep you in line, why should they trust me with their hard-earned money?"

"My God. They are offended because you're married to me?" The old, old shame crept up in Lucy. Once again she was the daughter who failed to please her parents, the last girl picked at every dance, an object of scorn and ridicule because she couldn't fit in. "You're lying," she said. But she could see from the look on his face that he was not.

She stared at the book in her hand. He would never understand why she could not abandon her cause for the sake of his bank. Still, she had gone to a great deal of trouble.

She handed him the small blue book. "I've been wondering if I'd find a right time to give you this," she said. "Now I'm beginning to think there isn't going to be a right time. But you should read it. Then you'd understand the sort of thing I'm fighting. And you might even learn to forgive." She went to the door between their rooms. "Getting married was supposed to make everything simpler," she said. "But it hasn't, has it?"

Twenty-Three

Thanks to his mother, Rand didn't finish dressing for two hours and wasn't ready when his visitors arrived. The moment Lucy had flounced from his room, he'd started reading, burningly curious about a matter she considered so important that she'd barge into his private chambers. Despite their antagonism, he was getting used to her lack of regard for propriety. But nothing could have prepared him for the contents of the book she'd delivered.

Seeing his mother's name printed on the title page sent a cold wind through all the empty places Pamela Byrd Higgins had left in her wake. He'd forced himself to turn the page, forced himself to start reading. The contents first startled, then infuriated him. This was no more than a litany of imagined slights from a discontented woman. What right had she, a well-off society matron living in a splendid house, to complain about her lot in life?

And yet, as he pored over page after page of the writings, he felt a reluctant affinity with the troubled writer. Like the sun warming a cold rock, understanding seeped into him.

"I starve with a full belly and die of thirst in a deep well. I freeze in an overheated house. I strangle on a rope of Asian pearls . . ." The haunting words on the page called across the years as Lucy must have known they would. As he finished the anguished essays and prose-poems, his fury died, replaced by a bitter comprehension. Trapped in a marriage of convenience, his mother had begun to suffocate. Lucy wanted him to see that a true marriage was not founded on creature comforts, but on mutual respect, genuine affection. *Love.*

He and Lucy had never promised each other that. Was she now saying she needed it? Lucy had said something else, too. She'd told him he had to learn to forgive. It wasn't enough to simply understand that his mother's pain had pushed her to do the unthinkable. He had to let go of his bitterness and forgive her. He didn't know if he was capable of that. But Lucy seemed to think he was, and Lucy's convictions were powerful.

"Papa!" Maggie's voice called from downstairs. "Look who's come to call."

He started to fling aside the book, but some mad impulse seized him. He picked it up, shut his eyes and pressed it against his heart. Then, embarrassed, he set it on the mantel shelf and hurriedly finished dressing.

By the time he went downstairs, the foyer resembled a disturbed anthill. Tom Silver had arrived with his two little ones, Dylan Kennedy with his twins and the other two. The children were in constant motion, chasing and playing in the fountain, running up and down the stairs.

"We got your summons," Tom said.

"Would've come sooner," Dylan explained, "but rounding up this lot —" he indicated the children "— was like herding cats."

Shaking off the overwhelming weight of his mother's confessions, Rand found it within himself to grin. He invited everyone to the kitchen for something to eat, and Mrs. Meeks obligingly filled the grubby, reaching hands of the children with biscuits and strawberries.

A consummate gambler, Dylan produced a deck of cards and slapped it on the table. "I don't suppose they'll leave us to play a hand," he said with a weary look at his red-haired son, who had just put a berry in his ear. "But we could cut cards. The loser changes Minnie's diaper."

Tom picked up the squirming toddler and passed her across the table to Dylan. "I don't like the odds."

Rand chuckled, enjoying an easy camaraderie with the others. While Dylan took his daughter to the back stoop, Tom set his elbows on the table. "I assume this is about the march today."

Rand's humor dimmed. "There's going to be a counterprotest."

"We expected that," Dylan called from the back. He herded the four older children outside to play and took a seat at the table. "What about this counterprotest?"

Rand told what he knew about the Brethren and their fiery opposition to women's suffrage. Lamott himself had organized the proceedings. The group intended to confront the marchers at the intersection of State and Madison. "I tried to convince Lucy not to go," he added.

"You'd sooner stop the tide," Tom said. "Men who call women 'the weaker sex' have never been married."

Rand stood and paced in agitation. "She wanted me to come to the march, and I refused."

Dylan and Tom exchanged a glance. "So did we."

Three seconds of silence filled the room.

Then they all reached the same conclusion at once. "Get the children," Rand said. "Hurry."

The suffrage marchers met at Fairfield Park to organize themselves into lines that resembled battalions. Energy ran high, sailing over the multitude of women — and quite a few men — like the summer clouds over the lake. Ladies with tin drums and brass trumpets waited for the signal to begin the march down State Street. Half a block away, Patience and Willa Jean rehearsed hymns and chants with the participants.

Lucy had been busy for an hour, going over the route with the guest of honor and leader of the march, Victoria Claflin Woodhull. Her notoriety as the first woman to trade stocks and run a bank on Wall Street, the first woman to run for president and the first to address Congress on the suffrage issue made her an intimidating figure. Yet she was thinner than Lucy had pictured her, with skin as pale as an invalid's. But under thick, straight eyebrows, her gaze was as challenging as her radical ideas. Newly divorced from her second husband, she traveled alone with her young daughter, Zulu Maud, a quiet girl of fourteen who looked ill at ease amid all the activity.

"We're so honored that you came," Lucy said to Mrs. Woodhull, bringing her to the front of the crowd.

"I was honored to be asked. I've always enjoyed our correspondence, Lucy, and I wanted to meet the person who named her bookstore after me."

"It was you who inspired me to strike out on my own. Hearing you called The Firebrand of Wall Street gave me the idea for the name."

"I'm pleased you picked that moniker, for some of the others are not so flattering." She grinned. "Mrs. Satan or Queen of the Prostitutes would not have suited at all."

Lucy admired her for making light of something that must have stung deeply. Standing beside the most famous and outspoken woman in America, she felt a surge of pride. But it was a hollow, empty feeling, robbed of its sweetness by her quarrel with Rand. She couldn't escape the thought that her cause alienated her from Maggie's father. Lucy's husband. Was it possible to reach the pinnacle of triumph even as her heart was breaking?

"Why the long face?" Mrs. Woodhull asked. "It's a grand day for the cause."

"I wish I could be impervious to our critics," Lucy confessed. "Is it terribly weak of me to let their opinions matter?"

"Certainly not. Just because your cause is just doesn't mean you're not human. What happened, Lucy?"

She flushed. "My husband's clients are threatening to pull their deposits from his bank," she said, slanting a sash lettered with the slogan I Will Vote across her chest.

"They probably will," Victoria said matter-of-factly. "Money is the most powerful weapon they have."

Lucy's stomach churned. "I could fix it," she said. "I could leave the cause to others, give up my shop —"

"You must love him very much, to be so concerned."

Lucy nearly choked. "I don't — it's not like that at all. In fact, ours is a difficult marriage."

"Trust me," Victoria said, "I've been married twice, and I can tell you firsthand that even a good marriage is never easy."

"There you are!" Kathleen Kennedy called, pushing through the crowd. She had Deborah Silver in tow, the two of them looking fresh and excited as they lifted their placards. Relieved to see her friends, Lucy introduced them to Mrs. Woodhull. The guest of honor stepped up to a horse cart draped in red, white and blue bunting.

"Your husbands didn't come, either," Lucy observed.

"They're sulking," Deborah conceded.

"And minding the children," Kathleen added. "But they know better than to stop us today."

A drumroll sounded, and the lead cart rolled. Flag bearers lifted their banners high, and the marchers surged forward. Linking arms with her friends, Lucy found herself at the head of a column. Accompanied by drums and whistles, they chanted verses of freedom and independence. Spectators lined the street and waved from open windows in the tall buildings. The summer sun blazed from a blue sky, warming Lucy's face as she lifted her voice in song.

The noise crescendoed to a fever pitch. As the parade progressed, the crowd of onlookers thickened. Among them, she saw a few faces pulled hard and taut with aversion and felt the occasional thrown fruit whiz past.

"Watch out ahead," Kathleen said, gesturing at the upcoming intersection. "That lot doesn't look too friendly."

Dressed in somber, Puritanical black, a horde of men advanced in a straight, unbroken line toward the suffragists. In ringing tones, they sang some hymn or other, but Lucy couldn't make out the words.

She felt a sick apprehension. It was a game of nerves, then. Who would move out of the way first?

Patience whirled to face the others and lifted her arms like a choral director. "Louder, ladies and gentlemen!" she shouted. "Sing louder!"

The song of freedom swelled from their ranks, but the deep spiritual dirges of the opposition rolled forth like black thunder. Deborah faltered, and Lucy squeezed her hand. "We must not flinch," she said. "We must not — Oh, no."

"What?" Deborah asked.

"That's Jasper Lamott from the bank." He stood shoulder-to-shoulder with the angry men, his face a mask of wrath as he boomed out his protest. Maybe it was her imagination, but she sensed his furious gaze focusing on her. He marched beside Guy Smollett, who sang with the fervor of a fanatic choirboy.

"And the Boors," Kathleen said. "We should have known they'd come to make trouble."

Suffragists and bystanders jostled each other at the edge of the crowd. Lucy couldn't tell who made the first move, but a fight broke out. For a moment it was a shoving match between two men only, but it quickly escalated like a flame being touched to incendiary oil. Mrs. Woodhull's cart horse bolted. Someone screamed, and the marching columns dissolved into confusion. Flags and placards were knocked askew like broken weapons in a mêlée. Lucy was caught in the middle, and though no one actually hit her, the mob of sweating, angry protesters and counterprotesters squeezed the air from her lungs. At one point her feet actually left the ground as she was buffeted between the warring factions.

"A riot," yelled Kathleen. "Saints and crooked angels, an honest-to-goodness riot." Her shout crescendoed to a scream as a powerful gush of water cut through the throng.

At first Lucy didn't understand what was happening. She took a faceful of water and choked, her hand torn from Deborah's. Then she realized that the police had turned the stream on the crowd. Using Chicago's new high-pressure water system, they separated the suffragists and righteous Brotherhood as if the two factions were fighting dogs. The stream hit fast and hard, parting the crowd, knocking some to the ground. The cowards of the Brotherhood rushed away, seeking shelter down a side street.

Drenched from head to toe, Lucy sat dazed upon the wet pavement. Over the crowd of thousands, a stunned hush hung like a pall. No one seemed capable of moving. Then the police took action, hauling away the most obvious of the brawlers — men with bloodied noses, women shrieking obscenities, crying children separated from their parents.

Groping for her ruined hat, Lucy felt a disquieting premonition. Dear God, were the police coming for her?

A long shadow dropped over her huddled form. She braced herself for the arrest and looked defiantly up at her captor.

"Rand?"

He held out his hand to her and drew her to her feet. She stood staring up at him, while all around, the marchers slowly re-formed their ranks. Mrs. Woodhull's driver brought the cart back in line, and she proceeded down the street.

"What are you doing here?" she asked.

"Seeing history in the making." He handed her a dry handkerchief. "Wipe your face. You've got another block or two to go."

As he spoke, Deborah's giant woodsman of a husband appeared, carrying their towheaded children. Dylan Kennedy held a baby on one hip while the twins and their sister followed him like ducklings in a row.

Lastly, Lucy's mother emerged, holding Maggie by the hand. Seeing her parents, Maggie gave a whoop and sped forward, grabbing Lucy's hand and then Rand's, joyously swinging between them.

Patience started singing with loud clarity. By the end of the first phrase, a thousand voices joined in as the song buoyed them to the end of the march.

Twenty-Four

That night, a huge crowd watched fireworks from the beach by the lake. Many of the suffragists still sang softly, the hymns riding the summer breeze. Sitting upon thick blankets spread over the sand, Lucy stroked Maggie's hair. "The last of the children to succumb," she said. "They were all so exhausted."

Next to her, Rand pushed a stick into the campfire the men had built. "How do they sleep through all this noise?"

Across from him, Dylan Kennedy stretched out, laid his head in his wife's lap and crossed his legs at the ankles. "Don't ever question why a child sleeps," he said. His own brood lay scattered nearby on a blanket, snuggled together like a litter of kittens. "Just be thankful for it."

"A child can sleep through anything if she's not afraid," Deborah said with quiet assurance. She leaned back against her husband's massive shoulder and tilted her face up to the night sky, where rockets and starbursts exploded in streams of color.

Lucy observed her friends covertly, and a stab of yearning pierced her. How wonderful, she thought, to be so relaxed and comfortable with one's husband, so secure in his love.

"Well," said Kathleen, stroking her husband's hair. "We're glad entirely that all of you showed up when you did."

Dylan winked. "I can usually count on finding you in the middle of trouble."

Lucy pulled her knees up to her chest, deciding the undignified pose was forgivable at this late hour. "We planned a peaceful demonstration. It's not our fault a group of ignorant philistines chose to pick a fight with us."

"They uphold their beliefs with the same passion as you uphold yours," Rand pointed out.

"They're probably ordinary men who play golf and go fishing," Tom Silver added.

"They can still be wrong," said Kathleen. "They can have obedient wives who enjoy looking after hearth and home, and they can still be wrong."

"We're lucky the police were right there with the fire hoses," Deborah said. "I wonder how they knew the precise location of the altercation."

From the corner of her eye, Lucy saw Rand shift and look away, out across the endless black lake.

"You knew, didn't you?" she said. "You knew they were planning a counterdemonstration, and you alerted the police."

"Jasper Lamott organized the demonstration," Rand said. "A bank is a gossip mill, you know that."

She understood then, and wonder welled up inside her. He had known he'd never succeed in talking her out of going. In his own way, he'd protected her as best he could. Protected her without taking away her freedom.

Until this moment, Lucy had never believed such a thing could be. As a rainbow fireburst blossomed overhead, she reached over and put her hand on top of his.

Lucy didn't feel a bit tired as she readied herself for bed. The usual rituals of bedtime still felt peculiar to her in this vast room where bedclothes were turned down by phantom hands and hot water appeared as if by magic in the ewer and hip bath.

A secret delight filled her. She adored the luxury of fresh bedding and hot baths and delicately scented soap, of water and coal she didn't have to fetch, of gaslight anytime she wanted it, fresh rolls for breakfast and daily newspapers delivered to her door.

But she would die before she'd admit these things to anyone but herself.

After indulging in a bath, loving it as though it were a private vice, she donned the white organdy nightgown her mother insisted on calling part of her trousseau. It was far too sheer to be practical, but she hadn't had the heart to tell her mother so. Besides, the night was balmy with the ripe warmth of summer.

Brushing her hair with absentminded motions, she went to the window and peered out. From this vantage point there was little to see in the soft dark of the summer night. A fine spray of stars lit the sky, and the sparse lights of the neighborhood spread out along the avenue below.

Her husband's room had a far better view. He could probably see the fireworks still going off over the lake. She pictured him standing at the French doors, looking out at the brilliant night. Despite the heated eddies of wind wafting in through the window, she shivered.

Swirling, tantalizing thoughts brought Lucy right back to a point where she'd been before, to a feeling she'd had before. Five years ago, she'd been so powerfully attracted to Randolph Higgins that she'd brazenly asked him to be her lover. Five years later, she still wanted that.

Five years ago, he'd been married to Diana.

Five years later, he was married to *her*.

How did one communicate these blazing needs to a man? She supposed she could simply ask him . . . but she wasn't sure what she was asking. She wanted — desired — an intimacy that had eluded her for years, mocking her efforts to subsist without it.

Lucy pressed her fingertips to the windowpane and then removed them, watching the foggy impression evaporate. Then, very slowly, she let herself make a decision at last, because she'd run out of reasons not to.

Before her conviction faltered, she hurried to the door dividing her room from Rand's.

She slowly turned the brass knob, encountered resistance. The knob seemed frozen in place. Her heart sank; the message was clear. Her husband had barred her from his room.

On the other side of the door, Rand turned the knob a little harder. It didn't budge. Fine, he thought. She'd locked it.

Obviously he'd misread her manner toward him tonight. In the amber glow of the beach fire, he'd dared to believe that she wanted his kisses, his touch . . . perhaps more. He'd felt a small measure of his old confidence, when he used to be certain of his appeal to women.

A case of wishful thinking, he concluded sourly, giving the knob one last twist.

This time, the latch yielded to his pressure and the door opened. Lucy stood there, mere inches away, snatching her hand from the doorknob as if it had burned her. She looked as startled and defenseless as a doomed rabbit caught in a steel trap.

"Forgive me," he said, rattled but intrigued. She must have been trying the door, too. "I didn't expect to find you standing so close."

"You might have knocked."

"But I didn't." He glanced pointedly at her.

"Oh." She was more flustered than he'd ever seen her, and he found this curiously appealing.

"Is something the matter?" he asked.

"No. I mean, yes. I mean —"

"Would you like something to drink?"

She regarded him as though he'd spoken in a foreign tongue.

"Brandy or port?" he said. "I have some in my room."

She nodded once and slipped silently past

him. He caught the whisper of a light soapy fragrance as she walked by. She wore the same nightgown she'd had on her first night in the house, only now it was covered with a modest robe.

A pity. In the sheer, revealing nightgown, she'd looked like a goddess. Now, with the robe buttoned to her chin, she merely looked uncomfortable.

"What would you like?" he asked.

"I'm not sure where to begin," she said, the words bursting from her in a nervous rush. "I have a few things to ask —"

"To drink," he interrupted, growing amused. "What would you like to drink, port or brandy?"

"Oh." Her shoulders sagged. "Brandy, please."

He poured a little from a crystal decanter into a snifter. The only light in the room came from a sconce by the bed; it was too warm for a fire. The diffuse glow fell like a veil over her, flickering in the folds of her gown as she paced over to the window and cupped her hands around her eyes to see out. "They're still letting off fireworks."

"As you pointed out this morning," he said, handing her a glass of brandy, "we only have one Centennial." He touched his glass to hers. "Cheers. Sit down," he said.

With surprising obedience, she not only sampled the brandy, but closed her eyes as she swallowed, and then took a seat. She looked so prim and proper, her robe buttoned from throat to hem, her hair in a loose braid down her back, yet the very modesty of her appearance made him want to peel away those layers, one by one.

When she opened her eyes, she was looking at the mantel shelf where he'd left his mother's book. "You read it, didn't you?"

"Yes." He pulled a reluctant admission from deep inside him. "I won't say it was the most uplifting material I've ever read. It was damned painful. But you were right to show it to me. There are things I never knew, never understood. My father painted a picture of an unfaithful wife and uncaring mother. Now that I've read her story, I understand. My father drove her away, threatening to put her in an insane asylum if she dared to contact her son. I didn't realize the burden I'd been carrying, and I never knew how forgiveness could lighten that burden." He helped himself to a glass of brandy. "Now. Is that what you came to ask me?"

"I wanted to ask you several things." Amazed by his candor, she took a quick gulp of brandy. "And for some reason, I've forgotten all of them but one."

"Which one is that?"

"It's something I've asked you before."

Rand wasn't sure he wanted to hear. In the past, she had asked him to lend her money for an enterprise in danger of failing, to support a cause he opposed, and in general, to change his life and his beliefs to suit hers. "What is it?" he said with weary resignation.

"Can you — will you — make love to me?"

It was the last thing he'd expected to hear from her, and he stood in complete, motionless silence for several moments.

She mistook his hesitation. "If you'd rather not or if you, er, can't, then I'll certainly understand —"

The old shame stung him. Damn Diana, he thought viciously. She'd made no secret of her rationale for divorce. Somehow, Lucy must have learned of the scandal. "What do you mean, *can't?*"

She took a bigger sip of brandy. "Why are you so angry?"

Because I'm afraid, his heart whispered. She thought she knew what the fire had done to him. But she couldn't, not really. Step by step, he'd reclaimed his life, building a career and a home, a place in society. Now he had his daughter again. He had his life back. He'd regained everything he'd lost, save one. He still lacked a true wife. Lucy was his in name only. So far.

"Rand?" she asked, confused by his silence. "If you'd rather not —"

"My grandmother told you about my mother. But I doubt she told you about Diana."

"I don't understand."

It was time she heard the truth from him, for it was only a matter of time before some other source informed her. The local scandal rags had reported the story in salacious detail. "In her divorce suit, my wife cited my inability to perform my marital duties."

"Your —" Comprehension dawned on her face. "Oh. Why would she do such a thing?"

"To facilitate the divorce." He could see the unspoken question in her eyes. "Yes, her claim was true. I lay in a semiconscious state, and I could barely make a fist, much less make love to my own wife."

Lucy finished the brandy and set aside the glass. "You can make a fist now."

A powerful surge of desire heated to a peak he hadn't felt since before the fire. He held out his own hand, demonstrating. "It's the second-best thing I do."

"What's the first-best?"

He hesitated, feeling as though he balanced on a sharp precipice. Then he took her hand and drew her close. Slowly he untied the ribbon holding the robe closed at her throat. Bending down, he whispered his answer in her ear.

"Heavens to Betsy," she whispered back.

He didn't let himself hesitate. Didn't think or analyze. He kissed her hard, sampling the brandy she'd just drunk, turned by some alchemy to pure nectar as it mingled with the taste of her. Each time he kissed her, he expected her to turn to stone, or to turn away. But instead, she became softer, more pliant. He pressed harder, parting her lips with his and the concealing robe with his hands. She tensed, and he feared she would draw back. He made a soothing motion with his hands until she relaxed against him. The fabric slipped off her shoulders and whispered down her arms, pooling with a delicate rustle on the floor.

He wondered what expectations she'd built up in her mind about him. She'd seen the scars on his face and hands. Surely she could guess his wounds didn't end there. He willed himself to stop thinking about his failings and concentrated on Lucy's needs,

Lucy's desires. He had been thinking about her for a long time. By now, he knew exactly how he wanted to love her, knew how he wanted to kiss and touch her, knew what he wanted her to feel.

He held and stroked her until she softened against him; then he changed the slant of his kiss, touching and pushing with his tongue, finding the pliant, brandy-sweet places of her. His hands skimmed downward, covering and then cupping her breasts. She gasped with surprise and, he thought, pleasure.

"Come," he whispered against her mouth. "Come to bed with me."

She seemed to tremble as she moved toward the bed, still holding his hand, stretching out her arm. In the dim light he could see that her lips were swollen and glistening, her neck and cheeks flushed. She hesitated as she stood by the bed, perhaps unable to decide what to do next.

"You don't have to do anything," he told her. "Just . . . let me . . ." He found the drawstring that fastened her nightgown. Pulling it loose, he skimmed the gown off her shoulders and down her body.

She wore nothing underneath. It was so startling, so unorthodox yet so typical of Lucy that he managed to smile despite the increasing intensity of his need. She folded her arms in an attempt to cover herself.

"Don't," he said, taking her hands and lacing his fingers with hers. "You look beautiful, just as you are."

"You needn't say that."

"Why not? I thought you believed one should speak one's mind." He was astonished to see doubt in her eyes. "Lucy. How can you think you aren't beautiful?"

Somehow, despite her unclad state, she managed to look prim. "If you must know, it has been reported to me as fact."

"By some life-form lower than a snail, I'd wager." Standing back, he outlined her silhouette with a long, delicate caress of his hands. "Believe this, Lucy. This." Kissing her, he pressed her back on the bed. A sound came from her — distress? Excitement? — and then she grew bold with her hands, pushing them inside his robe. Her touch was so wild and compelling, his need for her so great, that he nearly forgot what the fire had done to him. But when she sighed against his neck and slipped her hands inside his robe, he remembered. Her fingers were mapping the terrible rugged landscape of his wounded body, and would soon discover the horrors written in his flesh.

He pulled back, drew her hand away. "Lucy . . ."

She was too impatient, pulling at his robe. He kissed her until her hands stilled and she lay quietly compliant, for once not trying to take the lead. He reached up with one hand, twisting the knob to kill the flame of the gas lamp.

"What are you doing?" she said.

"Some things are best done in the dark."

She took his hand away and raised the flame again. "Not this."

"You don't want to see, Lucy."

"I demand my equal rights. You just lectured me about the relative nature of beauty," she said. "Will you not believe your own counsel?" She parted his robe and simply stared, saying no more. He waited for a revulsion that never came. "If you had the looks of a god I would still quarrel with you over the issues that matter to me. If you had the face of a wildebeest I would still want you," she explained. Sympathy flashed in her eyes, but it quickly turned to . . . he wasn't sure what, for she bent down, trailing her hair over his chest as she kissed him there, scars and all, with a compelling combination of reverence and heat.

Shaken, he accepted her tribute with a gratitude and tenderness too powerful for speaking. Laying her back on the bed, he pressed himself against her, and his flesh took fire. His kisses traveled over her, savoring the fragile contours of her body, the satiny breasts brushing against him. He closed his lips around the soft peak of her breast, eliciting a new sound from her, a sound he'd never heard before. One that spoke of yearning and abandon, one that drove away all attempts to control, to slow the pace. He parted her legs as he kissed her mouth. His tongue moved in and out, and his hand below echoed the rhythm. The motion of her hips beckoned and tantalized until he came to her swiftly, feeling a tight resistance and then a smooth fluidity as their bodies slid together. She felt like a virgin, he thought, but that was impossible. Or maybe not.

Bracing his arms on either side of her, he moved in a rhythm that ignited her as if he'd touched a flame to her center. She cried out with an explosive, deeply sensual sound that shook him. He felt her contract and then shatter into soft pulsations that drew from him an overwhelming response. He spent himself fully and deeply, joining with her in a bond forged of years-old, unbidden passion. The moment drew out in a long shock of sensation that left him panting, bathed in sweat and stricken to the heart.

He settled atop the covers next to her. Moonlight flooding through the window outlined her slender silhouette. He skimmed his hand over her and finally spoke.

"You're a virgin."

"Um, not anymore." A smile softened her voice.

"I thought you were . . . experienced."

She shifted, propping herself on his chest. "Most people who don't know any better believe New Women are promiscuous." There was a wry, gentle censure in her tone.

"You all but said you have a raft of lovers at your beck and call. You spoke of free love."

"That doesn't mean anyone was ever free to love *me*."

Unexpected tenderness took hold of him. Everything about Lucy startled and moved him. She was the last woman he could imagine winding up with, yet here she was in his arms, where he had never expected to find her. He laid the palm of his hand against hers, feeling the steady, strong cadence of their pulses mingling.

"I am," he said simply, not at all surprised to discover that he wanted her again.

"You're what?"

He pressed her down, kissed her, and she opened to him again, sweetly eager. He went slowly this time, using his hands and mouth at a leisurely pace, exulting in her ecstasy, feeling the wonder of something unexpected and new. "Free . . ." he said in answer to her question, "to love you."

Lucy kept the delicious secret of her new liaison with her husband hidden in her heart. There was nothing illicit about a married woman sleeping with her own husband, she told herself, yet this was something wholly her own, fragile as a soap bubble that could burst to nothingness at the slightest pressure.

She tingled with the sense that the world was brand-new, candy-colored, a place of whimsy and possibility. In the bookshop, she sang as she catalogued books and tallied accounts. On one unforgettable afternoon, Rand found her alone, halfway up the brass ladder, shelving books. Without saying a word, he turned over the Closed sign on the door and seduced her right then and there, with the ladder rolling back and forth and books dropping to the floor. Dime novels of love and adventure that used to seem so silly now had the power to move her to tears. She couldn't wait to get home each day, couldn't wait for night to come, for that was when she moved into the private, velvety-soft world encompassed by the bed she shared with Rand.

One morning, after he had gone to the bank, she and her mother had gone to the conservatory to tend the orchids, a project Viola had recently adopted. Surrounded by the lush growth of palms and cycads and helliconia, Lucy stood gazing out at the lake mist creeping across the lawn. Gradually she became aware of her mother's silent attention.

"What?" she asked, nervously fingering the leaves of a bamboo ginger plant. "Is something the matter?"

"I don't think so." Viola took out a pair of trimming sheers and snipped at an orchid's stray root hairs. "But you seem different."

"Do I?" Lucy ripped the leaf clean off the plant. The secret rose up inside her, wanting to be let out. "I suppose I am."

Viola froze, shears poised around a hank of Spanish moss. "Heavens, you've fallen in love with the man."

Lucy studied the hunting scene on the side of the china teapot. She couldn't deny it, not to her mother. "Believe me, I was the last one to expect that to happen. It's a bit frightening," she admitted.

"What, being in love with your husband?" The very thought of him ignited warm shivers inside her. "It gives him far too much power over me. He can make the sun come out with one smile. How absurd is that?"

"Completely. And it is one of life's sweetest joys." Beaming, Viola admired one of her favorite blooms, the dancing-lady orchid. "I think it might be catching. Eugene has asked Willa Jean to marry him."

Lucy grinned. "Bull and Willa Jean? It's about time. Did she say yes?"

"Of course she did." Viola winked. "You might find yourself in need of a new book-keeper soon."

"Why would she stop working at the shop?"

"Some women choose to direct all their energy to marriage."

"Are you implying I should be doing that?"

"Not at all. But I'm telling you to respect women who choose the traditional role."

"I do. I —" Lucy stopped. Could her mother be right? Was she intolerant of those whose views differed from hers? Overly critical of women who preferred tradition over innovation?

"Love is a gift," Viola said. "We each cherish it in our own way." She cradled a delicate arch of pale, yellow-lipped blossoms in her hand, taking care not to extract the body of the plant from its nest of bark. "I do love the moth orchid, don't you? This one can't exist without the tree to support it. On its own it would die."

Lucy turned away, the loamy humidity of the air in the glass room filling her lungs. An odd and unsettling perception nagged at her, tightening like a noose. She was starting to disappear. When she lay with Rand at night, she melded and fused with him, and even during the day, when they were apart, she felt a powerful connection to him. Because of the new bond growing between them, she ceased to exist as a separate entity; she'd become an adjunct that could not live apart from him.

That was it, she thought, working herself into a panic. That was how a man dominated and controlled a woman. He made her disappear. He transformed her from an independent individual into a clinging attachment dependent on him for everything, even the very air she breathed.

It was a frightening thing, Lucy realized, to be in love with her husband. She did not trust the idea at all.

"Don't go." Rand wrapped his bare arm around Lucy's waist and pulled her naked body snug against his in the bed.

His sleep-warm kisses tickled the back of her neck. "Ah, that's tempting," she admitted, stretching luxuriously, then drinking from a tumbler of water on the bedside table. He made her feel languorous and pampered; she wanted to lie abed and let him pet her all day as if she were a sleek cat. "I'm becoming lazy," she protested as he slipped his hand down in a clever, irresistible caress. His knowledge of her body was much too intimate. As the heated flutters of sensation started, she used the last of her willpower to pull away. "I have a lot of work to do at the shop today."

With much reluctant grumbling, he rose from the bed, walking across the room to the basin. As always, she was quietly mesmerized by his physique. The long, carved sinews of his limbs moved with innate grace, and the terrible scars that marred his right shoulder, back and chest didn't detract from his appeal but added to it. What he'd lost in perfection he'd gained in character.

At first, he'd been self-conscious about his scars, turning the lights down before disrobing and then covering himself hurriedly with a robe each morning.

But as the days passed, he came to understand that the scars were as much a part of him as the color of his eyes or the sound of his laughter. They represented the ordeal that had transformed him into the man she loved.

She leaped from the bed and went to him, wrapping her arms around him from behind. He turned, damp from his washing, his face half lathered for shaving. He bent and kissed her quickly, then gently moved her toward the bed, ignoring the weak, muffled objections she murmured against his mouth.

Sometimes, a chilly shadow swept over Lucy. The perfect abundance of their lives seemed too good to be true. There were still depths in him she hadn't plumbed, mysteries she hadn't revealed. He was a complex man of unexpected passions and temperamental nature. She wasn't sure of their love; it was too new. Too fragile. But strength would come with the years; her mother had assured her of that. They needed to create a history together, and building it would take time.

A distant knock sounded, followed by the tread of footsteps. "Who could that be, so early?" she asked.

"Probably Conn O'Leary, delivering the milk," he said, nuzzling her neck, opening her gown. "I want you again."

She laughed giddily and wound her arms around his neck. "Then you have excellent timing, my love, because I feel exactly the same —"

An urgent tapping sounded at the bedroom door.

Lucy and Rand broke apart like adolescents caught on the front porch. Rand strode to the door and opened it a crack. Lucy held her breath, uneasy that she might have to explain her presence here to his grandmother or worse, to Maggie. She wasn't ready for that, not yet. Their love needed to grow and deepen in private. It was awkward enough that her mother had guessed.

Rand spoke briefly to the caller, then shut the door, a folded note in hand. He walked swiftly to Lucy and kissed her fast and hard. "I've got to go."

"What's the matter?"

"Nothing for you to worry about," he said over his shoulder as he headed for his dressing room.

"Don't you dare hide your troubles from me," she said, pursuing him. "Don't you understand anything yet? Secrecy only

471

means trouble. You know that. You know."

"It's no secret," he said. "But there's no point in worrying you."

"I'm not a child," she said. "I am your wife and an equal partner in this marriage whether you like it or not."

"Fine," he said, shoving his arms into a starched shirt that crackled with each movement. "Late yesterday, the bank's wealthiest clients pulled their lodged deposits. I'm sure you can guess why."

Part Five

The reason husbands and wives do not understand each other is because they belong to different sexes.

— Dorothy Dix

Twenty-Five

The day's trials pressed hard on Rand as he returned home from the bank that afternoon. Failure cut like a knife between his shoulder blades.

The bottom line had been even worse than he'd feared. An influential group of depositors had withdrawn their money from the Union Trust. Then, fearing a run on the bank, others had followed suit. That action had triggered a panic, and by the close of the day, the bank's shares had dropped twenty-five percent.

At a special meeting of the board, the directors had issued an ultimatum — Lucy was to give up The Firebrand and her suffrage work, or Rand would lose his job.

He'd been tempted to stop off at Schultz's beer garden to douse the burn of failure with strong drink, but decided against it. What he wanted most was at home waiting for him.

What he wanted most was his wife and daughter.

The simple clarity of the realization buoyed him. Before Maggie and Lucy had come into his life, a blow like this would have knocked him flat. Yet somehow knowing they were there at the end of the day made even this disaster survivable.

But still, the bank was important to him. For years it had been his sole reason for living. Now the directors were forcing him to choose between his job and Lucy.

He walked up the front steps and let himself in. Standing in the foyer, he put up a hand to loosen his necktie. He envisioned a quiet meal, a rational discussion with his wife over coffee. They would find a way to solve this.

But instead of the tranquil refuge he needed now, he found his house in disarray, paint and placards littering the dining room and Lucy feverishly lettering a sign reading Union Trust Unfair To Women.

He gritted his teeth to forestall a wave of exasperation. "Lucy, what is this about?"

She looked up, her face flushed and hair tousled. "I'm organizing a protest, of course. They mustn't get away with this."

"There will be no protest," he stated. "It's uncalled for."

She set her hands on her hips. "It's absolutely essential, don't you see?"

"No, damn it, I don't see." All the frustrations of the day erupted inside him. "Everything has to be a battle with you, Lucy."

He turned on his heel and stalked out. He'd wanted to come home to peace and quiet, and instead had found her poised for combat. Not trusting himself to say anything more, he left the house, walking the eight blocks to Schultz's.

On the sidewalk outside the beer garden, a workman with a crate of kerosene drums passed by. One of the drums dropped from his load, splitting open as it hit the pavement. Rand acted instinctively, moving out of the way, but the kerosene spattered his shoes and trousers.

"Beg pardon, sir," the workman said, "it was an accident. "No one strike a match," he warned a group of men entering the bar, "or the whole building will go up."

Lucy spent a long time deciding which bed to sleep in. In the end she'd settled in Rand's, for doing otherwise would appear to be a retreat.

Everything has to be a battle with you. She'd been trying to help him. Couldn't he see that?

But when the clock struck ten and then eleven, a sinking disappointment tugged at her. She'd forced herself to face facts. He wasn't coming home. They had discovered the passion in their marriage, but passion didn't take the place of true understanding. What had she given him, after all, but failure at the bank? He had walked away from her. Maybe he was going to stay out all night, drinking and carousing.

The minutes seemed like hours as she lay waiting for him. She'd nearly given up hope when she heard the door open and shut. She didn't know what to say to him and so, for the first time in her life, she took the coward's way out. At the sound of his tread on the bedroom floor, she said nothing, simply pretended to be asleep.

The bed creaked softly when he got in next to her, and she heard his long, slow exhalation of — was it weariness? Indecision? She gritted her teeth to keep from asking him.

He stayed on his side of the bed, not touching her. She didn't move, but breathed evenly as if relaxed and sleeping.

As she stared into blackness, she became aware of two distinct smells. The faint odor of whiskey hung in the air, along with something she could not immediately identify. Wood smoke? No, this was harsher, a bit like lamp oil — or kerosene.

That was too much for Lucy. Pushing herself up to a sitting position, she set her hands on her hips. "Oh, I'm no good at this at all," she burst out.

He shifted, propped himself on one elbow. She could feel him peering through the darkness at her.

"No good at what?" he asked.

"No good at suffering in silence."

"But you were doing so well."

"There's no need for sarcasm." She clambered out of bed and raised the gas jet, then tugged on a robe. Pacing back and forth on the hearth rug, she said, "I must know what is going on."

He sat up in bed, weary resignation on his face. With his hair rumpled, his chest bare and his face shadowed by stubble, he looked dissolute, dangerous . . . and wildly attractive to her. Annoyed, she stopped pacing, folded her arms and glared at him.

"Well?" she prompted.

"Where would you like to start?"

"When you left for work this morning, you expected a problem at the bank, but the world as we know it wasn't ending."

"And it is now?"

She plopped herself onto a divan. "You tell me. You must be honest, and leave nothing out."

"I tried to earlier but you didn't seem inclined to listen."

"I am now."

He poured a small tumbler of water and took a drink. "I have to bring our depositors back to the bank, or I'll be required to resign."

"And they won't come back unless I close my shop. Cease my suffrage work."

His silence affirmed it.

She bit her tongue to hold in an oath. She could feel her temper escalating, so she changed the subject. "What is that smell on your clothes?"

"There was a kerosene spill. I went to Schultz's, and there was a mishap on the sidewalk in front of the place."

"You shouldn't have walked out on me."

"You shouldn't have concluded that the only way to contend with this is to stage a protest."

Restless, Lucy went to the tall French doors. The doors stood open to the summer night, and a light wind lifted the sheer voile curtains. Lights lined the lakeshore like a string of diamonds, and a few vessels bobbed in the harbor. She waited to hear more about the troubles at the bank, but a faint ringing sound distracted her.

Rand frowned. "Who the devil could that be at this hour?"

Exasperated, she tossed him a robe. "We'd best find out before they wake the whole house."

He swore between his teeth and shoved his arms into his robe.

She pulled open the door and hurried through the dim hallway to the stairway. The urgent, metallic *brrr* sound crescendoed as she approached the front door.

Sensing Rand behind her, she stepped aside and let him open it. A wire messenger held out a folded onionskin paper. "For Miss Hathaway," he stated, craning his neck to see into the house.

"That's me." A chill tingled over her scalp as she squinted down at the message. After reading the first three words, she knew the rest. Her mouth was dry with fear.

"Get the buggy," she said. "There's a fire."

Rand hitched the horse himself and drove the gelding hard across the State Street bridge. Beside him, hastily dressed, her hair flying wildly behind her, Lucy clutched the seat and stared intently at the road ahead.

When he turned the buggy onto Gantry Street, his heart seized up. The sight of the burning building sucked him back into nightmare memories, and though he gave no outward sign, his mind roared with fear. Flames shot from the windows of the bookstore, casting a livid glow that pulsed with a life of its own. Unnatural heat slapped at him, and the horse shied and tugged at the reins.

A hose cart crew was already there, aiming a stream at the flames. Some of the neighbors draped soaked rugs over their own shops to protect them from catching fire.

Lucy gave a choked cry and leaped out of the cart even before it rolled completely to a halt. "My shop," she said. "Dear God, my shop —"

He jumped down and grabbed her arm. "Don't go any closer," he ordered her. "Let the crew do its work."

She fought free of him. "But —"

"Can you for once in your goddamned life let someone else be in charge?"

His loud words shocked her into momentary silence.

The marshal came over, wearing oiled overalls with suspenders flapping down around his knees. He tugged them on as he spoke. "This your shop, sir?"

"It's mine," Lucy said. "What happened?"

"Mr. Birney called in the alarm. He heard a loud blast, then saw the flames. Foul play's involved. The police are holding a man who was caught fleeing the scene."

"But who would —" Lucy whipped around to face Rand. The look she turned on him made his blood run cold. "Oh," she said, that one accusatory syllable thrumming with wonder and hurt.

"For Christ's sake," he said. "You know better than that."

"But I know your friends at the bank. This morning, you told me that my shop and my politics were responsible for putting the bank in jeopardy. Do you think this is a coincidence?"

"Marshal, there's a flare-up on the second floor," a crewman yelled. "Must be a supply of kerosene or oil there. We can't get through with the hoses."

"Confound it," the marshal said, hurrying away. "I sent for a ladder cart but it hasn't arrived. The building's a loss for sure unless we get a stream up there."

Rand took one more look at Lucy's face, awash with firelight and suspicion. Letting go of her hand, he gave himself no time for second thoughts. He ran to the hose cart, grabbed a coil and plunged into the burning building.

At dawn, they came like mourners to a funeral, their wraithlike forms gliding silently through a street hung with fog and smoke. The clammy dampness of the morning plastered Lucy's hair to her forehead and neck, but she hardly noticed.

Deborah Silver and Kathleen Kennedy arrived first, escorted by their husbands. They shared embraces, shed tears, murmured words of sympathy and devastation.

Soon after, Patience and Willa Jean showed up, accompanied by Bull Waxman.

Holding her arm around Lucy's waist, Deborah said, "We're so sorry for your loss." Though blond and petite as a fairy princess, Deborah had always possessed a startling strength, a quality for which Lucy was grateful at a time like this. Unable to find her voice, she simply stared dull-eyed at the shop in Gantry Street.

The tradesman's shingle, which she'd once hung with such pride and hope, now dangled askew, flapping sluggishly in the breeze. The picture window that used to frame a cozy view of the shop lay in a thousand icicle-shaped slivers. Inside the jagged maw of the door, everything lay shrouded in a lifeless gray mantle of old smoke. The sharp odor of incineration stung Lucy's eyes and throat.

Even as they watched, the shingle fell with a *thunk* to the boardwalk. The sudden sound and movement laid waste to the last of Lucy's self-control. Her locked knees gave way; she staggered back and would have fallen, but a large male caught her — she didn't know if it was Dylan or Tom. Moving like an old woman, she slowly lowered herself to the boardwalk across the street.

Everything felt broken beyond repair. Nothing would ever be right again.

And Lucy, who never, ever cried, wept with every inch of her heart. She wept for lost hopes and shattered dreams, for the happiness that had been hers for such a brutally short period of time. She wept for all the times she'd tried and failed, for all the foolish things she'd done. She wept until she was completely barren, hollow as a porcelain doll, with nothing inside her but a cold, ringing emptiness.

The others seemed stunned to silence by her grief and kept a respectful distance. Tom, Bull and Dylan stood off to the side, speaking with an investigator for the Board of Fire. Eventually Lucy realized the world was not going to stop because of her loss. She had to take the next breath of air, had to take the next step . . . even if she wasn't quite sure where she was going. Through damp, grief-blurred eyes, she stared at the charred brick building.

"I can't believe it's gone," Willa Jean said. "There was a time when I couldn't read or write. Couldn't sum up the fingers on my own hands. But I learned, honey. I learned because I didn't want to be a maid all my life. And now —"

"You're a good bookkeeper with or without the shop," Lucy said. "You'll find another position." She tried to smile. "You'll find a place that can afford to pay you more."

"You'll rebuild," Kathleen said stoutly.

"No," Lucy said.

"What? No what?" Deborah asked.

"I cannot reopen. Ever."

"Of course you can," Willa Jean said. "You must. The Firebrand is too important to lose."

"A *life* is too important to lose," Lucy said, remembering the soul-freezing terror she'd felt last night, watching Rand plunge into the fire. It had taken the strength of two crewmen to hold her back. She'd barely felt their bruising grip on her arms, barely tasted the sharp, choking smoke that poisoned the air, barely heard the thin sound of her own voice, screaming her husband's name.

"No shop or idea is worth that," she concluded. "I'll not pursue an enterprise that endangers people." She had relived the night a hundred times already. Rand had fought the fire like a man possessed while Lucy had screamed his name, trying to follow him into the building despite the restraining hands. An explosion had blown out the upper windows, filling the night with white light and shattering glass. After the blast she'd been sure she'd lost him. Then he'd appeared out of the inferno, dragged the hose inside and fought for an hour to subdue the blaze. Neither he nor the crew would rest until the blaze died. Much later, he had limped to the wagon and collapsed in the back while she drove home. While he lay in exhausted sleep, she'd sent word to her friends and returned to Gantry Street.

"Then they've won," Patience said with quiet finality. "Those who oppose you have won."

Lucy nodded slowly, conceding defeat, possibly for the first time in her life. "Yes, they have."

Deborah and Tom drove her home. "Would you like me to come in?" Deborah offered. "If you want, I'll sit with you."

"Thank you, but no," Lucy said, hugging

her briefly. "I'll be fine." She bade them goodbye and went inside.

She made her way through the early-morning quiet of the house, pausing when she spied Maggie, Viola and Grace in the breakfast room.

Maggie jumped down and ran to her. "It's scary, Mama," she said, burying her face in Lucy's skirts. "Is the shop really gone? Why is Papa all sooty and sound asleep?"

Lucy struggled to gather her thoughts.

"He's all right," she said. "He was exhausted from fighting the fire." She propelled Maggie toward the kitchen door. "Ask Mrs. Meeks to get your breakfast."

"What a terrible catastrophe to befall your little shop," Grace said.

"How could this happen?" Viola asked.

Lucy swallowed, her throat tight with despair. "The fire marshal has confirmed it's a case of arson."

"Someone set the fire deliberately? But why?" asked Grace.

Lucy explained about the bank, adding, "A man can be fierce when his livelihood is threatened." Composing herself, she added, "The arsonist will soon find out that even though The Firebrand is gone, my convictions are not."

Twenty-Six

Over the next few days, life returned to an eerie normal pace in the Higgins household. It was as if The Firebrand had never existed, had never been filled with women's laughter and spirited conversation, a gathering place where women could feel safe and empowered by their convictions.

Rand went to the bank each day, and the crisis there continued. After the panic, the depositors hadn't come back, and Lucy knew he balanced on the knife edge between success and failure. Their tenuous bond felt weaker now, strained by the ordeal. They were both tense and short-tempered, their discussions frequently deteriorating into arguments.

Lucy mourned for the shop as though she had lost a loved one. There were hours when she was able to forget about The Firebrand and her cause for whole minutes at a time. But sometimes her heart constricted with unbearable grief. She'd built the bookstore from the ground up. She'd put her heart and sweat and soul into it. And in one night it had been taken away.

She felt impossibly selfish, knowing she had so much — a husband and daughter she adored, friends who cared about her and a new love she'd never thought would be hers.

And still it hurt. She could not bear to go anywhere near Gantry Street. Seeing the black scar of the ruined shop would be too much for her. She tried to content herself with looking after Maggie, minding the house and writing lengthy letters to the Legislature on behalf of women's rights.

But even defeat didn't stop her from making new plans. Secret plans. Rand's fury over her last protest had proven he didn't understand her way of doing things. Business must be attended to. Lucy believed she could do something to recoup the losses suffered at the bank. Its survival depended upon finding depositors, and she was acquainted with the most famous lady banker in America. She wrote more letters, rode out to meetings on her high-wheeled bicycle, and life went on.

Rand didn't get home until late one night, long after supper was over and everyone in the house was asleep. Everyone, of course, except Lucy and Silky. With the cat in her lap, she sat fully dressed, too wound up with doubts and worries to relax. Rand entered the room and stared at her for so long that she held her breath.

When she would have spoken, he held up his hand, the old scars white around the livid, fresh burns he'd suffered the night of the fire. "We have some things to discuss, Lucy," he said. "I'd prefer to do it without arguing."

"Why do you immediately assume I'm sitting here waiting to argue with you?"

He sent her an ironic look. "Because you're awake?"

"I have no intention of —"

"Do you want to hear who burned your shop or not?" he cut in.

She shifted to the edge of her seat. Disturbed by the movement, the cat dropped soundlessly to the floor and slipped away.

"It was Jasper Lamott," he said. "He paid Guy Smollett to set fire to the place. They've both been arrested, and with luck we've seen the last of them."

It's a blight on the neighborhood, and no decent Christian will be sorry to see it wiped out. She remembered Lamott's words, spat at her in a rage when she'd encountered him at the bank. "Are you surprised?" she asked.

"No. But don't expect all the lost depositors to come flocking back now. The bank's shares dropped again today. The Union Trust is still in trouble."

"Because of me," Lucy said.

"Because of themselves," he corrected her.

She caught her breath. Not long ago, he never would have admitted such a thing. Agitated, she got up and walked out to the balcony, letting the breeze off the lake cool her face. A full moon blazed from a clear sky, casting its blue-white glow over everything. The smells of the water and the rose garden filled the air, dizzying as a drug.

She felt him walk up behind her, felt his arms slip around her waist. Closing her eyes, she leaned back against him, feeling herself relax for the first time in days.

"I want everything to be all right," she said, her whisper mingling with the warm summer wind.

"It is when we're like this."

But even as she turned in his arms and let him lead her into the bedroom, she wondered if it would be enough.

"Mama, how come you started sleeping in Papa's bed?" Maggie asked, digging in the dirt of the kitchen garden later that day.

Lucy froze in the act of picking snap peas. The dreaded question caused her brain and throat to seize up. How long had Maggie known? Why did she have to ask today, of all days? There would never be a good time, she realized. She was bound to have to explain sooner or later.

"Why do you think?" she managed to ask, racking her brain for the proper response. How on earth had Maggie figured it out? Surely the help knew better than to discuss their employer's affairs in front of his daughter.

"Because he is new," Maggie said simply. "Whenever I get a new toy, I want to play with it all the time. I even want to sleep with it."

"I suppose that's as good an explanation as any." The hot afternoon sun beat down on her head. She should have put on a sunbonnet, but she'd been too distracted to bother with a hat today, or shoes for that matter.

Maggie harvested an abundant handful of pole beans and put them in the basket. "Well, I don't blame you," she said, her face sober with contemplation, "I just love Papa. Don't you?"

Lucy was unprepared for the flood of emotion that engulfed her on hearing her daughter's simple question. Maggie loved so effortlessly and so honestly. Lucy thought about the world of emotion and sensation she had discovered in the arms of her husband. She wanted to be certain, but true conviction eluded her. In some ways, he still held himself away from her, silent with private thoughts she could not fathom.

Instead of answering Maggie's question, she said, "So it's all right, then, that I . . . sleep in his bed?"

"Uh-huh."

"And you like living here?"

"Uh-huh." Like the kitchen garden, Maggie was blossoming, growing bright and healthy, drawn upward by the summer sun. We have something precious here, thought Lucy. We are building a home, a family.

But she had put it all at risk.

The idea enraged her as she stabbed a trowel down into the dirt to dislodge a stubborn dockweed. Damn the banking clients and their self-righteous ways.

Lucy put aside her discontent and gave her full attention to Maggie. The little girl had shouted with delight when Lucy had come down to breakfast in dungarees and an old shirt, with kerchiefs for their heads and gloves for their hands, announcing that she and Maggie would spend the day gardening. The truth was, the flower and vegetable gardens were among Lucy's chief delights in her new home. In the flat over the shop, she'd managed to tend a few potted herbs and African violets. The lushness of the lawn and gardens here were riches beyond compare.

Pulling off her kerchief to mop her neck, she wished it could be enough.

"Maggie, do you miss the shop very much?" she asked.

Sitting back on her heels, Maggie munched idly on a raw bean. "No. You were always busy at the shop. I like it when you're with me all day long."

The blunt reply startled Lucy, but she didn't say anything. The dockweed had a long thick taproot that had embedded itself deep in the soil. She dropped to her knees to scoop out the dirt around it. She paused to push a stray lock of hair off her forehead, knowing she'd smudged dirt there, but not really caring. The day was hot; she was sweating, but that only made the long bath she planned for later seem all the more inviting.

Digging deeper into the earth, she tried to imagine what Rand's day was like, with the bank shares slipping lower each day. Even after the disgrace of Jasper Lamott, things hadn't improved. The conservative clients still held her responsible, claiming Lamott would not have had to take such extreme measures if she had given up her shop and her cause. Would the board take action today? Would they censure Rand or — God forbid — terminate him?

He loved banking and he loved the Union Trust. What if she were responsible for taking that away from him? What would it do to her proud, brooding husband? To their fragile new love? What would it do to their comfortable way of life?

She looked down Bellevue Avenue, with its tree-lined parkway and endless view of the lake, and marveled at how quickly she'd come to regard this place as home.

Fitting both hands around the thick root of the dock-weed, she gave a tug, loosening it by scant degrees.

You can solve this, she told herself, tugging harder.

She could give up her crusading and stay home with Maggie. She tugged the weed harder. Was it so terrible, staying home to raise her child like a conventional mother? Maggie liked it. Lucy liked it. The bank directors and Rand were sure to like it.

With so much in her life, she didn't need the added burden of social reform, did she? Could she stay home and be a banker's wife? How long would she be content with that?

Forever. But even as her heart spoke the

word, her mind recognized the lie. There was room in her for other passions.

Frustrated by her efforts to extract the weed, she planted her bare feet in the sun-warmed soil and pulled with all her might. Grunting with the effort, she threw her weight into the task. The weed resisted stoutly, and she tugged again and again. It was suddenly a personal battle, her against the weed. She was not about to be defeated by a mere weed, for heaven's sake.

"Mama, who is that lady?" Maggie asked, standing up and pointing at the main driveway.

A woman in a peach-colored dress and matching bonnet alighted from a hansom cab.

"Hello!" Maggie called, waving. "Hello, over here!"

Lucy recognized the woman at the same moment the weed gave way. She ripped it from the earth, and the momentum sent her reeling. She landed on her backside, crushing a cucumber frame and several cucumbers beneath her.

For a moment she was too stunned to move. Then, picking up each arm like a marionette on a string, she climbed to her feet. She didn't bother brushing herself off as she hurried across the yard. She was far too sweaty and filthy for any brushing-off to help.

She hardly felt the gravel driveway beneath her bare feet, hardly heard the crunch and grind of the departing cab. Her entire being was riveted on the silk-clad caller.

Somehow, Lucy managed to arrange her sunburned, dirt-smudged face into a smile.

"Hello," she said in a voice she scarcely recognized. "We met once before, but you probably won't remember. I'm Lucy. Lucy Hathaway." Then she forced herself to do the impossible. She took off her filthy gloves, dropped them on the ground and extended her hand in greeting to Diana Layton Higgins.

Twenty-Seven

Maggie had seen the lady's face before. It was smooth and white, with sharply outlined red lips, like the face of the china doll Grammy Grace had given her. But there was something special about this face. Something familiar.

Then she remembered.

This was the lady in the old brown photographs. This was the lady in the fancy painting that used to hang in the parlor. Papa had taken that picture down and moved it to an upstairs room where nobody went.

There were bees in Maggie's stomach again, buzzing around like they did when she felt scared and shy. She clutched at her mother and hid behind her, peeking up at the doll-lady.

Her hat was enormously fancy, with feathers and flowers piled high as the sky. Long, glossy yellow ringlets hung down one side. Her stiff petticoats swished when she moved, and a gigantic bustle adorned her behind. Sally Saltonstall said bustles were fashionable, but to Maggie, they looked like a big bunch of bows and nonsense.

"I'm terribly sorry," the lady said in a soft, polite voice. "But you're right. I'm afraid I don't recall meeting you." She leaned to the side to get a better look at Maggie. "Is this your little boy?"

Maggie scowled. That again. Just because she didn't wear a dress, people were always calling her a boy. Worse than that, they always called her *little*.

"Miss — Mrs. Higgins," said Mama, "please come inside. We'll just get cleaned up, and then we'll join you in the parlor."

The lady puckered her forehead, but she went up the front steps with them and stepped into the foyer with its checkerboard floor and the staircase with the railing that was perfect for sliding down. She took off her skinny lace gloves and turned around slowly, looking at the naughty fountain of the boy peeing and the shiny woodwork of the staircase. "So this is Randolph's house," she said in a quiet voice.

Maggie didn't like it when people called her papa *Randolph* like he was a street or something.

"Please have a seat in the parlor." Mama's voice sounded tight, and her hand, which Maggie still clung to, felt all sweaty. "I'll send for some refreshments, and when we get cleaned up, we'll join you."

The white forehead puckered again. "I am here to see my — to see Randolph. And our daughter, Christine."

"Maggie," Maggie yelled before she could stop herself. She stomped her foot. "Maggie, Maggie, Maggie."

Mama held her shoulders to calm her down.

"You see," Mama said, "this is Maggie. I believe her father sent you a photograph of the two of them. Didn't you receive it?"

"Yes, but —" The fancy lady got very quiet. Her eyes grew as large as two blue marbles, two very wet blue marbles. "Dear Lord, *you're* Christine," she said, and she sank down low. Her skirts swished on the shiny floor as she put her face very close to Maggie's. "I didn't recognize you at first," she said. "But I do now. My daughter." To Maggie's horror, the lady started to cry. "My beautiful daughter."

Mama kept hold of Maggie's shoulders as though she knew Maggie wanted to run away and hide. Leaning down, Mama whispered very fast, "Everything will be fine. I promise."

Forcing herself to be brave, Maggie stepped forward.

The lady hugged Maggie, covering her in

a flowery smell that stirred up the bees in her stomach. She didn't know what to do about this crying lady, so she stood quite still and pressed her lips together until they hurt.

"You'll understand if she's a bit bashful," Mama said. "Please, if I could just get her cleaned up —"

"Of course." Sniffing into an embroidered handkerchief, the lady went into the parlor.

Mama told Nichol about the refreshments and hurried upstairs with Maggie. "We must be quick," she said. "We have a lot to talk about with Mrs. — Oh, I haven't the slightest idea what to call her." Mama was talking fast, more to herself than to Maggie. And the whole time, she was peeling off their clothes and scrubbing away with a damp towel. "Of all the times for her to show up unannounced."

Maggie brightened, tugging on her blue frock. "Let's tell her to go away."

"No." Mama brushed Maggie's hair and stuck a big bow in it. Then she did her own hair, twisting it into a braid. After that, with the shoe-button hook clenched between her teeth, she bent down to fasten Maggie's dress. Maggie had never seen Mama get them dressed so quickly.

"She's a very important person in our lives, Maggie, and we must be polite and gracious to her." Mama spoke around the button hook in her mouth. "Do you understand?"

Maggie stuck out her foot so Mama could put a shoe on and hook the buttons. They were the shiny black shoes she wore to church, and they pinched.

Mama pulled on a petticoat and plain blue dress. She checked herself in the mirror and scowled, taking up the towel to scrub her face some more. "All right," Mama said, grabbing her hand. "Let's go."

The lady was in the parlor where Maggie wasn't allowed to touch anything. When she saw Maggie, she smiled, but she cried again, too.

"My darling," she said, holding out both hands.

Mama gave Maggie a gentle shove and she went forward and put her hands into the lady's. "Sit here by me," the lady said, and Maggie obeyed, hoisting herself up to the cold, glossy silk of the best settee.

"So," the lady said to Mama, taking a glass of lemonade from a tray, "you must be the governess."

Mama sat down in another chair. "Actually, quite a bit has happened since I first discovered Maggie's father," she said.

"You're the one, then. *That* Miss Hathaway. The one who rescued my baby. How can I ever thank you?"

"You needn't, Mrs. —" Mama stopped as if she had forgotten the lady's name. "Well." Mama smoothed her hands over her dark blue skirt. "We didn't know you were coming. You must have left San Francisco before getting Rand's latest wire."

The visitor's forehead wrinkled when Mama said *Rand*. "He sent another wire?"

"He had some news for you. The fact is, we were married about a month ago," Mama explained. "Rand and I, that is."

The lady made a little hissing sound through her teeth. *"Married?"*

"With a flower and music *and* a kiss," Maggie said, unable to stay silent. She didn't like this visitor. She didn't like her at all. "She's my mother," Maggie yelled, jumping down from the settee and running to Mama. "Not you!"

The lady put her lemonade back on the tray. "Have you any sherry?" she asked.

Twenty-Eight

The bank was still on shaky ground, and foolishly, Rand was about to make things worse. Lamott was gone in ignominy but Crabtree, McClean and the others stayed on. Though less fanatic, the remaining directors were as stodgy and intractable as the departed Lamott. They wanted Rand to promise to keep Lucy in check, to promise The Firebrand would never be rebuilt. He hadn't given them that promise. He refused to sacrifice Lucy's dream for the sake of the bank, even if it meant losing his position and starting down an unknown path he'd never trodden.

The notion put an unexpected energy in his stride as he returned home that day and walked into the house, reaching up to loosen his tie. Female voices drifted from the formal parlor. They must have visitors, since Lucy and Maggie ordinarily avoided the fussy room, which his grandmother had filled with art treasures, fragile knickknacks and costly antiques.

Leaving his tie in place, he stepped into the parlor . . . and nearly stumbled.

His mouth dried as though he'd ingested cold ashes. Then, with a mechanical courtesy that masked his stunned senses, he bowed from the waist.

"Hello, Diana," he said to his former wife.

In a rustle of silk, she stood up, a blond goddess, every bit as lovely as she'd been the day he'd married her. The years had only deepened her beauty, polishing her with a sheen of sophistication.

He crossed the room and took her extended hand, raising it to his mouth. Why couldn't he remember the feel of her hand in his, the smell and taste of her? He had the distinct sensation of meeting a stranger.

"Dear Randolph," she said in a soft, beguiling voice. "I apologize for arriving unannounced, but I had the worst fear that — Oh, never mind. It's so silly."

As she sank back into her seat, he took a moment to greet the others in the room. Maggie jumped down from the settee and ran to him. "You're home!"

He picked her up in his arms, and instantly his heart thawed out. The familiar, welcome weight of her seemed to bring the world back into balance.

On another settee were Viola and Grace, the former looking as though she stood before of firing squad and the latter exhibiting a cautious pleasure. Grandmother had always liked Diana, mourning her departure more than Rand ever had.

Alone in an armchair sat Lucy, her dark dress and pulled-back hair giving her anxious face an unnatural pallor. She said nothing. He could not get used to a silent Lucy, for she always had something to say. Until now.

"When did you get here?" he asked. "Where are you staying?"

"I have rooms at the Palmer House," Diana said. "But I thought —" Flustered, she started again. "I've been simply overcome, seeing Grace and my darling Christine again." She pressed a lace-edged handkerchief to her flawless cheek.

"She thought I was a boy at first," Maggie said. "Just like you did."

He felt a flash of chagrin, recalling that day. "I suppose it's because you were so tiny when we lost you." Kissing her on the head, he set her down.

"When I saw you today," Diana said to Maggie, "you didn't look anything like the photograph your father sent me."

The photograph.

Suspicions swirled and started to harden inside him. What sort of coincidence was it, that she'd come to him after seeing the photograph?

An awkward silence descended over the group, punctuated by the ticking of the ormolu clock on the mantel.

Maggie shifted from one foot to another. She went over to Lucy to whisper in her ear.

"I'm sure you both have so much to discuss," Lucy said, standing up. "We shall leave you to it."

Taking their cue, Viola and Grace stood. Grace leaned over her cane. "We'll see you tomorrow."

"Of course." Diana's mouth curved into a melting smile. "That's ever so kind of you, Grandmother Grace."

As the four of them left the room, Diana's gaze lingered hungrily on Maggie. Rand wondered if he'd looked that way, so desperate with longing, when he'd first found out about her.

"She's absolutely gorgeous," Diana said.

"Yes."

"What a blessed, blessed miracle." All in a rush, she went to him, burying her face against his chest. "I never thought I'd feel this way again, ever," she said, weeping. "Oh, Randolph, where do we begin again? How do we begin again?"

He had no answer for her. His trying day

had extended into a nightmare. He did not recognize the feel of her, or her smell. The shape of her pressed against him was alien, awkward. He didn't remember her.

Except that she had given him a daughter.

He took her by the shoulders and held her away from him. "What are you doing here, Diana? What do you want?"

She searched his face with a misty-eyed gaze. He could feel her stare linger on the scars, but unlike she'd done years ago, she didn't recoil. He dropped his hands to his sides.

"I came because I want my baby back," she said at last, her voice breaking. "And my husband."

At one time, he would have sold his soul to hear those words. But that was a lifetime ago. "You were surprised, weren't you?" he said.

"I never imagined Christine —"

"By my recovery," he interrupted. "The photograph I sent surprised you, didn't it? You never expected me to get better."

"Oh, Randolph. I am more than surprised. I'm astounded and profoundly grateful."

"That you can bear to look at me?" He turned sharply away. "I'm very happy for you."

She pursued him, her face so dramatically pale that he suspected her distress was genuine. "Randolph, you must give me a chance. I'm a different person than I was so long ago. You cannot blame me for my actions when I was devastated by grief."

He said nothing to that. There was nothing to say that she would understand.

"I didn't expect to find you wed to a stranger," she said, her voice thin with woe. "Honestly, Randolph, what could you be thinking, marrying that woman?"

He'd been thinking of Maggie when he'd first done it, yet his marriage to Lucy had become something else entirely. But he wasn't about to explain himself to Diana.

"*That woman* saved Maggie's life," he said. "She raised her, and Maggie loves her."

"And I'll be forever grateful," Diana said. "But I am Christine's mother."

"You gave her life," he conceded. "But you lost her — wc both lost her — when she was so very young, Diana. She has no more memory of you than she does of being called Christine." He saw her wince. "Look, she didn't remember me, either. But our daughter has a loving heart. As time goes on, she's coming to know me."

"As she'll come to know me."

"Naturally you'll be welcome to visit Maggie," he said.

She pressed her small fist to her bosom. Then, without warning, she surged against him again, her arms going around his neck. She smelled of flowers and hair dressing, and she felt as soft and fragile as a bird. "It's not enough," she whispered against his neck. "I want you back, Randolph. I want us to be a family again."

"It can't be like that," he said. "Lucy is my wife."

"You can fix this, Randolph." Her fingers brushed through his hair. "You can change this and make things right. You don't need that woman anymore. No judge in the county would deny you a divorce. It's clear you only married her so you could be near Christine. An annulment might even be possible."

"Your understanding of the law has always been impressive. They say you managed to divorce me in record time."

She swallowed hard, tightened her arms around him. "Oh, Randolph. I was so terribly frightened, and so filled with grief for Christine that I couldn't think straight."

She'd thought straight enough to extract a huge settlement from him — a settlement he could ill afford at the time. Still, as she said, that was all in the past and he found he didn't care anymore. "I won't deny you a relationship with Maggie," he said, reaching up to unlink her arms from around his neck. "You gave birth to her and you have a right to be in her life. I'm sure we can arrange for Maggie to spend time with you."

She encompassed the room with a sweep of her arm. "I should have come back sooner, I admit that." In a swish of silk skirts, she turned to him. "Now I am home. This is where I belong."

"You made your choice," he said. "You fled from your monster husband. You only came back because you've learned that some wounds do heal." His gaze glided over her, head to toe. "But some others don't."

She had the grace to flush before turning away. "Must I beg you?"

"Don't bother. It won't work." He went to the door and leaned out into the foyer. "Mr. Nichol, have Bowen bring the buggy around." He caught a glimpse of Diana's expression and realized that he couldn't simply pack her off to Palmer House. "I'll be driving our guest to her hotel."

"What must I do to prove I'm sincere, Randolph?" Her voice rose in desperation. "I want things to be as they once were for us. Christine is back, my darling. Every-

512

thing will be perfect now, if only you'll remember the good times, and not the terrifying weeks after the fire." She ran a hand over the clock. That pale hand on the pale porcelain evoked a memory. At one time, all of this had been for her. He'd built this house and filled it with fine things for Diana, hoping to lure her back. And it finally had.

He went to the window to see if the buggy was ready. Hand in hand, Lucy and Maggie walked across the broad lawn toward Maggie's favorite climbing tree. Nimble as a squirrel, Maggie swung up to the first branch. Brushing back her skirts, Lucy followed, her head thrown back in laughter. Then the branch Lucy held bowed ominously, and she fell to the ground, still laughing as she brushed herself off.

"Things can change in an instant," he said quietly, turning to Diana, who was admiring the silver tea service now. "You know that. This could all be gone, and I could find myself living in a flat up over a shop."

"That's the silliest thing I've ever heard."

Nichol came in to announce that the buggy was ready. Rand led her, protesting, out to the front driveway. Lucy spotted them, and brought Maggie over. "I'll be driving Diana to her hotel," Rand said.

"Goodbye," Maggie said. "It was nice to meet you."

Diana's eyes glittered with tears. She went down on one knee, drawing her daughter close for a hug. Diana's love for the child was evident and genuine. Nothing about this situation was going to be easy, Rand thought.

He handed her up into the buggy, and took a seat beside her. He tried to catch Lucy's eye, but she avoided his gaze. Later, then, he thought. Later . . . but he had no idea what he would say to her. Lucy could move him with a single glance; Diana left him cold. But Lucy didn't seem to know that about him.

Clicking his tongue to the horse, he headed down the driveway. Diana ran her hand over the grain leather of the seat. The gesture filled him with a cynical understanding. She didn't want him. She merely wanted what he had. They drove in awkward silence across the bridge and into town. Pulling back on the reins, he rolled the buggy to a halt in front of the elegant hotel. A boy came forward to hold the horse, and Rand helped Diana down. With his hand at the small of her back, he guided her into the lobby.

The lobby was richly carpeted and furnished with gilt conversation chairs, potted plants and glowing chandeliers. Groups of guests spoke together in low, cultured murmurs. The resemblance to Sterling House was eerie.

Her face turned paper white, and he wondered if she still suffered as he did from memories of that night. She had been wounded, too, perhaps in ways he had never understood.

"Diana —"

"Honestly, I can't understand why you refuse to do the right thing, Randolph. I've come back, and Christine is back. We can be a family again." The color in her cheeks returned, and her bright gaze flashed over him. "You've done so well since we were last together."

A slight edge in her voice raised his suspicions. She had known about Christine for weeks. Why had she waited until now to make her appearance? "How would you feel if I told you my circumstances have changed recently?"

"I don't understand."

Playing his hunch, he explained, "At the bank. I expect to be dismissed."

"Nonsense," she objected, folding her arms in front of her. "You're just saying that to drive me away. Why would they want to be rid of you?"

"The bank board and its most important investors object to Lucy's political views."

"Just what sort of views does she hold?"

"She favors universal suffrage and believes in equality between the sexes. She owned a radical bookstore which was recently burned."

"That's a relief, at least."

"I doubt she'll stop organizing meetings and marches to support her cause." He remembered a time when he'd felt the same disapproval he saw on Diana's face, and marveled at how completely Lucy had won him over. "A number of the bank's clients objected to Lucy's behavior, and withdrew their deposits in protest."

"Then you must bring them back, of course."

"They won't come back unless Lucy gives up her cause."

"If that woman loved you, she would do so immediately." Diana pressed her point. "It's true, Randolph, you know it is. If she will not make this sacrifice for her husband, then clearly you're not as important to her as her cause."

Twenty-Nine

The local papers made much of Diana's return. Lucy read them with a sort of sick fascination. She pressed the heels of her hands to her temples, picturing their meeting the previous afternoon. She could not have been at more of a disadvantage — hatless, sunburned, sweating and dirty. In contrast, Diana had resembled a visiting queen. Cool and beautiful, she'd regarded Maggie with distaste until Lucy had explained that the little mop-headed boy in the garden was actually her daughter. Disapproval had turned instantly to adoration, and as far as Lucy could tell, it was genuine.

And why not? It wasn't every day a woman was reunited with the child she'd given up for dead.

Maggie had handled the reunion with typical aplomb, though she'd clung to Lucy's hand for dear life.

The papers described Diana as a returning heroine, the aggrieved mother back to reclaim her husband and child from the crazed radical who had stolen them both. Lucy longed to know what Rand thought of

517

this development, but he had stayed out late last night, leaving her to grapple with a new terror — the fear that Diana would win him back.

She had no chance to speak to him, for he went to work early, and then Diana arrived before breakfast.

"I know it's early," she said, "but you understand, I couldn't stay away."

Lucy studied the beautiful, hungry eyes, the exact same eyes she saw each time she looked at Maggie. "Of course." She asked Nichol to send for her.

Maggie came tripping down the wide staircase, still in her nightgown. When she spied Diana, she stopped. "Hello," she said.

"You haven't had your breakfast yet," Lucy said, her heart breaking even as she took charge of the situation. "And look who has come to see you." She led the way to the breakfast room.

Diana took a seat and opened her arms to Maggie. "Please," she said in a faint voice. "It's been so very long."

Maggie looked to Lucy for direction, and Lucy forced herself to nod encouragingly. The little girl climbed into Diana's lap. Mrs. Meeks served the tea and biscuits, her florid cheeks even redder than usual as she stole furtive glances at the former Mrs. Higgins.

518

And Maggie, bless her, took the situation in stride. Before long she was chatting away, recounting some exploit with Ivan while Diana listened with rapt attention. A chill shadow slid over Lucy as she stood in the doorway, watching them. They were so alike, Maggie and her natural mother. Both so pretty and graceful, as though they had been born to be in this room, this house, this life.

She wanted to shout at Diana to go away, to leave them alone to sort through this ordeal. But Diana didn't seem inclined to go anywhere. Lucy was at a loss. She didn't want to give the impression that she would allow Diana to simply push her out of the way, no matter how powerful a claim the other woman had, both on Maggie and on Rand. But at the same time, she didn't want to keep Maggie away from the woman who had given her life.

Lucy wondered if, under different circumstances, Diana might even be someone she could like. Rand's first wife was much like many of the young women of Miss Boylan's — well-mannered and educated, from a good family. As the moments passed, Lucy's confidence faltered. She felt herself slipping into the shadow of her former self, the outspoken misfit no one understood, or wanted.

"Nichol!" Rand's voice rang through the house. "Nichol, where did you put those papers —" He stepped into the breakfast room and fell silent. Lucy tried to read the expression on his face as he regarded Diana and Maggie, but his eyes were hooded. "Diana," he said.

She put Maggie down and hurried over to him. "Oh, Randolph!" She rushed forward and embraced him. "You're home."

"I forgot some papers —" he began.

"Then you can stay home with us all day," Maggie said. "Say you will, Papa. You don't have to go back to that old bank."

Lucy knew her heart was in her eyes as she watched them — Rand and Diana and their little girl, together again. What would it take for them to resume their lives together? Diana was more beautiful than the sun and filled with contrition about her past mistakes. She was the mother of his child. And she wanted her husband back.

Beauty, sincerity, history, commitment. How could Lucy compete with that?

In an agony of uncertainty, she slipped out of the room without glancing their way again. This was it, then, the thing her mother hadn't told her about being in love. The pain, when it came, was as intense as the ecstasy.

She went to the conservatory, hoping to find her mother there. Of late, she had come to depend on her mother's wisdom in matters of the heart, but Viola was nowhere in sight.

Feeling weary, Lucy sat down on a wrought-iron chair. Tropical plants filled the air with a lush, greenish haze. Grace's treasured palms, ginger and helliconias filled the glass-walled room with exotic life. Lucy studied the blooming orchids, their delicate pink lips parted to reveal the purple tongues at their centers. The long arching branches of delicate color exuded a fragrance that, for some reason, filled her with sadness. The clinging epiphytes could not exist without the trees that supported them.

Rand startled her, stepping alone into the long, glass room. "I've been looking for you," he said.

"I'm not hiding. I thought you'd want . . . some time with her."

He sat down next to her. Even with the smell of flowers hanging heavy in the conservatory, Lucy detected the cloying odor of Diana's perfume, lingering in his hair and on his skin. "I had no idea she would come back."

"But she has." Lucy took a deep breath

and forced herself to ask, "Where did you go last night? I waited up, but you never came." She hated the sound of her own words, so laced with suspicion and uncertainty. Was that what their marriage was to be like, with Diana back?

"Diana seemed upset by all the upheaval, so I took her to Anspach's for luncheon and afterward escorted her back to Palmer House."

Lucy had always wondered what it would be like to be the helpless sort, needing her hand held over every bump in the road. Now that Diana was back, Lucy suspected there would be many nights like this.

"Just what is it that she expects?"

"She wants to turn back time." The morning sunlight filled the conservatory with a diffuse brightness that played over every detail — his strong physique and glossy dark hair, his bold features; even the scars had a certain nobility to them.

Lucy took a deep breath, wondering if Diana saw what she saw when she looked at him. "You mean Diana wants to pick up where you left off. She wants to be your wife again. Maggie's mother."

A pause. Then: "Yes."

"And what will you do about it?" Lucy braced herself for the answer. This was probably the fantasy Rand had dreamed of for five years — his broken family made whole again. A daughter to love and protect, a beautiful wife who was content to fulfill tradition rather than striking out on her own as Lucy had.

She saw the situation with searing clarity through Rand's eyes. History was repeating itself. Just as Pamela Byrd had destroyed his family by following her ambitions, so was Lucy.

He had forgiven his mother, and he understood Lucy, but that didn't make it any easier to accept. Diana had arrived, holding out the promise of order and serenity. And tradition, which he'd yearned for since he was a boy.

Say it, she told herself. Just say it. Tell him you love him. Tell him . . . But her throat closed, and she couldn't speak. The fragrance of the exotic flowers nearly choked her. She was terrified that her love wouldn't matter enough to him.

"Lucy," he said, rising from the chair, "it's very complicated."

With those words, she knew. She knew he was preparing her for a blow. With both of Maggie's natural parents present, Lucy didn't have a legal leg to stand on. Before long, she'd be regarded as a kind stranger who deserved their gratitude, but not a place in their lives.

His choice was almost laughably easy. Did he prefer a beautiful wife in her traditional, feminine role, or an awkward, intense woman dedicated to a controversial cause?

"When you sort out all these complications," she said stiffly, "then you can let me know." Hurrying past him, she left the conservatory.

Thirty

In the middle of a lonely afternoon, Lucy sat looking at the wire message she had received from Mrs. Victoria Woodhull. Up until now, she had been afraid the response would never come, and had taken to haunting the Western Union Wireless office each morning, pacing up and down and worrying that time was running out. She shouldn't have worried; Mrs. Woodhull had come through for her. Lucy had received precisely the response she'd hoped for, prayed for.

But it meant nothing now. In the week since Diana's return, Rand had returned to the bank and Diana had gone off to her hotel. Today, Viola and Grace had taken Maggie on an outing. It was significant, Lucy thought, that she found herself alone at the darkest moment of her life.

She tried to talk herself out of her maudlin state, but nothing was working, and she found herself heading for the pantry, where the bottles of liquor were kept. Before she did something entirely foolish, Bull Waxman came to call.

"I have a buggy waiting out front," he said

simply. "You're to come with me, ma'am."

Lucy had always liked Bull. She liked the gentleness of his courtship of Willa Jean, and at the moment, she liked the fact that he had come to see her. "Where are we going?"

"Don't be asking me that. I'm not to tell. You'll see."

She suspected Willa Jean and Patience were going to try to cheer her up. But the moment she realized they were headed for Gantry Street, she protested. Loudly. She didn't want to see the wreckage of her beloved shop, to be reminded of all the struggle and triumph it had given her. Bull merely stared straight ahead, his big hands firm on the reins until they reached their destination. Only when she saw what was happening in front of the boarded-up shop did Lucy stop talking. She barely felt Bull help her down from the buggy.

"What is going on here?" she asked Willa Jean, who hurried over to greet her.

"Isn't it obvious, girl? We're saving the shop."

It was almost too much for Lucy to take in. Across the boards covering the broken-out window, someone had painted the message *Save The Firebrand Bookshop*. Tables draped with bunting were laden with various items for sale — berry pies, quilts and afghans, books and pamphlets. Lucy spied Patience, Deborah and Kathleen and all her dearest customers — Sarah Boggs and Mrs. McNelis, Lila Landauer and Dottie Frey, even cranky old Mrs. Mackey and others too numerous to count. They were the women who had found comfort and conviction between the pages of a book. Also present were the husbands of these ladies, men who knew better than to argue with the women they loved.

At the center of the table, seated before a line of patiently waiting admirers, sat Victoria Claflin Woodhull, autographing back issues of *Woodhull & Claflin's Weekly*.

"Mama!" Maggie broke away from a knot of people on the boardwalk. "Mama, we have a present for you. Come look!"

As if in a dream, Lucy allowed Maggie to lead her to the door. Rand emerged from the shop in a cloud of plaster. He wore old denims and a grin that offered no apology for working in secret without her consent. A leather pocket apron, filled with clanking tools, rode low on his hips.

"Show her, Papa," Maggie commanded him.

He handed Lucy a long, flat parcel. "It's not quite finished yet. Still needs a coat of shellac."

She didn't remember to breathe as she tore off the paper to find a new tradesman's shingle, sanded smooth and carefully lettered on both sides with The Firebrand — L. Hathaway, Bookseller. "Oh" was all she could say. "Oh." Then Lucy, who never, ever wept, burst into tears for the second time in her adult life.

Maggie looked horrified. "Don't you like it? Papa worked and worked, and I wasn't allowed to tell you anything."

Lucy smiled through her tears. "It's not that, sweetheart." She lifted her gaze to Rand. "I love it."

"A-*men* and hallelujah," Maggie said. "Now can I go play?"

Lucy nodded. Rand took her hand and led her inside. "Watch that beam there," he warned. "We've just propped it up." The place smelled of burnt paper and charred timber; the blackened furniture and shelves and ruined books were piled in a heap. A team of workmen with wheelbarrows and crowbars had cleared the wreckage. "Go and get some refreshments," Rand told them, and they stepped out.

Lucy's heart turned to ice. Now she understood. She stepped away from him, clenching her hands, digging her nails into her palms. The sunlight filtering through the broken windows suddenly blurred, smeared by tears. She clenched her jaw and blinked fast, fighting for control. "I see," she said. "You're giving me back my shop as a sop for your conscience because you're going to choose Diana."

His long shadow slipped over her as he stepped close and pulled her around to face him. "Damn it, Lucy, did it ever occur to you to listen before jumping to your own conclusions?"

The strength in his grip made her flinch, and she pulled away. "I'm listening."

"When Diana showed up out of the blue, I suspected her motives were less than purely maternal. During the week, Dylan Kennedy and I sent out some wires, and sure enough, she's run through everything she gained from the divorce settlement and is in debt. Naturally, I'll accept the responsibility of taking care of her."

Lucy took a step back. "Naturally."

"You're doing it again," he said, annoyed. "You're reaching a conclusion without hearing me out."

"Forgive me if I don't care to linger and hear your dreams of the future with Diana."

"Oh, for Christ's sake." Annoyance burgeoned to anger. "Of course there's a future with Diana. She gave birth to Maggie. In that way, she'll always be a part of our lives. She'll be paid a stipend — though God knows where that will come from if the bank fails — and we'll permit her to visit Maggie. I'll see to it that we have a legal arrangement so her role is clear and limited."

"And that's all she'll be to you?" Lucy forced herself to ask.

He took hold of her again, but there was no anger in his grip this time. He kissed her forehead with a tenderness that made her ache. "God, what do you take me for? You are Maggie's mother in every sense of the word, and you have been since the night of the fire."

"But Diana was your first love. Your first wife. The mother of your child."

"Two out of three are correct," he said, and she heard a smile in his voice. "Yes, she was my first wife. Yes, she gave birth to my daughter. But she's not my first love."

"She's not?"

"You're going to make me say it, aren't you? You're my first love, Lucy. I had no idea what love was until I found you. You're my life, my world, my . . . everything. The reason the sun rises and the moon shines, the reason spring comes and flowers bloom. You know you are. Who the hell else would inspire me to poetry like this?"

Relief and joy swelled inside her, and she could have sworn her feet left the ground. "I was so afraid," she said, pressing her cheek against the solid warmth of his chest. "I was so afraid you'd take her back."

"You're supposed to be fearless," he said gently. "Remember?"

She trusted the look shining in his eyes, trusted it despite the fact that her shop had burned, that he might lose his job at the bank. None of that mattered, not when she could look into her husband's face and see the whole world there. Trusting him was as simple as going where her heart led her. It all seemed so simple now.

"I know what it's like to be afraid," she said, pressing her lips to his big, scarred hand. "I know it all too well."

"Let's go outside," he said, "and let the workmen get busy. When the bank finds out The Firebrand is back, I might have to become your partner in business."

"Ah, there you are, Mr. Higgins." Mrs. Woodhull approached them as they went out to the street. "Your wife sent me a wire," she said. "She claims you are a man who can be trusted. A man who understands both money and women. Is that true?"

"I doubt Lucy would put up with me if it

531

weren't." He eyed Lucy with suspicion. "I didn't know you sent a wire."

"Of course she did," Mrs. Woodhull declared, "and I daresay you won't be hurting for clients much longer. The only thing more powerful than my convictions are my purse strings. I was once a banker myself, you know." She showed him a cardboard case of papers, stuffed with drafts and certificates. "I am going overseas to carry on a little adventure in England," she explained. "While I'm gone, I shall need a place to lodge my deposits."

"The Union Trust is an excellent choice, ma'am," Rand told her, looking amazed.

She swept her gaze along the line of admirers. "I imagine there are many ladies in Chicago who would like to find a banker who understands the needs of women." With the skill of a professional orator, she summoned them around and launched into a lecture on banking and finance.

"Mama! Papa!" Maggie came running over. "Look what I found. Just look." She opened her grubby little hand to reveal three dusty pennies. "I found them on the ground, Papa. Can I put them in your bank, Papa? Can I?"

Lucy and Rand exchanged a private glance. "It'll help," said Rand.

"I'm going to go look for more pennies!" Maggie ran off again.

"I love you," Lucy whispered, touching Rand's dear, scarred cheek. "Oh, how I love you. I love you for what you were willing to sacrifice for my sake."

"You would have given up the shop for me," he pointed out.

"But that's different."

"Is it?" He lifted one eyebrow. "I thought you believed in equal rights."

Thirty-One

Chicago
Spring, 1877

"Mama," Maggie said thoughtfully, "where do babies come from? *Really.*" Like a sprouting dandelion, she popped her tousled head up from between her parents in the big bed.

The reflected April sunshine off the lake created a watery pattern of shifting light on the ceiling. Lucy knew Rand was awake, though he lay very still with the covers pulled up, pretending he was asleep.

Coward, she thought.

She smiled and ruffled Maggie's hair. She loved Sunday mornings when they lay abed an extra hour before getting up for church. More often than not, Maggie joined them, letting the dog and cat follow her as well.

"Well," Lucy said, smoothing her hand over her belly, "this one is growing very slowly inside my womb."

She sensed Rand going rigid with mortification. He tried hard to endure her modern ways, but hearing her refer to body parts with matter-of-fact frankness always pushed his old-fashioned sensibilities to their limit. She loved him for gritting his teeth and letting her have her way, even if he didn't always agree with her.

Maggie put her small hand on the mound. "It feels hard as a rock."

"That's because the infant is growing strong and healthy. In a few weeks, the baby will come out, and we'll get to hold him and love him and care for him."

"Sally Saltonstall says the doctor brings the baby in his black leather bag."

"Sally Saltonstall is full of duck fluff," Lucy said. "The fact is, the baby's going to get out by —"

"I'll tell you who's full of duck fluff," roared Rand, springing awake, clearly unable to tolerate any more of the candid talk. "*You're* full of it." He grabbed Maggie and tickled her, and she loosed a loud stream of giggles. Grabbing a pillow, she held it up as a shield to protect herself. Ivan aimed his muzzle at the ceiling and howled.

Before Lucy could subdue her husband and child, she heard an ominous ripping sound. A fountain of feathers exploded into the air, and the breeze from the windows scooped them up and swirled them, a blizzard of softness settling over their three laughing faces.

Afterword

Section 1. The right of the citizens of the United States to vote shall not be denied or abridged by the United States or by any State on account of sex.

— Text of the Nineteenth Amendment
of the Constitution,
adopted by Congress in 1920